FIRST BORN

RICHARD LA PLANTE

Escargot Books and Music

ISBN-13: 978-1908191892

ISBN-10: 1908191899

Escargot Books and Music

Ojai, California

FIRST BORN

ACKNOWLEDGMENTS

This book could not have been written without the help of Dr. Steven Renzin, who not only supervised the delivery of my own first born but made himself available to answer a never-ending barrage of questions on medical procedures and "what if" scenarios regarding this book. Dr. Renzin is a combination of practitioner, listener, and advisor, everything a modern doctor should be. Most important, he is a lifetime friend .

My thanks also to:

- Peter, Ernest, and Escargot Productions. Long may you eat the olives and sip the wine.

- Nat Sobel, who worked on the manuscript nearly as hard as I did. Thank you also for the many talks in the garden.

- Abner stein for his dry humor, wet wit, and lasting friendship.

- Leonard Leokum and his white chair, and the countless hours and thoughts he puts into my mind.

- Tom Doherty, who gave this book a home.

- Melissa Ann Singer a terrific editor, who encouraged my idea from the very beginning.

- Midge Steadman and the Pendulum Newsletter.

- Budd Hopkins for his time on the telephone.

- Tom Janes, a believer.

- Bob Westfall and Patrick Hines for their knowledge and expertise.

- Richard Sullivan, Ph.D., for his time, ideas, and contradictions.

- The Colorado Springs Police Department's Public Relations Office, which answered lots of phone calls and many questions.

- Dr. Kevin Meachum, who made giving birth a party—if not for my wife—at least for me.

- Betina, my scathing critic, my ardent fan, my great wife.

- Jack Cameron, my inspiration.

- I began this book with a simple idea, yet as I researched and spoke to people I came to believe that the phenomena that I describe are neither simple nor fully understood within the confines of Western man's current frame of knowledge, even by those who have experienced them directly.

First Born is my effort to interpret, in the context of fiction, what I believe to be an evolution in human consciousness. An evolution that will lead us to the meeting place between science, religion, and mysticism.

This is dedicated to my son, Jack

I think we're property. I should say that we belong to something: That once upon a time, this earth was no-man's-land, that other worlds explored and colonized here, and fought among themselves for possession, but that now it's owned by something.

—Charles Fort, *The Book of the Damned* (1919)

PROLOGUE

september 12, 1984

ocean city, new jersey

The wooden lifeguard stands that had once perched like huge babies' high chairs in the sand were gone, along with the hordes of holiday-makers who had elbowed their way into the lives of the locals, swelling the checkout lines at the A&P and fighting for parking space at the Carvel ice-cream store. The vacancy signs in the motels were on again and most of the beach houses were closed, many boarded up for the winter ahead.

Labor Day was history.

Another season had ended, and it was Thomas Reed's favorite time of year. The midday sun was yellow warm and the nights were beginning to get chilly, enough to burn a few logs in the brick fireplace.

From the upstairs window of their Victorian-styled house, a block back from the beach, Thomas could see the Atlantic Ocean. He watched the waves, rolling and breaking, their crests whipped white by the tail of a dry northeast wind.

The water was still warm, in the low seventies; it was a perfect day to keep the promise he'd made to his son. "Alex, as soon as the crowds thin out and I can get out of the office, it's down to the beach, just you and me."

By the time they were in the water the waves were running at about three feet high and breaking ten yards from shore.

Thomas watched Alex catch a ride before he took the last in the set and body-surfed to the shallows. He stood up with Alex beside him. The boy had been long and slender as a baby but now, at twelve, he was filling out. His shoulders were broad and there was the hint of muscle beneath the tanned skin of his chest. Thomas felt a surge of love, mixed with pride.

"You had enough yet?" he asked.

Alex laughed and shook his head. "Just a couple more," he answered. His eyes were green, reflecting the sea, and his voice was on the edge of breaking, still more boy than man.

Thomas had promised Molly that they'd be home in an hour and that hour was gone.

"Your mother will be getting worried," he said, but Alex had already turned and plowed back into the surf.

"One more!" Thomas called after him, watching as the boy dove beneath a breaker and began to swim.

Thomas counted his strokes, reckoning Alex was about twenty yards from him before he stopped, began to tread water, and looked around. He understood that he was waiting for the next set to build, but as Thomas watched the blond head bob up and over a swell, adding more distance between them, he began to feel uneasy.

Then the wave came and Alex turned toward shore and began to swim. His arms churned, but not fast or powerfully enough to pull even with the break, causing him to miss the ride.

I shouldn't have let him go back out there alone, Thomas thought, wading deeper toward him.

He shouted, "That's enough, let's go!" But the wind had picked up and his voice was lost inside a roar that had become an echo all around him.

Alex turned seaward and dove deep to avoid the second wave in the set and when he resurfaced the third was directly in front of him. It was probably four feet from base to peak, and he swam hard toward it, up the side and over the top.

Thomas watched as Alex's head emerged beyond the spray. Then a fourth wave came and Alex disappeared. When

he broke the surface his right hand was raised above the
water. "Just one more, Dad, one more." Isn't that what he
was saying? That he was in control. That he was okay. "Just
one more ride." He was tugging at the air above his head, his
hand waving at the sky. And suddenly Thomas knew.

He's in trouble! It was his last thought before he dove,
staying shallow, swimming with his head up, trying not to
lose sight of his son. A wave broke, and for a moment
Thomas was inside the turbulence, fighting to keep eye
contact, catching the glint of reflected sunshine against the
gold chain and tiny cross that Alex wore around his neck.

Another four strokes. "Hold on. I'm almost there.
I'm coming." He wasn't sure if he was shouting or thinking it.
"Hold on." He was ripping the water apart with his hands,
crawling through the opening toward his son. Staring at the
blond hair, plastered tight to his head. Finding Alex's gray-
green eyes, locked on his own. That look. He hadn't seen that
look since Alex was a baby, learning to swim. He'd held him
then, high up in the water so that their eyes could meet.
Father and son. It was a look of pure trust. "You're safe with
me, Son. Nothing to be afraid of."

Three more strokes and he was close, his heart
kicking against the side of his rib cage, close enough to smile
with a confidence that he didn't feel. Close enough to reach
out with his hand, his fingers sliding from Alex's face.: down
his smooth neck, fingertips looping the gold chain. So close
that he never saw the wave till it broke on top of them,
catching them sideways, pushing them under. Still he held on,
gasping for air as he reached the surface, gripping the gold
chain and cross in his right hand.

Alex was gone.

Thomas fought for self-control, treading water as he
spun around, his eyes searching, lungs straining for breath.
He called Alex's name, over and over again. *God help me. Please
help me*, he prayed, releasing the chain and cross, as if it was an
offering to the sea.

Then he dove down.

There was hardly any visibility and it must have been
nine or ten feet to the bottom with nothing waiting for him
but sand. He went on like that, swimming and calling, diving

down, calling and swimming, till he was too exhausted to do anything but tread water. By then the current had swept him a hundred yards down the beach and he was a long way from shore. The waves were big now and his arms and legs were deadweight. For a moment, exhausted and gripped by fear, he forgot his son completely as another realization took hold. He wasn't going to make it. Thomas Reed was not going to survive. Then an angry, roaring wall of water crashed on his head, blackening his thoughts, forcing him under. He felt small and weightless, tumbling in space, not knowing which end was up, which was down until, gasping for air, he bobbed into the bright sunlight. A second later he was hammered again. That took the last of the fight from him. He'd lost. He wanted to stay under. It was peaceful down there, like some sort of slow-motion ballet, graceful and quiet. He didn't want to go up where it was loud and fast and angry. Didn't want to get hit anymore but there was just enough air left in his lungs to drag him to the surface.

It was then that he saw the boy on the shore. A boy with blond hair, wearing a swimming suit, pointing at him and waving.

Alex? The thought gave him heart.

Alex!

He couldn't swim; he was too weak and his lungs were shot, so he turned on his back, used his hands like paddles, and forced his iron legs to kick until finally, when the next wave came, swelling beneath him, he rolled over and rode it in.

He staggered, fell, then crawled to the beach, crying his son's name, "Alex? Alex!"

The blond-haired boy was gone. Maybe there had not been a boy at all. Thomas never found out.

Hours later, two fishermen hauled Alex Reed's body from the surf. He was naked, tangled in seaweed and dead.

It was a miracle that Thomas and Molly Reed had remained together. She'd never said it, but the feelings were always there. Thomas had been responsible for Alex's death; he'd wrecked their lives. She loved him, but she also hated him.

Vodka was Thomas's escape. He could mix it with anything and barely taste the alcohol that he'd always despised, and it did the job, numbed him sufficiently to wake up another day and shoulder his burden, trudging his way to nowhere. He and Molly had separated twice before they tried therapy. That, and Alcoholics Anonymous for Thomas, plus three changes in jobs and as many changes in cities, far away from the ocean, and they almost had a life again. The only thing missing was laughter. They were short on that.

Colorado Springs, in EI Paso County, Colorado, was their last stop. It was a town of 330,000 people, with a dry alpine climate, made beautiful by the Rocky Mountains, surrounding it like a great stone crown with Pikes Peak jutting high and proud to the west and the Garden of the Gods, a sacred Indian burial ground, laying low and tranquil at the northern base. It was a peaceful place and after ten years of selling apartments and condominiums in Chicago, Thomas enjoyed sleeping through the night without the barrage of car alarms and the wail of police sirens. He picked up his Colorado broker's license after a seventy-two hour course and a simple exam and sold his first property, a two-story shingled house off Cascade Street, in his second week with the new company. Molly found work in the school system, substituting at first, with the promise that a position in special education, her specialty, would be opening in the new term.

Then, ten months after they had settled, came the news that would disrupt the guarded monotony that had become their lives. At first they were certain that the gynecologist had made a mistake. It seemed impossible. Molly Reed was forty-five years old and her periods had been irregular for the past two years. She had been having recurrent headaches, her energy level was low, and she'd gone to the doctor in the hope that he would prescribe a course of hormone-replacement therapy. Besides, Molly and Thomas hadn't exactly been boosting the national average for frequency of sexual intercourse. They'd made love twice in the past year. But there it was, the scan of her womb with what looked like a tiny tadpole pulsating in the upper quadrant.

"Because of your age we're going to have to watch you very closely," Dr. Rose said, removing his glasses and rubbing his forehead.

Murray Rose was often mistaken for the talk-show host Larry King. Maybe it was his hair, thinning brown and slicked back, or his small, owly eyes, usually highlighted by square, thick-framed glasses, or perhaps it was his demeanor, very dry and matter-of-fact.

"But you look in good shape," he continued, "your weight is fine and your blood pressure is normal. I don't see why there should be any problems with this. If things run on course, your baby should arrive during the first week of January." He stopped and smiled. Then, as if he was coining a phrase, he said. "A millennium child. Congratulations."

"Very closely" meant frequent examinations and continued cautioning about eating properly, getting enough iron, gentle exercise, and plenty of rest.

The mental part was much harder. The Reeds already had a child. They rarely spoke of him but Alex was still with them, his picture positioned above their mantle, his baby book beneath Molly's side of the bed. They had never tried to have another baby; they had never wanted anything to detract from Alex's memory. Nothing could replace him. *Pregnant? How could she be?*

Thomas was the first to crack. It happened during his AA meeting. For the first time since arriving in Colorado Springs, he'd been asked to be a speaker, to talk about being clean and sober for nine years, to expound upon what it felt like to be in control of his life, and responsible for his future.

"And now I'm fifty-three years old and I'm about to become a father," he'd said at the close of his speech.

A father.

The two words hung in the air as he stared down into the faces and eyes of the group. They were expecting him to sit down, but he couldn't. He heard his own voice continue as if it was coming from someone else.

"Oh my God, Alex would be twenty-seven now. He'd be a man." Then his voice began to waiver and crack. "I watched him drown. I saw my son die. I couldn't save him. I couldn't."

No one at the Colorado Springs meeting knew who Alex was. In the months that he'd been coming, Thomas had never shared the fact that it had been his son's death that had triggered his alcoholism, and it was only after the meeting that he began to understand that he and Molly had been clinging to a ghost, packaging it in the name of Alex and hanging on.

Thomas changed. It was gradual at first but he could feel things opening up inside him and he grew to trust and follow his feelings. Molly's pregnancy was the catalyst for their future. He even saw some humor in being an older father. His auburn hair had receded by the time he'd turned forty, and even now, he couldn't read the label on a bottle of vitamins without glasses. On top of that, at five-nine and a hundred and eighty-three pounds he was hanging dangerously over the sides of his size 34 Levi's. He calculated that by the time his son or daughter graduated from high school he'd be pushing seventy. An old man. No, he wasn't going to let that happen. He was going to reform, at least fix what he could. Once he'd been an athlete and recently he'd seen a program on CNN about men his age and older who still participated in competitive sports. He went out and bought a set of dumbbells and a jump rope. Then he went on a diet. Between the lifting, the skipping, and the Atkin's regime, he dropped fifteen pounds of bodyweight, His energy was contagious.

Molly and Thomas Reed were alive again, even happy.

The bomb dropped sixteen weeks later.

They had driven together to the hospital, assured by Dr. Rose that the entire procedure, called an amniocentesis, would take no more than half an hour.

"Taking your age into consideration, this is a standard. I just want to make certain that there are no chromosomal abnormalities," the doctor explained.

Molly emptied her bladder, slipped into an examination gown, and a nurse positioned her on the table, her body draped with a sheet so that only her abdomen was exposed. Then Rose applied a small amount of gel.

"The ultrasound will let me look inside, to make sure the needle steers clear of the fetus and the placenta." His voice exuded confidence.

Molly had had the ultrasound before, in the initial phases of her pregnancy, but on this morning the clear blue gel seemed particularly cold. Then came the transducer, a palm-size device with its cable attached to a TV-like viewing screen. Rose ran it across her belly and Molly and Thomas watched the black-and-white images as they began to appear on the screen. The pictures were blurred and it was hard to say exactly what they were looking at but Rose seemed satisfied that everything was fine.

"Do you want to know the sex?" he asked.

Thomas was tempted but Molly said, "No, we want to be surprised."

"Well, one thing for certain," Rose continued. "You're going to have your hands full. That's one active kid in there. Really moving around. Look."

It was true, the image appeared in constant motion. Then with his free hand, Rose pressed a button on the keyboard next to the monitor and the picture froze.

"There. You can see the head." Molly and Thomas studied the screen.

"The dark shadows are the sockets of the eyes." Almost imperceptibly, the doctor's demeanor changed.

"Uhmm ... I just want to get a better shot of that," he continued, but his voice had lost its sense of fun. He moved the transducer and ran the index finger of his free hand over a small ball-like mouse at the base of the control panel. A set of calipers appeared on the monitor and he directed them to the portion of the sonogram that he had identified as the head.

"I need a couple of measurements," he explained, adjusting the calipers around the shadowed sphere.

Numbers came up at the upper right-hand side of the screen as a steady stream of numerated pictures rolled from the top of the machine, down the back, and gathered on the floor. Rose moved the calipers up and down and the numbers changed as the pictures continued to accumulate. He worked quickly, altering angles a half dozen more times, concentrating on the upper quadrant of the fetus's head.

Thomas wanted to say something, to ask if everything was okay, but was sensitive to upsetting Molly.

Finally, Rose spoke. "All right, now we know the baby can dance." He was making an attempt to lift the atmosphere. "Now let's see if we can get this finished without missing a beat."

He cleared away some of the blue gel with a tissue and swabbed an area of Molly's abdomen, below her navel, with an antiseptic solution. Then he picked up a long hollow needle from the tray of instruments beside the table.

"This won't take much longer than a shot in the arm," he said, watching Molly eye the needle. "And it won't be any more painful."

The sight of it seemed to invoke, in Molly, some deep-seated fear, something that screamed from below the threshold of her memory.

Rose lifted the needle above her abdomen and she began to squirm, closing her eyes and turning her head to the side.

"You have no right to do this to me," she said.

Rose responded gently, coaxing her. "Come on, Molly, this will be over before you know it."

She was somewhere else in her head. It was a terrifying, unfamiliar place. She was not talking to Rose at all. She was pleading with "them."

"No, no, no," she sputtered.

Rose slid the needle through the wall of her abdomen. It took twenty seconds to withdraw the fluid but by the time he was finished Molly was hyperventilating and Thomas was beside her, holding her hand and reassuring her, as gradually her breathing returned to normal.

"All over," Rose said. "That wasn't so bad, was it?"

Molly opened her eyes, taking in the doctor's office, the monitor, the smell of the antiseptic, Rose's face, and Thomas's warm hand on hers. She felt relief and a sense of embarrassment.

"I'm sorry," she apologized. "I don't know what came over me. I'm really sorry."

Rose waited several days before he called them both back into his office. He'd needed the time to study the ultrasound pictures carefully and to consult with his associates. He'd wanted second opinions.

Murray Rose hated giving bad news, especially when he was uncertain as to what exactly the bad news was, or, if indeed, there was any. In any case, he felt it was his responsibility to keep his patients apprised of all possibilities.

Once he had Molly and Thomas there, seated, calm and settled in front of his desk, he opened Molly Reed's file and laid out the clearest of the images.

"All right," he began, hesitating to clear his throat and using the tip of his index finger to outline the spherical shape inside the conical picture. Here you can see the fetus's head." He always used the term fetus as opposed to baby or child when he felt insecure. "First of all, the head size is quite a bit above the norm. That, in itself, particularly at this stage in the fetus's growth, is not uncommon. However, there seems to be an anomaly with the right hemisphere of the brain." He moved his fingertip to a shadowed area in the upper right side of the head. "This area here appears swollen or enlarged."

Molly studied the picture. It was hard for her to believe that what she was looking at was in any way related to the living, kicking child that she carried inside her. It didn't seem possible.

Thomas sat quietly, his face drawn, his eyes focused on the image. He felt doomed inside and Rose, sensing his anxiety, tried to lighten his tone. He was a good doctor but his forte was the operating room, not the office.

"Now I'm not certain at this stage exactly what this indicates. It could be hydrocephalus, water on the brain, but because the swelling is concentrated in the right hemisphere, and there doesn't seem to be any swelling in the ventricles, my hunch is that it's something else. We have to consider Down's syndrome or some other chromosomal aberration."

Molly's anger was beginning to cut through her angst. This was their child that Rose was talking about, their flesh and blood, their future.

"Are you trying to tell us that our baby will be born retarded?" she asked. "Is that what you're saying?"

Rose removed his hand from the image, looked up at her, and eked out a smile. His teeth were a sickly yellow in the halogen light from his desk lamp. He felt defensive.

"It may be that your son just has a big head," he replied, inadvertently giving away the sex of the child.

Thomas and Molly stared at him until the silence hung heavily in the room.

My son? Thomas thought. *I'm going to have a son.* Then he thought of Alex and his feelings dissolved in a pool of sadness.

"If there is something wrong, are you suggesting I abort the child?" Molly asked.

Rose held up his open palm as if to say "stop."

"I'm not suggesting anything," he said, lowering his hand to the desk. "When the lab results from the amnio come back, we can have a more informed discussion as to your options. I just wanted you to know what I've found so far. I don't want there to be any unnecessary surprises."

Thomas and Molly left Rose's office each locked inside their private thoughts, unable to speak, even to each other.

After that came the waiting, fourteen days for the cells from the amniocentesis to be cultured in the laboratory and the tests to be performed. *What if the child has Down's syndrome? What if he is born handicapped?* Molly's mind reeled with uncertainty.

How would it affect their lives? Would their marriage survive? Was abortion an option? The questions and anxiety came close to unraveling them, to taking everything that they had won back in their lives and destroying it.

Then one night, after his fourth AA meeting in as many days, Thomas sat alone in his car, watching the rest of the group drive from the parking lot. He had needed to share with them, to air his fears, but something had held him back. It was that feeling again, of being powerless. It was the knowledge that his words and emotions were inadequate to alter a fate that seemed predetermined, but unknown.

To him, the meeting had been a charade. The stories of recovery and strength hadn't touched him at all. What was the sense of staying straight if life was going to torture you anyway? It was better to be anesthetized.

He didn't want to go home. Didn't want to see Molly. She looked too much like Alex, with her blond hair, high cheekbones, and wide, gray-green eyes. Those eyes, looking straight into him. He didn't want to feel their weight, questioning and pleading for reassurance. He didn't have the strength and he didn't have the answers. He had nothing left and he was drowning again.

A screwdriver would do it. That would keep the lid on tight. Just a splash of vodka and glass full of orange juice. Well, maybe more than a splash.

There was a corner bar on Nevada Street, small and dimly lit. It was the kind of place he used to go, to get away from his feelings.

He was about to start the Camry's engine when Robert Barnes walked from the rectory and turned in his direction. The priest was a big man, not fat, just tall and broad, and his face was a character study in lines and creases. He looked well used, with eyes the color of paving slate.

"Thomas?"

He lowered the window of the Camry and said, "Robert, how are you?" He'd never felt that he could hide from Robert Barnes and now he felt he'd been caught red-handed.

"Car trouble?" Barnes asked.

"No, the car's fine."

"You seemed quiet in there tonight," the priest continued.

"Yes," Thomas answered. He didn't want to be prodded. "I didn't feel I had anything to say."

Barnes nodded his head. He was also a recovering alcoholic and he was Thomas's sponsor in the program.

"Yeah, I've had plenty of those nights myself," he said. "How's Molly?"

"She's okay," Thomas answered, trying to avoid the issue.

"That's good," Barnes said, but there was still a question in his tone.

Thomas felt something giving way inside him, a wall was about to crumble.

"She went in for another test last week. There might be something wrong with the baby, some kind of ... " he hesitated, "complication." He cut it short when he heard his voice begin to tremble.

"When will you know?"

Thomas cleared his throat.

"The results will take a couple of weeks," he replied, looking up at Barnes. The wall was giving way.

"Jesus, Robert ... " Then, more firm, almost demanding. "I want a drink."

"I'll bet," Barnes replied.

"That's where I was going. There's a bar down on Nevada. I've driven by it a thousand times. That's where I was going." As he spoke he realized how close he'd come. He'd almost slipped and it made him feel raw and vulnerable. The feeling scared him. Everything scared him. He turned his head away from the priest and stared out of the car's windshield. His voice echoed the vacancy he felt inside. "What happens if they find out the baby's handicapped? What do we do?"

"In terms of what?"

"Do we keep it or do we—" He nearly said "get rid of it," but choked back the words.

Barnes walked another step closer and bent down to the window.

"First of all, why don't you come inside. Call Molly, tell her you'll be a bit late. Let's just talk for a while. C'mon." He reached in and touched Thomas's shoulder.

Thomas got out of the car slowly. The night air was warm against his skin as he followed the priest back to the rectory. There was a small cemetery behind the wood-framed building and the late summer moon gave a silvery glow to the tight rows of headstones. Thomas thought again of Alex. They'd buried him in a family plot in Saratoga Springs, New York, next to Thomas's mother.

He stopped.

It had been just the two of them in Saratoga, standing above the fresh grave. Molly had read something aloud. He wasn't sure who had written it or where it had come from but he remembered a few of the lines. He would always remember them. "I have only slipped away into the next room. I am I, and you are you, whatever we were to each other, we still are, and always will be."

Sometimes it felt that way, as if Alex was close by, as if he could still talk to him.

"What am I going to do now, Son, what am I going to do?" he asked the shadows. Then he trailed Robert Barnes into the rectory.

The priest was waiting for him, holding an opened bottle of beer in each hand.

"Here, have that drink." It sounded like a challenge.

Before he could answer Barnes handed him one of the bottles.

"Go ahead," he urged.

Thomas balked as he watched Barnes lift the other bottle to his lips and gulp the beer, suddenly concerned for the welfare of the priest. He felt responsible.

"Robert, don't do that."

"Why? You said you wanted a drink. Don't you think I ever feel that way?"

Thomas reached across and took hold of Barnes's arm, preventing him from lifting the bottle again.

"Robert, this is crazy."

Barnes looked at him.

"What are you talking about?" he asked. There was the hint of something in his eyes.

Thomas looked down at the brown bottle. "Kaliber." He'd never heard of Kaliber. He let go of the priest's arm and lifted his own bottle. "All natural ingredients."

"This doesn't have any alcohol in it."

"Of course not!" Barnes answered and for the first time Thomas actually saw the man behind the clerical collar, the craggy face and crooked smile, standing there with a bottle of alcohol-free beer in his hand. It had been a test, a small test but a deciding one.

"You son of a bitch," Thomas said.

They both laughed. It made Thomas feel easier, lighter, not so isolated. Afterward they talked, about the pregnancy, the tests, and about Thomas's fears for the future.

"It might sound trite, especially coming from me," Barnes said at the end of the evening. "But I don't believe God's going to give you anything that you and Molly can't handle. You've been through a lot already and you've made it. Whatever happens here, you'll be equal to it. Have faith in that."

The following night Thomas listened to The Father Barnes Radio Talk Show for the first time, surprised at the number of call-ins and the subjects covered, everything from teenage steroid abuse to gay parenthood. Father Barnes was not only a good friend and a liberal, he was a happening act on public radio.

Then, on Sunday, Thomas took Molly to St. Anne's Episcopal Church. It was the first time in fifteen years that either of them had set foot in a chapel and they sat in a pew at the rear. At first Thomas felt self-conscious, as if he was somehow an intruder, but as the service got under way, he began to relax. It felt good to be there, as if he and Molly were about to begin building something together, some kind of safety net for whatever was about to happen in their lives.

Molly felt it too, stronger and more confident, as if they were no longer alone.

They attended regularly after that and several times Thomas went to the chapel by himself, at the end of his working day or after a meeting. The side door was always open and the place was usually empty. He'd go in and sit in the exact spot that he and Molly had on their first visit. Sometimes he'd pray for the future and at other times he'd just think about it. It gave him peace.

The results of the amniocentesis arrived in Murray Rose's office thirteen days after he'd performed the procedure. It was the single notation written on the chromosome sheet of the two-page report that disturbed him. It read, "The top arm of chromosome 10 appears significantly longer than normal." Which meant that one of the sets of chromosomes in the twenty-three set chain contained more genetic material than it should have. It followed, to Rose, that the DNA contained in those genes was almost certainly dictating the hyperdevelopment of the right hemisphere of the fetus's brain, but aside from that abnormality there was no indication of hydrocephalus, Down's syndrome or any metabolic disorder.

Rose was confused and frustrated. He reopened Molly Reed's file and removed the folded printout containing the eight pictures he'd taken of the fetus's head with the ultrasound. Opening it, he laid the relevant shots beneath his desk lamp then used a magnifying glass to study them.

The fetus's brain was enlarged, that was confirmed by every picture and every measurement, and unless the technicians at the lab had made a mistake and somehow contaminated the amniotic fluid, there was also a significant abnormality with one of the sets of chromosomes. There had to be a connection and it made Rose nervous. What was he going to tell the Reeds? What if he delivered a bad baby? Yet, even with the long chromosome, the anatomy appeared normal. There had to be a mistake somewhere. Maybe a filament of one of the sets of chromosomes had broken loose and attached to chromosome 10, causing a translocation. That would explain the added length. Maybe the lab had failed to pick it up. Rose could smell a malpractice suit a mile away.

He considered scheduling another amniocentesis, which meant another two weeks of waiting. Then, if there was something wrong and the Reeds wanted to terminate the pregnancy he couldn't do it. They would have to go to Kansas City; it had one of the only two hospitals in the country licensed to abort a fetus after six months. But what if the lab had not made a mistake? What the hell was growing inside Molly Reed?

He shuffled through the glossy pictures, his eyes not completely focusing until he got to the fourth image, which included a portion of the placenta. He noticed a small shadow, and beneath the magnifying glass he could make out a definite shape. It looked like a tiny section of wire. He went to the next picture and found the same thing. What the hell was it, and how could he have missed it during the ultrasound? He was sure that Molly Reed was not using a coil or any other form of IUD. In any case, it did not resemble any intrauterine device he'd ever seen. So, what was it?

Twenty-four hours later Rose met with Molly and Thomas in his office. He laid it out for them as plainly as he could, explaining the role of DNA in directing the development of the fetus and talking them through the lab's findings regarding the abnormally long chromosome.

"We don't know what it means," he confessed. "The baby seems healthy, there's no sign of Down's syndrome or anything else. There does, however, appear to be something asymmetrical about the right hemisphere of the brain, and I want to keep a close eye on it in the next few months."

By then the Reeds had made their decision anyway. There would be no abortion, no termination of the pregnancy.

"Also," Rose added, "I've found a shadow along the wall of your uterus."

There was a short silence before Molly repeated the word, "Shadow?" She was thinking of cancer. Her father had died of it and the first thing he'd been told by the doctors, after a routine X-ray, was that they'd found a shadow on his right lung.

Rose recognized the anxiety in her voice.

"I don't think this is anything serious," he said. "Here, I'll show you what I'm talking about." Pulling the picture from the folder, he laid it flat on his desk.

Molly and Thomas stood and looked down.

"This area here is the placenta and behind it is the wall of the uterus. See that dark spot?"

They studied the picture.

"It doesn't look like much," Rose continued, removing the square magnifying glass from his drawer and placing it above the image. "See, right there, that little dark line."

Rose indicated the area with the tip of his pen.

"Yes, I can see it. Are you sure it's just not the way the thing's been printed? It almost seems the paper's been scratched," Thomas said.

"No, it shows up in the next one too," Rose replied.
"I was wondering, Molly, have you ever used an IUD for
contraception, a coil?"

Molly answered quickly. "No, never."

"How about abdominal surgery?" He was wondering
if another surgeon had left something behind. It could have
even been an old stitch.

"I had a hernia operation."

Rose had never noticed any type of scarring and
certainly hadn't seen it indicated on her medical records.

"Oh, and when was that?" he asked.

"I was seven years old," Molly answered. The scar
was hardly visible anymore and what there was of it was
concealed by her pubic hair.

Rose nodded his head. "Well, whatever it is, it isn't
bothering you so there's no need to do anything about it now.
I'd like to take a look again with the ultrasound just to make
sure it's not affecting the baby, and then when I do the C-
section, we can get to it."

"What do you mean, C-section?" Molly asked. It was
the first she'd heard of a cesarean section and the thought
frightened her. "I want a natural birth."

Rose had already thought it through and had planned
to discuss his reasoning and allow the Reeds to come to the
obvious decision. Now he realized he'd jumped the gun and
needed to backtrack.

"I would advise against a natural birth," he answered
calmly. "One reason is your age. Even though you're in good
shape, your muscle tone isn't what it once was and labor
could be dangerous. It would certainly take longer and there
could be all kinds of complications, but the main thing is the
size of the fetus's head. I don't believe it will clear your birth
canal without trauma to the baby's skull. We don't want to
end up with an emergency ... I'm as concerned for your safety
as I am for the baby's." He paused until he was satisfied that
his message was getting across. "The bottom line is, I want to
minimize the risks, and we can do that with a cesarean. We
can plan this delivery."

Molly and Thomas sat silently and considered, both understanding that there were no legitimate grounds for argument.

Molly spoke first. "January second. That was my mother's birthday. How about that?"

Rose smiled, relieved. "Perfect."

~ 1 ~

december 30, 1999

montauk, long island

Lonely, isn't it?" the driver asked. Then, without waiting for an answer he said, "It's like everything's dead. The trees. The sky. Not many people around either. A lot of them are scared about the power cuts. You know, all that stuff about the computers going down when the clocks hit 2000. Most of the big houses are locked up and the rich people have gone to Florida, just in case there's no heat here. Still, I figure they've got that all worked out by now. Just a lot of panic over nothing."

"I hope so," she answered, wondering who the driver thought "they" were—the mysterious "they" who were in control. She looked from the back-seat, beyond his head and out onto the main street of Montauk. It was different from the last two towns that they'd passed through during their ride down Long Island, much less manicured than East Hampton, and lacking the expensive shops of Amagansett. It appeared altogether more working class, with its parade of fish restaurants, diners, and motels. There was less Christmas decoration, too. Not so many colored lights climbing the lampposts, just a few wreaths here and there and a single lit tree on the island in the middle of the traffic circle at the end of town. Casey noticed a sign in the window of a department

store that advertised a MILLENNIUM SPECIAL ON
ALPINE PARKAS GUARANTEED TO THIRTY
BELOW. $89.99 WHILE THEY LAST. And several more
shops advertised bulk buys on bottled water while the
hardware store was running a special on kerosene lamps and
stoves. Obviously, not everybody thought that the Y2K bug
was a panic over nothing.

"Dick Cavett lives out here," the driver continued,
knowing that many of his clients enjoyed a bit of celebrity
chatter. "I've driven him into town a couple of times. Very
nice man. Paul Simon's out here too, you know the
musician?"

Casey didn't watch much TV, and Dick Cavett hadn't
had a regular show in over twenty years; his name didn't
mean a lot to her, but Paul Simon's did. His CD Graceland
was one of her favorites.

"Yes, I love his music," she replied.

To her right, through the tinted windows of the
Lincoln and beyond the flat brown rooftops of the buildings,
she could see the gentle rise of the sand dunes, covered in
sparse shrubs and sea grass. Then her eyes caught on a red
neon DELI sign as they passed the big plate-glass window of
one of the shops.

"They do a nice turkey-cranberry sandwich in there,"
the driver noted. "Guy got the recipe from some place in San
Francisco and brought it home with him."

Casey nodded and smiled.

"I'll keep that in mind."

Breakfast had been half a grapefruit followed by a cup
of coffee during her twenty-minute briefing. She hadn't eaten
since and she was starving. Turkey-cranberry sounded like an
exotic delicacy.

Main Street was less than a mile in length and by the
time she'd looked back at the deli sign, wondering if the place
was still open for business, they were out of town and
climbing the last of the thousand foot overlook before their
final destination. From the crest of the hill she could see the
Atlantic Ocean to the south and Block Island Sound to the
north. The water looked dark and alive, swelling and
churning, capped with splashes of white.

The driver glanced again in his rearview mirror. His passenger couldn't have been much more than thirty, and he wouldn't have called her a beauty. Her features were a bit too strong for his taste, her mouth very wide and full and her nose slightly flat against her face, accentuated by her jet black hair, cropped close to her head. He usually liked blondes, with little noses and rose-petal mouths but there was something about this one that held his interest. He wondered what her eyes looked like behind the dark glasses. It was already dusk so maybe she'd take them off before the ride ended. His attempts at conversation hadn't gone far either but, on the other hand, he'd never felt that she'd objected to his chat.

"Loads a' money to keep a place by the ocean," he commented. "Lots and lots of upkeep, plus the beach is eroding. My house is two blocks back off the old highway, but I figure it'll be waterfront in the next ten years. All's we need are a few more big storms." He slowed to twenty miles an hour as they entered the one-way system of the state park.

"I guess that will do it," she replied. Her eyes were now focused on the lighthouse, which stood at the very end of the Island, about five hundred feet directly in front of them. She leaned forward, resting her elbows against the top of the front seat.

"So that's Montauk Point?"

The white towering building looked desolate against the sky.

"That's it. You sure that's where you want to go?" the driver asked.

"I'm sure," she answered.

"You got people meeting you there?"

"I'll be fine." Her voice was clear and self-assured.

He'd been instructed by the car service to pick up a Ms. Emerson from La Guardia, arriving on the 2:30 American Airline flight from Washington, D.C. Her destination was the parking lot of the Montauk Point State Park. He'd assumed it was a meeting place but as he drove into the crescent-shaped lot there wasn't another car in sight. He stopped, put the Lincoln into park, and turned to his passenger.

"Looks like you've been stood up," he said.

"I'll be fine," she repeated.

"There's nobody here. I don't feel good about just dropping you off," he insisted.

"Don't worry about me."

"I don't have another pickup till nine so why don't I wait with you? You can stay in the car where it's warm."

Casey took off her wire-framed Ray-Bans, folded them, and slipped them into the fleece-lined pocket of her leather jacket. Without the glasses she looked more formidable. There was something about her eyes. It wasn't hardness; it was more a determination. In the dwindling light they looked steel gray. The driver reconsidered his original evaluation. Ms. Emerson was a beauty. Her eyes, set wide above prominent cheekbones, made all the difference; they seemed to bring the other features of her face together. There was also a slant to them, just enough to add a feline awareness, quick and intense. So intense that they seemed to bore right into him.

Casey smiled and her eyes changed, turning from gray to dark green, steel to water, softening.

"I appreciate your concern," she said, "but I'd prefer to be on my own."

Reaching into the pocket of her jeans, she pulled out a silver money clip and peeled a twenty-dollar bill from the top of the pile, handing it to the driver.

"Here, it's been a nice ride."

"No, please, that's all been taken care of," he protested.

She pushed it into his hand. "Take it anyway."

He felt embarrassed accepting the extra tip since there was already 20 percent built into his fee, but he didn't feel he could say no to her. She had a kind of force, a presence that seemed to reach out and take hold of him. He stepped from the car and walked to open her door but by the time he arrived she was already out, so he followed her to the back and lifted her duffel bag from the trunk, handing it to her. It was bulky and looked well used, almost beat-up, out of context with the stylish lady who took it with one hand while offering him the other. Her grip was dry and firm.

"Thanks again," she said.

"Good luck," he replied. It was said without forethought but that was the kind of atmosphere she inspired. As if she were about to climb Everest.

He got back inside, shifted from park to drive then back into park, lowering his window.

"Ms. Emerson?"

She turned as he extended his arm.

"Please, take my card," he said. "If you're ever up this way and need another ride ..." His tone was warm and not solicitous.

She took it from his hand and glanced down at it. JAMES RENO. HAMPTONS LIMOUSINE COMPANY.

"Okay, James.

"Ask for Jimmy. That's what everybody calls me."

"I will," Casey promised as she slid the card into one of the side pockets of her duffel bag.

"And Ms. Emerson?"

Casey turned again.

"Have a happy New Year."

She smiled and her smile seemed to ignite the darkness, like a sudden burst of flame.

You too," she replied.

Reno glanced at her a couple more times in his rearview mirror, as he drove slowly away. His ex-passenger's jeans were not particularly tight and her jacket covered most of her rear end but her legs were long and she moved with the grace of an athlete, a runner or something. She was walking with strong purposeful strides toward the pay phones at the edge of the lot. He almost lowered his window again, to ask one more time if she was all right, out there all alone, with night coming on, but he knew what her answer would be so he kept driving.

Casey dropped a quarter in the slot and dialed the number that she'd been instructed to memorize. Whoever picked it up at the other end didn't say a word.

"Armstrong speaking. I'm here."

The phone clicked and went silent. She sighed as she returned it to the receiver. She hated all the cloak-and-dagger

stuff but it was often part of the private contracts. She'd
walked away from her last two assignments without even
knowing what she'd been tasked to do or what exactly she
had seen. It was that way. There were things happening on
the planet and to the planet and as the millennium neared, the
pace was quickening. There were more targets and more
taskings. The people outside, the civilians, glued to their TV
screens and lapping up *Unsolved Mysteries* and reruns of *The X-
Files* didn't suspect the half of it. Christ, they didn't have a
clue. She thought a moment of her father, Henry. Holed up
in his cattle ranch on the outskirts of Perth, in Australia.
Married to a twenty-eight-year-old and trying to start a
second family at the age of fifty-nine, Henry was blatantly
uninterested in life beyond his wife and his cows. Simplicity.
Maybe he had it right. She'd spoken to him on Christmas
Day. It had been a short conversation. They hadn't had a lot
to say to each other in the seven years since his retirement
from his criminal law practice in Los Angeles. He'd seen
enough of "the ways of men." That's what he'd said when
he'd walked away from the L.A. firm that bore his name, with
a three-million dollar handshake from his two younger
partners. He had traveled halfway around the world before
landing in Sydney. His postcard had read, "I love the
Australians. They're honest. A rarity where I come from."

Susan had been working as a receptionist at the
Regency Hotel and Henry had stayed a month. When he'd
left, Susan had gone with him. After the initial shock of
seeing her father with a younger woman, Casey had accepted
his new life. She understood that he had paid a heavy toll for
whatever happiness he'd found. Casey's mother, Rebecca, had
been devoured slowly by multiple sclerosis. Once a concert
pianist, by the time she was Casey's age, thirty-three, she had
been confined to a wheelchair. Casey could remember her
sitting in the front row of the high school auditorium while
Casey had performed, her hands twitching in spastic rhythm
as her fingers attempted to mimic her daughter's on the
keyboard. Her death, in 1986, had been an assisted suicide.
Casey wasn't supposed to have known but she'd found the
prescription pill containers by the side of Rebecca's bed.
Sleeping pills. Her mother had never taken sleeping pills. Not

till the night she had died. After that Casey had had no one to play her music for. No one to please. Psychotherapy could not resurrect either her desire or her talent. It served only to make her question why she had played to begin with. Perhaps it had been to fulfill her mother's ambitions.

Her therapy had led to an avid interest in the workings of the human mind. She'd studied psychology at Berkeley, then gone on to Stanford for a Ph.D. It was there that she became acquainted with the Human Research Institute in Menlo Park, volunteering initially for a series of tests in what was known as "remote viewing," the ability to recreate, by audio recording and drawing, remote places, or objects, known as "targets," guided only by latitudinal and longitudinal coordinates. She had scored higher on the HRI tests, or taskings, than even the renowned psychic Uri Geller had in 1973, and within a month had received a call from the US Army, offering to subsidize the rest of her education in exchange for a three-year stint in their RV program.

Casey'd had no idea at that time that she had just been recruited into a clandestine military operation designed, almost thirty years ago, to develop the perfect spy. Human beings, trained at a minimal cost, who could penetrate the most secretive and heavily guarded locations on earth.

■ ■ ■

She adjusted the strap of the duffel bag against her shoulder, pulled the collar of her jacket tight to her neck, and walked against the wind to the main entrance of the lot. There she crossed the road, turned right, and continued up the macadam path toward the lighthouse. They'd been very specific during her briefing as to the pickup point. "When you reach the top of the rise, the lighthouse will be ahead of you. There will be a patch of lawn in front of you and a wooden bench on the lawn. Sit down on the bench and wait."

Casey sat down, breathed in, and listened to the waves pound steadily against the shore. The salt air was heavy and her lungs devoured it, like an infusion of pure oxygen, solid and satisfying.

She hoped they took a long time to come to get her. She loved being near the ocean, having grown up next to it, in Long Beach, California. The sea was her friend, her ally. Its waves had lulled her to sleep as a child, their rhythm against the shore a soothing lullaby.

In the past year, whenever things had been on top of her, whenever she thought she'd implode from the pressure, she had taken a weekend at Virginia Beach and rented a room by the sea. Sometimes she'd smoke a joint, just like she'd done when she was a teenager, before walking to the water's edge and sitting down in the sand to practice the breathing exercises she'd studied in Menlo Park, at the institute. The sea was like a metronome, a natural pulse of energy. Once she was in tune with it, she, Casey Lee Armstrong, was gone. It was like losing the boundaries of her physical body, and being released from the prison of life. She needed the ocean, particularly before a tasking. Sometimes it felt as though her mind were a fist, bunched so tight it hurt, as if it had been overtrained and overused. She'd tried yoga and meditation, even a sensory-deprivation tank with piped-in Zen music, but nothing relaxed her like the sound of the surf. That and the sight of it, building and rolling, surging forward, white spray against the deep blue.

Above her head the moon was new, just a hazy yellow aura around a circle of black, and the stars seemed small and far away while the beacon from the lighthouse revolved slowly, casting its beam seaward. She breathed in the solitude of the place.

Solitude was different from loneliness. Loneliness was separation, the yearning to belong to something or someone; solitude was the opposite. It was a sense of wholeness and connection. Her discipline was getting through the loneliness to discover the solitude; it was a discipline that her life had required. Time alone, to gather herself in, to recover and regroup her energies, to prepare herself to go out there again, into a place that was uncharted, a place that many said did not exist at all.

She turned at the sound of the approaching vehicle, listening as it slowed down with the narrowing road, headlights flickering through the barren trees as the road

snaked, tires grinding against gravel and sand, winding toward
her, bringing her back to the present, and to the business at
hand. She wished Nick was with her. He was her rock, her
foundation. He'd helped her put it back together more than
once in the past year. It wasn't that way for all of them in the
program, some of them could walk through a tasking, there
was no disorientation at all, but they weren't the talented
ones. They were the ones who had learned the technique and
performed it by the book. The true sensitives often folded
after a dozen or so jobs. Something inside their minds
seemed to lock open and the voices and images wouldn't stop
until finally there was nothing solid to hold on to. After that
they were of no use to anyone. Casey had been told that a few
were still there, in a special mental facility near the military
base at Fort Meade, drugged to oblivion and wandering the
corridors in white robes and cloth slippers. The thought
broke her connection with the night and suddenly she was
cold and her legs felt cramped from too much sitting in cars
and planes. Planes? *God*, she thought. *What's going to happen to
air-traffic control tomorrow night?* She didn't want to fly on New
Year's Eve, not till "they" got their glitches worked out. What
had the driver said? The rich folks had headed south.
Probably in their Hummers, loaded with tins of caviar and
blue bottles of designer water. Insecurity. Everywhere was
insecurity.

She was looking forward to going home, back to
Meade and back to Nick Hughes. They'd been together only
nine months but she felt like she'd known him a lifetime.
Their physical attraction had been instant, but Casey, on the
rebound from a failed relationship with a Washington-based
journalist, had been cautious and it had taken Hughes nearly a
month to get a date. He'd been persistent, but what really
clinched it was where he'd taken her the first time, Ocean
City, Maryland, for a picnic on the beach. It had been a box
lunch, sandwiches and a salad, with no pretense, nothing
fancy, except the '95 chardonnay. He'd looked great in a
swimming suit. Nick Hughes. Nature boy. She wished he was
with her now.

She stood up as the green Toyota Land Cruiser
rounded the final bend and turned left into the lot, inching its

way toward her. *Here we go again.* The realization carried her across the threshold of fear. That was bad. Fear was her mortal enemy. It could get her stuck, like an iron gate, blocking her safe passage home.

The window of the Land Cruiser's driver's side lowered silently.

"Captain Armstrong?" The man's voice was sharp and demanding.

"My name is Emerson," she replied, playing the game, just in case.

She already had the Myotron in her hand, inside the pocket of her jacket. It was a device about the size of an electric razor that when activated in contact with the human body delivered an electric charge that disrupted the autonomic nervous system, stopping the heart and lungs for an instant. Not intended to be lethal, it was certainly disabling.

"My orders are to transport Captain Armstrong to the base," the man continued.

In the darkness she couldn't clearly make out the features of his face but she hated his tone of voice, pumped up with authority.

"What base?"

"Black-Out," he answered.

It was the correct code name so she released her grip on the Myotron, picked up her bag, and began to walk toward him.

"I'll handle that," he said, opening his door and stepping down onto the pavement. He was at least an inch taller than Casey's five-ten and she reckoned he outweighed her by fifty pounds, packed tight into a khaki-colored pullover, jeans, and high Timberland boots. In spite of the civilian clothes he looked like a professional soldier. Never casual, something was always too polished or too starched. In this case it was his jeans; there was a fresh crease running down the front of either leg. Aside from that, he was broad-shouldered and lean and she noticed the muscles of his chest ripple beneath the fabric of his shirt as he hoisted her duffel bag and carried it to the back of the Land Cruiser. Casey liked men with good bodies, not all blown-up and overdone, but

strong and functional. Nick's body was like that and so was
this guy's. It was his face that bothered her. He had short
sandy hair, small deep-set eyes, a large nose that would go
bulbous with age and a tight thin mouth. Her grandmother
had always warned her about thin-lipped people. "Never
thrust them," she'd warned. Casey thought about that as she
followed him to the passenger side of the car.

"And you are?" she asked as he opened the door for
her.

He stared at her as if he didn't understand her
question.

"Your name?" she tried again.

"Please get in the car." There was a veiled threat to
his tone and a new wave of bad vibrations swept over her.

She slid her hand back into her pocket and cupped
the Myotron. She had heard of remote viewers being
kidnapped, even tortured for information. There was a lot of
greed and money in psychic espionage; there was also a lot of
competition and desperation. She held the weapon loose at
her side, concealed in her hand. If she had to, she'd hit him
directly in the chest, through his shirt.

"Let me see some identification," she demanded,
stepping toward him, gauging her distance. "I'm not going
anywhere till I'm certain of who I'm going with." She
disengaged the safety on her weapon.

He stared at her and for an instant she could sense his
anger. Then, as quickly, it subsided.

"My name is Roy Ames and I'm not carrying ID."

She looked down at his creased jeans then up at his
badly cut hair.

"What's your rank?" She was nervous but holding her
line. He hesitated and she pushed. "I asked you a question."

His lips softened into a passable rendition of a mouth
and his posture eased. He looked vaguely amused.

"I was in the Army Special Services until last July,
now I'm employed by Black-Out. It's a classified agency and I
have no rank." He glanced down at his jeans then back at
Casey. He was almost smiling. "I've been in the military since
I was seventeen years old. I run an iron over everything; it's a
habit."

His honesty relaxed her enough to say, "Okay then, let's go."

She stepped up and into the Land Cruiser, pocketing the Myotron as they drove out of the park area and back onto the main road.

About a mile later she was feeling better. At least these people hadn't insisted she wear a blindfold. She was thinking of her last assignment, outside of Des Moines. She hadn't known exactly where they'd taken her or what she had targeted; it looked like some type of fiber-optical instrument but that was just a guess.

The Land Cruiser slowed as they swung left off the main highway and down a stretch of road lined on either side by a mixture of white oak, cedar, and evergreens.

"Where are we going?" she asked.

"Camp Hero."

The name meant nothing to Casey.

"Is that a naval base?" she asked, thinking of their location and proximity to the water.

"Air force," Ames answered.

"Air force? I've never heard of it."

He glanced at her quickly, assessing to see if she was prying or just trying to make conversation.

"Probably because it's been closed down for thirty years," he replied.

"So who's running Black-Out?" she asked. Knowing that if he answered, he was a lousy soldier.

"I don't know." It was actually true. He'd been working for them for two months and didn't know a damn thing. He brought people in and took people out, controlled security, and got an envelope with two thousand dollars in it on Friday morning of each week. That, alone, inspired his loyalty. He'd met only one of the men in charge and knew him by the name of Mr. Dix. The others, two of them, were like ghosts, wandering around silently in lab coats like characters from a sci-fi movie. They gave him the creeps.

Casey rode the next hundred yards in silence, past a sign that read, CLOSED TO THE PUBLIC. NO UNAUTHORIZED VEHICLES, through an open gate and on to the broken surface of an old road. It ended with a crescendo of potholes and Ames, after shifting into four-wheel drive, continued to follow a dirt trail into the darkness.

A desolate feeling added to the dull dance of nerves in her belly. She didn't like the man beside her but conversation at least humanized him.

"Look at that damn thing," she said as they reached the crest of a small hill; her eyes fixed on a radar reflector the size of a football field, looming above them like the black spreading wings of a giant bird.

"World War Two stuff," Ames answered.

Casey nodded, saying, "Biggest one I've ever seen."

Ames kept quiet. In his own way he admired his passenger. She was a sexy bitch with balls, and very confident; he could tell that by the way she'd lined him up for the stun gun or whatever it was she was hiding in her pocket, eyeing his chest and making her distance. Not that she'd have had much success with an attack, but it was a good indication of her character.

Another fifty yards and they arrived at the seven-foot-high gate of a barbed-wire perimeter. Ames stopped, lowering his window in time for the beam from a Maglight to illuminate his profile.

A man, dressed in a black jumpsuit, aiming the light and armed with an M14 rifle, stepped from concealment and walked toward the Land Cruiser.

"Everything is in order," Ames said, his voice flat against the night.

The man nodded, switched off the Maglight, opened the gate, and Ames drove on. A hundred yards later and the procedure was repeated at a second perimeter with another man, identically attired and carrying a similar weapon.

"These people are very serious, whoever they are," Casey commented.

Ames did not reply. Now that they were inside the guarded area of the compound, he seemed very much the soldier, silent and alert.

They were moving at a crawl by the time the headlights from the Land Cruiser lit up the tight group of buildings ahead of them. One appeared out of context to the others; it was almost residential, a shingled bungalow with a front porch and a chimney, something that looked as though it had been transported from one of the nearby towns, old and quaint like a fisherman's cottage. It was also the only building with the glow of light from its windows. Behind it, maybe thirty feet back, was what resembled a small aircraft hangar with corrugated iron walls and a high curved roof adjoined by a cylindrical tanklike structure that Casey assumed to be some type of fuel-storage facility. The last in the cluster was L-shaped and sided with clapboard. All told, with its lack of trees and vegetation and dark perimeters of barbed wire, the place looked foreboding; it also looked temporary, like a stage set, as if it all could be quickly torn down or vacated.

Ames pulled to a stop in front of the fisherman's cottage. He switched off the headlights and the night closed in around them.

"Wait here," he ordered, moving the shift lever to park, turning off the engine, then removing the keys before he climbed out of the Land Cruiser.

She sat back in the cream-colored leather seat and watched the door of the cottage open as Roy Ames went inside. She recalled her early morning briefing with Col. Parnell Stevens. Stevens was in charge of the Remote Viewing Unit at Fort Meade, known as Etherworld, and he had explained to her that she'd been requisitioned by an agency with "above top secret" status.

"Requisitioned to do what?" she'd asked.

Stevens had appeared at a loss to answer, even guilty, which was out of character for the cut-and-dried military man.

Finally, he'd responded. "The tasking is on a need-to-know-only basis, and, obviously, I don't need to know."

She'd pressed on. "Why me?"

He'd smiled then, but his smile was somehow guarded, almost sheepish.

"Because of your success rate in the Gulf. It seems to trail you like a banner."

The Gulf offensive had been her first assignment, nine years ago. Casey had targeted over a dozen of Hussein's mobile SCUD launchers and saved the government millions of dollars in aircraft sorties and reconnaissance missions. Most people, including military people, had had no idea that a team of psychics was actively scouring Middle Eastern coordinates for weapons and Iraqi troop placement. General Schwartzkopf had been the hero of the military campaign, but twenty-four-year-old Casey Armstrong had become the hero of the psi community.

Still, that hadn't saved the Remote Viewing Unit from extinction, and in 1994, after failing to receive new funding from the CIA's Office of Research and Development, the psychic-spying program was officially canceled. It was followed by a barrage of negative mainstream publicity, claiming that it had always been a mixture of fraud and delusion.

What the public did not know was that the program, scaled down and refinanced by a faction of the National Security Agency, had remained operational, and that a select group of psychics, most unknown even to each other, were still active.

Finally Ames reappeared. Walking straight to Casey's side of the car, he opened the door.

"Mr. Dix is waiting for you inside."

Casey met his eyes. She hadn't had a clear view of them before, but now in the yellow glow of the car's interior lights she could see that they were sharks' eyes, dead and cold. She hung on a second longer than she should have, trying to read them. That's when the rush came. Catching her unprepared, like a concealed blade, poker hot against her heart. She went suddenly rigid, gasping for breath, thinking, *He's going to kill me.*

"Is there a problem?" Ames asked. He'd been awake since 4:00 A.M. and he didn't feel like hassling with another one of these temperamental guinea pigs, no matter how long her legs, or how tight her ass.

Casey pulled herself back through what felt like a fissure in the surface of time. Her stomach closed around the fear and she was whole again. Frightened but whole.

"No problem," she replied, stepping down from the car. Ames attempted to assist her but she pulled away from his arm. "I'm fine," she said, but inside she was anxious. Maybe she was losing it, like the others. Maybe it hadn't been a true precognitive flash. There was such a fine line between imagination and future reality. It was when that line disappeared that you had to worry. She'd been working hard in the past six months, really stretching herself, and perhaps this acute paranoia was the toll. But what if it was not paranoia? She had always wondered if one day she'd sense her own death. Was this it? Was this ugly man her executioner? What was she really doing here? She stumbled slightly on her next step. *Get it together*, she told herself, reining in her thoughts and concentrating on her breathing and the muscles of her body. Her calves were still sore from a long, uphill exercise run she'd taken two days ago. She thought about that. Sore calves, a little pain, a good way to get back into the here and now.

Ames held the door as she entered the cottage. The main room was to her left, illuminated by the glow from a single table lamp. The floor was dark oak and the furniture, two chairs and a sofa, looked cheap and disposable, like something bought from a cut-rate mail-order catalogue, with a beige fabric and thin cushions. The fireplace was clean and empty, as if it had never been used.

"Dr. Armstrong?"

It was the first time she'd been called "doctor" in years. Her Ph.D. in experimental psychology from Stanford seemed a long way behind her. She turned to see a tall gray-haired man walking from the adjoining room, using a carved wooden cane and carrying a whiskey glass.

"I'm Preston Dix, how do you do?" he continued, placing his cane to rest by the side of the chair nearest him, and extending his hand.

The first thing that Casey noticed about his clothing was his shoes, or rather carpet slippers; they were black velvet and monogrammed, the silver thread of their entwined initials very ornate and almost impossible to read, obscured by the break in the cuff of his dark woolen trousers. The trousers were held in check by a set of green plaid suspenders, which fit snug against his cream silk shirt.

Like some eccentric country gentleman, Casey thought as she took the long, thin hand in hers, shaking it lightly while casting a sideways glance at Ames, who remained in the tiny entrance hall, his back to the door.

"Please, sit down. May I offer you a drink? Something to eat?" Dix asked, following her eyes to the cheap sofa. Then, as if by way of an apology he said, "Not exactly my taste in decor but, with any luck, we won't be here much longer." His voice was hard to place, but Casey distinguished traces of the South, smoothed over but still there.

She was too on edge to eat, anxious to know what her tasking was all about. On top of which she felt uncomfortable in Dix's presence. He seemed to be assessing her, staying one step ahead of her thoughts. Or, maybe, it was the way Ames was standing, as if he was on guard duty.

"I can have something brought in, fish or pasta," Dix continued.

Casey eyed his glass. She needed to level out.

"I wouldn't mind a whiskey. It's been a long day."

Dix hesitated, studying her. She seemed very young. More the organic rice and distilled water type. Whiskey? He was surprised she had requested alcohol before a tasking but then, these people always fascinated him, peculiar in one way or another. This one, as his inquiries had promised, seemed particularly sensitive.

"Certainly, would you like a blend or a single malt?" he asked.

"A single malt," she replied, "just a little ice."

"Is Glenmorangie acceptable?" Dix asked.

"That would be perfect," she replied. Her father had been a whiskey drinker and had educated her to the various blends and malts.

"Please sit down," he repeated. "It will only take a few seconds." He placed his glass on the table, picked up his cane, and walked to the kitchen. There was no trace of a limp, and Casey wondered if the cane was more cosmetic than functional.

The whiskey soothed her, buffing the edges of her nerves, and after the second glass she was drowsy.

Preston Dix had done his homework. He knew as much about the Remote Viewing Program as Casey did and had a way of talking that gave away precious little about himself. There was an indication that he was working on a top-priority multinational project yet he never committed as to who he was working for or the exact nature of the project.

"I believe you'll find it most challenging," he repeated on several occasions. His pattern of speech was relaxed, almost a singsong, and after twenty minutes Casey was wondering where her sleeping quarters were and how she could politely end their meeting.

As if on cue Dix said, "You must be tired." He was studying her eyes in a way that she found uncomfortable. It felt like an invasion of her privacy. Reaching over from his chair he took the glass from her hand, then looking toward the door where Ames was still standing, said, "Would you show Dr. Armstrong to her quarters."

Casey stood up from the sofa and accepted the skeletal hand for the second time. This time she held it longer than on their initial meeting. Dix's skin was thin, dry, and cool and she flashed momentarily on the first time she'd touched a snake. The thought made her pull away. She didn't feel "right," not with Dix and certainly not with Ames. She tried to rationalize her feelings: hunger, fatigue, too many assignments in the past month. None of it worked to allay her unease.

Dix cleared his throat.

"I'd like to begin the tasking at 0800 hours, the mess hall opens at 0600," he said. It was the first time he'd said anything that sounded truly military. "Sleep well," he added.

She followed Ames out of the house. The stars were brighter than they had been half an hour ago and the air seemed colder and incredibly heavy; she could smell the ocean on the night breeze, a blend of seaweed and salt. She felt a long way from Nick and very alone.

Ames led her to the L-shaped building which was about a minute walk from Dix's headquarters. The door was not locked and she trailed him through a dimly lit corridor. There was a series of closed doors to either side; they looked light and flimsy, not enough to keep her safe. *From who or what?* she wondered. *Why am I having these thoughts?*

"Toilet and washroom are here," Ames said, indicating one of the doors. "And you'll be in here." He stopped outside the room closest to the toilet and bath facility and laid her bag on the floor. "You need water, or anything?"

She met his eyes and waited, as if the feeling from before, that sense of death, was going to recur. She didn't want it to but she was drawn to its possibility, as if she was testing it. Nothing happened.

Ames stared at her. She looked like she was losing it, before they even got started on her.

"Are you all right?" he asked.

"Fine," she answered, too quickly. "No. I won't be needing anything. Thank you."

"Good night then," Ames replied, watching as she hoisted her bag, opened the door, and entered the room.

She did have a great ass. He'd seen it as she'd bent over. He'd never fucked anything that looked quite as good as Casey Armstrong. She was right out of the Victoria's Secret catalogue. He wondered if he ever would.

~ 2 ~

Casey often had the same dream before an assignment. She was in a subway car, up front with the motorman. They were traveling fast, through a giant metropolis, steel bridges and skyscrapers, rivers and glass-fronted buildings. Through them. That was the essence of the dream. Nothing was solid. It was all illusion, reflections of light, creating form. The motorman kept telling her to wake up and see life for what it was, a dream, images projected by the mind. "Strawberry fields. Nothing is real." Wake up. Wake up.

When she did, it was just after six o'clock in the morning. She had a moment of complete disorientation, that kind of jet-lag moment, when the sleep has been too deep and the mind too far away. She looked around the small room, her eyes adjusting to the diffused light from the hallway, seeping from the crack beneath the thin door with its single bolt lock. The bolt was in place. She remembered locking it last night, then she remembered Ames and her premonition. It seemed less threatening now, almost absurd. A heavy sleep had caused it to shrink in perspective.

She slipped out of bed, put a black silk robe on over her bare chest and underpants, slid back the bolt from the door, and peeked out into the hallway. It looked prefab and dingy: white painted walls, a gray linoleum floor and a low flat ceiling. She could get no real sense of the place, wondering who else was inside. Was she alone?

It was dead quiet as she walked to the bathroom. Locking herself in, she used the toilet then returned to her room. There, she removed a digital timer from her bag and a leather jump rope, pushed the cot tight to the wall, making space, took off her robe, and jumped six three-minute rounds with a minute rest in between each. It was her away-from-base ritual. A good sweat seemed to flush her system in preparation for the mental exercise that would inevitably follow. After that, she replaced her robe, grabbed soap, shampoo, and a towel from her bag and headed back to the shower room.

By 6:45 A.M. she was dressed in a loose, white cotton training suit and a pair of Asics running shoes, her preferred working uniform.

She stepped into the hallway and inhaled the aroma of fried bacon and eggs that wafted on the heavy, heated air. After twenty-four hours without food, the smell of the grease and fat was nauseating. Still, curious as to exactly where she was and who else was there, she followed the smell from her room, down the hall, and into a larger room, which had been converted to a dining area.

Dix and two other men were seated at one of three folding tables beside a small buffet. He nodded his greeting but made no sign for her to join them or meet the others so she walked to the buffet and piled as much fruit onto her plate as it would hold. Then she took a bottle of spring water and walked past Dix on her way to a table. He was mopping the yolk of an egg from his plate with a thick slice of toast and stopped only long enough to say, "Good morning, Dr. Armstrong, sleep well?"

She replied, "Fine thank you," and kept walking. She felt like the new kid at boarding school.

The fruit was out of season and the slices of honeydew were cold from refrigeration and hard and rubbery in texture. She passed on them and was attempting the first in a pile of pale strawberries when Dix and the two men got up from their table. She hadn't really paid any attention to the others, but now, standing beside Dix, she noticed that one was heavyset with a full beard and the other was Asian, unusually tall and as thin as Dix, with a set of half-lensed reading glasses hanging by a cord around his neck. Both wore lab coats and the Asian was wearing what appeared to be a badly fitted toupee, dark brown and loose to the sides of his head.

They stopped as they got to her table.

"Dr. Armstrong, I'd like to introduce you to my colleagues," Dix said.

She swallowed half a strawberry and began to get up from the table.

"Please, don't stand, enjoy your breakfast," Dix continued. It was the first that she'd seen him smile and she noticed that his teeth were small and yellow like old ivory.

"This is Professor George," he said, indicating the larger of the two men, "and this," turning to the tall Asian, "is Dr. Mishima."

The Japanese man performed a polite bow.

"Dr. Mishima and I will be observing while Professor George will monitor your session."

Casey met the eyes of Professor George, brown with just a streak of gold in the irises.

"It's a pleasure to meet you," George said, holding her gaze. "Should be an interesting experience."

Casey smiled politely, noting the hint of sarcasm in his tone.

"Is there anything in particular that you'd like at the session?" George continued.

Casey was uncertain as to what he meant and it must have registered in her face.

"Some of our RVs have wanted ginseng tea, incense, that kind of thing."

"Thanks. I'll bring along another bottle of water. That's about all I ever have while I'm working," she replied. Her own voice sounded phony to her, like some spaced-out health junkie. In fact Casey could knock back a pint of Haagen-Dazs with the best of them. The clean regime was reserved for working days, when she wanted no interference from her digestive tract. Plus, she was covering for the fact that she wasn't comfortable with any of these men. There was just something insincere about them, their bearing and attitude, so stiff and condescending. They were like cardboard cutouts of actual human beings. She was going to have to work hard at relaxing, which was a contradiction in itself.

"As you wish," Dix answered. "We'll be starting," he checked his watch, "in just under an hour. I'll have Mr. Ames collect you from your room."

"I'll be waiting," she replied, manufacturing a smile that she passed on to the group, then watched the three of them walk briskly from the makeshift cafeteria, Dix leading, tapping the floor lightly with his cane, like a blind man, followed by George with the Japanese doctor taking up the rear. It was a strange procession and she wondered what the three of them had in common, what interest had brought them together here, and what part she was supposed to play in it. She looked around. There was no one else in the room, not a cook, not Ames. *Ames?* What was that all about, last night's paranoia? The whole damn thing was getting to her and she wondered if she could pull it together for the tasking. What if she couldn't? A loss of face and they'd send her back to Meade a few hours early, for New Year's Eve with Nick. That would be worth the humiliation. New Year's Eve at the Tante Claire restaurant. Very sexy.

She held the thought as she walked from the empty room and back down the hall. Locking her door she sat down on the bed and tried to piece her feelings together. She'd never felt this bad before a tasking. Why? What was she sensing? She was tempted to open up then, right there in the room, to use her energy, to put her mind behind her feelings. Sheer professionalism held her back. She knew that if she tranced out, she'd have nothing left for the session. Instead, she did what she always did before an event; she took off her trainers, lay back, and concentrated on her breathing, controlling her breath from her lower abdomen, drawing it up through the energy points of her body, retaining it at the chakra midway between her eyes, then sending it out through the crown of her head. The exercise, which she had practiced for almost a decade, had the effect of both centering and emptying her and after a hundred rounds of inhalation, retention, then exhalation, her thought process had slowed and she had the sensation of being a hollow tube; she was a breathing apparatus made of flesh and blood. The next phase was complete relaxation. Had it not been for the persistent knock on the door she could have drifted for hours.

Ames's face looked younger than on the previous night. Pinker and fresher. Maybe it had been the darkness, or maybe she had been tired, but in the morning light he looked like a kid. A very tough kid. He was wearing a white T-shirt, which clung to his torso, and his arms were roped with veins, crisscrossing his biceps and running down the pale skin and into his pop-eyed forearms like lengths of blue steel cable, ending just before the large knuckles of hands that resembled bony mallets.

"Ready, Dr. Armstrong?" he asked, his tone matter-of-fact. It was less a question than an order.

"Yes. Let's go," she replied, noting as he turned that his jeans were freshly pressed.

They walked out of the building.

Above, the sun was pushing hard behind a thin layer of cloud and the sky was silver gray; it made the kind of light that caused everything to look old and unwashed. They turned right, toward the rusted cylindrical structure she'd thought to be some type of fuel depository. It was about thirty feet in diameter and windowless but as they got closer she could hear the low rumble of what sounded like an air-conditioning unit and saw a door cut into the metal siding. She felt claustrophobic just looking at it.

"This is a bit severe," she said as they walked toward the door.

Inside, the place was a labyrinth of small adjoining rooms, lit by soft, yellow light. One room in particular caught her eye. More a chamber than a room, it had a heavy metal door with a wheel lock that looked as if it had been borrowed from a submarine. The door was open and inside the room she could see a beige carpeted floor, a tan leather club chair, and a folding table with paper, pencils, and what appeared, at a distance, to be a metal cigar tube on top of it. An audio headset lay on the seat of the chair. Aside from two air vents and a single spotlight, which had been fixed into the apex of the ceiling, the room was a perfect pyramid of galvanized steel.

"We've tried to achieve as near to complete isolation as possible."

She recognized Dix's mild drawl before she turned to see him emerge from the room directly facing the chamber.

"Look comfortable?" he asked.

Working conditions were paramount to an RV and Casey sure as hell didn't like these.

"The chair and table are fine but the rest of it is a bit tight," she replied.

"Don't worry, it's perfectly ventilated and the pyramid shape was designed to maximize mental energy. You'll get used to it," Dix said, then stepped to her side and placed his hand high on her shoulder. "Come on, Doctor, let me show you in."

She felt more like she was being shoved than guided as she stepped up and over the lip of the door and down into the chamber.

Dix removed the headset from the seat.

"Just sit down, relax, slip this on, and Professor George will take charge. Your water? Did you forget your water?"

The chair was worn and had the good reassuring smell of old leather.

"I'm fine for the time being without it," she replied, settling comfortably against the high back and rolled arms.

Dix handed her the headset, watching as she put it on and adjusted the mouthpiece so that it was positioned directly in front of her lips.

The next voice she heard belonged to Professor George.

"Hello, Dr. Armstrong." It was very resonant through the earphones. "Can you hear me clearly?"

Casey sat back and felt the first trickle of cool air from the vents.

"Loud and clear," she replied.

"Right, let me get some levels in here and we'll begin."

That meant they were recording the session. It was a common practice.

"Please, Doctor, say your name a couple of times. Just till I get the levels."

"Casey Lee Armstrong." Lee had been a family name. "Casey Lee Armstrong." Her mother had been Hawaiian and her ancestry was Chinese. The slight slant of her eyes was Casey's only legacy.

"That's fine, keep talking please."

Casey turned to see Dix step from the chamber and swing the door into place behind him. Then she thought she heard the locking wheel turn and the bolts click into place.

"He's not locking me inside here, is he? I'm not comfortable with that if he is."

"That's good, Doctor, we've got the levels." George spoke as if he had not heard her.

"If you have the levels then maybe you could answer my question," Casey replied. She sounded firm and unruffled. "Have I just been locked inside?"

Dix's voice answered. "It is simply to seal the room. We don't want any outside interference, no noise, no disturbance. We like to work in a controlled environment."

His reassurance didn't do a lot for her.

"I've never worked in these conditions," she said. "I'm not sure I can."

"Shall we attempt the target?" Dix asked. There was no concession in his tone.

Casey sat back in silence. Obviously, they weren't going to bow to her requests. *Let's get it over with*, she thought.

"Yes," she answered curtly.

"Do you need a little time to relax?" It was George speaking again, all smooth and breathy like a two-hundred-dollar-an-hour shrink.

"Relax," he repeated as the overhead light dimmed.

She had an image of the three of them, Dix, George, and the silent Japanese doctor, what was his name? Mishima, yes, that was it, Mishima, like the fascist novelist. She thought of them sitting in their tiny room, testing her as if she was some kind of laboratory animal. A rat, locked inside a metal drum, performing for them while Ames prowled the perimeter of the building like a guard dog. She didn't like it at all.

"Would you care for some music over the headphones?" George asked.

"No music, please," she replied.

"All right, I'm going to ask you to pick up the cylindrical metal container, which should be directly in front of you on the table."

Casey hesitated. She had expected to be tasked with a set of coordinates, longitudinal and latitudinal settings that would act as a bridge between the physical universe that the monitor was concerned with and the mental universe that she would inhabit during the session. The coordinates provided a specific target for her psychic abilities.

"Have you done that?" George continued.

Casey looked at the tube. It was the first time since she'd noticed it that she'd paid it any particular attention. It was actually beautiful, about four inches long and the color of dull silver, not shiny but perfectly polished, rounded at both ends and with no visible joins in the metal. It reminded her of a surgical instrument, something built for a specific purpose, with no frills or waste in design. Perfect in its simplicity. Still, she had an aversion to actually touching it. It was a sensation, not of danger, but of something else, almost a reverence. She couldn't quite pinpoint the feeling.

"I'm accustomed to working with coordinates," she said, stalling. "I don't understand what this has to do with that."

George hesitated and she could sense him thinking. Finally he spoke.

"We're going to do this a little bit differently today."

"I don't get it," Casey said.

"Psychometry," George replied. It was the ability to divine events concerning an object or a person associated with it by contact or proximity to the object.

"That's not what I do," Casey answered.

"Please, there's no need for modesty. We have all your tasking results on file. Your record with the CIA is most impressive."

Casey held back a groan. She'd worked several times with the CIA on cases concerning political kidnappings, when the only shred of evidence was an article of clothing or a personal effect.

"Doctor," Dix intervened, "will you please cooperate."

Reaching forward, she touched the tube gently with her fingertips. The metal was cold and incredibly smooth. It was also extremely hard, glasslike in the consistency of its outer surface.

"I'm making contact with it now," she said.

Lifting it from the table, she held it lightly in her right hand, gripping gently with her fingers, caressing it with her thumb. Then she placed it between her palms and rolled it back and forth, as if she were aligning herself with the cold metal. Her first sensation was that it contained something that was alive.

"Now, if you'd care to open it," George coaxed.

Casey was already getting flashes.

"The tube is man-made. It's just a case, it's what's inside that's important. It has been examined before," she said. "Several times."

"That's correct, Doctor. Now if you'd care to proceed."

"Professor, I need to work in my own time," she answered.

There was a brief silence before George replied, "Carry on."

She squeezed the cylinder as she let her head recline against the back of the chair, closing her eyes.

"This has been all over the world," she said softly. "I feel all kinds of—" she hesitated. "Scientists, mostly scientists have examined this. Except in Peru. Something strange happened in Peru."

"Yes, but that's of no consequence now," Dix answered as if he were talking to her when in fact she couldn't hear the men in the monitoring room unless the TALK button on their console was depressed.

"In the Amazon," she said. "Death? Did somebody die there?" Her voice was low, even though it was amplified by the hundred-and-fifty watt speakers.

Before George could depress the TALK button, Dix said, "Don't answer, just let her keep going."

"Peru? The Amazon? What is she talking about?" Mishima cut in. His English was as precise as his manicured fingernails, clipped and polished.

There was nothing Japanese about his accent. It was all Oxford.

"An Indian shaman," Dix explained, although his tone was reluctant. "He was supplied by our British sources, about six months ago. Damned idiot took some kind of sacred, hallucinogenic drink, opened the capsule, and had a coronary."

"His heart. It was his heart," Casey said abruptly and suddenly there was a sharp slapping sound from the speakers as she placed the tube back on the table. "I don't want to go on with this." She removed her fingers from the metal and sat staring at it. It seemed to reflect her stare. Challenging.

"What happened?" Mishima asked. "Did she hear us?"

"Impossible. That's impossible," George replied, checking the button on the console, finally depressing it. "Dr. Armstrong, are you okay in there?"

"There's something wrong," Casey said. "Something feels very wrong."

After that the only sound coming from the speakers was of her breathing, fast and shallow.

"Same as the others, goddamn it," Dix said. "What do we do with her?" He looked hatefully at the wall that separated them from the RV chamber, as if he was staring straight through it, at Casey. Frustrated, he spit the words. "These people are all useless."

George turned toward him. "Hold on a second." Then, lowering his tone, he said, "This one is different. Let me work with her." His forte was behavioral psychology and he'd had an excellent feeling about Casey the moment he'd seen her enter the cafeteria. It was more than her credentials or her background. She'd looked confident, emotionally strong. It was written in her body language, the way she'd walked, as if she was sure of the connection between her feet and the ground, and the way she carried herself with her shoulders back and her neck straight. There was something animal-proud about her, combined with a wariness. "I'm sure I can get something out of her," he added.

Dix pushed back in his chair. "Then by all means get on with it."

George pressed the TALK button on the console. "Dr. Armstrong?"

By then Casey had regained control of her breathing.

"Yes, I'm here," she answered, but she was still trembling and she couldn't explain it. She'd never been shaken during a tasking. This was a first. The object in front of her possessed a unique energy; it seemed to have probed her as she was probing it, pushing right in against her mind. She'd never felt anything like it before.

George spoke slowly and reassuringly.

"Do you want to take a break? Listen to some music? How about that water?"

Casey looked at the tube. Harmless again now that it was out of her hand. What the hell was inside it anyway? She inhaled, held the breath and exhaled slowly. It was a professional matter now. It had nothing to do with the men in the monitoring room. She'd been trained at this; she was talented. She couldn't afford to freeze up. She'd heard about viewers who'd seized during a tasking. They were never the same again, not quite whole.

"I'd like to try again," she replied.

Dix muttered something under his breath that sounded like "Thank God" as George answered, "In your own time, Doctor."

Casey picked the tube up quickly with her thumb and forefinger, as if she was handling a dangerous snake, keeping her mind away from the fear, concentrating her awareness on her breath. Breath was everything. Breath was consciousness.

Open it, she told herself. *I don't know how it opens.* Even as she thought it, the metal seemed to separate between her fingers, dividing on near-invisible joins, popping slightly as the vacuum was broken.

The woofing sound transmitted through the speakers.

"She's inside," George whispered.

Dix nodded his head. "Finally."

In the lower section of the tube, nestled in a soft transparent gel, was a small object, about a quarter of an inch in diameter. It was encased in some sort of flesh-toned fabric, or skin, with tiny black threads, or legs, protruding from its upper quadrant. Was it an insect? There was something live about it. Something animate.

She asked, "May I touch it?"

"Please, Doctor, feel free," George replied.

The gel was soft but not sticky and Casey removed the object with the thumb and index finger of her left hand.

Placing it in her palm, her initial sensation was one of warmth, as if it was giving off heat. She closed her hand around it. At first she thought it was her own heart beating, the pulse was steady and strong, but it was not her heart. The pulse was actually coming from the object. It was moving, undulating. There was something unnatural, repulsive, about it and she withstood a desire to throw it on the floor and get rid of it. Instead she moved closer to her fear, squeezing tighter. It felt like it was burrowing inside her skin, entering her.

"What is it?" Her words were barely audible.

George replied softly. "Dr. Armstrong. You tell us."

The first flash of light exploded directly between her eyes, throwing her backward against the chair. Then a second. On the third she dissolved. That's what it felt like when she detached from herself and entered the "zone," a place where Casey Armstrong ceased to be and the division between internal and external stimulus temporarily vanished. Sometimes, but not often, it was violent like this.

She looked down, onto a city milling with people. There were hundreds of buildings and mountains all around. And people were staring up. Looking at her. Waiting. Waiting for what?

"Ninety-nine degrees north, nineteen west," she said.

George turned to Dix and Mishima. "She's got it."

"Ninety-nine north, nineteen west," she repeated it like a mantra as she closed her eyes and drifted.

Casey moved in the chair as if she was listening to the slow, dreamy beat of some distant music, her head swaying in gentle rhythms. The images came like that, as if they were

floating on waves of light, swimming in her mind. She
opened her eyes and leaned forward, picking up a pencil with
her free hand. She had done this so many times in so many
different places that she was barely conscious of her own
physical movement. It had become a reflex action at a certain
point during a tasking. Once the target was firm and active in
the right hemisphere of her brain, the left functioned as a
recording device, analyzing and transmitting data.

She began to draw, as if the act of recreating on paper
aided in the recovery process, pulling form from the ether.

She drew a sun, then she blacked it out, leaving only
the borders.

"What's this? An eclipse. A solar eclipse." She spoke
as she drew but the questions and answers were directed at
herself. "Is that what everybody's watching? A total eclipse of
the sun. A lot of energy here. Masses of energy. It's hot. Hell
of a time to be in Mexico. Summer. Summers are hot in the
city. Too hot."

Dix knew all about the '91 eclipse. It had coincided
with one of the best-witnessed and most-documented
accounts of unidentified aerial phenomena in history. A light
dancing in the sky, coinciding with the blackout. Hundreds of
people had witnessed it and numerous civilians had taped it
with camcorders. His organization had analyzed seventeen of
the cassettes and the results had been inconclusive as to what
exactly the object had been.

Casey drew a triangular shape to the left of the sun.

"That's beautiful, really beautiful. Looks like a stone,
skipping across water. Are we watching that or are we
watching the eclipse? Are they connected? What the hell is
that thing up there with the sun? We're watching it. Forget
about the sun. We're watching the light. It's putting on a
show." She spoke her next words as if they were some sort of
revelation. "I'm part of that light."

After that, she experienced a mild nausea, which
rapidly became more intense.

"I've got that light inside me," she continued. Then,
her voice changed, expressing pain. "I'm not sure I want this.
It hurts."

It was burning, like a hot probe.

"Hey, I don't want this goddamn thing inside me." Her voice blasted the speakers. "It's not natural. Not natural!"

"Relax, Dr. Armstrong. Relax. Keep going," George soothed.

"Jesus Christ. I can't take this!"

A moment later it broke inside her, all the pain and fear purging in one cleansing burst. After that her voice eased.

"It's out. Thank God. It's out. I'm okay. Okay."

She felt groggy, as if she was waking up from a general anesthetic.

"I'm in a big building. Lots of beds. I think it's a hospital. I don't feel well."

She could smell flowers. Roses. Sometimes she had olfactory sensations and the sweet aroma came as a relief.

"My stomach still hurts. God, they pushed that thing right inside me. Way up. They had no right. No right." Even as she spoke she was writing, as if she was divided cleanly between the person undergoing the experience and the person recording it.

"Dr. Armstrong?"

"Thirty-eight north, one hundred four west." Her voice was clipped.

Dix and George exchanged glances as Casey drew a triangle. Then sensing something not quite right with her drawing, she erased the upper quarter, toward the apex, and put a straight line across the top, to connect the sides so that they formed what looked like a funnel, then drew a sphere inside it, and another, close together so that the two spheres joined. She shadowed the top one, until it resembled a face with eyes, nose, and mouth. Staring down at it, she had a feeling of recognition, as if she was linked to it, both psychically and physically. The feeling was overpowering.

"Where are you now, Dr. Armstrong?" George asked.

"Inside a place that is warm and dark. I feel a heart beating. I see a face. Not human. Not yet, but close. Very close—" She stopped speaking and closed her eyes. She could sense something gripping her mind. Opening and entering.

"Dr. Armstrong?"

It was a triangle of light, pulsing with a steady rhythm, linking her to something vast, some great collective gathering of energy.

"Talk to us, Dr. Armstrong," George ordered.

"It has to look like us. We wouldn't accept it if it did not look like us."

"Explain," George continued.

"We come from them. Dear God. Oh, my God. It's manifesting in terms that we will accept, like a disguise, a camouflage."

There was silence before her voice cut back into the room.

"I don't know if I can handle this." Escalating in pitch she said, "I can't channel this energy. It's too much. It's distorting my perception. I'm going to lose it. Colors. I see all kinds of colors. I'm looking at my hand. I see red. I don't like that. Blood. I'm swimming in blood!"

She could hear George's voice through the speakers, but it seemed far away, on the other side of some great divide.

"We're coming to get you."

"Thirty-eight north, one hundred four west," she blurted. "There's a building. A hospital. A rose. A blood red rose?" Then frightened. "I don't understand. Something's not right with this. What the hell is this?" She lifted the pencil, touching the lead to the paper. "Thirty-eight north, one hundred four west." She was bearing down so hard that she tore through the white sheet and into the top of the table, breaking the point of the pencil.

There was blood dripping onto the desk, trickling between her fingers. Then pain, like something eating her flesh. She opened her hand.

"Oh my God! My God!" she screamed, leaping up from the chair, knocking over the table, trying to shake it loose. "Get it off me!"

They were inside the chamber within seconds. George held her while Mishima rammed the needle through her shirt and into her arm. The antipsychotic was laced with a sedative.

"Lay her out here, on the floor," Dix instructed, pointing with the tip of his cane.

George positioned her on her back, legs spread slightly apart, and arms to her sides. She trembled slightly as she lost consciousness.

Dix had been this far with a viewer only once before. There had been a delay then and it had turned into a real mess.

"We've got to get it out before it assimilates completely," he said, looking at Mishima. "Are you ready?"

Mishima nodded. Of course he was ready; this was his moment. He was going to get close to the thing. He propped his glasses onto the bridge of his nose and squatted down beside the bleeding hand as George pried it open.

"It's nearly in," George stated. Already pieces of Casey's flesh had bonded with the membrane. "You see how the tentacles synthesize with the host's flesh until they become part of the body?"

Mishima used a scalpel to cut the skin of the surrounding area. He had to go deep and the operation took a full minute.

"Incredible, incredible," he kept saying, as he studied the device.

"Where did it come from?" he asked.

Dix replied. "A girl in Mexico City. It was in her uterus. Surgeon removed it in 1994, during a routine C-section. He had no idea what it was. None."

"Where are they now?" Mishima asked, working the device free.

Dix pursed his lips and shook his head.

"The mother and the child," Mishima said, believing that Dix hadn't understood his question.

Dix's mouth tightened.

"Dead. Both of them," he answered. "It was a traffic accident, a hit and run."

"And the father?" Mishima asked.

"There was no father."

"I don't understand," Mishima continued.

"The girl was a virgin."

"But—"

"That's all we know." Dix's tone was sharp and left no room for speculation.

"I see," Mishima answered. Then, using a pair of surgical tweezers he lifted the device from Casey's palm, dipping it into a tube of saline solution to clear her blood and flesh away, before returning it to its titanium casing.

Dix scanned the papers that were scattered on the floor. He picked up the sheet with the funnel-like drawing on it. It was torn at the top and the coordinates were indecipherable but that didn't worry him; everything that Casey had said—including the new set of coordinates—had been recorded on tape. It was the drawing that caught his attention.

George looked down.

"What do you make of it?" he asked.

Dix turned the paper in his hand, so that the shadowed areas of the sphere were uppermost on the white sheet.

"I'm not sure."

Mishima looked over his shoulder at the drawing and asked cautiously, "Have you ever seen a photo print of an ultrasound examination?"

George's mouth was suddenly dry. "Are you suggesting that it might be a fetus?"

Mishima was a newcomer to the project and he wanted to be respected. He spoke slowly, careful with his words.

"It is the correct shape for a scan, almost like a funnel, and that upper sphere certainly appears to be a baby's head. See the shadowing around the eye sockets?"

George looked at Dix. "Do you think it's possible?"

Dix met his eyes and held them a moment without answering. Then he turned away, looking back at Casey's drawing. He was thinking fast. He'd need a survey of all the hospitals in the areas corresponding to the new coordinates. Doctors. Delivery dates. Especially planned cesareans. He'd have to lean on people in the private sector to gain access to medical records, and that could be done only with full compliance from his own organization. He'd have to act quickly.

Turning to Mishima, he asked, "Are you ready for the stretcher?"

Mishima met Dix's gaze. It was all business, nothing savored. Then the Japanese doctor bent down and lifted one of Casey's eyelids, peering at the enlarged pupil.

"Yes, anytime."

"I'll get Ames in here to help you," Dix said.

"Do you want a complete dissolution?" Mishima asked.

Dix looked down at Casey. Her mouth was open and there was a bit of white foam around her lips, a symptom of the heavy sedation.

"I don't want anything left," he answered.

~ 3 ~

It was December 31, 11:20 P.M.

Forty minutes before the year 2000.

They were dancing. Trying to anyway. That's what made it fun. Moving around the living room, in front of the blank television screen, with the CD player turned on, swaying to an old Van Morrison song.

Molly's head just about reached his shoulder, if she pushed her hips hard and his hands were wrapped around her waist, fingers barely able to clasp.

"Something's come between us," Thomas said, pressing himself gently against her belly.

That made her laugh. It felt good to laugh.

"Not for long," she answered. In two days they'd be parents again.

The first pain hit her a few seconds later. It was sharp, stabbing, like period cramp, but much more intense, causing her to hunch forward.

She jerked away from Thomas, saying, "I've got to sit down."

He looked at her. Even in the dimmed light from the overhead spots, she looked suddenly pale and drawn.

"Here," he said, taking her arm and leading her to the side of the room.

She sat down as another contraction hit. The pain made her gasp, "I think I'm in labor."

Then, aware of a wetness beneath her skirt, she reached down and rubbed up, along her thigh.

"My water just broke."

When she looked at her hand, she noticed a trace of blood. Her voice betrayed her fear as she looked pleadingly at Thomas and said, "This isn't supposed to happen, not now."

Thomas was already on the phone, Murray Rose's business card in his hand, dialing the number of his service.

At midnight, with fireworks exploding over Pikes Peak, car horns blaring, and people dancing at parties and charity balls all over town, Molly Reed was wheeled into the operating room of the maternity unit at the medical center. She had been shaved, intubated, which meant a tube had been run through her mouth and into her windpipe, to supply the gas required to anesthetize her, a catheter had been inserted into her bladder, and an IV infusion started, providing her with the fluid she would need during the surgery.

The doors closed behind her, leaving Thomas Reed alone in the hallway. Waiting and praying.

He had wanted to stay with her. To be right there, beside her, but it was not permitted, not when they were using a general anesthetic.

Inside the operating room, Rose's assistant, a tiny Filipino nurse, named Carmelita Rodriguez, finished arranging the sterile drapes around Molly Reed's exposed abdomen.

Rose already had the scalpel in his hand, while Rodriguez, who at fifty-six had participated in as many deliveries as most of the doctors, including Rose, picked up a sponge in preparation for the procedure.

Rose looked at David Lesh, the thirty-five-year-old anesthetist who had been on duty at the hospital.

Lesh knew and respected Rose. He also sensed his nerves, which he found unusual, since he'd seen Rose deliver a dozen babies in more dangerous circumstances. Checking his monitors, he increased the gas slightly.

"Everything's fine here," Lesh said.

This was the moment of truth. The moment that Murray Rose had secretly dreaded. What was inside Molly Reed? What was he going to find?

He made his first cut along her bikini line. Then, using his hands, he carefully pushed through the muscles of her abdominal cavity and exposed her bladder, which he cut from its attachment to the surface of the uterus to create a flap, allowing him to push it down and gain access to her womb.

Exchanging the Metzenbaum scissors for a scalpel, he instigated a second incision, this one in the lower segment of Molly's uterus, cutting laterally to expose the amniotic sac.

He could see that it was torn and leaking, but not completely ruptured, so, with an Alyce clamp, he completed the tear of the membrane and released the last of the fluid.

Exposing the baby.

Lying on its back. Its skin shiny and gray, covered in the vermix that had protected it during its gestation in the uterus.

Rose stared down.

It was one of the most unnerving things that he had ever experienced. The newborn's eyes were clear blue, and wide open. The baby was looking up at him. It seemed poised. Waiting.

Noticing Rose's hesitation, Lesh asked, "Is everything all right?"

Rose swallowed and replied, "I'm not sure."

Lesh eased closer.

Recovering, Rose said, "I'm going to take him out."

At first, Rose believed the baby's eyes to be without pupils, but as he reached in, he noticed a tiny pinprick of black at the center of each. Then he noticed the dilation of the black as his body shadowed the baby and the eyes moved. They were working in unison to follow the motion of his body, which meant the baby's vision was already binocular, a sign that the controlling muscles were developed, something that Rose had never seen in a newborn.

Lesh asked again, "Is everything okay?"

"So far," Rose replied, doing his best to hold steady. As he said it, the baby's arms reached up and its tiny hands gripped his. The baby was holding onto him. It was a cognizant movement, as if to aid in the recovery from its mother's womb. After being lifted out, its pale eyes looked around as if to take in everything within its new environment.

Rose was at once frightened and repulsed. It was as if he had some kind of alien creature clinging to him, alert and calculating.

Carmelita Rodriguez said, "He's so strong. And his eyes. *Que precioso.*"

Rose was amazed at the strength of the small fingers; they seemed more like claws, digging into the side of his arm.

"He's incredibly developed," Lesh said. "I've never seen anything like it." He had a strange feeling. It was as if the atmosphere of the room had changed and grown heavier with the addition of another presence. Another mind. He kept glancing at the child, as attracted to the sensation of the newborn's mental presence as he was curious about his physical features.

Following his initial shock, Rose was relieved. The head was large but not deformed in any way; the swelling was due to its positioning in the uterus, so he could not be certain as to its specific shape, but it appeared relatively normal.

He nodded to Rodriguez and she suctioned the baby's nose and mouth.

His first cry sounded like that of a wounded cat, almost a screech, and even then, the boy's hands and feet kicked out against the intrusion of the instruments.

Rose glanced up at the wall-mounted clock. "Twelve-ten. We got the first one. The millennium child." Then, he added, "And he's a fighter," as he passed the struggling infant to Rodriguez, before double-clamping and cutting the umbilical cord.

Rodriguez wrapped him in a blanket and carried him to the far corner of the room, placing him on the scales as Rose returned to Molly Reed, moving his hands gently inside her, removing the placenta. As he did, his fingers felt something hard, protruding from the muscular wall of her uterus.

Rose remembered the object that had turned up in the ultrasound. With all the nerves surrounding the delivery, he'd almost forgotten it. Turning to Lesh, he said, "Looks like a stray suture in the uterine wall. I'm going to remove it."

The anesthetist replied, "No problem here."

"I'll need some oxytocin," Rose added. It would help contract the uterus and control the bleeding. He watched as Lesh hooked the additional bottle up to the IV.

Then, attaching a hemostat for traction, Rose used a fine scissors in an attempt to resect the object. Nothing budged. It was embedded in the muscle. He was tempted to leave it alone but, afraid of infection, he tried again. This time he held it taut with the scissors while going in with his scalpel to cut delicately around it. He pulled again.

The baby screamed, as if somehow, he was connected to the object.

Rose turned quickly to see Rodriguez checking his heartbeat with a stethoscope. She met his eyes and nodded to indicate that everything was fine, normal.

Rose returned to his work, pushing inward with his scissors, gaining a better grip. Pulling harder.

The baby shrieked.

Rose turned again toward Rodriguez.

"Take him to the nursery," he ordered.

"Kid's got some lungs," Lesh said.

"Sure does," Rose replied, as the object came free, taking more of Molly Reed with it than he had anticipated.

It wasn't like anything that either Rose or David Lesh had ever seen. It resembled a tiny insect, something with tentacles and its host's flesh attached to it.

"Could be a suture wrapped inside a fibrous cyst," Rose said, unconvinced as he dropped it into the steel tray beside his table, while the newborn's cries faded to a whimper.

Then he went back to work, suturing the gap that the object had caused before closing the two layers of Molly's uterus and moving to the last incision in her belly.

What the hell is going on? he wondered. This pregnancy had him spooked. First the abnormal chromosome and the hypertrophy of the right hemisphere of the brain, then the baby with his alert eyes and advanced motor skills. Now this. He glanced over his shoulder, into the metal tray, telling himself, *Clean it up and get it down to the lab for analysis.* They'll know. But the damn thing reminded him of something. The bulk of it was small and circular. It looked fat, like it was about to burst. Blood? Maybe it was full of Molly Reed's blood. Then he remembered his dogs, boxers, a male and a bitch. He used to let them run in the woods at the base of the mountains, near the national park. Sometimes when they'd come back, he'd have to pull the ticks off them, out from their ears or from the soft folds of skin beneath their jaws. He'd needed surgical tweezers to remove them; that's how embedded they'd become in the hour or so that the dogs had been free, their razor-sharp pincers burrowing right into the animals' flesh. Ticks. Revolting little creatures, pumped full of stolen blood. Really grotesque. That's what this thing reminded him of, a tick.

"John. His name is John," Molly said, lying in the bed of her private room. She was laughing, lightheaded with relief upon seeing her baby for the first time. John Reed. It had a nice ring, and she and Thomas had agreed on it a month ago. After that they'd never talked about names again, just in case something went wrong.

"He's got some face," Thomas said. "Look at his face."

It was the first thing that he had noticed when the nurse had carried

his son from the delivery room. The child's features had seemed incredibly

defined, in spite of the surface swelling. There was something else, too.

Thomas remembered Alex as a newborn. His physical movement had

been very jerky by comparison to this one, who seemed to be hanging on

to the nurse's arm like a chimpanzee. There was nothing awkward at all

about him.

Not like a normal baby, he thought.

This baby was different, very different, and inside Thomas was trou-

bled. He had no desire to reach out and touch him, to hold or to bond

with him. He was reticent on all fronts and he felt
guilty because of it.

"He was the first born of the new millennium," Molly
said, reaching
out to take the child from the nurse, looking at
Thomas. "We won the
hospital's prize. A year's supply of diapers."

She took John in her arms and held him tight to her
bosom, smiling
up at her husband.

"Come on, be happy," she said. "We've got a son."

~ 4 ~

Preston Dix hated steps, particularly stone steps, and the hundred and seventeen that he had to climb each time he visited G4 at Albany were the most unforgiving in the world. Bone rubbing against bone as he forced his sixty-one-year-old knees to mount another then another on his assault at the summit.

The British weather didn't help either. The country just about lived under water, and when it wasn't raining the sky was lead-heavy and the color of a dirty shirt collar, and so low overhead that he felt he could poke a hole in it with the tip of his walking cane. He took a break on the last three landings, gathered his resolve, and then hiked the final leg to his destination, a nine-foot-high wooden door with G4 etched into a brass plate beneath the knocker. No bell, no video surveillance, no security—with the exception of the uniformed doorman in the lobby who kept a cricket bat on hand for protection—just a knocker that had been fashioned to resemble a judge's gavel.

Dix took a few breaths to insure his equilibrium then used the gavel against the brass plate to announce his arrival. He felt like he had entered a time warp.

Albany was England at its very best and very worst, eighteenth-century tradition blended with eighteenth-century plumbing. It was sheer irony, Dix thought, that Neo Tech, funded by the black budgets of four governments, with direct financial links to Vatican City and private industry, would be controlled from a place without an elevator. Neo Tech? He knew that he was not much more than a field rep, a front-line officer and had no idea of who the real players in the organization were, and who was actually calling the shots, but he also understood the way it worked. If you didn't know who was behind you, you couldn't give them away under pressure. It was a safety measure.

His musing was interrupted when the door was opened by a very tall, elegant woman. She was dressed in a blue pin-striped suit by Chanel and had dark red hair, piled high in a bun. At one time, during the 1970s, the woman had been a high-ranking MP and, although blood-replacement therapy, human growth hormone, and plastic surgery gave her a fiftyish appearance, Dix estimated Lady Eleanor Blythe-Saxon to be in her middle seventies. She had been a stalwart in Parliament, narrowly missing an election to prime minister in the early '80s, then falling from grace when the press discovered her links to a conglomerate selling cargo containers of cigarettes to Third World countries, after the anti-tobacco lobbies had successfully sued the big American companies because of links between smoking and cancer.

Now she was Dix's immediate superior.

"Hello Preston," she said, extending a hand that had been impossible to reshape. Even though she had attempted to have the skin tightened and bleached, it looked like a wrinkled leather glove, marred with prominent broken veins and misshapen joints.

"Hello, Eleanor," Dix replied, grasping the dry, tough flesh.

"Nice flight? No problems at Heathrow?"

London's Heathrow, like Chicago's O'Hare and New York's Kennedy Airport, had experienced a couple of computer malfunctions in the past two days, but nothing as serious as the train wrecks in Russia, where the funds had been inadequate to deal with the Y2K bug.

"No, no problems," Dix replied.

Blythe-Saxon smiled like a patient auntie. "Come in, Preston."

Dix entered an entrance hall with pearl-white plaster walls, a fourteen-foot ceiling, and an original Picasso hanging to his right. It was one of the artist's later self-portraits, done

with pencil and white chalk, and depicted a face in the shape
of a figure eight that looked, to Dix, like a ravaged skull.

"Alarming, this business in Colorado," Blythe-Saxon
said, making alarming sound like alahming.

"We've got it under control," Dix assured, entering
the main reception room with its Ming Dynasty wooden
furniture and fawn hide sofa. From the street-side, double-
plated, bulletproof window, Dix could see Saville Row, the
heart of the hand-tailored clothing district, a hundred feet
below him.

Blythe-Saxon's tone iced over his view. "I do hope
so."

She was staring at him through the thick lenses of her
glasses and her eyes looked very dark and very close to him.
"We don't ever want the tabloids getting hold of this. It's too
flammable."

Neo Tech had been funding experiments in
pharmaceutical drugs and genetic engineering for two
decades. Ultimately, they intended to filter patents into the
private sector for chemicals and genetic procedures to control
disease, particularly cancer. It was an insidious enterprise,
considering that it was Neo Tech that was buying up most of
the commercial nuclear power plants that the governments
were unloading to private businesses—the same reactors that
were leaking radioactivity into the water and air, poisoning
the food chain, and causing leukemia and genetic deformities.
Disinformation and confusion had been Neo Tech's game,
and now, they were confused.

"I'm very serious," she added. "Very serious."

The last thing that the organization had anticipated
was that another faction, terrestrial or extraterrestrial, would
meddle in the area of genetic engineering.

"Sit down, Preston."

Dix sank into the cushion of the sofa while Blythe-
Saxon took a higher, opposing seat in a honey gold Ming
chair that looked like a delicately carved wooden throne. She
picked up a small brass bell from the low table between them.

"Tea?" she asked.

Dix shook his head and Blythe-Saxon placed the servant's bell down.

"What are the latest lab findings on the device?" The word device ended in a hiss.

"They can't get any further without cutting through it, then they can do the x-ray diffractions, but since the Soto implant is the only one we've got—"

"How about Colorado, is there one there?"

"From what my sources have gathered, I believe so," Dix replied.

"Rome is getting very antsy," Blythe-Saxon stated. Antsy. It was a term that Dix hated. Very English.

"We don't need this kind of problem again," she added.

It had been difficult enough to debunk the Mexican situation. An immaculate conception, a miracle? If the Soto child had matured and word had spread, the religious implications would have been enormous.

The termination of the mother and her son had marked the inception of Black-Out and been Preston Dix's first assignment for Neo Tech. He'd been spearheading the team ever since, tracing and interviewing witnesses to the Mexico City sighting, analyzing videotapes and photographic data, silencing the press, and organizing the eventual acquisition of the implanted device from the Mexican government.

"We want more intrusive tests done on the implant, as soon as that becomes feasible," Blythe-Saxon continued.

"Absolutely," Dix agreed.

"And the child—" she broke off, shaking her head.

"I'll deal with everything," he assured.

The Concorde flight from New York this morning had been quick, three hours and ten minutes, but Dix was still tired and resented traveling the distance to hear what could have been said by phone.

"Whatever the technology behind this is, Preston, we want it."

"I understand," he answered, beginning to feel obedient. The feeling didn't agree with him.

"And we want this situation in Colorado contained.
No press, no leaks. Do you understand that?"

"Yes," Dix replied. "I do."

"I sincerely hope so."

Blythe-Dixon was used to having the last word.

Molly Reed was fed up with doctors. She'd been
pushed and prodded for three days, looked at inside and out.
God, was she the first forty-five-year-old in the world to have
a baby? Why wouldn't these medical people just leave her
alone? All she wanted was to go home with her husband and
her son. To hold John and nurse him and rest.

Poor Thomas was beat, too. He'd been trying to close
on a deal in the new housing development in Manitou
Springs, spending his days on the phone with clients,
contractors, and mortgage brokers and his nights with her in
the hospital, bringing her Chinese food—her favorite—being
so caring and looking so drained. Enough was enough, and
now, to top it off, one day before she was scheduled to be
discharged, she had another pasty-faced doctor sitting at the
end of her bed asking her more questions.

The interview had begun with the postnatal care of
her son, particularly about her decision to breast-feed, which
the doctor had strongly endorsed, leading to what felt like an
interrogation concerning her personal life.

The man took detailed notes as he continued.

"Mrs. Reed, prior to your pregnancy, did you ever
experience rapid shifts in mood, say, from extreme joy to
unexplained depression?"

Molly stared at him for what felt like a long time. His
eyes seemed to reflect the dead gray color of his tweed suit
and he carried a walking cane, old and carved with an inlaid
silver handle. She hadn't seen anyone use one like that in
years, not since ninth-grade history class. That was it. He
reminded her of a school teacher she'd once had. He'd
walked with a cane, too, and he'd had the same hollowed,
jaundiced look, and terrible breath. Mr.? What was his name?

"Panic attacks?" The steady, practiced voice continued, pulling her back to the moment. "Perhaps a deep and irrational fear ... ? This is important, Mrs. Reed."

Molly recalled a period of acute depression, directly following Alex's death, but remained silent.

"Have you ever used any form of prescription, mood-altering drugs?"

Finally, Molly spoke. "What has that got to do with my baby?"

"I am trying to ascertain the reason for the chromosomal anomaly," Dix explained. Actually, he was trying to compile a profile of the host women. Lucia Soto, the Mexican, had been an hysteric and a religious zealot. Dix was looking for something similar here. Some factor that would link them.

"Not that there is any reason for alarm," he added. "The records indicate that John is superbly healthy."

Molly didn't like the feel of this man; she resented him even talking about John.

"Please, Mrs. Reed," Dix urged. "I understand your discomfort, but this is for the good of your child."

Finally she replied. "I used lithium for a brief period. Following a family tragedy."

"And when was that?"

"1984," Molly stated.

"May I ask the nature of the tragedy?" Dix probed.

His question provoked images of Alex. It was the last time she'd seen him alive. Standing there, his tanned bare feet a shade darker than the pine boards of the kitchen floor, thin legs sticking out from the bottoms of his billowing blue and white surfer-style swimming trunks, waiting for his father to bring the beach towels. He'd laughed when she'd warned him about the rough surf. "Don't worry, Mom, I can handle myself." She could still hear his voice. She choked back a sob.

"Mrs. Reed?"

"It was my son. My first son. He drowned in the ocean ... I'm not comfortable discussing it." Who was this man, this horrible, intolerable man?

Dix nodded his head.

"I understand," he said. "And I don't believe it's particularly relevant anyway." Then, continuing with hardly any pause he said, "Think back to the approximate time of ... " He hesitated, checking his notes, "John's conception. It would have been ... " he hesitated again, "sometime around April of last year. Is that correct?"

Molly looked at him. Why did he make her feel so uneasy? What was it about him? She told herself to relax.

"Yes, that's correct," she answered.

"Did you have sex during that time?"

The question stung.

"What the hell are you getting at, Doctor? ... " She paused and regrouped, willing herself to calm down but unable to hide the indignity in her voice. "Of course, I had sex. I conceived, didn't I? I must have had sex."

The truth was that the question had struck a nerve. When she'd first learned that she was pregnant she'd tried to place the time of conception and failed. Even joked with Thomas that it could have been an immaculate conception. The joke hadn't gone down well and for the first time in their marriage he'd asked her if she had been having an affair.

"I don't understand what these questions have to do with my health," she continued. Her tone was sharp and she knew it. "They just don't seem to be particularly relevant to anything and, actually, I'm very tired."

She wished Thomas would arrive. He'd know what to do with this guy. Toss him right out the door.

"Dr. Rose has all my medical records anyway," she added. "A lot of the stuff you've asked me I've already been over with him. I'm sure he would show you his files."

The man put down his pencil, folded his arms, and settled back in his chair.

"I'm very sorry if I have disturbed you, Mrs. Reed. Perhaps just one more question?"

Dix tried to smile but he was no good at it.

She sighed. "What is it?"

"Have you ever been to Mexico City?"

The question took her by surprise and she answered quickly. "Yes, once. Why?"

Dix leaned forward, a trickle of energy sparking his eyes.

"And when was that?"

"It was the summer of 1991," she replied. She remembered it well. It had been during one of her bust-ups with Thomas that she'd taken a cheap off-season holiday.

"Why?" she repeated.

"And what was the nature of that trip?" he continued, ignoring her question.

"I went to see the solar eclipse."

"You saw the eclipse?" He sounded genuinely excited.

"Yes."

"Did anything unusual happen to you during or after that time?"

In fact it had. It was an incident that she had pushed way back in her mind, denying the fear that it still provoked.

"No," she said.

There was a quaver in her voice and Dix was quick to note the dilation in her pupils, a sign of deception. His own eyes widened and there was again the faintest spark of light inside them, visible for an instant then gone.

"Did you lose time?" he asked. "By that I mean is there a period of time, an hour, a few hours, that you can't remember, like amnesia?"

Who was this man? He'd introduced himself as a doctor, working with the hospital, but he wasn't wearing a nametag like everyone else, and where was the female nurse who usually accompanied the male doctors? Now he was grilling her about something that had happened nearly ten years ago.

"Hours, a day, anything out of the ordinary?" he pressed. "Please, think about it."

It was a place that she did not want to go.

"I don't know," she answered abruptly.

"Mrs. Reed, have you ever experienced a lucid dream. By that, I mean a dream that was particularly vivid. Think, please. Dreams of lights, or shapes, a triangle of white light?"

His voice was hypnotic, creating images in her mind. Lights. Blasting down at her from above, exposing her, all naked and raw. Then she saw the hollowed needle; she could hear Rose's voice, "This won't take much longer than a shot in the arm." There was pain in her belly, hot and fast.

"No."

"A medical procedure?" he prodded.

She shouted. "You have no right to do this to me!"

Dix stood up with both hands on his walking cane, balanced, studying her reactions, knowing that he'd just unearthed another piece in the puzzle.

"I'm sorry if I have disturbed you," he said flatly.

Molly centered her attention on his eyes, using them to pull her back into the present.

"I'd like you to leave now," she said.

"Certainly," he replied. "But before I do, I would like to see John ... "

Molly stared, sobering. "What?"

"John. Your son," Dix said, restraining his voice. "I'd like to take a quick look at him."

She felt anger swell in her chest as he added, "You see, you may have contracted a virus in Mexico and—"

"No," she replied firmly. Then reaching down, she pressed the call button on the side of her bed.

"I want you out of here. I don't care who you are, I want you out."

Preston Dix walked from the room as she pressed the button a second time, keeping it down until the ward nurse bustled in.

The woman looked relieved to see Molly sitting up in the bed, then annoyed that she was still pressing the button.

"Mrs. Reed, are you all right?"

"Who was that man?" Molly demanded.

The nurse, whose nametag read NANCY ANDERSON, looked confused.

She asked, "Which man?"

"That doctor. What the hell was he trying to do, what right did he have to be in here?"

Nancy Anderson walked to the bed.

"Please, Mrs. Reed, please calm down."

Molly continued, "Asking me personal questions, all kinds of questions, come on, what kind of doctor was he? Doing research for the hospital? Tell me."

Anderson gently took the call button from Molly's hand. She hadn't seen anyone either come or go from Molly Reed's room.

"First you'll have to tell me his name," she said.

"Cannon," Molly answered. "I think he said his name was Cannon."

Anderson thought a moment.

"Well, as far as I know you've had no scheduled visits and the only Dr. Cannon in this hospital is in the orthopedics unit, so I doubt it was him. Let me look into it."

"I want to lock my door. Can I do that? And I want my child in here with me."

"I can certainly bring your baby to you, but you can't lock the door to this room. There is no lock; it's a safety precaution."

"I want my baby and I don't want that man, whoever he was, anywhere near him," Molly insisted.

"I'll go get you your son right away. Then I'll telephone Dr. Rose. Okay?"

Molly nodded her head. She was calming down, slowly.

"Thank you."

"The other thing I'll do," Anderson continued, "is to call hospital security. We can see that you don't have any more visitors you don't want, how's that?"

"I'd appreciate it," Molly replied. "I'm sorry if I was rude to you."

"Don't worry about it. Now let me go get John for you."

Molly watched the nurse walk from the room, her fat ankles bursting from the sides of her white rubber-soled shoes. Then she waited, nervous at every footstep in the corridor, telling herself that her fear was unjustified but unable to control it.

Finally Nancy Anderson returned, wheeling John in a bassinet. The sight of the child soothed her.

John was special, so special, and already Molly was
certain he was interacting with her, raising his arms to be
held, focusing his eyes, and he was strong, incredibly strong.
As soon as she took him in her arms she felt at peace. He
seemed to have the ability to anchor her emotions. She'd
noticed it before but now she really felt it, as if she was
protected by him.

"Thank you," she said. "I feel better now. I'm sorry
about all that."

"I completely understand," Anderson replied. "I've
spoken to security. You won't be disturbed again, I promise.
By the way, is Mr. Reed coming in later today?"

Molly felt good again. She looked down and found
John's eyes fixed on hers. He was talking to her. That's how
she thought of it, as a mental thing, like a telepathy, at least
that's what it felt like, a little tickle in her head. She'd noticed
it on the first day, when they were alone in the room
together, the first time she'd breast-fed him, just something
between them. It was a private communication. She couldn't
quite understand what John was saying to her but it felt good.
Wonderful.

"Is your husband—"

It felt like she was being interrupted.

"Yes he's coming when he gets finished at work,"
Molly answered.

Anderson looked at the two of them on the bed.
She'd never seen a three-day-old child who was so alert.

"'Okay, I'll tell them at the desk. To expect Mr. Reed.
Nobody else."

Molly was smiling and cuddling her baby when Nancy
Anderson left the room.

Anderson had already checked on Dr. Cannon with
Obstetrics and Gynecology. He didn't exist as far as the
Colorado Springs Medical Center was concerned and there
had been nothing scheduled in the way of consultations or
examinations for Molly Reed. That had disturbed her, enough
to call for extra security on the wing. But the thing that
disturbed her more was that Murray Rose was not responding
to his emergency beeper. That wasn't good at all.

~ 5 ~

It was 2:10 in the afternoon when Jane Simpson parked her Honda Civic in the small lot behind the medical building. She turned off the engine, removed her seat belt, and pulled down the visor above her windshield. Checking herself out in the small, attached mirror, she ran her fingers through her short hair, pushing it back off her forehead and wondering if the new, almost masculine cut really suited her heart-shaped face. It had looked good on the actress Ellen Degeneres but, then, Ellen had a stronger jaw. It was hard to tell anyway, since the mirror was so narrow that she could only see her face in thirds. Besides she could always grow it out again and she was between boyfriends anyway, so it was a good time to experiment. She lifted a stick of lip gloss from her handbag and tilted her head back, pouting her lips as she applied it, wishing they were more full and wondering if collagen actually worked, how much it cost, and if Dr. Rose knew anyone who did that kind of work.

Twenty. Maybe that was a little young to get into cosmetic surgery, she thought, smiling at herself in the mirror; then lowering her body in the car seat, she met her own eyes. They were good, her best feature, soft blue, and the dark tint on her lashes really accentuated them.

As she stepped from her car she noticed the new black Lexus parked about thirty feet from her, adjacent to the driveway that separated the white-painted side wall of Sparrow's Pharmacy from the parking lot. It looked like the doctor's car. Yes, it was. She could see the MD plates on the back and she could see a man whom she assumed to be Dr.

Rose sitting in the driver's seat. She studied him for a few seconds, wondering what he was doing out there on his own, just sitting, so still. The doctor was a man whom she associated with activity. God knows he had never once been on time for any of her appointments. There were always women waiting to be examined and he was always running late. But he was a good doctor and she'd been coming to him for three years, since she'd been on the pill.

Besides, he looked like Larry King, and for some reason, maybe because her mother was an avid fan of King's show, that made her feel as if Rose was a bit special, like a celebrity. She was tempted to approach his car, tap on the window, and remind him of her appointment, but glancing down at her Swatch, she saw that she was early by twenty minutes so whatever he was doing, having a cigarette, although she'd never seen him smoke, listening to music, or resting, she decided to keep a respectful distance.

Jane walked down the driveway, her high-top, rubber-soled Reeboks quiet against the macadam, arrived at the main street, and turned right, continuing along the front of the red-brick, single-story medical building until she got to the entrance door. There were four names on the brass plate above the buzzer, Rose's and the three other doctors with whom he shared the practice. She pressed the button, gave her name when the entry phone crackled to life, and was buzzed in. There were two women behind the desk in front of her and six more in the green-carpeted reception area, sitting either on one of two long sofas or in the fat, upholstered armchairs. Four of them were reading magazines, taken from a stack on the glass-topped center table, while the other two appeared impatient, one eyeing the woman seated at reception while the other, a heavily pregnant African-American wearing a loose silk blouse and several chains of gold around her neck, cleared her throat and glared at her wristwatch.

Jane walked straight to the desk and to the silver-haired receptionist. The woman was fiftyish, wearing glasses, and a starched, white blouse, very prim and proper. Her nametag read B. J. WILLIAMS.

"Hi," Jane said. "I have an appointment with Dr. Rose at 2.30. My name is Jane Simpson."

The older woman looked at her, then down at her appointment book.

"I know I'm early," Jane added.

"As long as you don't mind waiting, Miss Simpson. Dr. Rose is not in yet." She glanced quickly in the direction of the seated women. "And he's got two appointments ahead of yours."

Jane was an apprenticing beautician and this was her lunch break; she didn't want to be rescheduled.

"But he's right outside," she insisted.

"Is he?" B. J. Williams asked, looking up.

"I just walked past .him, sitting in his car. He's got a black Lexus, doesn't he?"

B. J. Williams disliked covering for Rose when he was late. She breathed a sigh of relief, saying, "Yes, he does .... Please, Miss Simpson, take a seat. I'm sure he'll be right in."

A quarter of an hour passed without sign of Murray Rose. Finally, B. J. Williams walked from behind her desk over to Jane Simpson.

"Would you be kind enough to show me where you saw the doctor?"

Murray Rose was seated in the driver's seat. He was wearing an Armani suit, a white shirt, and the navy blue, silk tie with white polka dots that his oldest daughter had given him on the last day of Chanukah. He was leaning back against the soft leather and his hands were gripping either side of the wheel as if he was driving, eyes wide open, staring straight ahead. He really did look like Larry King. It was his mouth. Jane had never noticed how full and wide it was, but now everything looked somehow exaggerated, as if all his features had been carved in yellow wax.

"What's the matter with him?" Jane asked.

B. J. Williams didn't answer. Instead, she tried the door and found it locked.

"Go to the other side, see if that's open," she said, trying to stay calm, then began rapping with her knuckles against the window. "Dr. Rose! Dr. Rose!"

The car was locked from the inside and by the time the police and emergency fire crew responded to the receptionist's 911 call, a small group of spectators had gathered.

Jane recognized a couple of the men from the pharmacy and noticed that a few of the doctor's patients were also in the crowd. She felt like some kind of voyeur, but there was a fascination to what was happening and she was compelled to stay. She'd never seen anyone dead before, not like this. She'd been to a wake once, for her mother's sister, seen the body in the open casket, all made-up with her hair permed like plaster. But this was different; this was like some television drama, *N.Y.P.D. Blue*, or *Homicide*. This was real.

She stayed back, behind the police lines and stared as the locksmith opened the door and the paramedics confirmed that Murray Rose was dead. She was struck by the fact that they made no attempt to move him, and also by the delicacy with which they handled his body, one calling the other's attention to an area above the collar of his jacket, on his neck.

While all this was happening the sky segued from a cold blue to a gunmetal gray and a light sprinkle of rain started and stopped as more people gathered, until finally, one of the police officers walked from behind the line and took a position in front of them.

"It would be easier, people, if you'd let us get on with our work," the officer said. "It looks like the man has had a heart attack. That's about it."

He was a short, fat man, his belt was let out to the last hole and his uniform was stretched tight to the belly, but there was a calm, matter-of-fact authority to him and after a minute or so people started to walk away. In the background Jean could hear B. J. Williams talking to the officers closest to the late doctor's car. The receptionist was very upset and although Jane couldn't make out her precise words, she could hear her muffled sobs. Then, just as she was about to turn and go, a man in a well-worn, dark-brown corduroy suit walked from behind the cordoned-off area and approached her.

"Are you Miss Jane Simpson?" he asked, looking straight at her with eyes that matched the color of his suit.

His dark hair was swept back, offsetting a wide forehead above a straight nose, prominent cheekbones, and a strong, square jaw.

"Yes, I am," she answered, suddenly nervous.

"I'm Detective Caruso, and, according to that lady over there," he said, glancing in the direction of B. J. Williams, "you were the first person to see Dr. Rose in the parking lot."

"Yes, I guess I was. Well, probably not, I mean a lot of people walk by on the main street. I just knew who he was."

Her nerves escalated. What was happening? Was she being accused?

"He was my doctor. That's all."

Caruso smiled and Jane noticed that his teeth were tobacco-stained but it was his eyes that really got to her. They had an intensity that made her feel that they could see things in more detail than ordinary people.

"Jane," he said, focusing on her. "All I need are a few specifics, like the time you first noticed Dr. Rose sitting in his car and how long after that before you told Miss Williams that he was out here? Simple stuff, okay?"

While they were talking a white Chevrolet van arrived, followed by a sedan with official plates. They parked in the driveway and a new team of men got out, some dressed in blue overalls.

Jane watched as they walked toward the Lexus.

"Forensics people," Caruso commented.

Jane knew enough from *Homicide* to know what forensics implied.

"That means that Dr. Rose was murdered, doesn't it?" she asked.

Caruso smiled and shook his head.

"No. It means we consider his death suspicious. Now, let's go over the details. You first saw Dr. Rose in his car at—"

His manner was very precise, and seemed to help her recall.

"Two-twelve," she answered. "I know, because I checked my watch to see how early I was for my appointment."

"Did you see anybody else in the parking lot at that time?"

Jane hesitated, feeling suddenly disconnected from what was going on around her, the sound of police radios and the milling people. It was as if she'd stepped out of real life and walked onto the set of a movie. She was observing things but not feeling much. She wondered if she was supposed to be sad.

"No," she replied in a vacant voice, looking toward the Lexus. "I didn't see anybody. Except for Dr. Rose. He was just sitting there, like he is now."

Caruso noted it in his book and was about to continue with his questions when another man in street clothes walked from the Lexus to the taped boundary and gestured with his hand for Caruso to join him.

"Hold tight, I'll be right back," Caruso said, noticing that she had begun to shiver, either from nerves, or the cold. "Just a couple more things .... You all right?"

Jane nodded, then stood and watched as the two men spoke. She was only six or seven feet from them. The second man was taller than Caruso and thin, with eyes that moved constantly, darting from the doctor's car, to the forensics van, and, a few times, at her. She put him at about thirty or thirty-five years old, maybe ten years younger than Caruso. His sandy hair had been grown long on the right side, then combed to the left, all the way over, and glued down, but there was just enough breeze to lift the loose strands up, exposing his bald head beneath. He kept patting the rogue hairs back into place, all the time speaking in a nervous kind of voice, thin and raspy.

Jane watched for a minute or so, then, not wanting to appear to be eavesdropping, she turned her head away, but she could still hear him.

"Wife's going to meet us at the morgue for the ID. ... She sounds pretty messed up," the raspy voice said.

Caruso's tone was lower and his words harder to decipher but Jane figured they were talking about Mrs. Rose.

She thought Caruso asked something like "What do you mean by that?"

The flyaway hair detective, whose name was Neil Adams, continued, "She sounded confused. Kept going on about this being the biggest day of the guy's life. Said he'd just made some kind of medical discovery."

Caruso's voice sounded clearer after that, and louder. "Medical discovery?"

"Don't know. His wife said he got a call early this morning. He told her it was some government agency. Some kind of top-security bullshit. She thought he was joking. Said he was hardly the secret-agent type, but, according to her, he was dead serious. Enough to go to the lab at the hospital to meet whoever was on the phone. He called her from there, all excited. Said she wouldn't believe what he'd found out. He wanted to wait till he got home to tell her."

Jane sneaked a couple of glances at the two detectives as their conversation intensified.

"What government agency?" Caruso asked.

"His wife didn't know."

"What was he working on?"

Adams shrugged his shoulders.

"As far as we know, the usual stuff, examinations, delivering babies. Nothing special."

Caruso looked intrigued.

"Have we had anybody at the lab yet?"

"Not yet."

"I'll go then," Caruso said.

"Right," Adams replied, then he turned toward the Lexus. "Word is, so far, it looks like a stroke. I mean he was inside the car, locked up. Only strange thing is that bee sting or whatever it is on the side of his throat. Anyway, they'll cut him up downtown and let us know." He glanced over at Jane. "What's she got to say?"

She saw that they were both staring at her, then flyaway winked and she lowered her head again as Caruso lowered his voice.

"Not much, other than that he was alone in the car with the engine off. She thought he was resting between appointments, or listening to music or something."

Adams nodded, caught a fresh handful of hair and
battened it down, saying, "It's probably a natural cause. His
time was up. End of story."

"Maybe," Caruso replied. "But I'll run down to the
lab and have a poke around."

He turned, ducked beneath the tape, and walked back
toward Jane.

"We're almost done," he said. "How are you feeling?"

Tired, like she felt when she'd had a long day in the
salon, drained in the way that interacting with lots of people
often drained her.

"I wouldn't mind sitting down," she answered. "I'm
cold."

Caruso smiled and motioned with his head toward a
dark green Corsica.

"We can sit in my car and finish up this report, then I
want you to go home and rest."

"Dr. Rose is dead?" she said, as if she was really
realizing it for the first time.

"I'm afraid so," Caruso answered, putting an arm
around her shoulder to guide her to his car.

The lab was on the second floor of the Colorado Springs Medical
Center and there was an office in the corridor leading to it.
Caruso stopped there, identified himself, and asked the young
woman behind the desk if she remembered Dr. Rose coming in
early that morning.

"I didn't get here till noon," she answered. "But if
you hold on, maybe Irma will remember."

Caruso waited while the woman walked down the
corridor and disappeared behind the white double doors. He
noted that she had a good set of legs, long and well rounded
at the calf and for a moment he contemplated her ass, then
stopped himself. Ass obsession had caused Michael Caruso
enough trouble in his forty-seven years. In fact, at eighteen
years old, he had married his first wife, primarily for her ass,
then found shortly afterward that it had precious little to
contribute in terms of conversation. The marriage had lasted
a year and a half. He'd managed twice that length of time
with his second, their longevity due primarily to the fact that

he had been overseas for two of the three years, serving in a recon unit with the Special Forces in Cambodia. By the end of the war he was addicted to the rush of adrenaline and for a time considered prospecting for a South Florida chapter of the Outlaws Motorcycle Club. In the end, family tradition won out. His dad, Martin, had been a cop in Miami and his father's father before him. Besides that, his mother Ethel was still alive, living alone in Boca Raton. He'd felt a responsibility toward her.

Caruso met wife number three, Josie Ann, during bike week at Daytona Beach, where she worked the local clubs as a stripper. It was possible, if she held her back in the correct position, to balance a glass of champagne on the ledge between her lower back and the upper quadrant of her ass. On top of that, she was a dropout from one of the snobby New England girls colleges. At last, an ass that could talk back to him. It was too much for handsome Mike. He had to own it.

The mixture of his jealously and her refusal to hide her physical assets was purely nitrous and their marriage had ended in a public brawl at the neighborhood 7-Eleven, costing Caruso a small piece of his left earlobe, a lasting memento of Josie Ann's passion.

Then came the move to Colorado Springs, and his attempt at a clean slate. Asses were a thing of the past, or so Caruso told himself as the foxy little blonde walked back through the doors and toward him. He noted the name on her tag, SUSAN WALKER.

She spoke as she stopped in front of him.

"Ms. Willis saw Dr. Rose in here at about eight-thirty this morning."

"In where?" Caruso asked.

"He went to the lab for something," she replied, her voice a little harsh for his taste.

Caruso nodded. "Would you mind introducing me to Ms. Willis?"

She looked at him. Her eyes were blue and mean, set close together. She seemed impatient.

"Certainly. Follow me."

He trailed her through the swinging doors without letting his eyes drop below her waist.

"The lab is in there," Walker said as they passed a closed door with PATHOLOGY stenciled above the frame. "And that," indicating a big woman, walking toward them, carrying a specimen jar, "is Ms. Willis."

"This is the policeman," Walker said, before she walked away.

Caruso gave his name and rank and began to extend his hand to Willis in greeting when his fingers started to twitch. It was more a sensation than a visible tremor, like an electricity behind the muscles of the metacarpals, causing a slight paralysis.

He stopped and stared down.

"Is everything all right?" Willis asked.

Caruso withdrew his hand awkwardly. Three times this week it had happened. It was his right hand, the hand he shaved with, wrote with. His shooting hand.

"Yes," he replied. "I think so."

"Then what may I do for you?" Willis asked.

Suddenly Caruso felt a bit disoriented. What was it, the tingling, the paralysis? The beginning of a heart attack? He was in a hospital, with professionals, maybe he should ask. Pride held him back. That and the fact that in his business denial was nine-tenths of the law.

"I understand that Dr. Rose was in here earlier this morning," he said. "I'd like to know who he was with, and what he wanted."

"Is there some kind of problem?"

Caruso studied the wide pink face as if he hadn't understood her question. He could still feel his hand twitching. What the hell was it?

Finally he spoke. "There's been an incident involving the doctor and any information you can give me could be vital."

"Dr. Rose was in here at about eight-thirty this morning and he was by himself," Willis replied.

"By himself?" Caruso repeated, clenching his hand into a fist then releasing it, over and over again. It was probably nothing more than a muscle cramp. The district handgun competition was coming up and he'd been at the range three times in the past five days. That made sense, a cramp.

"Yes," Willis confirmed. "By himself."

Caruso stood silent a few seconds. He was disappointed. He'd hoped for something that would lead him to the government men that Rose's wife had mentioned.

"Do you know what he was doing here?"

"He was in the lab," she replied.

"Could you please take me there?" Caruso asked.

His right hand was hanging down, to his side, and he clenched his fist once more, just to test it, to make sure. It felt good, fine, nothing to worry about. He pushed it out of his mind.

"Please, follow me," Willis said.

They walked about ten yards back to the door marked PATHOLOGY and she opened it. There were two men working inside the large rectangular room. Willis deposited the specimen jar on the table, opened a registry book that was positioned beside it, and quickly made a notation, then escorted Caruso to the older-looking of the two men.

"Dr. Carlson, this is Detective ... " she hesitated. Irma Willis could never remember names, even important ones.

"Caruso," the detective filled in, trusting his hand enough to offer it to the silver-haired pathologist with the long, worried face. "I'm interested in whatever it was that Dr. Rose was doing in here this morning."

"I didn't even know he was in," Carlson replied, looking accusingly at Irma Willis then back at Caruso. "What's happened?"

Caruso was trying not to open up an unnecessary can of worms. He held the baggy eyes of the pathologist and replied, "Dr. Rose has had a stroke."

"How serious?" Carlson asked.

There was nowhere else to go. "He's dead."

The pathologist's mouth dropped and, almost reflexively, he lifted his glasses from the breast pocket of his lab coat and slipped them on his nose, as if he needed a clearer view of the bearer of the bad news. He stood shaking his head.

"He was only fifty-one years old. Too damn young to die."

Caruso let the moment settle, then asked, "Did you know him well?"

"For as long as I've worked here, about ten years," Carlson answered.

The detective turned to Irma Willis. "Thank you for being so cooperative, Ms. Willis. Now I'm going to need to speak privately to Dr. Carlson.

He waited till she left the room before he turned back to Carlson.

"What I'm trying to do is retrace Dr. Rose's movements up till the time of his death."

Carlson looked at him curiously and asked, "Since when does a death by natural cause become a police matter?"

Caruso relaxed his manner.

"I wouldn't be down here but for a couple of things his wife said on the telephone," he explained. "Something about a medical discovery, and that he was going to meet some government people here at the lab. I'm just trying to put the pieces together." He smiled. "I'm suspicious by nature."

Carlson's initial shock drifted to a mild sense of irony.

"With all respect to Murray, he wasn't exactly the pioneering type. I can't imagine him involved in any type of breakthrough."

"What would he have been doing in here this morning?"

Carlson shook his head and gave a slight shrug.

"Had he sent anything down for you to examine lately?" Caruso continued.

Carlson thought for a moment. "That thing that came out of one of his C-sections?" Walking past Caruso, he stopped above the registry book on the table. "I only examined it briefly. Couldn't make any sense of it and I didn't want to run a drill through it or crush it so I was going to send it to the pathology department in Washington."

Carlson opened the book and ran his finger up along the lines of recent registrations.

"Came in three days ago. Patient's name was Molly Reed."

"Let me have that again, will you please?" Caruso asked.

Carlson repeated the information and Caruso wrote it down in his notebook.

"I'm curious," the detective said. "Why are you sending it to Washington?"

"It's a standard practice with anything of unknown origin," Carlson answered. "They've got a more sophisticated setup down there at FBI headquarters."

Caruso felt a wave of excitement.

"Has it gone yet?"

Carlson looked back in the book. "No, we're backlogged in here and didn't think it was urgent. I've got it down to leave today."

"May I take a look at it?" Caruso asked.

Carlson led Caruso to a shelf in the far corner of the lab. There were three rows of plastic specimen containers on the shelf, all numbered. Carlson stroked his chin, adjusted his glasses, and lifted down a couple, then replaced them in order. Then, he checked again.

"I'm sorry, Detective, but it doesn't seem to be here anymore." Turning, he addressed the third man in the room. "Mark, has anything been shipped out this morning?"

"Not that I know about," the other man answered.

"Well, I'm missing a specimen container. Remember, we took a look at it a couple of days ago. You thought it might be a suture encased in a fibrous cyst ... Murray Rose sent it down."

The other man smiled. He was young, Caruso put him at half Carlson's age, maybe twenty-eight or thirty but already he was going bald at the crown of his head. He was also overweight and his freshly shaved face was lush with white flesh.

"This is my assistant, Mark Jewel," Carlson said.

Caruso accepted the assistant's meaty palm then watched as Jewel took a quick look through the containers on the shelf, finally turning to Caruso and shaking his head.

"It's definitely not here."

Inside Caruso's mind, the wheels were turning. What was Murray Rose's discovery and what did it have to do with whatever it was that was now missing from the lab. Where had it gone? With the government men? Who were they?

He was anxious to get the autopsy results on Rose. He could smell a homicide, his first in eleven months.

Reaching into the inside pocket of his jacket Caruso pulled out his wallet then peeled two of his cards from a small stack.

"I want to thank you guys for your time," he said, handing each of them a card. "My private number is there and if, by any chance that thing turns up, I want you to call me." Then looking at Carlson, he added, "I'm sorry about Dr. Rose."

Caruso's next stop was Maureen Dobson, the thirty-four-year-old who guarded the reception desk of the maternity unit. She looked up, drinking him in through the thick lenses of her prescription granny glasses while twisting a few strands of dyed, orange hair. When he asked for Molly Reed and before he could explain that he was a police officer, she commanded him to wait and picked up her phone.

Thirty seconds later, a bull-necked man in a blue security uniform appeared. He carried a Maglight in place of a weapon but what he lacked in firepower he made up with aggression, standing eye-to-eye with Caruso so that his cheese-and-onion breath pelted the policeman's face.

"What do ya' want with Mrs. Reed?"

Caruso actually enjoyed moments like these. He hated intimidation and he knew he couldn't lose, so he purposefully let the moment play, sizing up the stocky guard without saying a word.

"Maybe you'd better leave the premises," the guard continued, attempting a side step that would have positioned him behind Caruso.

Caruso noted the name on the white ID tag and matched the sharpness of the man's tone.

"Mr. Rudge, maybe you'd better take a look at this."

Moving with him, he slid his jacket to the side to reveal the detective shield that was clipped to his belt.

Billy Rudge stared at the shield and put his hands in the air as if he was surrendering.

"Sorry Officer, I'm just doing my job. We've had people in here lately who shouldn't a' been here."

Caruso felt his senses heighten again.

"What people?" he asked.

"Some guy impersonating a doctor," Rudge answered.

Caruso felt a pull in his gut. He was onto something.

"Was he here to see Mrs. Reed?"

"Yes," Dobson interjected from her chair behind the desk. "That's why I called security when you came in."

Caruso turned to her and said, "Would you please take me to see Mrs. Reed? Now."

Molly Reed was in bed, resting, when Dobson led Caruso into the room. He introduced himself to her, showed his police ID, and asked to speak with her privately, then waited till Dobson left the room before sitting down in one of the two chairs against the far wall.

"I wish you wouldn't sit there," Molly Reed said.

She was older than Caruso had expected and she appeared extremely nervous, fidgeting with her hair and glancing frequently at the door.

"That's where he sat," she continued as Caruso stood. "That man. That's why you're here, isn't it? To tell me who he was. Isn't it?"

Caruso dredged up a smile and tried to appear matter-of-fact.

"Let's take this a step at a time," he replied.

"Then why are you here?" she asked. There was a different emphasis on the "why" this time.

"The first thing I think you should know," Caruso said, "is that your doctor, Murray Rose, died earlier today."

"Dr. Rose is dead?" she repeated, as his words settled. "Yes."

Molly Reed didn't blink. Staring into Caruso's eyes, she asked, "Was he murdered?"

Caruso shook his head and took another three steps toward her bed, until he was beside her.

"So far, it appears he suffered a stroke," he answered.

She shook her head. "No, no. John warned me. He warned me."

"John is your husband?" Caruso asked.

"John is my son," she replied, relaxing slightly.

"And where is John now?"

"In the nursery, down the hall. John is my only child. He's my baby."

Caruso kept his voice soft, treading carefully. "I don't understand how he could have warned you."

"John is psychic."

"Are you telling me that your three-day-old child talked to you?" He was unable to keep the skepticism from his tone.

"Of course not, but he communicates."

After that there was a silence between them, until, finally, Caruso replied, "I see." It sounded lame but he was at a loss.

Molly Reed looked up at him.

"The man who killed Dr. Rose wanted to take my child."

"How do you know that?" Caruso asked.

Molly Reed reached out and grabbed his hand, pleading. "I don't want him coming back for John. Promise me that you won't let that happen."

Caruso felt the desperation in her grasp.

"Why would he do that?"

"I told you, John is special," Molly answered.

On the way out of the ward, Caruso felt compelled to stop at the nursery. Considering everything that had taken place, and the things that had been said, he needed to see the baby for himself. He introduced himself to the nurse in charge, displayed his police credentials, and followed her to the crib in the far corner of the room.

"Try not to wake him," she whispered, before leaving him alone with the infant.

Caruso looked down at the sleeping baby. He was struck immediately by the infant's fine face with his full, red lips and wide, high forehead. It was not a newborn's face, not exactly. It seemed somehow more refined, expressive, even in

repose. He continued to stare and as he did, he was swept up
in the feeling that he knew the face, had seen it somewhere
before. He just couldn't place it. The infant reminded him of
someone. *That's crazy*, he told himself. This was a newborn,
not yet formed, but looking down, Caruso felt something
inside himself stirring, as if a part of him, long asleep, had
begun to reawaken to some memory, some déjà vu.

He continued to gaze at John Reed's closed eyelids, as
if he could penetrate the mystery with his stare. What was this
feeling? And where was the link between this newborn and
the dead man in the parking lot? Was there something truly
special here? Without thinking, he closed his own eyes as if
that single act would bring him closer to his intuition and in
the darkness he could feel something pulling at his mind,
demanding entry. The feeling grew stronger and with it came
a fear; he was about to cross a border, into an unfamiliar
place, a place with no reference points, nothing to hold onto.
He opened his eyes to break the feeling and found the child
looking up at him.

John Reed's eyes were light blue and perfectly clear,
yet so deep, as if they were twin apertures, opening into a
different world, far beyond the patina of Michael Caruso's
reality. They were drawing him inward, to the place he had
been frightened to go. Then his thoughts stopped and it was
as if a trapdoor in his mind had opened and a part of him had
dropped through. He was falling, trembling like a leaf as he
descended. But where was he going? And what was this
energy that drew him toward it? Was it good or bad? He was
thinking again. Fear thoughts.

He braced himself, trying to get a grip, grasping the
sides of the crib, feeling his hands, aware of the sweat
beneath his palms. He was back in the room, inside his own
body and both his hands were shaking. Jesus Christ, what the
hell was happening to him? He stood there, captive to his
malady, willing the shaking to stop, but his muscles were
cramping and he couldn't let go of the crib.

He turned his head toward the door of the nursery.

The nurse was talking to a coffee-colored man in light
green scrubs. No, he wouldn't call out to her. Thank God she
wasn't looking at him, as if her acknowledgment would be the

final verification of some black truth. He turned back to the crib.

The baby was still looking up, into his eyes. Knowing? But that was impossible. *How can a baby know anything?* Caruso thought. Still, the blue eyes searched and calmed him, pulling him back from his fear as the seizure ebbed and he regained his balance, both physically and mentally. After that he turned and, without saying a word to the nurse, walked from the room.

It was six o'clock and dark outside when Caruso returned to his desk at Homicide, telling himself that whatever had happened to him in the nursery had not been related to the two episodes earlier in the day. It had been something else. Caused by John Reed. What had the baby's mother said? He was psychic. He did seem to have some sort of power, some force that exuded from his eyes. Caruso couldn't get those eyes out of his head. But had John Reed really caused the trembling in his hands? Or was he sick? He didn't have time to be sick. Not now, at the beginning of a case.

There was a message waiting on his machine. It was from the medical examiner's office and as Caruso dialed the number he was anxious with anticipation. Something big was going down, something extraordinary, and he felt part of it.

The voice on the other end of the line doused his fire.

Medical Examiner Fred Gilespie didn't get called out on police business often, not unless the circumstances of death were suspicious, but when he did, he liked to act quickly and today, rushing from his home, he'd forgotten his nasal spray. He had a cold. He'd had it for a week and his nose was blocked.

His voice was high and whiney anyway, but with the added congestion he sounded like he'd inhaled a balloon full of helium.

"Murray Rose had a stroke," he said.

Caruso asked, "What caused it?"

"An embolism." Then, aware of the hollow silence on the other end of the phone, Gilespie added, "Sorry, Mike, but an artery gets clogged, blocks the flow of blood to the brain. It could happen to anybody."

Caruso sank back against the black leatherette cushion of his chair. There was something wrong here; he could feel it. Murray Rose had died with a secret.

"How about the blood work?" he asked.

Still got a little to do there, but, so far, it's clean."

"Yeah, but there was that mark on the side of his throat. What was that? He sounded desperate and he knew it.

Gilespie was aware that Homicide had been running thin on cases but he wasn't about to feed Caruso's fantasies. He inhaled hard and swallowed, an act that served to give his voice the hint of resonance.

"I don't know. It seems insignificant at this point."

"Insignificant?" Caruso barked.

"Mike, I don't know what you want me to tell you, but so far, that's all I've got. A portion of a clot lodged in the main artery leading to his brain and the man died."

Caruso felt like he'd just been rammed headlong into a stone wall.

"Well, if you get anything else, anything new on the blood work—"

"I'll be on the phone to you faster than you can whistle," Gilespie replied, searching through the debris on the top of his desk for a box of decongestants that he was sure he'd left there following his last cold.

Caruso signed off and sat there, alone in a room containing seven desks, other than his own. His brain felt knotted.

He pulled his notebook from the pocket of his jacket and studied the pages, then picked up a pencil and began putting things in order, trying to establish a sequence. He began with Murray Rose's wake-up call from the unidentified government agent, followed by his trip to the lab and the apparent theft of whatever it was the doctor had removed from Molly Reed's belly. Then there was Molly Reed's description of the gray-haired man with a walking cane, asking questions about the baby.

There was a pattern, leading to Rose's murder. Caruso was certain of that, and deep down, he suspected that the baby, John Reed, was the reason behind it.

~ 6 ~

January 13, 2000

Casey Lee Armstrong looked old. It was in her eyes, a deadweight tiredness, without shine or luster. She could see the capillaries behind the whites, like finely threaded cobwebs. She had that wasted appearance that she'd seen a few times with people about to die of cancer, when the flesh recedes against the bones and every feature is made more prominent, the nose appearing broader, and the mouth wider and the eyes further back in the head. Her hair looked bad too, like it had been drained of some vital fluid, as if the shafts were empty. No energy. That was it. A vampire was drinking her energy. Every night when she slept he'd creep into her mind and devour her dreams, so that when she woke, she was emptier than the day before, and this vampire had a face. She could almost see him now, staring back at her from the mirror. Maybe, when his work was complete and he'd stolen her soul, she would see only him in the mirror. She would be gone.

"Case, what are you doing in there?"

Nick's voice broke the spell.

It was seven-thirty in the morning and they both had things to do.

"Brushing my teeth, I'll be right out," she answered, noticing that the toothpaste had fallen from her brush and lay like a shiny slug against the white enamel of the sink. It was

Nick's toothpaste. She'd run out. Green stuff, some kind of gel, with a candy white stripe running through it. It looked like something that had been made for a kid. She scooped it up with the bristles of her brush, turned the tap to cold, and started on her tongue, scrubbing the surface with the spearmint-flavored paste. Anything to get the metallic taste of a bad night's sleep from her mouth. Scrubbing. Tasting the spearmint. Spearmint. ... She gagged, then retched, spitting it out.

There was the sound of the doorknob being turned and the door holding rigid against the bolt lock.

"You all right?" Nick asked from beyond the barrier.

She recovered and placed the brush down. She could still taste the toothpaste, smell it. Jesus, it was nauseating stuff. She was suddenly furious with him.

"How can you use this shit!?" she demanded.

He was still outside the door, listening, and his voice sounded close, as if it was inside her head.

"What are you talking about?"

He was right. It didn't make sense. If he wanted to use green and white toothpaste which tasted like spearmint, that was his business. What the hell was the matter with her anyway? She looked at herself in the mirror again, using her reflected eyes as an anchor, something with which to tether her emotions. She'd been riding a roller coaster for the past two weeks, up and down, up and down. Her stomach was falling out and she wanted the ride to end.

Pulling herself together, she replied, "Nothing. Sorry, I'll be with you in a second."

She'd become a real pain in the ass and she knew it. Particularly in the bedroom. She just wasn't interested. Not that Nick was pushing or anything, he wasn't the kind of man who pushed, but she could tell that he sensed her aversion to sex. Actually, as she thought about it, it was more than sex. She didn't want any kind of intimacy, no hugs, no kisses, no touching, nothing. She didn't know how to explain her feelings to him. It wasn't him anyway; it was her. She just wasn't there; that's how it felt. It wasn't just the lack of energy. There was more to it than energy and fatigue. She was missing something. A piece of her had vanished. Maybe today would help bring it back. She was working today.

She wiped the dribbled remains of the toothpaste from her lips with a towel, brushed her hair back with her fingers, averted her eyes to avoid another confrontation with the stranger in the mirror, turned and walked to the door, sliding the bolt from the lock and wondering why, in the past couple of weeks, she'd begun to lock everything. Doors. Windows. Even when Nick was with her.

She opened the door.

Beneath the lights of the room Nick Hughes looked like a model for an anatomy chart, his long frame covered with beautifully defined muscles, vascular and striated. He looked like a gymnast who could run a marathon, but it was his rear end, round and tight, that usually stimulated Casey's most erotic fantasies. That and his tattoo. It was a faded blue bracelet, like old denim, circling the bicep of his right arm, a tribal piece of Hawaiian design, wrapping in tight geometric patterns, like a blue filigree. It was the only tattoo that Casey had ever found erotic. Maybe because it looked out of place on his pristine body, like a lascivious intruder. But today, she felt nothing as she studied him from behind. Nothing except a certain vacancy inside herself, as if she had perpetrated some form of crime or violation and had been stripped, not just of her dignity but of her right to even desire intimacy, as if she were no longer worthy of it.

She watched as he put on a blue oxford cloth shirt, buttoning it up then tucking the tails into his khaki trousers, before finger-combing his dark hair. He turned toward her.

"What's up with you?" he asked.

She bit her lower lip and stood there in her underpants like a naughty schoolgirl, trying to affect a lightheartedness she didn't feel.

"I don't feel so good lately," she replied. "Not since that night."

He feigned an order. "Come here."

She walked toward him, stopping cold when he reached out for her with his arms. He shook his head. "Case, what the hell's the matter?"

She stared at him, feeling as if something was trying
to push through from way back in her head. The feeling was
not pleasant and it held her poised, as if she was on the cusp
of some ugly revelation. Then the sensation faded to a vacant
sadness. She caught herself on the verge of tears and in an
effort to control her voice, her words came out flat.

"I don't know."

Nick stood and she let him hold her but she couldn't
let herself settle into him the way she used to. Something had
been damaged between them, a part broken; that's how it felt.
She knew she was about to anger him but she did it anyway,
asking the same question she had asked him dozens of times
in the past two weeks. "What happened to me?"

He did not reply.

"Something happened to me that night. I'm changed.
That's how I feel. Changed."

He gripped her tighter but there was more muscle
than love in his posture. His tone hardened. "Drop it, Casey,
just let it go."

She pulled back and met his eyes. There was
something there, barely hidden. "What do you mean 'drop it'?
What's there to drop?" It was the first time in their
relationship that she'd sensed a lie.

"What's going on?" she continued.

He shook his head. There was dismissal in the action
and that angered her.

"What is going on?!" she repeated, her anger building
quickly to fury as the roller coaster began its descent, faster
and faster. "Goddamn it, tell me!" she said while pushing him
away and bunching her fists as if to strike out at him.

"How many fucking times do we have to go over it?"
he shot back.

"It" meant New Year's Eve at the Tante Claire, and it
had been coming back to her in fragments, like a torn
photograph that she was reassembling bit by bit. She'd had
too much calvados, way too much. Apple brandy didn't agree
with her anyway, but Nick had ordered it and she'd knocked
it back. She remembered a Japanese waiter with a bad hair
piece and breath that stunk of spearmint mouthwash who'd
kept pouring more. Till she was so drunk that she couldn't

walk. That's when she'd fallen, smashing her glass against the table and ramming the broken base into her palm. It had taken ten stitches to close the wound. She couldn't remember the trip to the emergency ward, or the trip back to the town house, but she had the bandaged hand as proof. It was the first time in her life that she had ever blacked out.

"Did you tell me everything?" she asked suddenly.

"About what, Case?" His tone was abrupt.

The question angered her. He knew perfectly well what she was asking him. Why did he want to avoid it?

"That night," she answered.

"Do you really need more?"

She felt suddenly defensive. "I've never blacked out before, that's all. Do you think I ought to call the restaurant to apologize?"

It was about the tenth time in as many days that she had suggested calling the restaurant.

His mouth tightened a fraction and he shook his head. His voice was flat. "You don't know when to quit, do you?"

"Quit what?" she pressed.

He looked hard at her, and she felt a dangerous energy rise from him.

"All this bullshit, the questions, the inquisition."

"But I don't feel right—" she began.

"You're exhausted, that's all, I'm going to get you some stuff to take."

"What stuff?" she asked.

"A relaxant, maybe something to help you sleep," he replied.

"Why? Why do I need sleeping pills? I've never had any trouble sleeping, and I've never felt like this before."

"It's probably your work. Sometimes it happens. You know that."

"Not to me," she answered. "I haven't had an assignment in nearly
three weeks anyway. It's not the work."

He stood there looking helpless and in that moment she felt sorry for him. She exhaled and the roller coaster flat-lined, running smooth for as

long as it took her to walk over to him, to put her arms around his body

again and her head against his chest. She could hear his heart beating and

the sound soothed her.

"Casey, I love you. You know that," he said softly. "We're going to

get through this patch. Whatever it is, it will pass."

"I know," she replied, believing it for that moment.

She left the town house first, with him sitting at the glass-topped breakfast table sipping a cup of coffee and reading the entertainment section of the *Washington Post*. There was a familiarity to the scene, a sense of balance.

He put the paper down when he heard the engine of her car start up. The yellow Toyota was about ten years old and had over a hundred thousand miles on the clock, but Casey still loved it. Maybe because it had been her first car and she'd driven it cross country to get to Meade. "My baby never lets me down," she often said. She was sentimental that way and Nick loved her for it.

She'd been good for him, too. She helped him to accept himself for who he was, without even knowing that she was affecting him in that way, because, although he never admitted it, Nick Hughes had never been completely secure inside. He had the looks, the body, the smarts, but he was a bit of a fish out of water, a passionate man in a job that, more often than not, required the ability to calculate coldly and quickly, a job whose loyalty lay within its shadowed perimeters, and personal relationships rarely fell within those confines.

Nicholas Douglas Hughes had been a "Navy brat." His father was an admiral, six times decorated, and four times married. Nick's life had been anything but secure, more a traveling circus. Five different schools before he was fourteen, and three different mothers. The original, a former debutante from Baton Rouge, was a raging alcoholic and his last memory of her was a drunken kick to the Admiral's groin, thrown on the night prior to the custody hearings for himself and his older brother Arthur. Then he watched as she was hauled screaming from the house by two policemen. He'd been eight years old at the time. When he'd last contacted her by telephone, on Christmas Day of 1994, she was living with a car salesman in Aberdeen, Texas and kept confusing Nick with his brother, a marine lieutenant who had been missing in action since the official close of the Vietnam War.

"So Arthur, how was Saigon?" she kept asking, as if he'd just returned from a lengthy vacation. She slurred her words till they sounded like a vodka-laced slush. Finally he'd hung up the phone on her.

In his early teens Nick had been a rebel—smoking pot, tooting a bit of coke, skipping school, and hanging with the surfing crowd around La Jolla. The admiral wasn't actually aware of how far off the rails his son had gone till the tattoo. The admiral termed it, "Low-class swabby shit," when he'd happened to spot Nick coming out of the shower. That, followed by a room search that uncovered a half pound of Acapulco Gold stuffed inside a shoe box in his closet, resulted in a military academy in New Jersey.

Nick had hated it at first, the uniforms, the discipline. Until Ben Smack.

Smack was an Afro-American giant, black as coal, six-five, and weighed in at an even 300 pounds. He was also the football coach and he and Nick had a rapport from the start. "Whitebread." That's what he'd called him the first time that Nick, unusually pale from an overcast August, had turned up for mandatory football practice.

In two years Smack had helped pack Nick's gangling, six-two frame with forty pounds of muscle and taught him the "art of football," "Just like the art of war," he'd said, quoting from the two thousand year old teachings of Sun Tzu, a Chinese warrior-philosopher. "There are five important things: the common desire to win, the weather, the terrain, the leadership, and the discipline."

By the age of sixteen, Nick Hughes was an all-state quarterback and a year later, in his last year at the academy, he was being scouted by the top college teams.

Texas A&M won the bidding war and after two seasons leading the Aggies he thought he'd found his vocation. Football was something he loved.

His dreams of being a professional ended with a torn medial cartilage in his left knee during training camp for the New York Jets. The bucket handle tear wasn't a serious injury, but it had sidelined him for the duration of the camp. Not making the final cut for the Jets was the greatest heartbreak of his life. It left him in a tailspin as to what to do next. He'd wandered, working as a bartender in Boston, driving a cab in New York, and finally taking off for Costa Rica, intending to spend the winter surfing and sorting out his mind.

That's when the admiral had stepped in, pulling strings to secure his son a position at Officer Candidate School in Pensacola, Florida, then arriving in Costa Rica to coerce Nick into accepting it—really leaning on him.

Nick had performed well during the thirteen weeks of training, tested high and displayed the kind of psychological profile—an IQ of 153, a propensity for self-reliance, and the ability to perform exceptionally well under pressure—that caught the attention of several more clandestine government agencies.

After OCS he'd gone to Fort Hachuca in Arizona. It was an espionage school. That followed with two undercover assignments for the navy in the Middle East. Years later, and following a recruitment into the National Security Agency, he was working on stuff with above-top-security status, but nothing like the thing he was involved with now. This was bad business. Very bad.

The Remote Viewing headquarters was located in a four-roomed bungalow about three miles from Casey's town house. The rectangular, wooden building had once provided temporary housing for army staff but now had fallen into disrepair. The gutters of its flat roof needed renewing, and consequently several seasons of rainwater had dripped down its walls and eroded the white paint, also adding the vague hint of mildew to the stale aroma within. Sited on a side street, several blocks back from Meade's main arteries, the bungalow's most distinguishing feature was that all but one of its seven windows, that one containing a rusted 3,000 BTU air-conditioning unit, were closed and shuttered. It was a ghost of a place and very few people knew, or cared, that it existed at all.

Casey parked in the dirt lot behind the back door and got out of her car. She was worried. The way she'd been feeling lately made her wonder if she'd be able to perform. She considered a request for a temporary leave of absence as she walked to the door, punched her code into the security lock, and entered, coming face-to-face with Col. Parnell Stevens, the head of Etherworld.

Casey had always thought Stevens to be the least likely man ever to wear a military uniform, in the looks department anyway. His thinning hair was carrot red and short, although with no apparent cut or style, as if he may have trimmed it himself with a pair of office scissors, and his forehead was high and usually shiny, even in the cold of winter. He had a small pink nose, actually a reconstruction following a war injury, which was disproportionate to his long thin face, and served primarily as a support for his glasses. His lips were beef-steak red. All this was set against a canvas of skin so pale as to appear, when seen occasionally in the daylight, translucent. Casey had speculated that half an hour in the California sun would have incinerated Stevens completely.

His body was equally spectacular. Standing a hair under six-four, he was shaped like a V, unfortunately inverted, with his hips being substantially wider than his stooped shoulders, his posture indicating a man who had grown up ashamed or at least self-conscious of his height, not exactly prime for a recruitment poster. But his voice was a pure contradiction to all of this. It was firm and assured, as in fact was Stevens himself, who had been a highly respected intelligence officer and a decorated veteran of both the Vietnam and Gulf wars before his assignment to Etherworld.

Casey liked and respected Parnell Stevens. Somewhere over the years he'd learned to laugh at himself and certainly didn't treat his work with the near-religious fervor of some of those who had preceded him. No, Stevens was a nuts-and-bolts kind of man, as much as anyone could be in a business like theirs, and Casey rated him as one of the best monitors she'd ever worked with, unbiased and unflappable, solid as rock.

He greeted her from behind his beat-up wooden desk, which fit right in with the worn green carpet and faded white walls of the bungalow's main office. Greeted her with a smile, not a salute. They were very informal at Etherworld.

"Ready for a little trip?" he asked.

Any plans of a postponement evaporated with his voice. His authority spread like an aura outward from the mahogany on which he rested his hands.

She answered by reflex. "I am."

She had a fair idea of what part of the ether they'd be invading. Ten to one the coordinates would guide her to China, in an attempt to locate new nuclear weapon facilities. Since the plans for America's most advanced warhead, the W-88, had been stolen from Los Alamos, the escalation of China's nuclear capabilities had become a priority.

Stevens surveyed her quickly.

"What happened?" he asked, looking at her left hand.

A thin strip of adhesive tape held a gauze pad over the circular wound. It had begun to itch, which Casey had interpreted as a sign of healing.

"Nothing serious," she replied. She didn't want to talk about it.

Stevens nodded and looked up, into her eyes. "I've got your water inside. Couldn't get Evian, so it's Polar Springs today."

Attention to detail. That was another of the things that Casey respected about the colonel.

"That'll be just fine," she said, slipping off her leather jacket and hanging it up on one of the four metal hooks to the side of the front door.

The leather coat looked small next to the colonel's green jacket, heavy with ribbons and metal. Nobody in the unit ever came in military uniform, except Stevens, and Casey wondered if he even owned a civilian suit.

She felt his eyes on her as she turned.

"You look tired, Captain," he commented. "Any problems?"

"No," she lied.

Stevens cocked his head, pushed his glasses back on his nose, and brought his lips together, scrutinizing her.

She felt self-conscious in the line of his thick lenses, as if they could magnify her confusion and make it evident.

"Let's get started," she said, walking by him quickly to open the door behind his desk.

"Okay, Captain, see you in half an hour."

Stevens knew her routine, or ritual, or whatever it was. They all had them, each of the four RVs who still worked in the program. A couple liked to do yoga exercises before a session, and Martin Olive, the newest and youngest of the space cadets, as Stevens referred to them with his peers, enjoyed six rounds of shadowboxing.

The ready room was the only room freshly painted, a pale, pastel green, the color rated most conducive to relaxation. The wool and acrylic carpet, green also, but a shade darker than the walls, was also relatively new. In the center of the wall, hung and framed, directly across from a seven-foot sofa, was a large Indian mandala, comprised of blue and gold patterns of interlocking triangles and concentric circles. It was intended, if used as a point for visual concentration, to center the mind.

Casey turned on the overhead track lights, then lowered them with the dimmer switch before making a minor adjustment to the thermostat beside the door. It may have been a bright, crisp winter day in Meade but it was seventy-two degrees and twilight in Etherworld.

She slipped off her trainers and lay down on the sofa, placing her arms to her sides and closing her eyes.

Precisely half an hour later the door opened and Parnell Stevens entered the room.

He always lowered his voice when he worked, and listening to it with her eyes closed, as Casey was doing now, it sounded like a late-night radio announcer, all hushed and confidential.

"Are you ready?"

The breathing exercise had relaxed her and Casey felt good, all things considered. Maybe getting back to work was exactly what she had needed.

"Yes," she replied, getting up from the sofa and following Stevens through the door and into the monitoring room. The carpets were thicker in the monitoring room than in the ready room, and they were red, the color designed to keep the monitor's mind focused and alert.

"Water's on the desk inside," Stevens said, opening the padded door to the RV chamber.

He stepped aside and Casey walked through and into the dimly lit space, its floor cushioned by an old and threadbare Persian carpet, which had faded from pink to a flesh tone in color. The walls had been soundproofed and painted in the standard conducive green and the smell of incense, a mixture of sandalwood and lavender, clung to them like a musky perfume.

She'd done close to two hundred sessions in this room so she felt right at home sitting down in the high-backed chair.

An old school desk, like a flat board on top of spindled legs, sat in front of her and everything she needed was laid out on its surface—her bottle of spring water, a drinking glass, paper, and pencils. Pretty simple and inexpensive equipment considering the magnitude of the tasks that had been attempted from inside the chamber.

They finished the sound checks on her voice, then Stevens eased into business, his words falling like warm rain from the Bose speakers. "We're okay for sound in here. All right from where you are?"

If Casey hadn't known what he looked like she would have sworn he was handsome.

"I'm fine," she replied.

"Okay, let's run a couple by, just to loosen up a bit."

She picked up the pencil, holding it lightly between her fingers.

"Ready when you are."

He gave her the coordinates, seventy-four north, forty-one west, then repeated them again slowly.

As was her routine, she wrote them along the top right-hand corner of the paper.

"Got it," she replied.

After that there was a sharp click from the speakers and she knew that Stevens had switched his mike off, leaving her alone in the silence.

She leaned back and inhaled. The smell of the spent incense soothed and relaxed her; as she exhaled, she focused her complete attention on the coordinates. In words and on paper, they were numbers and letters—symbols, mankind's means of representing a specific place in his physical world—but as she left that world and traveled in an inner, far more infinite space, the coordinates served as homing devices, directing the path of her flight and eventually, calling her back to the physical plane. Why this technique worked was open to speculation, yet all theory pointed toward the reality of dimensions beyond the world of human perception, beyond the collectively agreed structure of human consciousness.

In truth, the brain and nervous system served as reduction valves for the bombardment of stimulus from the great multidimensional mind of the universe, and the remote viewer, for a limited period of time, was capable linking with this larger mind and traveling within it, unencumbered by the brain's constraints of time and space.

Seventy-four north, forty-one west.

The image evolved like a photograph in the developing tray, becoming more defined as she sketched it on the sheet of white paper, undergoing metamorphosis, shaping with lines and angles, to become the hull of a massive ship. It was not a battleship. There were no gun turrets, and no armament and there were lots of people on board. She drew the people sticklike, in fast clean lines, standing, looking down over the rail of the promenade deck, windows below and banners flying from the rigging above them. The ship was afloat, but not at sea, because there were buildings to its starboard side. Then Casey began to get another image. It was of a letter in the alphabet, or was it a question mark; no, it was a set of letters. She relaxed and concentrated simultaneously. The feeling was electric, like a surge of sheer power, vibrating, taking her to a new level. Her mind opened wider, allowing a greater exchange of energy with the mind-at-large, allowing her to slip completely through the portal of space and time. She was there. Standing on the dock. The massive ship was sitting in front of her, languishing in the water; people were laughing, celebrating. There was animation, human life.

"I'm looking at the *QE II*," she said, and with her pronouncement the portal closed, as if the voltage had been cut.

Casey felt a quick fatigue passing through her in the wake of the electricity. Then she heard the microphone click back on.

"Well done," Stevens replied. "It docked this morning in New York."

He was always impressed with Casey. Most viewers would have stopped with the identification of the target as a ship, not pushing any further. Armstrong went all the way.

Casey felt a tinge of anger. Why was Stevens wasting her energy with games? She had been scheduled for a tasking. What was he doing?

"What now? Do I get a free ride to England and a seat at the captain's table?" she asked..~

Stevens made a low guttural sound that was not quite a laugh but as near as he ever came to one.

"No, you get another set of coordinates," he said, then hit her with them before she had time to lose concentration.

Stevens liked Casey Armstrong. He'd never married and, aside from the occasional prostitute, he didn't have much to do with women. He felt uncomfortable in their presence, but he and Captain Armstrong had, on occasion, shared a joke, and over the course of the two years he'd been running Etherworld, they had established a certain rapport. Besides, she was one of the two best viewers he'd ever worked with, and of the two, was the most emotionally stable. Sometimes he wondered what had happened to the other, Damon Raye. There were rumors of Raye's suicide and

others of his confinement in a psychiatric facility, but both
were unconfirmed. One way or the other, the man had been
used and discarded.

    Stevens sat back in his chair. The sound system in the
monitoring room was very sensitive and he could hear Casey
breathing, slow and steady. In his own rather dispassionate
way, he was routing for her. He didn't want her career
terminated, or worse, but that was not his decision. It was
beyond his control.

While Casey worked, oblivious to the world beyond her mind,
another vehicle pulled into the parking lot of the bungalow and
parked between her Toyota and Stevens's Jeep. It was a white
Ford sedan with military plates, one of the many nondescript
vehicles that were made available to Meade's higher-ranking
personnel. The man who stepped from the driver's seat was
clothed in a topcoat that had been expensively tailored on Saville
Row, and its gray fabric, a fine soft wool, matched the color of
his skin. He stood outside the car, balanced with the aid of a
walking cane, sniffing the scent of dead leaves on the cold air.

    An hour and a half of driving, from deep within the
mountains of Virginia, had provided plenty of time for him to
ponder the lab findings on the Colorado implant.

    In the preliminary analysis with the electron
microscope, the implant had appeared to have the same
collagen-based outer skin as the original device, while x-ray
diffraction revealed the inner core to be a thin, quartz-like
cylindrical object composed of silicon, potassium, calcium,
small traces of iron, and trace elements too small to be
identified. But the most intriguing fact was that the core was
conductive to electricity—speculation as to why included its
structure, like an elongated diamond with small grooves
etched into its surface, or the possibility that the unidentified
trace element were electrically conductive. Then came the
identification of microscopic twin valves, one on the core's
anterior section, the other on the forward posterior section
and the discovery of a residue of Molly Reed's blood, leaving
Dix to wait anxiously for its analysis.

Stevens saw the green light go on above the entrance to the monitoring room and knew that someone had entered the office. He glanced at the digital display of the clock on the console. It was 9:22 A.M. He was late by a full two minutes. That pleased Stevens. Any slip in form on the part of his visitor pleased him.

Stevens did not like Preston Dix. He found him arrogant and pompous, but above and beyond that, he was frightened of him. Dix did not seem to possess a heart. His manner was as cold as his handshake, and his interactions with people ruthless. He had absolute power, answering to no one, including, it was rumored, the president of the United States. Stevens had made discreet inquiries about him and come up with a number of blanks. Maybe people were reluctant to talk and maybe they truly didn't know, but Stevens found it impossible to believe that a man in charge of a classified government agency, with carte blanche into his and most other departments in the community, had no available military record or personal history.

Dix simply came and went, taking what he wanted, and Stevens had lost two talented viewers to him in the past eighteen months, including Damon Raye. *And after today*, he reminded himself, looking at the wall that separated him from Casey, *I might just lose another.*

Three quick raps against the thin door to the office interrupted his thoughts. He got up from his chair to open it, seething inside, as he always did, at Dix's habit of using the silver head of his walking cane to signal his arrival.

Pretentious son of a bitch, Stevens thought as he nodded a silent greeting.

"Morning, Colonel, how are things moving?"

"We've done one set so far, » Stevens replied. "Took her three minutes and twenty-three seconds. She seems fine."

"Excellent. I'll join you for the others."

By the time they were seated Casey had begun to speak, her voice possessing a light, musical quality as it drifted from the studio monitors.

"What I've got looks like houses, small, lots of them, line after line."

She was drawing a grid of interconnecting roads or walkways, lined by rectangular structures.

"There's a gate leading into the ... " she hesitated. "Park. What is this? Some kind of park?"

Stevens didn't answer. He knew she was not speaking directly to him anyway; in fact she may not have been conscious of speaking at all.

"And there are people here, inside the little houses. No, they're not houses, they're vaults, and these people have no energy. These people are dead."

There was a silence of about thirty seconds.

"I'm in a graveyard. The names on the vaults are not written in English, looks like Italian, maybe Latin."

"That will be enough for this target," Dix responded. "No need to continue."

Stevens switched on his mike and spoke.

"That's fine. You've got it."

His voice jolted Casey. It wasn't like Stevens to interrupt her before she had finished. He was too experienced for that.

"I could have gone further," she answered.

"Recoleta," he continued, trying to smooth it over.

She still sounded agitated. "What?"

"Recoleta," he repeated. "It's a cemetery in the heart of Buenos Aires, Argentina. That was a good hit."

Dix sat back and folded his arms across his chest. He had chosen Recoleta as part of the tasking. He knew the place, in fact he made it a point to stroll through the tombs whenever business took him to Buenos Aires. It gave him a rare feeling of peace to walk among the dead.

"What do I win now, a burial urn?" Casey asked, her humor returning. She found the exercises futile, but, at least, she felt more like her old self. Functional, almost whole. She uncapped the Polar Spring and took a long drink from the bottle before placing it back on the table.

Stevens ran her successfully through two more targets before looking down at the top page of his notepad. There were six remaining sets of coordinates written beneath the four he had already used, plus the correct answers to all of them on the next page. He was about to choose another when Dix slipped him a sheet of paper, folded in half.

Stevens took it and opened it, revealing the coordinates 38N, 104W.

It was written by hand, but small and neat enough to have been confused, at a glance, for type. He assumed correctly that it was Dix's writing, very anal, and he shrugged his shoulders—indifference being Steven's only weapon under the circumstances—and repeated the coordinates into the microphone.

Casey wrote them down, repeated them again, and Stevens confirmed that she was correct before switching off his mike and turning to Dix.

"A minor variation on the original assessment," Dix explained, adding casually, "let's see what she does with it." This left Stevens with no idea of how critical the situation had just become. Life-or-death critical.

Casey leaned back, closed her eyes, and concentrated on the coordinates she'd been given. She was almost sure she knew them, because the feelings surrounding her were all familiar; it was as if she was about to begin a journey back to a place she'd been before. She inhaled and exhaled in a slow rhythmic pattern, letting herself slide, once again, through the funnel of time and space.

Thirty-eight north, one hundred four west.

She picked up the pencil. It was starting to come, images forming against a background of white. Snow? Mountains? High, snowcapped mountains. Jutting peaks.

She drew quickly, sketching the outline of the peaks, high and jagged, at the top on the paper.

Then she began picking up images of a shape, more orderly than the random peaks, but still asymmetrical, like a lopsided pyramid. More shapes adjoining it. Maybe a set of triangles, placed side by side.

She drew the shapes as they came to her, watching them form on the paper, an angle, a straight line, another angle with a different pitch. It was man-made. Some kind of structure, a building, or possibly a house?

She almost began speaking then, to report into the microphone, when a wave of new sensation caused her to hold her tongue. She sensed a contact inside the building,

another mind, reaching to her across time and space. The
feeling shook her slightly, because the sensation was so
powerful. She had worked with telepathy in the past but this
was different; it felt like a higher pitch, an elevated resonance.

Casey lay the pencil down and attempted to enter a
deeper state of relaxation.

Stevens sat and waited. He could hear her breathing
but so far, which was unlike her, she hadn't said a word and
for some reason that made him nervous, He cast a furtive
glance at Dix, sitting straight against the stuffed fabric of the
office chair; his features were relaxed, as relaxed as his tight,
thin mouth could be, but his eyes were sharp and focused
with anticipation.

The first image came. It was a face, unusual in that its features
were refined but not fully shaped or formed. As she concentrated
she saw that it was the face of an infant. The eyes, however, were
a different story. They were pale sky blue, and it was as if they
did not belong to the baby at all, but to someone else, someone
old and infinitely wise. They projected a sense of knowing and as
her awareness became more centered Casey felt herself being
drawn into them, until her perspective shifted and the scene
hardened to become a reality.

She could see the baby clearly: his flawless skin and
fine blond hair. She had the sensation that she knew him. He
was hers, inside her now, a dream yet to be fulfilled. She
studied him, lying there in his crib, as he began to stir, his tiny
arms and legs stretching, his fingers extending toward her.
She could feel him awakening, the beat of his heart, the
rhythmic pulse of his mind. How clear his thought. How
clear his vision of her, unencumbered by form. She was the
light in his eyes.

She could sense herself awakening.

Then the dream changed, and she saw herself inside
the crib. She was looking up and Nick Hughes was standing
above her, looking down. He was talking to her, calling her
name, over and over again, anxious. "Case, Case. Can you
hear me? Case. Case." He was telling her to relax, asking if
she wanted another drink. A drink? The thought sickened
her.

It was a bad dream. She needed to wake up from this. She had the power to end it.

"What really happened, Nick?" she asked. "Tell me."

Another voice entered, "Would Madame care for a brandy?"

This was followed by the taste of calvados, the smell of spearmint, a flash of white light, and the face of the Asian waiter, like a mask. It flared, then burned, then melted away leaving her skin cold and her mouth dry, as an emptiness swallowed and devoured her.

"Oh God, I'm going to be sick." Her voice sounded feeble through the monitors. Then she retched.

■ ■ ■

Stevens moved to get up from the console and Dix stopped him with a reach of his arm, his fingers locking tight on Stevens's biceps, surprising him with their strength.

"Talk to her," he ordered.

Stevens turned to argue and was met with a glare as the pressure on his arm increased. The fingers relaxed only as he settled back into his chair and turned on his mike.

"Casey, what's going on in there?"

"I lost it," she answered. Her head was beginning to throb, as if a tight band was constricting around her temples.

Dix motioned with his hand, as if he was lifting something in his palm.

He wanted more.

"I don't follow you?" Stevens continued.

Casey tried to stand but couldn't. She was dizzy and disoriented. Whatever had happened had been like some kind of short circuit in her mind.

Her words sounded emotionless and flat.

"Sorry, I was onto something, but it was more an abstract than an actual target." She stopped, unable to describe what she had seen or felt. "It started out okay, but then it got confused, one thing spilling into another." She looked down at her drawing paper. "I didn't get much on paper either. Looks like a broken pyramid, badly defined. Just a bunch of lines and angles."

She purposely stayed away from the Japanese waiter. There was no point in telling Stevens any more of anything, not till she understood it herself.

"My head aches, I don't think I can continue. I'm sorry. It's just not going to happen," she said.

The steel band slackened and the headache receded, replaced by something else.

"I think I want to go home and lie down."

The feeling had started again. That gnawing in her gut that told her something was missing. That she'd left something behind. It was something important. She reached to the table, took the bottle, and sipped the water; the liquid felt uncomfortably heavy as it hit her empty stomach.

"Sorry," she repeated, looking down at the paper once more, studying the coordinates and puzzled by her drawing. Nothing came, no memory, no connection.

"Sit tight, I'll be right in," Stevens said. "Do you want some aspirin, some ibuprofen?"

Casey noted a compassion in his tone of voice that she'd never heard before. It added a new layer to him, touching her.

"No thank you," she answered. "I'm just going to sit here a minute, then I'll get going, if that's okay with you."

Stevens felt protective, and guilty.

"Take your time," he said. "No hurry."

He didn't want her walking in on them, as if by accidentally laying eyes on Preston Dix, Casey would somehow, and irrevocably, seal her fate. He looked across at his visitor, unsure of what had just transpired in the RV chamber and what it all meant, but he could sense the man's mind turning, weighing things up.

Finally Dix spoke, softly but with a dull edge. "And you believe that she's still the best RV you've got?"

Stevens had answered the same question three weeks ago, when Dix had requisitioned Casey for the first time. He knew no more now than he had then, nothing of where she had been taken, or of what she had been tasked to do. He did know that she had been the subject of some form of memory block, and that today's assessment had been a test to gauge its effectiveness.

His answer, also, was exactly as it had been then, but his tone, if anything, was more emphatic, as if his assurance might save her from the gray man.

"Yes, Captain Armstrong is the best I've got. She is irreplaceable."

Dix nodded, as if his decision had just been made final. He was pleased that the erasure had been effective, while apparently leaving her psi capabilities in working order.

"Good, because I shall be requiring her again," he stated, standing up from the chair.

Grasping his cane from its leaning position against the console, Dix hesitated a moment, as if to make sure his knees and ankles were all connected, then walked to the door.

He opened it, turned, looked one more time at Stevens, and said, "Colonel, don't you work Dr. Armstrong too hard. I want her fresh, understand?"

Stevens nodded and Dix was gone. But a feeling of inevitability remained. The gun was loaded, and the hammer was cocked. It was only a matter of time for Armstrong. The same way it had been for Damon Raye.

~ 7 ~

The "house of cards," as Thomas Reed liked to call it, was a two-story, three-bedroom contemporary, made of red cedar. The nickname stemmed from the first time he'd seen it, driving by in a local agent's Dodge Suburban, en route to view another property. It was an eccentric masterpiece, or monstrosity, depending on individual perception, with a high shingled roof, rising straight from the ground and pitched at a seventy-degree angle to overhang the bank of dormer windows that constituted the entire south-facing side. Another roof with a less acute pitch made up the north face, covering a garage and shed. It was joined to the main part of the house by a third, skylit, flat roof. A single chimney rose from that, and the sides of its cedar cladding had been cut to match the pitch of the slanted roof lines.

Looking at it from the road, it was hard to find a single right angle to the place, and the overall appearance was that its pieces had been cut, laid together, and balanced one against the other, like a house of cards, giving the entire structure a jagged, off-kilter appearance, modern in a way, but without a particular period. It was an original. As if its creators had designed it as they'd been building it, changing an angle here, adding another there, trying to make it all stand up, while evolving some form of spontaneous symmetry.

The property agent, a wily old widow who'd been selling property in the Springs area for twenty years, had noticed Thomas looking at it and explained.

"Morris Madden built that—" almost slipping to say "thing," but catching herself at the last to change the word to house. "That whole south side was once a solar panel, but Morris hadn't reckoned on the winter shadow from the mountains so it never quite worked. He pulled out the panels about five years ago and replaced them with the dormers. That was just before he flipped his pickup coming down from the Peak. His sons have been trying to sell it ever since he died."

Thomas Reed had purchased the house on impulse.

To him, it brought to mind something that should have been hanging on the edge of a cliff in Big Sur, California, overlooking the Pacific, and not staring up at the Rockies. It looked very unloved but the price, a hundred and seventy-five thousand, was right. He enjoyed renovations, if not the hassles with the builders, at least the end result. It had turned him a decent profit in the past, when it had become time for him and Molly to move on.

And now, with the arrival of their son, John, it was time again. Not to leave the Springs, but to consider a house that was more child-friendly, because, inside, the house of cards was mostly open space, the ground floor a series of interconnecting areas on two levels, joined by four, wide crescent-shaped stairs.

The lower level was divided by a spiral staircase, leading to the second story of the house. It was not dissimilar, in living space, to a New York loft, and no easier to childproof. Sooner or later, John would be crawling, and eventually walking, and it was easier to address the issue now, particularly since the house would probably take some time to sell, requiring a buyer with a similar vision to Thomas.

The problem was, that since John's birth, Molly would not permit the house to be shown. She didn't want strangers near her, or near her child. Not since the episode with the unidentified man in the hospital, and not since Murray Rose's death. She was convinced that the two events were connected.

In the days that they'd been home, the curtains had been drawn, and the doors and windows locked. She'd even had Thomas install a bolt lock on the door of the bedroom on the top story. When he returned from work he'd find her in there, locked up, bottles of water and packets of prepared food, yogurt, and crackers beside the bed, nursing or cradling their son. That didn't stop people from coming. Each day Thomas would find gifts laid on the wooden porch, in front of the entrance door, flowers and baby clothes, religious ornaments, icons and rosary beads, a hand carving of Jesus on the cross. He'd carry them inside and up to the bedroom, then sit in the chair beside the bed while Molly read the attached cards. Some were from the few friends they had made during their time in Colorado, but most were from people at the hospital, doctors and nurses who had had occasion to care for or spend time with the child.

"I don't get it," Thomas had said, time and again. "These people don't even know us."

And Molly had answered, "Yes, but they know John."

She seemed in a state of bliss with her son and the closer their bond became, the more excluded Thomas felt. In the first days, he had moved to the guest bedroom on the ground floor of the house, with the excuse that, at his age, he needed his sleep. But the real reason was that he wasn't comfortable in close proximity with the baby. He felt that there was something unnatural about him; it was intuition more than anything else, but he didn't sense a connection to the boy. He'd held him only a few times, and then had avoided looking into the strange blue eyes.

The result of his reticence was a rift between him and Molly.

When, seeped in guilt, Thomas had spoken of his problem to Robert Barnes, the priest had suggested a visit to the Reed house, thinking that he could act as a bridge between the parents.

The priest had been his usual confident, joking self and Thomas had felt a sense of relief. If anybody could rescue the situation, it was Robert Barnes.

Thomas led him up the spiral staircase, then waited while Molly unlocked the door to the bedroom.

After a short while he left them alone with John and went back downstairs to make coffee. It took a few minutes and during that time Thomas listened hopefully for sounds of conversation from the room above the stairs. He heard nothing and finally, he went back up upstairs to rejoin them, surprised to see the priest sitting, cradling John in his arms.

The baby was big, nearly twelve pounds, and Thomas was certain that he had grown noticeably longer since he was born. He was definitely more coordinated, able to sit and hold onto things, like he was doing now, his small hands gripping the priest's arms while his head remained erect, his eyes alert as if he knew what was happening around him. His hair was white blond. Alex had been blond, too, but not like this, so thick and long, already falling to touch his shoulders. There was something very strange here. Why couldn't the rest of them see it? Robert Barnes sat, shaking his head and smiling.

It was his smile that irritated Thomas more than anything. Barnes had that look of ignorant bliss that Thomas associated with the newly conned and converted, like some babbling Hare Krishna disciple.

The priest's first statement incensed Thomas even more.

"You have something very special here, very special."

Thomas stood, feeling more alienated than ever. He didn't get it.

"Your son is a miracle," Barnes went on, looking down at John, then smiling radiantly at Molly. "A miracle of life."

Thomas stared at him. He felt like he'd been double-crossed by a friend. Barnes had come to help him, to patch things up, what the hell was he doing?

"A miracle?" There was more cynicism in Thomas's voice than he'd intended. "What do you mean by that?"

"Look into John's eyes. I mean, really look," Barnes continued, holding the baby toward him. "Have you ever seen what's inside?"

Thomas took a step forward and looked down, into the blue eyes. They were focused and unwavering, and there was something there, inside them. It was something familiar, yet unresolved. Something that he didn't want to face. He turned away.

"The coffee's getting cold," he said, before walking from the room.

He was sitting sullenly at the dining table when Barnes finally appeared.

"What's going on?" Thomas asked.

The priest turned toward him and Thomas was struck by the look of his face—younger, his skin more fresh, as if the lines and ridges had been relaxed and smoothed, and his eyes, they contained a mixture of awe with a touch of fear, and something else, like a rapture.

"Do you want to know something about me? You want to hear my story?" Barnes asked. Then without waiting for an answer, continued. "I've been a hypocrite. Your priest, your sponsor. The man who gets his congregation together every week and preaches to them. I've been a scholar, understood things intellectually; I've memorized parts of the scriptures, underlined the words that I've felt were relevant. I've counseled and I've recited the gospel, but I've never gone to sleep at night with any true faith in what I've spouted. 'Cause I've never taken that big leap of faith, and because of that, I've paid the price. I've never had any real peace of mind. That's been my burden, my secret. I've covered it with alcohol, guarded it, disguised it with a collar and robes, but the truth is, I've been a fake, a cynic and a liar. Till right now. I'm going to sleep well tonight, because I found my religion. Right here, in your house."

The words and manner were completely out of context with the dry, humorous man Thomas had come to know. He resented the change.

"Robert, what the hell's going on with you?" he asked. "What kind of bullshit—"

"You have a miracle here, right upstairs. Your son is the miracle. Look inside that child's eyes."

Thomas stared into his coffee cup and replied, "I didn't see anything."

Barnes looked at him with compassion. "You're so close to it; you don't want to acknowledge its presence. It

must be a frightening thing, to have it so near, such a
responsibility—"

"I don't know what you're talking about," Thomas
said. When in fact, Barnes had hit it exactly. Fear. That was
what he'd felt. Fear and confusion. The infant's eyes had
begun to unearth something inside him, before he'd turned
away.

Barnes continued to look at him, studying his face as
if he was waiting for him to come clean. Prying, until finally
Thomas spoke again.

"I don't feel like he's my son. Do you understand me?
I can't look at him because it's like ..." His mouth tightened.
"He's not my son."

Barnes nodded his head, reached out, and gripped
him gently by the arm.

"I understand. It's natural to feel that way."

Thomas met the priest's eyes. What did he mean by
that? It had been natural enough with Alex. What did Barnes
know? What had Molly said to him?

Barnes held him by the arm, intending to quiet him,
to make him think, to aid him in some deep understanding.

"I'd like you to come to church on Sunday. Please.
It'll do us both good."

Thomas looked at him with resentment. Church was
the last thing on his mind. It seemed like a different world.

"I don't think so," he answered.

"Please. Promise me you'll come," Barnes insisted.

Thomas hesitated. All he wanted was to be left alone.

"We'll all need each other before we can accept this,"
Barnes added.

Thomas held his eyes. It was as if Barnes had gone
upstairs as someone who he had known and trusted and
come down a different man.

"Yeah, sure Robert," Thomas said. Anything to get
rid of him.

Barnes smiled and removed his hand from Thomas's
arm.

"Good, see you in church. God bless you, Thomas."

Thomas felt like shouting "Asshole!" at his back. The simpering son of a bitch. Then he listened as the car engine started and Barnes drove off.

Barnes knows. Molly knows. What did they know? Running around smiling, nodding their heads. Whispering. Sharing the big secret. Whose kid was it anyway?

He stormed up the steps.

The sight of Molly and the child made him feel even more aggressive.

"What the fuck is going on in my house?"

Molly pulled the baby closer to her, as if to protect him from the anger.

"Please, Thomas. What's the matter with you?"

"Me? Me! What's it with you? And what's it with that baby. Who the hell is he? Or should I say whose is he!"

She hadn't seen him this way for years, since his boozing days, abusive and irrational. He frightened her.

"What are you talking about?" she asked.

"I'm not sure, exactly. Maybe you'd like to let me in on it," Thomas continued, walking toward her, his eyes on the child.

She pulled back against the head of the bed.

"Where's Father Barnes?" she asked.

"Gone."

Then a thought struck him, crazy, but once it bit, it wouldn't let go.

"Barnes," Thomas continued. "Was it Barnes? Were you fucking Robert Barnes!"

All at once she realized what he was talking about. It was so ridiculous that, in spite of her distress, she laughed, making a low, nervous sound, more an expulsion of air.

That set him off. Enough to make a grab for them. Intending to shake the truth from her. Getting his right hand on the baby's shoulder when John turned toward him. His movement was uncanny, his neck twisting, apparently under complete muscular control.

He locked eyes with Thomas.

The flash of light was inside the blue. It hit Thomas hard, and for an instant, he was back in time, in the churning water off the Jersey shore, reaching out for Alex. Seeing the shining gold cross hanging around his neck, feeling his smooth skin beneath his fingers before the contact snapped.

"Leave us alone! Get away! You've got no right!" Molly shouted, pulling John back from him, withdrawing against the pillows. And for that instant, she, also, seemed locked in a different place in time. Then her eyes refocused and she was staring at him.

There was fury in her voice. "Don't you ever touch him again. Ever. Do you understand me!"

Thomas was too stunned to argue. He felt lost and hollow. His knees were trembling and he thought he might collapse on the floor. He looked again at the baby, clinging silently to its mother's bosom. The eyes were still aimed at him, and the light was still there, but it was smaller now, and further away.

He looked at the infant and asked, "Who are you?"

"Please, Thomas," Molly answered, recovering her composure. "Please leave us alone."

With the traffic, it took Casey forty minutes to get to Georgetown, and then another fifteen to find a place to park, along a quiet side street three blocks from the Four Seasons Hotel and a ten-minute walk from the Tante Claire.

She felt like she was marching to battle.

The Tante Claire was gearing up for trade and Serge Le Blanc, the maitre d' with the Belmondo profile, was busy assuring that the thirty tables were set and the staff accounted for and properly attired. Sometimes prominent politicians used the restaurant for a quick dalliance with a secretary or an associate's wife. Dangerous liaisons, as Le Blanc called them, but he always held two discreetly located tables in the back of the large room, away from the kitchen, just in case.

He was seated at one of them, going over his reservations for the afternoon, when Casey entered. At first he didn't recognize her, not in her leather jacket, sweatpants, and trainers. In fact he was on the verge of asking one of the waiters to inform her that they were not yet serving lunch and politely showing her the door when he remembered the short cropped hair and unusual eyes. He was just a bit embarrassed that he could not remember her name. That was a fatal flaw in his profession.

Casey stopped at the table and smiled sheepishly at him. She was half expecting some sort of reprisal and she was squirming inside, trying hard to hold her composure, aware that every waiter in the restaurant must have seen her performance.

"Serge, when you have a moment, may I speak with you?"

Le Blanc returned her smile, determined to cover for his lagging memory with a well-polished charm.

"Of course," he said, closing his book, then standing to extend his hand and kiss her on both cheeks. "And how is Madame today?"

"Better," she replied.

Le Blanc looked at her, mildly confused, then noticing her bandaged hand. "Has Madame had an accident?"

Casey smiled, thinking he was being discreet. "Thank you, Serge, you are very kind."

This confused him more, as he fought to recall her name. He had family money and was better dressed and better educated than many of his clients but he still had a fierce professional pride. He knew her face. But her name, her name?

"And what may I do to be of service?" he asked. Then it came to him. She was the woman from the army base, the one who wore the sexy stockings and spiked heels.

"It's about the other week," Casey began, then stalled, searching his face, waiting for him to take up her lead.

Armstrong. Ms. Armstrong. That was it. And her boyfriend was the big, good-looking man, the one that Charles, the head waiter, couldn't keep his eyes off. Le Blanc was 90 percent sure, so he chanced it.

"And how is Mr. Hughes?"

Casey sensed his discomfort and it heightened her own.

"Fine, Nick's just fine." Then, to the point. "Serge, I'm very upset about what happened in your restaurant on New Year's Eve. I've come to apologize." Which was not exactly true. She'd come for answers, any kind of answers.

Again, Le Blanc was taken aback, and again she misinterpreted his hesitancy as politeness.

"I've never done anything like that before, and it has disturbed me a great deal," she continued, turning to scan the room, searching for the Asian waiter.

"Ms. Armstrong, I am sorry, but I do not know this incident to which you refer," he replied, wracking his brain to recollect the last time she'd even been in.

Le Blanc's accent was still strong, even after ten years in the States, but it now sounded, to Casey, thicker than usual, as if he was laying it on.

"I appreciate your kindness but it's not necessary. I just came by to apologize to you and also—" She looked around again. "I'd like to say I'm sorry to the gentleman who took care of our table that evening."

Le Blanc was confused.

"He's Asian, very tall," she said.

"Never," he answered, shaking his head and raising both hands, palms open. "I have never had anyone like that working for me. Never."

Casey didn't seem to hear him.

"Maybe Japanese, a tall Japanese man?"

"I am sorry, but Madame is mistaken. All our staff are either French or American."

"It was New Year's Eve. Maybe you just had him on for the night," Casey continued.

She could feel the anxiety building. She needed something to hold onto. Needed to make this real, to confront this demon, to bring it out into the open, to get clear of it.

Le Blanc studied her from the side, noticing the intensity of her eyes, the tension in her posture. The lady was going to explode, right there, in front of his prized tables, at the beginning of lunch hour, with his first customers filtering in. He had to do something to defuse her.

"If Madame would care to come to my office and sit down, it would be my pleasure to serve her a glass of wine."

Casey turned and her look genuinely frightened him. It was a wild, haunted look.

"Calvados. I was drinking calvados that night," she said.

"Mais oui, but of course we have calvados, if that is what Madame desires," Le Blanc replied, catching her attention for a second, drilling into her eyes. "But, Ms. Armstrong, I assure you, we do not have the man that you have described working here. That I promise."

Casey tried to swallow and noticed that her mouth had gone dry again. She was caught inside a nightmare and couldn't wake up. This wasn't real. Nothing seemed real. It was all as artificial as it had been on that night, like a blur of lights and voices, actors and stage sets. Nick, where was Nick? She stared at the dark-haired maitre d', his eyes were coffee brown and he was sweating, just a trickle, forming on his brow. Nervous. That was it. She was making him nervous, scaring him; she could feel it and the feeling gave her a sense of grounding, just enough footing to keep her from giving way completely. She dug deep inside herself and grabbed the last of her reason, pulling it forward to use as a brace.

"Serge," she said, extending her hand and leveling her voice, "I'm sorry to have troubled you. Obviously, I was mistaken."

Le Blanc watched as she walked from the restaurant, feeling somehow, that he had just averted a crisis, but not knowing the nature or magnitude of the event, simply that he was extremely relieved.

Once on the sidewalk, Casey turned once and looked back at the Tante Claire, through its tall windows and into the dining room, at the vacant tables with their white linen cloths and sparkling crystal glasses. In a single flash of clarity, the kind of pristine clarity that sometimes breaks in the wake of great confusion, she remembered the last time that she and Nick had eaten in there; it was late in November, Beaujolais Nouveau season. The wine had just arrived from France and they'd shared a bottle. That was it. The last time. The Asian waiter was from somewhere else, not a restaurant, but some place in her mind. Like a figment of her imagination, but not quite, more a disembodied memory, something that she had attached to this particular place. The disconcerting part was that Nick was an accomplice to this phantom union.

She recalled New Year's Day; the manner in which he had woven the story, recanting the episode in the Tante Claire. Creating the scene, filling in gaps, painting by number until the illusion was complete. In the past two weeks he had become short-tempered, even aggressive, whenever the subject of New Year's Eve had arisen.

Casey walked toward her car. Another ally had stepped forward from an arsenal devoted to her self-protection, her anger, hard and strong. Capable, for a time anyway, of holding her demons at bay.

She drove fast. Now she wanted to get back to the town house. She wanted to get inside and barricade the doors. For the moment, she did not fear her own mind. Her anger was securing the fissures and demanding that she step forward, closer to the truth.

She drove to the rear of the town house, down a small road that gave access to the back door. There, she parked, out of sight from the building. She wanted privacy, particularly from Nick Hughes.

She entered through the kitchen, locked the door behind her, and went straight to her bedroom. Within fifteen minutes she had torn it apart, tipping drawers and emptying her closet, tossing Nick's clothes, along with her own, all over the bed and onto the floor. Searching for something that would give her a clue, rummaging through her handbag, his pockets, looking for what?

As her passion ebbed, the confusion began to return, in short quick spurts at first, just enough to unsettle her, to make her stop and look around, to ask herself what she was doing. Then the spurts became more sustained. Until finally, sitting there on the floor, amidst the rubble of her existence, she suffered the great dread. Maybe this was it. Insanity. Stalking her, making her sick in the body and mind. It was not the way she had imagined it. Not some state of dull acceptance in which the soul had died. There was lucidity here, naked and raw, but too brief, offering only quick glimpses from the window of a runaway train. Into the tunnel, loud with voices, shouting, and the frustration of almost recognizing them, but then, they too were gone, echoing in the darkness as the ride went on. If only she could

slow down and think, but the more she struggled the faster it
became, until there was only speed and blurred image.
Memories, flawed and disjointed. What had happened to her?

She was weeping, with her head hanging, and tears
rolling down her cheeks, into her mouth, tasting the salt and
the sorrow of her frustration. Remember? There was
something in there. Something to remember. What was it?
She took her head in her hands and held it, as if she could
slow down the spin.

I need help. Maybe Nick would come. He'd take her
away. Put her some place safe and warm. Someplace where
they could not get to her. They? Who were they? And Nick.
The thought of him made her angry.

She opened her eyes, then picked up a white cotton
sock, one of a pair that Nick used for the gym. He loved
those socks, Ralph Lauren, thick and heavy; she wiped her
tears with it, then blew her nose. For some reason that made
her smile. She did it again, before dropping the sock beside a
duffel bag, which was sitting open in front of her, unzipped
and gaping. She took the bag everywhere, on every
assignment. It was her traveling companion, a piece of her
life. She'd already checked it thoroughly and it had been
empty, but still, she lifted it again. She was transfixed by it, as
if it was compelling her to touch it. Slowly, she ran her hand
down one of the side pockets, as if the missing piece of her
life would be contained inside the worn canvas. She felt
something with her fingers and pulled it out. It was a business
card, white with embossed lettering, printed in black. JAMES
RENO. HAMPTONS LIMOUSINE COMPANY.
SOUTHAMPTON, NEW YORK. There was a phone
number beneath the name.

She sat there a minute with the card, staring at it,
trying to figure out how the hell it had ended up inside her
bag. Southampton, New York? She'd never been there. She
wasn't even sure where it was.

Getting up from the floor, she walked to her bed,
sitting down beside the night table with the portable clock
and the telephone. She looked at the card again, rubbing it
between her fingers. She sensed something far away, one of
the voices in the tunnel was calling to her. She had touched

this card before. It had meaning, significance. Then a wave of panic threatened to sink her again. What if she called the number and it was like the restaurant? A dead end. There could be only so many dead ends and her time in the maze would be up. She would have failed to find her way out. Then they'd come for her. Take her away. They. They. Who were they?

She picked up the phone and dialed the number.

A woman's voice came on the other end of the line. "Hamptons Limousine, may I help you?"

The voice had a New York accent. Brooklyn, or Bronx, it didn't matter. What did was that it sounded normal and sane. Worth the call just to affirm that the world outside her room had continued with business as usual.

"May I help you?" the voice asked for a second time.

Casey cleared her throat.

"Yes, please." She wasn't sure where to begin. "I'm calling to speak to a ... " she looked down at the card and read the name, "James Reno."

"Jimmy's out on a job right now. If you're calling to book him for a pickup, I can do that from here," the woman explained.

"Have you got a log book there, something that would confirm past jobs?" Casey asked, suddenly very nervous. This was it, another moment of truth.

"Depends how far back you're talking."

Casey replied. "December 31."

"That shouldn't be too hard."

"Have you got anything down for Armstrong?" Casey asked.

The woman working the switchboard was Peggy Taylor and it was only her third week working for the company. They carried some pretty important clients, rock stars, prominent writers, show-business people, and Wall Streeters; she wasn't sure if she should be giving out information. Maybe this was a private detective or a divorce lawyer. There were plenty of them working the Hamptons beat.

She shuffled back through the pages to Friday, December 30.

"May I ask why you need this information?"

Casey didn't know how to answer.

"I just do," she said, sounding desperate, then in a quick reversal, her voice sounding more aggressive, "My name is Armstrong and I can't locate my personal diary. I'm trying to see if my secretary booked me a car on that date. I may have had her do it, then missed the ride. I need to know for my own records."

Peggy Taylor thumbed down the line of bookings; there was no Armstrong recorded.

"I show nothing here under that name," she said.

"Are you sure?"

Taylor looked a second time. "Yes."

Casey felt like she was sinking again. She reached out one last time.

"How about James Reno?"

The switchboard was lit up and Taylor had other calls to take.

"He's out on a job." Repeating herself.

"When is he back?"

Taylor wanted to get rid of her, but, at the same time, didn't want to risk offending a client.

"I'm not certain," she answered. "An hour, maybe two, it all depends on traffic."

"Actually, this is very important," Casey said. "James usually drives me and I need to talk to him. It's urgent."

Taylor hesitated. All the drivers had car phones. If this was one of Jimmy's client's, then what trouble could she get in?

"I'll give you his number," she said. "You should be able to reach him."

Casey grabbed the notepad from beside the phone and picked up a pencil, writing it down as the woman spoke. She thanked her and put the phone down, then sat a moment, trying to think through what she was going to say. How was she going to approach James Reno? She finally realized that it didn't matter what she said; he either knew her or he didn't, and there was only one way to find out. She dialed and waited.

"Hello, this is Jimmy."

She'd hoped that his voice would trigger something but it sounded thin and far away. Maybe hers would.

"This is Casey Armstrong."

Reno was halfway up the Long Island Expressway, between the Oyster Bay exit and Lake Ronkonkoma using the carpool lane and trying to make up some time after the jam coming out of Kennedy Airport. He had Saul Becket in the backseat, a literary agent known for his abrupt manner, short arms, and long pockets.

Reno had no idea who he was talking to, but he was always professionally polite.

"Yes, Ms. Armstrong, what can I do for you?"

Casey felt a ray of hope.

"This may sound a bit strange," she said. "But I found your business card in my traveling bag and I'm trying to figure out how it got there. Have you given me a ride recently?"

Reno slowed behind a Durango with a single passenger, wished a cop would grab the guy for illegal use of the carpool lane, and wondered what kind of nut case he had on the phone. Still, he was polite.

"To be honest, your name doesn't ring any bells," he replied.

"It might have been December 31. New Year's Eve. I live in Washington," Casey continued.

"You got me there," Reno answered. "Haven't been to Washington since Nixon was in office." Becket was smoking a cigar, one of the Cuban Monte Cristos he bragged about but never offered and the smoke was snaking over the front seat, making Reno feel nauseous. He wished he'd brought the limo, with the dividing window.

"I'm wondering if I was in New York," Casey said.

Reno considered the possibility that he was being set up. One of his buddies messing around. Maybe Freddy Wren from Hampton Bays, a small-time bookie. Also a practical joker.

"Well, with respect, if anyone should know, it would be you," Reno answered, a little lighter, beginning to enjoy the game.

"I'm thirty-three years old, tall, about five-ten, short dark hair, gray-green eyes. I always wear sunglasses if it's bright, aviators with wire rims," Casey continued, trying to think of some distinguishing feature that would click his memory.

Reno was pretty sure Freddy Wren was behind the call, pulling his chain. He was just about to lower his voice and ask Casey her bra size, when she said. "I always carry an army duffel bag when I travel, an old canvas thing. Khaki-colored. That's where I found your card."

And suddenly Reno remembered the flight from Washington and the ride to Montauk. "Ms. Emerson?"

"Armstrong. My name is Armstrong," Casey replied.

"Well, I took a Ms. Emerson to Montauk on the thirtieth. Late in the afternoon. She looked like the lady you just described."

Casey felt a surge of emotion. Something was clicking, finally. "Did you give her a business card?"

Reno remembered the episode very clearly now.

"Yes, I did, and she put it in the side pocket of an old canvas bag. I remember the bag."

"I'm pretty sure that was me," Casey answered. Then, before Reno had time to digest her remark, she said, "James, I'd like to book you for another ride."

"Sure," Reno answered. He'd thought about Ms. Emerson a couple of times since he'd driven her, wondering what she'd done after he'd left. Now, he was more curious about her than ever.

Casey straightened her back, sitting more upright. She felt suddenly that she'd found a thread, something to follow through.

She said, "I'm going to grab the next plane to New York." Glancing at her travel clock she said, "If I'm lucky I should get there in three or four hours. I know it's short notice."

Reno checked the time on the dashboard. The display read 2:45. This was his second airport run since five this morning and he was tired. He'd finished for the day and counted on dropping Becket off in Wainscott and going home to relax. But he'd liked Ms. Emerson, or Ms.

Armstrong, or whoever she was and he was buzzed by the intrigue.

"I don't know if I can get back to Kennedy or La Guardia in time."

"That doesn't matter," Casey replied. "I'll sit and wait for you." She heard him hesitate. "I'll pay you whatever you want."

"It's not the money; it's the traffic," Reno answered. "Shouldn't be too bad going west, though. I should be able to get there by seven. You got to let me know your flight number, and which airport."

"Can I call you back with those details?" Casey asked.

Reno could hear Becket making grumbling sounds in the backseat. The cigar smoke had dissipated and the great man obviously wanted to sleep.

"I'm driving a client right now," he answered, aware that he'd been on the phone too long as it was. "Call it through to Peggy on the main number. Don't worry I'll get it ... By the way, where do you want to go?"

She replied, "The same place as last time."

"Montauk Point?"

"Yes," she answered.

"You got it."

Casey felt better, as if she had finally acquired an ally. "See you later, James."

"Jimmy. Call me Jimmy."

She had the vague sense that she'd had this conversation, or part of it before. "Okay, Jimmy. See you."

~ 8 ~

In his dream Michael Caruso was back in the old stucco house in Hialeah, directly under the flight path from Miami International and a few minutes walk from the Greyhound Bus terminal. He was wearing his number 9 baseball jersey and standing in front of his father. His mother, Ethel, was there too, sitting in the big, red upholstered chair by the television.

His father was wearing his police uniform and looked just as he had on the last evening that Michael had seen him. He was forty-one years old but looked much older. In the preceding year he had begun to walk with an awkward, unsteady gait, his speech was often slurred, and his hair had turned from jet black to a ghostly white. There was a vacancy to his brown eyes, as if they'd been drained, leaving them sad, dry, and sometimes frightened. His olive skin had sallowed and the area above his cheekbones was etched with deep lines, like cracks in the surface, fissures caused by some internal pressure.

Michael stood in front of him and asked, "It wasn't an accident, was it, Dad?"

His father looked confused, shaking his head.

Michael continued, "You shouldn't have done it. We needed you."

Then he turned and looked at his mother, Ethel, sitting in the chair, staring at him. She appeared younger than he had remembered her; her eyes were emerald green, her face was full and pale, and her dark hair was soft, and fell naturally to touch her shoulders.

Her voice was a melody. "Michael, you don't understand. Try to understand."

The sound had come from the bedroom, like the pop of a cork from a champagne bottle, except there had never been any champagne in the bedroom of the Caruso house. It was fast and final. Everything completed by that single sound. Pop! They'd told him that it was an accident. Sergeant Martin Caruso had died while cleaning his handgun. Even then, Michael had suspected the truth. It was something that he and his mother had never spoken of again. A sacred taboo. Yet its legacy had been an indelible sorrow between them.

"I've always known," he said as the images vanished.

He had awakened with it fresh in his mind, lying there on his back, staring through the darkness at the white ceiling. He'd had the identical dream three times since he had seen John Reed, since the infant had opened some portal in his mind, setting free the ghosts that had lived inside.

Caruso slid from beneath the duvet, his bare feet soft against the carpeted floor and walked from the bedroom, down the corridor, continuing down the stairs, his mind struggling to interpret what he had been experiencing.

As he entered the living room he saw the red upholstered chair.

It was the same chair that his mother had been sitting in on the night of his father's death. The chair from the dream. It was an artifact from Miami, occupying a corner of his life, directly beneath a wood-framed mirror, also a memento from the old house, and it was in the mirror, in the dull morning light, that Caruso saw the reflection of his face. It held the same frightened look that his father had had on that night.

He walked to the chair and sat down, attempting to rationalize what he was feeling, recalling John Reed's eyes. Ever since that day in the hospital he'd felt them, as if they had become a companion to his ,always there, guiding him to this place.

He picked up the phone from the table beside him and dialed a number from memory.

As soon as he heard the familiar voice he said, "Mother, it's me ... "

It was five o'clock in the morning in Florida. Not the usual time for a call from her son and Ethel Caruso's voice was suddenly alert.

"Michael, has something happened?"

Then, in a sudden flash, he knew exactly why he had phoned. He'd known that his assumption had been correct for many years, but now he needed the whole truth.

"Why did my father kill himself?"

There was a long hesitation.

"I need to know."

Ethel spoke to Mike regularly, usually on Sunday mornings, but never about her late husband. It was the first time she'd realized that her son had even suspected that his father's death had been a suicide. It had been half a lifetime ago, gone and buried with the pain.

"What happened that night?" Caruso continued, as if she required prompting.

His mother's words were soft but clear.

"Why now? It's over. It's been over a long, long time."

"Because I need to know," he answered. "What happened in our house? What happened that would make him do that?"

There was silence from his mother's end.

"Why did he shoot himself?"

Nothing.

"Mother, are you still there, are you listening to me?"

Her voice came suddenly, filling the hollow between them.

"Your father had ALS, Lou Gehrig's disease. It's a neurological disorder and it's fatal."

Caruso sat stunned as she continued.

"The symptoms were getting worse, some days he could barely walk, and his speech was starting to slur. He was going to end up totally paralyzed, everything but his mind. That's what's so terrible about it. It doesn't affect the mind; he was going to be aware of everything that happened to him. He didn't want that. He didn't want to go through the suffering, didn't want us to go through it, to see him lose his dignity. That was just the way he was. But believe me, he

loved me and he loved you." She was weeping by the time
she finished. "His friends on the police force, the ones who
knew, called it an accident to spare me the questions, and
because ... because of his pension and the insurance."

There it was, the truth, cold as the winter morning.

"It was something I should have told you years ago,"
she added. "I had no idea that you suspected anything. No
idea. Oh, Michael—"

"It's okay," Caruso replied softly. Thinking, *so that's
what it is, the trembling in my hands, the cramping in my feet. The
beginning of Lou Gehrig's disease.* He didn't know much about it,
just that there was no cure. He'd been handed a death
sentence.

"It's hardly ever passed on through the genes," Ethel
continued. "Hardly ever." She hesitated. "Michael, there's
nothing wrong with you," saying it as if it were a fact. Then
her tone changed. "Is there?"

"No, Mom," Caruso lied. "I've just been thinking
about Dad a lot lately, even dreaming about him. I felt like I
had to call, but there's nothing wrong with me, nothing at
all."

He wondered how long he had if it was true. Maybe it
was just coincidence, the trembling and cramping, but
something inside him said not.

"You promise me that," his mother continued.

He could hear the worry in her voice.

"I promise," Caruso replied.

He wanted the call to end, needing time to sit alone
and think, to take stock of his situation. He'd see a doctor, a
brain doctor, or a neurosurgeon, or whoever it was who dealt
with this kind of thing, this disease.

"Okay," Ethel answered softly, as if she was agreeing
to something she was unsure of.

Caruso forced a last grain of energy into his voice.

"Mom, I'm fine. I'll call you Sunday, just like always."

"Okay, Mikey, I'll look forward to that." She sounded
relieved.

That had been five days ago, before he'd had any idea of the
diagnostic workup required to detect Lou Gehrig's, or

amyotrophic lateral sclerosis, as the neurologist had termed it.
Blood and urine tests, electro diagnostic tests, X rays, a muscle
biopsy, and a spinal tap.

The tap had been the worst of it, the long hollow
needle, pushed in between the vertebrae of his lower back.
Even though he'd had a local anesthetic, the thought of what
they were doing scared him. And now the wait as the
neurologist attempted to rule out the other diseases that
mimicked Gehrig's. They were all bad, but Gehrig's was the
worst, and because of his symptoms, which had persisted,
and the fact that his father had been afflicted, the doctor was
not optimistic. Caruso had done a little research himself and
found that he'd probably have two to five years before it got
bad, then with the care required in the final stages, when the
paralysis of his muscles had spread to the trunk of his body,
canceling his ability to speak, chew, swallow, or breathe—at
that point he would need permanent ventilatory support—
then it would cost a couple of hundred grand a year to
maintain his brain. He wondered if his police insurance would
cover it. Then he thought of his Smith & Wesson. One bullet
through the roof of his mouth would be cheaper, a few
pennies worth of powder and lead, just like his dad.

So here he was on a Saturday afternoon, sitting in his
Corsica, feeling more alone than he had ever felt in his life,
contemplating suicide while staring across the road at the
front door of the Reed house.

He'd been parked there for half an hour, not long
enough to come up with a legitimate reason for knocking on
the door and announcing himself. He wanted to see John
Reed again. The baby had touched something inside him. In a
way, the infant had foretold his fate, and Michael Caruso
wasn't sure if that was the work of God or the devil.

Caruso remained sitting and staring at the house for
another ten minutes, telling himself to get out of the car, to
walk down the driveway and knock on the door, but unable
to justify those actions in a professional sense, in the sense
that he was a policeman.

Finally he drove away.

~ 9 ~

The placard read ARMSTRONG and the man holding it was of medium height and wiry, dressed in a rumpled blue suit. His head had been shaved so cleanly that the overhead lights of the arrival lounge reflected off its surface.

Casey's first impression was that she'd made a mistake by coming to New York. She didn't know this guy. Had never seen him before, but as she walked closer, his face lit with a smile.

"Ms. Emerson, nice to see you again."

She shook his hand and it all felt like some ridiculous joke.

"Jimmy?"

He took the duffel bag. "Surprised you recognized me," he said. "With the new hairdo and all. Shaved it on a bet." It had been his sister's wedding, and Freddy Wren had bet him that he wouldn't shave his head. He had and Wren hadn't paid up.

"Is this all you brought?" he continued, lifting Casey's duffel bag like a dumbbell.

"That's it," she confirmed.

"I'm not kidding, when you called I had no idea who you were. None at all. Thought it was a buddy of mine setting me up."

Reno carried on speaking as they walked down the carpeted corridor of the lounge and toward the exit doors. All the time Casey was struggling to click the pieces into place and getting nowhere.

She followed him through the revolving door and to the curb of the sidewalk. It was loud with the bustle of people and traffic.

"If you wait here, I'll bring the car. I got the limo this time." He noticed the confusion in her eyes and misinterpreted it. "Don't worry. It'll be the same price as the Town Car, just thought it would be more comfortable for you."

He often used one of the limos, if it was available, for clients that he liked.

She watched him weave through the tangle of cabs and airport buses, across the street and toward the parking lot. She was sorry he'd brought the limo. She had wanted everything to be the same as last time, if, in fact, there had been a last time. One thing that was reassuring was that he seemed to know her. Then she had a rush of pure paranoia. What if the whole thing was a setup, the business card, the driver. What if they were going to kill her. They? She waited for five minutes, checking her wristwatch, and twice wondering if she should turn and walk away, make a run for it, but to where? This thing, this feeling, was following her. There was no place to run. Then she saw it coming, long and white, with Jimmy Reno grinning at the wheel.

Reno pulled to the curb, jumped out, walked to her side, and opened the door so that she could climb in. It was only her second time in a limo. The first had been in Washington, with Nick; it had been a political fund-raiser, some kind of five-hundred-dollar-a-plate dinner for the president.

The door closed and the airport sounds faded.

Inside, the limousine was upholstered in a cream-colored leather and as she sank back into the seat she had another touch of nerves. She hadn't stopped to clean the town house. She'd just wanted to get out and move, away from the mess in her mind. What if Nick was an enemy? The thought upset her, but the evidence was building.

Reno closed his door and hit the button for the central locking system. The mechanism clicked as it engaged. The sound reminded her of the trigger of an Army Colt being cocked. The sense of finality.

"Everything okay, Ms.—" Reno almost said Emerson. "Ms. Armstrong?"

Casey smiled at him. He looked about fifty yards away, up there beyond the dividing window.

"I feel like a rock star," she replied.

"Funny you should say that, 'cause this is the same car I drive Billy Joel in," Reno confirmed. "By the way, there's whiskey back there, beer, diet coke, take anything you want. Traffic could be a little heavy for a while so why don't you relax?"

Relax? She hadn't done that in a while, or slept properly either. She untied her trainers and took them off, then stretched her legs, and closed her eyes, feeling the car move beneath her like some great ship at sea, out of the airport and into the slow moving stream of automobiles, their lights penetrating her lids like muted strobes. She dozed for a few minutes then pulled herself back up to the surface. She didn't trust it down there anymore, below the level of consciousness.

She looked up. Reno was on the phone. He was talking quietly, glancing in the rearview mirror as he nodded his head. Who was he talking to? Was it Nick Hughes on the other end of the line, or the Japanese man with the spearmint breath? The limo suddenly felt like a hearse, all quiet and locked vault-tight, carrying her to her own funeral.

She shifted seats, moving forward, getting closer to the partially opened divide.

Reno caught the flicker of movement in the mirror.

"Hold on a second," he said into the phone, turning his head. "I'm sorry, Ms. Armstrong, if I disturbed you. Really sorry." He was realizing that he was getting into a bad habit, using the phone while he was working. Laying bets on everything from the fights to the rise or fall in the Dow Jones.

"Who were you talking to?" she asked, trying to make her question sound casual but hearing the edge in her own voice.

Reno glanced quickly back at her.

"My bookie," he answered.

Casey was about to reply when Reno continued. "I was in a program once, up Island. Gamblers Anonymous, do you believe it? Like AA. It's serious, very serious. Thought I had it licked, besides it was a long way to drive every Tuesday. Maybe I should go again. I can't afford another slide .... " His voice drifted lazily through the space in the partition and his tone was soothing to her. By the time he had finished his story, they were free from the traffic and rolling along at a steady seventy miles an hour. Casey was nearly asleep again.

"So, if you don't mind me asking, how come you use two names?" Reno asked finally. He knew it was pushy but he was dying with curiosity.

Casey snapped back to attention.

"If I told you, I don't think you'd believe me," she stalled, looking up through the windshield. The exit sign read 61. "How much further have we got to go?"

Reno checked his odometer. "About another sixty-five miles if you still want to go all the way to Montauk."

"I want to go to the exact place as last time," Casey replied.

"The parking lot behind the lighthouse?" Reno asked. It was dark outside and getting cold.

"Same place as last time," Casey confirmed.

This was all very strange, so he pushed again.

"What line of work are you in, Ms. Armstrong?"

The question annoyed Casey but she could understand why the man was curious. Besides she needed him. He was the sole link to her recent past, and he had no idea of how important he was to her.

"I'm a government employee, and sometimes I travel under a different name," she answered.

Reno smiled. "Are you being straight with me?"

"Yes."

He turned and grabbed another look at his passenger.

"What, some kind of secret agent?"

Casey laughed. "Hardly that. I work mostly on contracts. Sort of a business consultant, but it's pretty high-level stuff. There's a lot of money involved. I just didn't quite finish my work here, in Montauk."

"Then maybe they'll be on time tonight to pick you up," Reno said. Let's hope so."

"What do you mean by that?" Casey asked, realizing that Reno knew more than she did about her recent past.

"I felt really bad leaving you alone in that parking lot," he replied. The place was deserted."

Casey felt like she was sinking again. Riding through the darkness en route to another dead end.

"And if they're not there, this time at least let me sit with you till they show up," Reno added. "I'm not going to charge you for sitting. It's too cold to hang around outside."

"Okay," Casey replied, trying desperately to remember.

They got off the expressway at exit 70 and took the link road to Route 27. After that, the highway turned into a single lane and it was a smooth ride into the Hamptons, and out to the tip of the Island.

■ ■ ■

The lighthouse looked desolate, casting its orange-yellow beam out to the black water beyond, and the parking lot was big, cold, and deserted.

"Where do you want me to stop?" Reno asked.

He had the same feeling as he'd had last time. Something didn't make sense. Where were the people who were supposed to meet his passenger? Except now it was later, darker, and colder and Ms. Armstrong, or Emerson, didn't seem quite so sure of herself.

"Same place as before," Casey replied, playing it down to the wire and hoping for a revelation.

Reno pulled into the same space that he'd used before, about fifty yards from the public restrooms and phones and stopped the car.

Casey sat there. She felt dazed; it was a mixture of feeling lost and feeling like a fool. She didn't know what to do next.

Reno shut off the engine, switched the interior lights on, and turned toward her.

For an instant she thought, *This is it. He's going to pull a gun and shoot me.*

"Now what, Ms. Armstrong?"

Reno was late for the third night running and he knew his wife was going to crucify him. There would probably be a blanket thrown on the sofa by the TV and a cold Hungry Man dinner sitting on the table by the phone. Then she wouldn't talk at breakfast.

He said, "I don't mean to be rude but it's 10:30 at night."

She looked at him. She was tired, too. And lost. More lost than ever. She nearly burst into tears, biting down hard on her lower lip. There was nothing else to do but continue the charade.

"I don't know where they are," she replied. She began thinking maybe it was a government contract, or a military target. "Is there anything military around here, some kind of base, anything?"

Reno thought a few seconds and shook his head. "Not anymore."

She was grasping. "What do you mean 'anymore'?"

"Used to be an air force base back up the road, maybe a mile or two. Camp Hero. But it's deserted now."

"Camp Hero," she repeated. She thought she'd heard the name before, or maybe she just wanted to have heard it. "Will you take me there?"

Fifteen hours at the wheel was enough for a day.

"There's nobody there," Reno answered. "Anyway, I can't drive this thing inside the gates. The roads are too rough. On top of that, it's illegal to trespass. Sorry, but no way."

"Tomorrow then, will you drive me tomorrow, at least to a place that I can walk in. I need to see Camp Hero."

Tomorrow was Jimmy Reno's day off and he'd been planning a trip to Jersey, to play the horses, giving the excuse to his wife that he was working overtime. He felt almost righteous when he answered.

"Okay, I can do that. I can drive you tomorrow, but right now, tonight, I'm not leaving you here."

She thought a moment. "I saw a place back up the road, on the other side of the village. I think it was a motel."

"Yeah, the Memory Motel. You ever hear that song by the Rolling Stones, it was written about that place, the memory—"

"Take me there," Casey said, cutting him off before the lyric began.

Reno pressed down on the accelerator, happy to be moving. Montauk Point gave him the jitters at night. It wasn't like the rest of the Island; it was out on the end of the earth, all cut off.

"One more thing, Jimmy," Casey said. "I'd like you to find out who paid for my ride last time."

"It'll probably be a credit card," he replied.

"Would you check the name for me? Please, it's important."

Earlier that same night, at nine o'clock, Thomas Reed, alone in his bedroom, tuned his radio to the public broadcast station. Desperate for answers, he wanted to hear Robert Barnes.

And there it was, with its usual jazz introduction, Miles Davis on the trumpet, trailing out with John Coltrane, blowing blues on a tenor sax, and into "Good evening, this is Father Robert Barnes, on PB101. Tonight I want to talk with you about God. Please, hear me out. Don't turn me off. It's not the kind of religious discussion you may be anticipating. Have you ever met him? Heard him in the notes of a trumpet, or a saxophone, or a piano. Seen him in the eyes of a child? Or are you, like I was, running so hard, intent on survival, that you'd miss him if he was staring you in the face. Do you believe in the second coming? What would it take to convince you? Or would you pass him off as a prank, a money spinner, another charlatan, another New Age guru ... Think again. What is God? A power? An energy? Something tangible? Yes. Yes. Yes. You see, it happened to me. It stopped me dead in my tracks. Changed the way I see, and understand.. I met the son of God.. I'm telling you about someone made like you and me, in the mold of man, fashioned in flesh and blood, someone so pure that looking into his eyes bathed my soul clean, baptized me in a new religion. It's a religion without

ego, without walls. No divides. Take my word for this. I saw
him. Touched him. Felt the warmth of his body. Felt the
warmth of his mind. This child. This Christ child. But did he
come from the loins of man, or was he created from the
higher energy of the universe? Or is that all the same thing?
Are we not, mankind that is, in the process of some great and
inevitable evolution? Are we not in the process of realizing
that we are beings of the spirit, not of the flesh ... Because
that is what I feel tonight. That is how I feel. My emotions
have been my guide, and in my feelings I trust, like I have
never trusted before. This child turned the key. He was pure
energy. He opened the door in my mind that held back the
truth, a truth that had been bogged down in dogma. He
turned water into wine. I could taste its sweetness as I held
him. He made me believe in my own spirit, in my own
redemption. Truly this must be the second coming. The
catalyst for the change. Water to wine. Flesh to spirit. The
realization that we are all part of the whole. So tonight I say,
tear down the walls. Tear down the walls that divide us. I
want to hear from you out there. I want to talk about this—"

Barnes was taking calls by the end of his introduction.

"Are you saying that Jesus has been reborn?" Snicker.
"Here in Colorado Springs?"

"No. That's not what I'm saying."

"What are you saying?"

"I'm saying that my revelation, the thing that has
become clear to me is that religion divides us. I'm saying that
I have been divided inside, and now, I'm whole. I'm saying
that old religion is dead."

"Are you on drugs, Father?"

"No, better than drugs, I'm on truth."

"Where is this incarnation of the light. This child?"
Hesitation.

The caller's voice became more insistent. "You can't
just tell us about some miracle and then hold back on us.
You're talking about the truth, so I'm asking for the truth."

"John ... " He paused as the name slipped from him.
"He is here, with us in Colorado Springs. I can't say more

now, but you will know when the time is right. The world will know—"

Thomas turned the radio off. *Fucking Barnes. What was he saying? What was he doing? Was he mad?* He felt like getting into his car, driving to the radio station and throttling the idiot. How dare he spout off at the mouth about something that was destroying his life. Bringing attention to them, his family, his child. His child? Goddamn it, John didn't feel like his child. He felt like an intruder in his home.

Thomas stood up from the bed; he still had his clothes on and his shoes clumped hard against the oak floor as he walked to the spiral staircase and took the steps two at a time to the top.

"Molly, open the door." He controlled his voice, keeping it gentle but there was nothing gentle about what he was feeling. This was it. He was going to get to the truth. No shouting, no hysterics, just the truth.

"Please, open the door. We need to talk. We really do."

The door opened and the sight sickened him—Molly standing there, backlit by the moon from the window, with the baby attached to her breast. That was the only way he could describe it. Attached. As if the "thing" was hanging on to her like a chimp or a tiny ape, legs wrapped tight to her abdomen, fingers gripping the lapels of her flannel nightgown like claws, head buried deep in her swollen bosom, sucking ravenously, making loud, slurping animal sounds.

He held his revulsion in check, averting his gaze from the baby, looking into Molly's face, at the shadows beneath her eyes.

"You've got to tell me what this is all about," he said. "It's destroying us, it's destroying me. I think I'm going crazy. I've got to know about John. I'm not mad anymore. I'm scared. Tell me, whose is he?"

She looked back at him and there was a look to her that Thomas had never seen before. All the fear had vanished from her face and in its absence there was a soft, yielding compassion. Her voice was hardly above a whisper.

"A long time ago, something happened to me," she said. "It was while I was in Mexico."

"Mexico?" He didn't know anything about Mexico. What had that to do with the baby anyway?

"Come in and sit down, please."

The slurping stopped as they sat on the side of the bed and the baby raised his head from her tit, still facing forward into her chest, but listening. Thomas could feel him listening.

"It happened nine years ago. We weren't living together then and I needed to get away, to think my life through—"

She paused and Thomas could feel his heart sinking. It was a tangible sensation, as if the part of him that pumped his blood, his life, was receding inside his chest, leaving an empty cavern.

"Are you telling me that nine years ago you started seeing someone else?"

She smiled and shook her head.

"No."

"Then what are you saying?" he asked.

"I had an experience ... "

She hesitated again. It was beginning to anger him, the hesitations, the cryptic answers.

He asked sharply, "What kind of experience?"

"I'm not sure. I don't remember all of it."

"Come on, Molly, I'm trying to understand this, really trying, so give me a break." His patience was wearing thin and he'd started to think about Robert Barnes again. The man was totally irresponsible.

"All right ... I'll tell you what I remember ... It started in Mexico City in July of 1991."

Thomas looked at her silently. What could a trip to Mexico City in 1991 possibly have to do with the thing she was holding in her arms?

She continued. "I went because I thought that traveling alone would be good for me. I'd never been particularly independent and I needed to believe I could do something on my own. I'd read in the newspapers that there was going to be a total eclipse of the sun and that Mexico City was one the best places on Earth to see it. It sounded exciting and I got an off-season package deal that included a room in the center of town, right near the old red-light district, the Zona Rosa ... I hated Mexico City when I got there, it was hot and humid, and loud, all day and all night, car horns and bumper-to-bumper traffic, and radios blaring, no wonder the room was cheap. I'd never seen more people crammed into one place in my life. The sidewalks were elbow-to-elbow, the air stunk from exhaust fumes, and riding in a taxicab made me feel like I was risking my life. God, they drive fast ... There were even more people there than usual, because they'd come from all over the world to see this eclipse. On the day it happened the whole city was shut down and there were crowds of us outside, very friendly, and quiet for once, like we all were sharing some kind of magic, everybody staring up at the sky, waiting. At first it was cloudy and I thought I was in for a letdown, then, right at the last minute, the sky seemed to open up. That's when it started, at first it was just the edge of the moon, cutting into this brilliant orange ball, taking a piece away from it. It was the only time in my life other than when Alex was born that I'd ever had a real sense of awe. It made me realize how small we are and how little control we have over nature. By the time the sun was halfway gone, the city that had been so hot actually started to feel chilly to me; it was like someone was digging a cold blackhole up there above our heads, and all the rising heat was being sucked into the hole. After that it started to get dark, really dark, and in a few more minutes it was pitch-black. You couldn't see the person standing next to you and I got very frightened. I was having these strange, irrational thoughts, like the sun was never going to come back out and that we were all going to die in that darkness. There were other people who must have felt it too, because a few of them began praying out loud, some in Spanish, some in English. Their prayers felt good to me, comforting, and I remember thinking that that was what prayer was about, humility, acknowledging that God is the boss, not us, and I started praying too, saying the Lord's Prayer to myself. It was while I was praying that the lights began. They appeared suddenly, three of them, like bright stars; they seemed to come out of nowhere then to skip across the black sky, like stones across water, back and forth, making all kinds of impossible turns, veering off at angles, getting big then small, changing color, as if they wanted us to see them. Some of the people started to take pictures or tape them with their camcorders, others got down on their knees and prayed louder. A man next to me started ranting on about flying saucers and another guy said something about the star of Bethlehem. We didn't know what we were looking at, but it had the feel of ... It's hard to put into words, but it had the feel of something that was deliberate, but not done by man."

"Why are you telling me this now?" Thomas asked. "I don't understand—"

"The longer I watched them, the bigger they seemed to get, and the closer. Until pretty soon I was concentrating so hard that I seemed to lose all sense of where I was. And then this incredible thing happened. It was like the three stars merged into one huge spinning wheel of light, coming down right on top of me. I had the sensation of being drawn up into it, then nothing—"

"What do you mean, nothing?" There was skepticism in his voice; there was also real concern.

"I don't know what happened to me after that. When I woke up it was past midnight and I was lying in a ditch beside the highway, about ten miles from the center of the city. At first I thought that I'd been hit over the head when it was dark, robbed and dumped, but I had all my belongings with me so I knew I hadn't been robbed. Then I got another feeling. It was terrible, like a deep sense of violation, and the big fear hit. Maybe I'd been raped, maybe that's what had happened. And there I was, stranded in the dark. How was I going to get back to the hotel, or to a doctor? I've never been so scared in my life, but it's funny what you do when the chips are down. I ended up hitching a ride in an old pickup truck that looked like it was held together with chewing gum and string. There was no room in the cab so I rode in the back, with two fat white pigs, but it felt like paradise because it was something that I understood. It was real. Not like whatever had happened to me."

"It's a terrible story, Molly, but what has it got to do with John?" Thomas asked softly.

As he said the baby's name he turned his head and looked in the direction of the window. The moonlight was streaming in and the infant's face looked suddenly changed, like a very old, wrinkled man.

"I believe that John was conceived inside that light," Molly replied.

"What?"

"For weeks afterward, I kept dreaming about being in some kind of doctor's office or operating room, with bright lights shining down on me.

There were people all around but I could only sense their presence and they were doing something to me, right up inside, and I was terrified and then a voice, a woman's voice, told me not to be frightened, that I had been chosen."

"Chosen by whom, and for what?"

"To have this child," Molly replied.

"Nine years later? Come on, Molly, don't talk like this."

"Time isn't the same inside the light."

Thomas started to pull away from her.

"I didn't believe it either," she continued. "Not till John came. I've never been unfaithful to you, whether together or apart. That's the truth, so how do you explain it? And how do you explain the light, and the missing time, and the dreams. I've denied it for years, never told a soul. It made me scared that I was crazy, but John is proof that I'm not. Something happened to me; it actually happened. He's here."

"Oh, Molly," Thomas said, reaching to touch her shoulder, keeping his hand far away from the hands of the thing that clung to her. "Let me get you someone to talk to, a proper doctor, someone who understands this kind of thing."

"I don't need a psychiatrist," she answered. "I need you to believe me."

He removed his hand, feeling the first stirring of anger.

"How can you expect me to ... " He searched for the word. "How can you expect me to accept this insanity."

Molly's eyes met his as the baby turned toward him. The infant's face no longer appeared old, the light from the moon was hitting him full on and the shadows were gone. There was another quality to him now, something disturbingly familiar.

"John knows you," Molly said. "You were also chosen."

"Please stop it," Thomas said.

He wanted to leave the room, to get far away from this feeling that everything that he believed in was about to cave in around him. He began to stand up when Molly spoke.

"I have seen you through John's eyes," she said. "You are drowning."

Thomas felt immediately drained and exhausted, his mind and his body, the same way he had on that day, in the water, the day that he'd lost Alex.

"John is here to save you."

"Stop it," he choked.

"Remember the boy on the shore?" Molly asked. "Look at John. Do you see him?"

Thomas stared down at the infant. The hair, the eyes. In the cascade of moonlight he had changed again; he could have been Alex, or he could have been the boy on the shore, the boy he had always thought that he had imagined. It seemed impossible. All of it. He had never told anyone, not even Molly, about the boy on the shore, the boy who had never been.

"He wants you to swim, to live again."

Thomas let out what sounded like a garbled, "I can't!"

Pushing himself up from the bed, he turned and ran from the room. What was this thing that had come to their home? This thing that dug into their lives and brought such confusion, such torment? This devil thing.

~ 10 ~

C asey had the subway car dream. Traveling through the world of illusion, through walls and rainbows, with the Japanese conductor pointing the way. Until the last building, the last wall. It was a beautiful structure, mostly steel and glass, a skyscraper, but as they approached it, in their silent vehicle, like a long snake of winding metal, Casey knew that there was something different about this one. It was an illusion but of a different substance than the ones that they had passed through previously on their journey. She could see her own reflection in its mirrored glass, looming larger as they sped forward, toward it. The Japanese man had turned and he was staring at her. He was wearing half-lensed reading glasses, poised on his nose. Studying her. The building was only yards away. They weren't going through this illusion. This illusion was solid. They were going to crash. Her vehicle, the one she always traveled in, was going to be obliterated. Her mind would be destroyed.

She woke up drenched in sweat, her heart hammering, too frightened to move.

It took her a second to remember where she was, to adjust to the white walls with the photos of fishermen holding up their catch, and a framed, yellowed map of Montauk, ending like a jagged finger pointing out, into the Atlantic. She was in the Memory Motel. The heavy smell of salt hung in the ocean air and the early light peeked through the curtains. She rolled over and looked at her travel clock. 7:23. Reno wasn't due till eight. She thought of phoning Nick, to let him know that she was okay, to apologize for leaving

like she did. Then, knowing that she couldn't, she felt a sense
of loss and loneliness. Somewhere, a trust had been broken,
and she was bereaved. Nick. She'd wanted to have children
with Nick Hughes. She'd never had a moment of doubt about
him. Her instincts had never wavered. She loved him. Then
she felt the twist inside her heart. She didn't know who Nick
Hughes was, not anymore.

She got up, stripped off her clothes, and walked to
the bathroom, reaching into the shower stall to turn on the
tap, gripping a little too hard with her injured hand. She
withdrew and stared down at the circular wound. Had it really
been an accident?

The car pulled in at ten minutes before eight, its tires grinding
against the sand and gravel in the lot. Reno had brought the limo
again.

He smiled when he saw her.

"You get some sleep?" he asked.

"Enough," she replied.

Reno stepped out and took her bag.

"I got some bagels and coffee," he said. He was
feeling good. Sandra had been awake watching TV, not mad
at all, and had cooked a red wine risotto, his favorite, plus
he'd seen the definite shadow of hair on his head in the
mirror.

Casey intercepted the duffel bag before he'd had a
chance to put it in the trunk, saying, "That can come in the
back with me." Her tone was a lot more resolute than it had
been last night, reminding Reno of the way she'd sounded the
first time he'd driven her. Not rude, but firm.

She slid across the leather seat closest to Reno's.

"How long to get to Camp Hero?"

"Five minutes," he replied, passing the bag from the
Bagel Shop to her through the partition.

Casey sipped the harsh, black coffee and took a bite
from a warm, doughy bagel that tasted of sesame seeds and
onions. "Remember what I said last night," Reno reminded
her, as they cleared the village and passed a horse ranch on
the left, en route to the Point. "I can't drive through the
entrance gates at Hero."

"Please, just get me there. Then wait outside," Casey answered.

Reno drove in silence for several more minutes then slowed in front of a small, tree-lined road.

"This place is easy to miss," he said, turning right, and continuing about two hundred yards down, before pulling to the side and stopping. "That's it, up ahead. And this is about as far as I'm comfortable going."

Casey looked through the windshield. Ahead there was a sentry box and two cement posts, but the gates were gone and the paved surface leading beyond the derelict, wooden house was cracked and broken. Nothing looked familiar to her.

"I'll walk from here," she said. "Are you going to be okay sitting? I mean you're not exactly inconspicuous. Does anybody patrol this place?"

"I doubt it, but if they do," Reno lifted a copy of *Homes and Land*, a Hamptons' property magazine, and said, "it's a quiet road and I'm taking a rest before my next pickup. There's no law against that."

Casey said, "Fine," reached into her duffel bag, and slipped the Myotron from the folded pile of yesterday's clothes. She slid it into the pocket of her leather jacket and got out of the car.

"How long are you going to be?" Reno asked from his window, wondering what she wanted in Camp Hero but professional enough not to ask.

"Depends on how big the place is inside, and what I find," she replied.

Then, thinking more carefully, she added, "If I'm not back in two hours I want you to get the police here and tell them I'm inside. Will you do that?"

Suddenly the tone of the morning became somber.

"Yes, I'll do that," Reno answered.

"Thank you," Casey said.

Reno watched as she started walking, past the gateposts, and beyond the signs that warned against trespassing. There was something about her that frightened him.

Casey continued until the macadam degenerated into clumps of stone and sand, ending in an old dirt road. Ahead she could see a cluster of small buildings and above, a huge radar reflector, casting a shadow like the wings of a giant bird.

Casey stopped in the shadow and closed her eyes, trying desperately to get some sense of the place. She could envision it all in her mind, the reflector above, the buildings in the foreground, but nothing came so she continued walking, over a rise and down a gentle decline. The buildings ahead looked vacant and deserted, but as she walked toward them the feelings began, dull at first; it was as if she was sensing a presence, like a barrier, in the air around her. Still she pushed on, finally arriving at the closest building.

"Looks like a cottage. A fisherman's cottage," she said out loud. Her voice was her assurance. She wasn't alone here. She didn't want to be alone.

The front and back door were closed and locked, but the window on the porch was open. She pushed it up and climbed through, onto the hard wood floor of the kitchen.

There was a bottle of Glenmorangie on the butcher's block surrounding the sink. The bottle was half empty. She picked it up and pulled the cork, sniffing the whiskey. It reminded her of her father. He was a good man. He had a wry sense of humor. He was a real gentleman. A gentleman?

She had the flashing image of a tall gray-haired man with a walking cane. The image came and went as her stomach suddenly soured and she replaced the bottle on the work top, then walked from the kitchen into the main room and sat down on the sofa. The springs sagged beneath her hips.

Something was coming back to her, trying to fight its way through the amnesia, but she needed more stimulus.

She exited the cottage through the window and walked down the steps from the porch and toward a building that looked like a large, metal cylinder. The door was held closed by an iron bar, which she removed and dropped to the ground. Entering, she walked into the first room, spotting the old mixing console below the wall-mounted speakers, and the three chairs lined up in front of it. *Looks like a monitoring room*, she thought as she continued to a second door that resembled a hatch, walked across the threshold, and down a step into the next room.

And here's the RV chamber.

There was a folding table directly in front of her and a leather club chair behind it, positioned sideways, as if someone had risen from it abruptly. She walked to the chair, and felt compelled to sit down in it. The smell of the old leather triggered a new rush of sensation; everything was beginning to feel familiar. Looking down at the arm she noticed the blood stains ingrained in the tanned hide. Was that her blood?

Look around. Pay attention to every detail, she told herself, noting the shallow scratches in the enamel surface of the metal table. They were letters and numerals. She stared at them, at first not recognizing her own handwriting, the N that looked like it had been laid on its side, the unusually wide W.

Her eyes remained fixed, 38N 104W. Coordinates? Of course, she recognized them as the identical set that Stevens had given her yesterday, before she'd cracked up. So this was it. This was the heart of the mystery. 38N l04W. Etched now in her mind as surely as it had been scraped into the metal.

She stood and walked from the chamber, quickly through the adjoining rooms and out into the light. Checking her wristwatch, surprised to see that she'd been gone forty-five minutes. She thought of Reno, waiting for her in the white stretch. It felt as though he had remained on the surface of some deep sea while she had gone below, holding her breath.

You ought to go now, she told herself. You've got something. Take it and go.

She turned to leave, then turned back to see the long, corrugated structure that adjoined the RV unit, sitting in the cold sun, beckoning. Fear was telling her that she'd seen enough, felt enough, retrieved enough, but the gnawing in her gut had returned also. The sensation of loss, the missing piece of herself that demanded reconnection.

She walked toward the building. The door was secured by a rusted padlock but the shackle was open. Reaching out, she removed it from the ring and pulled back the latch, leaving nothing but the thin plywood between her and what waited inside.

She experienced a wave of vertigo as she pulled the door open, then stood there as the stench of rotting flesh spilled outward from the mouth of the building, washing over her as she stared down a thin shaft of daylight.

Finally, she began to walk.

The passage was long and narrow and there were open rooms to either side, like small shallow cupboards with empty shelves. She shivered with nerves, continuing against every instinct to turn and run. Into a silence that was alive. Her lungs became bellows, sucking the putrid air through her opened mouth and her heart was slamming. One step, another, groping. The crash came like an explosion behind her as the front door slammed shut. She spun round but could see nothing but a haze of black. Freezing her with fear. Who was inside the building? Who had followed her?

A second gust blew the door back open and she could see that she was still alone. The knowledge revived her courage enough to continue walking, to the far end of the passage, to a second door. She tried to open it, but the wood, warped at the base, caused it to stick, forcing her to push harder. When there was still no give, she kicked at the jam and the door exploded inward, slamming against the wall of the room, leaving her facing a metal vat.

She stared. It reminded her of a baby's crib, with solid walls. She'd been in that crib, looking up at Nick Hughes, begging him to save her. She could recall his voice. "Case. Case. Can you hear me? Relax, have another drink."

The memory fired a sequence of disjointed images. Knives and forks flying through the air, a champagne glass tumbling in slow motion, a Japanese waiter? No, he was not a waiter. He was wearing a white apron, like a doctor's coat; it was a lab coat and he was holding a syringe. His face was close to hers and his breath smelled of spearmint. Stank of it.

She took another step forward, toward the vat. There were discarded bottles scattered on the floor, with rubber caps and the names of chemicals written on them and an intravenous unit, a stand and tubing, pushed against the far wall. Another step and she was looking down, into it, at the decomposing body of a rat. It was the size of a small house cat and its teeth were embedded in the rubber cap of an empty vial. Its hollowed eye stared up, into hers, breaking the great block of fear that she had stored, suffered, and withstood—turning it loose on her like a savage animal.

She ran from the horror, out of the room, sprinting the length of the corridor, through the door and into the light, continuing without looking back, running with her mind on fire and her heart pumping like it would burst. Away from the fear, away from the memories and the truths, running beneath the shadow of the metal bird. A hundred yards, two hundred, three. Don't die now. Keep going. Her stomach muscles were cramping. A hundred yards more and she had a stitch in her side. Don't stop. Until finally she could see the gateposts ahead.

Then she was on the other side of her nightmare, standing on the macadam, beyond the sentry box and warning signs, bent over, with her hands on her thighs, almost sick, heaving for oxygen, her throat rasping as, mercifully, all her rampaging thoughts ground to a halt. She was out and clear. The fear was behind her, beyond the borderline, behind the gates. She hadn't conquered it, but for the time being, she had outrun it. She straightened up, her hands on her hips, drawing deep breaths, regaining her control.

Casey Lee Armstrong. She was a little more whole than she had been before she'd gone down, below the surface of the murk. She was a bit more complete.

She turned and walked; she could see the white limo, sitting beneath a big scrub oak, facing in the opposite direction, ready to leave.

Reno saw her coming toward him and got out of the car.

"Are you all right, Ms. Armstrong?"

She didn't look all right. She was flushed and her nose was running. She looked like she'd been crying.

"What happened in there?"

She answered. "I'm okay, thanks. Nothing happened in there ... nothing at all."

Reno was curious but her tone of voice stopped him from probing.

He opened the passenger door and she got in, then he slid in, behind the wheel, and pressed down on the locking mechanism.

The bolts snapped shut and Casey felt more secure, as if another gate had closed behind her nightmare.

Finally Reno turned toward her and said, "The name of the company was Blueridge Travel."

"Pardon me?" Casey replied.

"Blueridge Travel paid for your ride from La Guardia to Montauk on the thirtieth," Reno answered.

Blueridge Travel. It took a few seconds for it to settle in. Casey knew the name. She had seen it on a credit card inside his wallet. Had even asked him about it. It was one of the front companies for the NSA. Untraceable. Nick booked his business trips through Blueridge Travel.

She huddled in the backseat, wishing she'd had a blanket to wrap around herself. Blueridge Travel. That did it. It was confirmed.

Her reply sounded vague and far away. "Thanks, Jimmy."

After that they were moving, driving slowly up the road and away from Camp Hero.

The quiet of the big car was soothing, and the further they traveled, along stretches of beach and ocean, the more perspective she gained. She had been lied to, used, drugged, brainwashed, or whatever they called it these days, but she was still alive and functioning. She could go back to Meade and pretend it had never happened. A few people, particularly Nick Hughes, would be very relieved. She could get on with her job and her life, and live the lie. At least she'd know that she wasn't insane, at least she'd have gained that much. She could go on, waking up beside a man she would never trust again, a stranger. But what would happen if she carried on, pushing to find the truth? Would they kill her? Maybe Nick would be her executioner. Maybe he'd do it while they were making love, while she was thinking of having his child. He'd squeeze a little too tight and break her spine. Nick Hughes?

Who are you? With her fury came the first tides of real resolve.

"Jimmy, I need a map of the United States, do you know where we can find one?"

Reno answered, "Sure. Book Hampton'll be open. We can get one there."

38N 104W. Casey was determined to go all the way.

~ 11 ~

It was two hours earlier in Colorado Springs than in New York, and Father Robert Barnes was sitting in the chair beside his bed. His Bible was beside him on his night table. He had opened it once, begun to read, then put it down. There was nothing for him in the old scriptures, nothing but the interpretations of men before him, inspired by truth and vision, yet weighted down with the fear, anger, and the uncertainties of the times in which they had lived. This was a new age and perhaps he, Robert Barnes, was a new prophet. The idea both humbled and exalted him.

He had been the recipient of a great gift. He had seen the child with his own eyes and felt the truth awakening inside him when their minds had touched. For Barnes it had been a religious resurrection and now he viewed it as something with the potential to bring people together, something alive and vital. It was what he had been thirsting for, starving for, not the symbolic wafers and wine; this was flesh and blood. He had spoken of the child in his radio broadcast and the switchboard at the station had lit up. People had been calling in from all over the region. He had touched a nerve. There was so much isolation out there, so much doubt and insecurity, so much fear. Attachment to symbols, wealth, and status, that was the disease of modern man. Tear down the walls. That was Robert Barnes's message. Resurrect the human spirit.

Last night's broadcast was only the beginning. Barnes could feel the energy building. It was inevitable. He had to talk, to tell the people what he had experienced. After his years in the wilderness, he was finally home. He would speak of the child again today, in his sermon. John Reed was his purpose, his calling. Old religion was stale. He'd seen something fresh and vibrant in the infant's eyes. He'd seen a pure, knowing soul, a soul that had reached into him, cleansing him of his doubt.

Robert Barnes was determined to spread the word.

Thomas Reed had not slept well. The phone had rung five times during the night, and each time the caller had hung up when Thomas had answered. He'd pressed *69 and been told, via a recorded message, that the number, or numbers, were unlisted.

He felt frightened by what Molly had said to him about Mexico City, worried for her sanity, and furious with Robert Barnes. The man had gone off half-cocked, acted irresponsibly, and now Thomas and his family had been made vulnerable. Attention had been called to them and he blamed the priest. Everything that he and Barnes had built up over the past year. the honesty and the trust, had been decimated by his betrayal.

Thomas had a gun; it was a matte black, pump-action shotgun with a handgrip. Not a sporting gun, but a cheap hundred-and-eighty-nine dollar short-barreled weapon that had been designed for self-protection. Euphemistically called, by the four-hundred pound bozo with the Hitler mustache who'd sold it to him, a streetsweeper; it was the kind of thing that would have better complemented a member of an L.A. street gang. He only fired it once, into the lake at the base of the mountains, just to make certain it worked. Then, and against Molly's protests, he'd kept it loaded, and stowed away in the closet of their bedroom. A "what if" kind of thing.

"What if somebody broke into our home and it was our last resort?"

All that had changed since the child had been born. He'd bowed to Molly's wishes, unloading the streetsweeper, wrapping it in a bath towel, and relocating it to the garage, stowed in a locked storage box.

Until last night, following the hang-ups.

He'd called the police, spoken to a sergeant on desk duty and, without going into detail, reported the telephone calls. The man had been patient and recorded Thomas's complaint but could offer nothing in the line of reassurance. It was not officially a police matter, not till a threat had been made. He'd suggested that Thomas report the calls to the telephone company.

After that Thomas had gone to the garage, retrieved the shotgun,and loaded it. Then lay awake most of the night, with it beside him on the bed.

By 9:20 A.M., he was dressed in his flannel slacks and blue woolen blazer. His shoes were cordovans, his shirt was white oxford cloth, and his tie was deep blue with small, white diamond-shaped patterns running through it. It was his Sunday best and he was going to church. He was leaving Molly and John in their locked fortress upstairs and going to the house of God, but he was not going to ask forgiveness; he was going to grab Robert Barnes by his clerical collar and ask him what the hell he'd meant by coming into his home and convincing his gullible and emotionally fragile wife, that this infant—this devil—was in some way divine. And then to go on public radio and broadcast his name? It was inexcusable.

As Thomas walked out the door of the house, he remembered he'd left the shotgun on the bed. That was a bad idea, with Molly half crazy anyway. He turned around, walked back inside, to the bedroom, picked up the gun from the blanket, and rewrapped it in the towel. Then he returned to his car, laying it down on the floor, in front of the passenger's seat. Thinking that for the time being he'd keep it with him. He still felt he needed protection. Fuck the police. Fuck the phone company. He'd heard the Barnes show. He'd picked up the telephone. He'd heard the clicks on the other end of the line and sat listening to the silence. He wasn't going nuts. This was real.

As he pulled out of the driveway and turned right, he noticed a black Jeep Grand Cherokee parked about a hundred yards down the road, behind him. It was the newer model, with the rounded grill; the way it was parked, half up on the grassy verge, engine off—there was no smoke coming from

the exhaust—made him suspicious. In such a small
neighborhood, Thomas knew most of his neighbors and
most of their automobiles and he could not recall seeing the
Jeep before. He looked again, this time through his rearview
mirror. He could make out the silhouette of a person in the
driver's seat.

Why's he sitting there, is he waiting/ or someone? The
question sparked a fresh rush of paranoia.

A ribbon of white smoke curled upward from the
Jeep's exhaust as it began to move slowly in his direction.
Thomas pulled to the shoulder of the road, to allow it go
around him, telling himself that he was being crazy, but as he
did, the Jeep followed, crawling behind, keeping its distance.

Thomas accelerated and the Jeep did the same.
Finally, he braked and stopped, thinking of the streetsweeper,
and keeping his eyes on the mirror. The license plate? It was
spattered in mud. GV something, or was it GU? To hell with
the plate. Look at the driver's face. It seemed to be
shadowed. Or maybe the driver was wearing a dark hat, or
hood? Closer. Still, he couldn't make out a face. Reaching
down, so nervous that he banged his forehead against the
tape deck, Thomas got a grip on the gun, bringing it up,
fumbling to get it out of the towel, pointing the wrapped
muzzle out the window before he noticed that the Jeep had
turned off the road.

Thomas could see the rear end of it, one taillight
broken, going down a small side street, less than fifty feet
behind him. Disappearing.

He sat there sweating, staring down at the gun, with
his hands trembling and his head cut. He'd panicked. What
was the matter with him? The answer came with a flood of
anger. It was this baby, this thing that had come into his life,
into all their lives. It was making him crazy. It was making
everyone crazy.

He remained still long enough to believe that the Jeep
was not going to reappear. Long enough for his heart to slow
down and for him to wipe the blood from the small cut
above his eye. Then he lay the gun back down on the floor,

concealing most of it beneath the passenger's seat, and drove off.

Casey drank three tiny airline bottles of Johnny Walker Black on the short connecting flight between Chicago and Colorado Springs. The whiskey had a settling effect on her nerves, enough to hold her steady while she walked from the arrival lounge and down the corridor, past the newsstands and coffee bars, and into the main area of the terminal building, following the signs for baggage claim and car rentals. She checked her watch—7:20 New York time—5:20 in Colorado. She'd picked up two hours. Somehow that made her feel better, like she'd gained on her imagined pursuers. Stolen something back.

She walked to the Hertz desk. If she was going to do anything she was going to need to be mobile. She hoped that the woman behind the counter didn't smell the whiskey on her breath as she produced her driver's license and credit card before answering the questions on the company's checklist.

She was given a map of the city, along with the keys and the directions to find the vehicle.

The Neon was in a numbered space.

Casey got in, locked the doors, and started the engine. She didn't feel safe, not like she had, locked inside the limo, with Jimmy Reno at the wheel. She felt like she was way out there, on the edge, and this time, she was all on her own.

She drove out of the airport and left onto Academy Boulevard, a wide road with lots of traffic lights, all the while assuring herself that whatever she was looking for was here, in Colorado Springs. She could feel it, the missing piece. The thing that had called out to her in the RV chamber in Montauk.

A few miles later she spotted a Holiday Inn. It was off the main road and to the right, so she followed the signs until she came to the rear entrance of the parking lot, found a space, parked, and shut off the Neon.

Inside, the motel was smaller than she had anticipated, and much less citified. It was more a simple, homey place, with an entrance lobby that doubled as a lounge, fitted with a soft-drinks machine, a coffee percolator, folding chairs, several tables, and a television set. The television was turned on and there were a handful of people seated in front of it, watching a news program.

Casey placed her bag down beside the desk and registered, managing to get the last of the "no smoking" rooms on the third floor, and had just handed over her credit card when she noticed that the woman handling her business seemed more intent on the television screen than on her booking.

Casey turned toward the set to see the caption BREAKING NEWS. The volume was too low for her to make out what was being said but she could see a man, with his jacket pulled up to disguise his face, being hustled by two uniformed police officers from the back of a brick building to a waiting car. A third man, Michael Caruso, dark and handsome, his features just on the rough edge of pretty, turned to face the camera, shouting something like "get the fuck out of here," while angrily pushing his palm against the lens, blacking out the screen. Casey was drawn to the energy, about to walk closer to the set to hear the story when one of the other hotel guests turned up the volume by operating the remote control.

A newscaster's voice crackled, sharp and authoritatively. "This is Tennyson Albright with Breaking News. Minutes ago, a local man became the only suspect in the murder of priest Robert Barnes."

The camera cut from the video footage of the departing car to the newscaster, seated behind his desk, complete with a cityscape backdrop. He was dressed in a dark, shiny suit, and bright yellow tie, and was coated in pancake makeup and hair spray, reading from a teleprompter. Nothing about his face appeared to move but his lips.

"The execution-style murder took place earlier today, just minutes following religious services at St. Ann's Episcopal Church, after a heated and public argument between the two men. A shotgun belonging to the suspect was found at the crime scene, and is alleged to be the murder weapon. More on this story as it breaks. And now, Ed Carbone with the regional weather forecasts."

There was a quiet murmuring from a couple of the residents as the channel was switched in favor of Arnold Schwarzenegger, painted in silver , playing Mr. Freeze in *Batman and Robin.*

Casey turned from the screen and walked back to the reception desk. She had a strong intuition about what she had just seen on the television. It was as if, somehow, she was connected to it. Then she had another thought. Maybe she was supposed to have seen it? Perhaps it had been staged. Maybe everything was being staged, or maybe it was all part of some preprogrammed memory, some mental manipulation that had been set in place at Montauk.

Come on. That's ridiculous. Impossible, she told herself. But it was a terrible feeling. She looked over again, toward the television. Mr. Freeze was aiming a huge, silver gun at Gotham City. Freezing everything with a tubular gush of iced energy, buildings and people, cars and a dog, its leg lifted against a fire hydrant, pissing.

Five people were glued to the screen, backs turned toward her. Five frozen minds. Could they feel her? Did anyone know where she was? A man turned and glanced over his shoulder, in her direction. His face looked ill-defined and sinister in the darkness, highlighted only by the flickering light from the television. Mr. Freeze laughed. God, she'd left an easy trail. Booked reservations in her own name, used a credit card. Shown her photo ID at three airports.

Turning back to the desk, she focused on the woman's face.

April Foster said, "Terrible thing to happen in a town like this. Just terrible," as she handed Casey back her card and the receipt for her to sign.

"Yes, it is," Casey answered, scrawling her name and meeting the sad blue eyes.

"I knew the man who was murdered," the flaxen-haired receptionist added.

"Robert Barnes?" The name fell from Casey's lips.

April Foster looked surprised. "You knew Father Barnes?"

Casey shook her head. "No, I just heard his name on the television."

"Oh … well, he was a good man. Me and my husband go to St. Ann's. Terrible thing. The church won't ever be the same. I mean, how awful. Murdered by somebody so close to him."

Casey's stomach tightened. The feelings were becoming more intense. Something was trying to break through. Resting her hands on the desk, she asked, "Do you know the name of the suspect?"

April Foster nodded.

"His name is Thomas Reed." She leaned closer, then whispered, "Alcoholic." As if that single word provided both motive and proof of guilt.

"That's a terrible thing," Casey said.

"Yes, but he'll pay for it," April Foster concluded, handing Casey an envelope with a coded room key inside. Then with a smile, she said, "Enjoy your stay in the Springs, Ms. Armstrong."

Thank you," Casey replied, picking up her bag and glancing quickly at the group in front of the television.

The man was still looking at her. He was thin with gray hair and she couldn't begin to estimate his age in the darkness. He smiled. Who was he? What was he doing? Were they a step ahead of her? How could they have known that she was coming here? Was Jimmy Reno working with them after all?

She turned and walked from the reception desk, out of the entrance lobby, and down a short corridor with service rooms to either side. There was a room marked GYMNASIUM to her right and a metal water fountain to her left, beside the brushed steel doors of the elevator. She pushed the arrow for UP and waited. Nervous. She turned to see the gray-haired man walking toward her, maybe thirty feet away. He was carrying a small, black briefcase and he was still smiling.

Up close, beneath the overhead lights, he looked younger than she had imagined. It was his gray hair that aged him. The bastard. She wasn't going to go easily. She unzipped her bag enough to get her hand inside and fumbled to find the Myotron, gripping it and slipping it out, concealing it by her side as he reached her. The bell chimed and the elevator door opened.

She walked into the metal box. He followed. It was tight enough inside that she could feel his body heat. Standing there, waiting for the door to close, felt like an eternity.

He asked, "Are you traveling on your own?"

"No," she replied without making eye contact.

There was a moment of edgy silence, as if he was assessing her response. He was taller than Casey by half a head, and skinny, with black sprouts of hair on the knuckles of the hand carrying the briefcase.

The elevator arrived at the second floor, stopped, and the door opened to a vacant corridor. He raised his free hand, hairy knuckles, ugly joints, and pressed again for the third floor.

He seemed to have a Southern accent. "Here on business?"

"No."

The elevator clinked to a halt and the door opened again.

He said, "I am." He indicated that she should step out ahead of him.She turned and faced him, then, as gracefully as she could, took a step backward, out of the elevator.

He smiled. "You wouldn't fancy a little nightcap? A drop of whiskey?"

She looked at him, confused.

His smile broadened. "I'm a rep for Seagrams. I sell it; I might as Well enjoy it. Just one drink?"

"Sorry," she said, turning away from him, seeing the signs for rooms 301-320.

She felt his eyes against her back as she walked to room 312, slipped the card in the lock, and waited for the click. When she looked again, he was gone. She waited another minute, then walked to the emergency steps, and back down to the lobby where April Foster exchanged her room for one in the smoking section on the second floor.

The carpet, the bedspread, the pillows, the upholstered furniture, everything stunk of stale tobacco.

Casey laid her duffel bag on the floor and walked to the bathroom. Even in the forgiving glow of the soft lights, she had a look that both disturbed and fascinated her. It was in her eyes, staring at her from the mirror, as if they belonged inside another face. She'd seen the look before, on street people, people who were hanging on by a thread, clutching to some last vestige of hope, yet knowing that there was none. It was developing, growing from the whites of her eyes, as if the seed had been planted in them, spreading with an exquisite circuitry of red veins, like a fine spider's web, taking root, poisoning the green, causing the softness to glaze over and lose its subtlety, then hardening to form confusion.

She thought of the man in the elevator, tall and gray, with a Southern accent. It was the accent. More than anything else about him, the accent had repulsed her, reminding her of someone, but she could not remember who.

She stared once more at the face in the mirror and said, "I'm not afraid of you." Then she switched off the lights, walked back into the room, and picked up the remote from the top of the television.

Pressing the power-on button, she stood watching the dark screen break up into flecks of white light as the picture crackled to life. Compelled, she searched the channels till she found the man with the canary yellow tie and plastic face, the man with the animated lips. She wanted to see the video footage again, needing to hear more, to learn more. The name? What had the woman at the desk said? *Reed. Thomas Reed.* That was it.

She walked to the bedside table and picked up a telephone book.

~ 12 ~

John Reed was inconsolable. Wrapped in a blanket, screaming, he clung to his mother while she stared down from the upper window of the house at the woman in the white trainers and black running suit. She was a tall, athletic-looking woman and it was taking the uniformed police officer all his strength to contain her as she fought. Finally, amidst the scuffling and the shouting, another officer ran to assist and together the two men pulled the woman backward, off her feet, and wrestled her to the ground, rolling her onto her stomach before they cuffed her hands behind her back. Still, she struggled against them, even as they hauled her up and began to march her along the driveway, toward the squad car.

Once, before they had reached the car, the woman turned and looked up at the window. Her eyes were wide and focused, but not on Molly; they were aimed at John. That's when he stopped crying, so abruptly that Molly was certain that he'd fainted, but when she looked at him she saw that his eyes were wide open, staring down, directly at the woman with the short dark hair. His body was rigid and he seemed to have stopped breathing.

"John!" she shouted, shaking him.

By then the woman was in the car and the baby had begun to wail again.

"No, Mama, no!" he bawled.

Molly didn't believe it. John had spoken, formed words and spoken. It was impossible. Maybe she had imagined it.

"No!" John screamed again, just as Thomas made it to the top of the stairs.

"What's going on up here?!" he demanded.

Molly answered, "John just said his first words."

Thomas stood in front of them with his hands down at his sides. He felt like breaking down and sobbing; he'd only been out of the police station three hours and his anxiety had settled to a dark depression. How much more insanity could he take?

"Yeah, well maybe you should feed him," he replied. "Maybe he's asking for food."

"He said a word, he said 'Mama,'" Molly continued, pulling the child closer to her body.

Thomas looked at them, Molly in her beige cotton nightgown—she seemed to wear it continually now—holding the baby tight to her bosom. She was standing there so protectively while he, Thomas Reed, was a suspect for murder, spending his hours hiding behind locked doors while stalkers were hauled off his property. Had his whole world gone crazy? Didn't Molly care? Didn't Molly care about anything but the thing in her arms?

People had been showing up at the Reed house all afternoon. It was amazing to Caruso how they'd figured it out. Then again, there had been seven witnesses to the verbal exchange between Barnes and Reed at the front of the church, and seven mouths could lead to a town full of gossip and speculation. Most were curiosity seekers, drawn to the morbidity of the circumstances. A few were religious freaks, and then there was the satanist, who had thrown a severed and bleeding pig's head at the Reed's front door with the words "Anti-Christ" carved into its skull.

Following that episode, Caruso had doubled up on the police guard and tried to convince the Reeds to allow him to take them into protective custody. Nothing doing. Molly Reed was staying at home, with her son, while her husband, after his release, wanted to be left alone.

The murder weapon, which Thomas Reed had admitted owning, was with forensics and, to everybody but Michael Caruso, it was an open-and-shut case, just a matter of time till they made the arrest. Open and shut. The same way that Murray Rose's "death by natural causes" had been open and shut.

Caruso wasn't so sure. There were things that didn't ring true. Motive for one. Witnesses had testified that although Reed had shouted at Barnes, he had never threatened him in any way, given no indication that he was premeditating his murder. Instead, according to the sources, it had seemed an argument between friends, at the end of which the two men had shaken hands.

To Michael Caruso, Thomas Reed did not have the feel of a cold-blooded killer. He seemed a warm, emotional, if somewhat fragile man, which was in itself a direct contradiction to the method of the priest's execution: Robert Barnes had been tied to a chair in the front room of the rectory, and a shotgun had been forced inside his mouth, so hard that it had shattered his front and bottom teeth, before the trigger was pulled.

There were no clear fingerprints at the crime scene, just a few smudges on the handgrip of the abandoned weapon, and a few more on the priest's clothes, which had already been sent to the lab in Denver, along with a set of prints that Thomas Reed had provided voluntarily. Now Caruso would have to wait for Denver's more sophisticated equipment to decipher them, a process that could take days, even weeks, depending on their caseload. Caruso was left with a pile of circumstantial evidence and no confession.

The Barnes case was Caruso's worst nightmare, loud and glaring, since the television footage of Reed leaving the police station. The department had injuncted the tape and put a restraining order on the local station, but the damage had been done. The Barnes case had become public knowledge. It was the first time in their history that there had been a media leak in a murder investigation, and the weight had fallen right on top of Michael Caruso.

The woman, sitting beside him in the Corsica, didn't look like a freak. She was clean and good-looking, too calm and articulate to be just another whacko. Casey Lee Armstrong. What was her story? An officer in the United States Army? Her credentials looked real enough. So what was she doing in Colorado Springs, picked up by a patrolman while trespassing on Thomas Reed's property? Whatever it was, she wasn't talking, and Caruso knew that once back at the station, he'd have to slap her wrist and let her go with a warning. Thomas Reed wasn't going to come downtown again, not to fill out a complaint form, and press charges. He had other things on his mind.

Caruso glanced quickly at her. What had she been trying to do? Get a glimpse, a feel, a thrill? There was nothing like human tragedy to draw a crowd, but that didn't make sense to him. No, she didn't have the feel of a curiosity seeker. Caruso felt a purposefulness to her, a sense of mission. She was stoic, answering only when spoken to. Captain Casey Lee Armstrong? He'd know more about her after they'd run a check on her military ID.

He pulled a pack of Camels from his pocket, and ignored the tremor in his hand as he banged the pack against the steering wheel, forcing a cigarette up, and clenched it between his teeth. He was still trying to quit. That was a joke. A dead man trying to quit smoking? *Stop thinking like that,* he told himself. The doctor hadn't come back to him yet with the test results. Nothing was final.

He didn't light up, just chewed on the filter, sucking the flavor from the tobacco while glancing to his side, at his passenger. She was staring straight ahead, out the window, her face a crisscross of the oncoming lights from the highway. She was good-looking, but there was something else about her, an energy, a craziness that made Caruso uneasy. It was as if she was combustible, about to explode.

Casey Armstrong was trying to hold the reins on her thoughts, but they were galloping. She knew she was in trouble, but there had been no other way to the truth, and now more than ever she needed sanctuary, an ally, but how much could she trust the man sitting beside her? She'd recognized him from the television as soon as he'd stepped from his car, sensing an honesty, even a rapport with him, but he was a policeman and he'd already phoned her name and army identification number into his office. She'd been caught.

Caruso turned again from the road and stole another glance. He was attracted to her, but not in a way that he'd ever been attracted to a woman before. This one was different. That's the only way he could put it. She had a presence, a weight.

Their eyes met and he felt suddenly awkward, as if he had to say something, to explain himself. He turned back to the highway and spoke to her reflection against the glass.

"So, do you want to tell me what brings you all the way from an army base in Ft. Meade, Maryland, to Colorado Springs, and why you picked that particular house to visit?"

"If I told you, I doubt that you'd believe me," Casey answered, testing him.

"Yeah, but I might," he said. His tone was matter-of-fact but sincere, and his voice and demeanor reminded Casey a little of Nick Hughes, at least the Nick Hughes she'd thought she'd known. A straight Nick Hughes.

She decided then that she was going to risk it.

"I'm a professional psychic," she said, half expecting him to react with a laugh, or a groan. She waited, but he remained silent so she continued.

"And there's someone or something inside that house that's drawing me to it. Something important is happening there."

Her words caught Caruso cold. He thought immediately of John Reed, and of his experience with the baby. Yes, something was happening. Still, he held back.

Probing, he said, "I thought you were in the military. That's what it says on your ID."

"I am," Casey answered. "I work for the army's Remote Viewing Program. I'm an RV, a remote viewer. That's the name they give to psychics, to people who do what I do."

The term remote viewer rang familiar. Maybe he'd seen a book in the drugstore, in the paperback section, something with those words in the title, or a program on TV? Or maybe this lady was pulling his chain. His voice bore a shade of skepticism.

"Are you telling me that you're on some kind of military assignment?"

"I'm telling you that I've seen that house before; I've even drawn a picture of it. I remember the shape, the angles."

"How could you have seen it?" Caruso asked.

"In my mind," she replied.

"And how, exactly, does that happen?"

"I was given a set of geographical coordinates, latitudinal and longitudinal, and they triggered a vision of that house," Casey answered.

Two weeks ago, Caruso would have discounted her as a crank. Now he wasn't discounting anything.

"And what's so important about it?" he asked.

"That's what I came to find out," Casey answered.

Murray Rose. A medical breakthrough. The unidentified man in Molly Reed's room. Robert Barnes, and now some psychic from the army. Caruso's mind was churning.

Interpreting his silence for disbelief, Casey became defensive.

"Listen, what I've told you is real," she said. "I'll give you my clearance code with the RV Program. You can reference it. I'm not lying about any of this."

She caught a glimpse of his eyes as he turned toward her. They were hard and centered, drilling into hers.

"What about the baby?" he asked.

She flashed on the infant's face in the window, the eyes that had locked onto hers and another piece of the jigsaw snapped into place.

"A baby?" she repeated, feeling something stir inside her, as if a dredge was at work, clearing clumps of rubble from the slate of her subconscious.

"Yes," Caruso answered. "John Reed."

"When was he born?" She asked.

"New Year's Day."

Casey sat back against the seat. That would have been two days after her tasking at Montauk. It made sense. The signal was getting stronger.

"So that's who they're after," she said.

"What did you say?"

"John Reed," Casey answered. "Take me back there." Her voice had an urgency. "Take me back to that house. Let me see the child. Let me get close to him. I think I can help you. Please."

Caruso slowed the car. He'd heard of psychics being employed in murder hunts, but he had always been skeptical. Now, desperate for answers, he was tempted. But what if she was another crazy? He'd screwed up enough already. He was a mile from the station on South Nevada. There was a press leak to be contained and a furious boss to contend with.

"I can't do it," he said, accelerating. *Christ, a psychic, if the media got a hold of that, on top of everything else ...*

Casey had sensed vulnerability in his hesitation.

"I've got to get back to that house," she insisted. "It's important for me, and it's important for you."

He slowed, thinking of stopping the car, letting her walk away. She'd get back on her own. Then, the uniforms would pick her up for a second time. No, it wouldn't work.

"I'd have to clear that with Thomas and Molly Reed," he answered. "And I'm not sure that's possible."

"It is important that I see the child," she insisted.

Caruso didn't answer and a few minutes later they were entering the parking lot of the station and driving into a space with his name on it.

Part of him believed Casey's story, the other part, the logical, rational side of him, wanted to see something more on Captain Casey Lee Armstrong, something in black and white, pictures and identification, verification. If that checked out he'd do what he could about getting an audience with the Reed family.

"We're going inside the station," he said, opening her door.

Casey walked ahead, through the entrance to the four-story building. The door closed behind them. She was scared now, sensing a loss of control, within herself, and within the policeman. Things had changed. She had become property of the system.

Caruso led her to the main desk and recorded her name and time of entrance with the public-service representative, then to an elevator and up to the second floor, past the curious eyes of several men in plain clothes, down a corridor, and to another door, with black stenciled letters on it. The letters read HOMICIDE.

Inside, the room was stark, with white wails, no pictures, three computers, a printer, a metal filing cabinet, and the faint smell of human sweat in the air, not clean and flowing, but stale and stagnant, carried on the dry heat from the radiators. There were seven desks, three of them occupied by men in plain clothes, two were on the phone and one was shuffling papers. Each looked up as Caruso guided her by and into an interior office that was available for privacy.

He closed the door behind them.

Casey stood by the desk as he picked up the telephone and pressed the extension for the records department.

"This is Detective Caruso in Homicide. I'm expecting something on a Casey Lee Armstrong. Has it come in yet?"

The man on the other end of the line sounded nervous.

"Yes sir, it has, but you'll have to talk to Captain Lochart about it."

Caruso gripped the phone tighter, as if it had become suddenly hostile. He spoke again, his voice harder.

"Officer, I phoned in a request for information. Give it to me, will you please?"

"That information is with Captain Lochart, sir. He's dealing with it."

"Put me on to him," Caruso demanded.

"He's not here."

Caruso placed the phone back on the desk and looked at Casey. He had a bad feeling.

"Maybe you'd like to sit down."

She felt as if they were wasting time. She intended to get back to the Reed's house. It was more than desire; it was a need.

"How long do I have to stay here?" she asked.

Caruso replied, "Till I check you out. Make sure you are who you say you are. I'm waiting for—"

The door opened.

Yale Lochart was a short man, wearing an expensive-looking leather jacket and brown woolen trousers, narrow at the cuff, so that they bunched over the instep of his lizardskin cowboy boots. Up close, he looked older than his forty-four years, and battle-weary, with bags that looked like bruises under his sunken eyes and brown hair parted to the side and matted, like he'd missed his morning shower. His body was more wide than fat and his voice was gruff.

"Hello, Mike. What's she doing in here?"

Caruso, like everyone else in the department, was wary of the captain. He was a tough, by-the-book boss, but there was something else that made him distinct. After six months on the street, Lochart had grabbed a job in community relations and come up the ranks from there; he didn't cut any extra slack for street cops. There had been no bonding and there were no favors.

Caruso answered warily. "One of the patrol officers picked her up outside the Reed house. I'm waiting for an ID check on her."

Lochart's mouth tightened to a slit.

"I don't think so," he said.

Caruso was confused.

"What do you mean?"

Lochart continued as if Casey was not present.

"Her name is Armstrong, and she's a military officer. She's not part of your investigation. "

Caruso held his line.

"Yale, I don't understand."

"You don't need to," Lochart snapped.

Caruso felt like he'd been smacked in the face; he studied the captain's small, beady eyes, until he was certain he wasn't going to get anything from them.

"You get back to your case, Detective," Lochart continued. "I'll take care of the lady. Are we clear?"

Without waiting for an answer, Lochart turned to Casey.

"Now, Dr. Armstrong, if you'll come with me, maybe we can resolve this."

Dr. Armstrong. Doctor? Where did he get that? Casey wondered as the warning flags went up.

"I want police protection," she said suddenly, looking to Caruso. " I believe my life is in danger."

"I'm sorry, we can't help you there," Lochart answered, gripping the back of her arm. "Let's go."

Caruso watched, confused, as Lochart led Casey from the room. This thing, whatever this thing was, was staring him right in the face, defying him to put it together—providing him with half clues and possibilities, then snatching them away. He stepped out of the office and walked across the room to Neil Adams.

"Neil, can I see you a second?"

Adams stood up from his desk and followed Caruso to the corner, out of earshot from the other detectives.

"What's going on with Lochart?" Caruso asked.

Adams replied, "I don't know."

"Come on, man, he's got a rocket up his ass. What's it about?"

Adams eyed Caruso.

"Because he wants to close this fucking priest case," he answered. "He's getting killed by everybody on top of him because of that video footage on the television. If enough people see it and hear about the verbals in front of the church, we won't be able to get Reed an unbiased—"

Caruso stopped him there, saying, "We haven't even arrested Reed. What are you trying him for?"

Adams face hardened. "Murder. It's his weapon. He had motive. Come on, Mike, why prolong the dance?"

Caruso was frustrated. "Because maybe he didn't do it."

"Then who did?"

Caruso was lost for words. He thought of Casey Armstrong. Dr. Armstrong? What the hell was going on? Then he got angry.

"What the fuck kind of game is this?"

"Don't know, Mike," Adams answered with an edge. "I've been working on the Barnes case. Hoping to put it to bed before it gets any uglier. I don't know what else is happening. Who was that woman, anyway?"

Caruso looked at the door that Lochart had closed on his way out of Homicide.

"I don't know," he replied. He was thinking about Murray Rose, again, and the Reed baby. It was starting to feel like some kind of conspiracy. What did Lochart know? He felt like trailing after him, collaring him for answers, but he knew that would be a terminal move.

He turned back to Adams.

"I don't think Thomas Reed is guilty. That's what my gut tells me. And before I do anything, before I arrest anybody, I want to hear from Denver about the smudged prints, and, fuck it—" he looked at the closed door again, "I want to know who Casey Armstrong is."

It was then that the telephone on his desk rang. It was his private line, but he was so wrapped up with what had just happened that he barely gave it a second thought as he walked across the room and grabbed it.

"Yes?" His tone was clipped.

A friendly female voice replied, "Is this Mr. Michael Caruso?"

"It is," he answered, standing with his back to the room.

"I have Dr. Rogers for you," the cheerful voice said.

That's when he got the sick feeling in his stomach. He'd known this call was coming, but still it had taken him off-guard.

The seconds passed slowly and his thoughts of Casey Armstrong receded with them, until finally a dry male voice filled the line.

"Mr. Caruso?"

"Yes."

He felt like every man in the office was watching and waiting when in fact no one with the exception of Neil Adams was paying any attention to him.

"Hello, this is Dr. Rogers."

"Hello, Doctor," he answered.

"I've got the results from your tests," Rogers continued. "Do you think you could stop in here and see me?"

"Any problem?" Caruso asked, trying to pour a casual tone down the line.

"I really do want you to come and talk to me," Rogers insisted.

It was bad. Caruso could sense it. It would have been easy for Rogers to have said "nothing to worry about," but he hadn't.

"When?"

"Today, if that's convenient with you," Rogers answered. "I've got an opening at noon and another at 4:30—"

"I'll come at noon," Caruso answered.

He didn't want to put it off. He wanted to know, one way or the other, he needed to. He looked down at his wristwatch. It was 11:35 and he was only about fifteen minutes from the doctor's office.

"Fine, I'll see you then," Rogers said in the same pleasantly flat voice.

Caruso listened to the dead line another few seconds while he composed himself. Finally, he placed the phone down and turned toward the door of the room.

"You all right, Mike?" Adams asked.

"Fine, why shouldn't I be?"

"Just asking," Adams replied.

"Sorry, Neil, it's been a lousy morning," Caruso said, patting Adams on the side of his arm as he walked past him and out the door. *I'm fine. Gonna be fine. Fine. Fine*, he told himself with every step.

~ 13 ~

The truth, in the opinion of Dr. Norman Rogers, who sat behind his glass-topped desk, wearing a blue cashmere jacket on top of a white cotton shirt and Liberty-print tie, was that Michael James Caruso was not going to be fine. He appeared to be in the first phases of ALS, before the weakening and paralysis spread throughout the muscles of his body. It was not news that the forty-nine-year-old neurologist dispensed lightly, but in his silent assessment, the one he withheld from Caruso, he believed that the man in front of him would be a mentally alert quadriplegic within five years and probably dead within seven.

Caruso sat cold and expressionless in front of Rogers, in much the same way that he had seen convicted felons sit in front of the judge, at sentencing. There seemed to be something distant and detached about what he was hearing. The guy wasn't talking about him. Not Michael Caruso, ex-special Forces, decorated combat veteran, decorated cop, dead-eye with a thirty-eight, oh please Lord, not him, not that Michael Caruso.

His only question was, "What do I do now?"

Rogers tightened his small, tight mouth and cocked his head as if he was considering a request for leniency.

"You get a second opinion," he said. "I have a colleague in Denver who deals specifically with ALS and I'd like you to see her. Her name is Adrian Mitchell and I can set up an appointment for you."

"Sure, thanks," Caruso replied.

His head had begun to spin. He was going to die. Not
quickly or unexpectedly, and not of old age. He was never
going to find love, never have children. It was over. He was
going to die miserably, lying frozen in a bed somewhere, with
every sensory function intact, while piece by piece his body
packed up.

"Listen, I'm sorry to be so pessimistic," Rogers said
sincerely.

"It's all right, it's not your fault," Caruso answered
quickly before getting up and walking from the office.

Then he was in his car driving west along the
highway. He couldn't remember the spaces in between, the
little details, like starting the car or where he was going. He
was just going, with the hum of the tires and heavy gray
clouds up ahead.

He wanted to be alone, to sit and think things
through.

He thought of his father, and wondered how his old
man had felt when he'd first learned that he was a goner,
because it was the most solitary, most terrible feeling that
Michael Caruso had ever known, and it was his alone; no one
could ever share it.

Then he realized another thing. His father had had a
lot of courage. He'd turned a gun on himself and pulled the
trigger, not out of despair or driven by fear, but out of
consideration for his family. He'd picked his moment, said his
good-byes, and taken care of business, clean as a whistle.
Caruso wondered if, deep down, he had that kind of
backbone. If, at the moment of truth, he would be able to
pull the trigger.

He stayed on Highway 24, driving through Cascade,
stopping at the gate to pay his toll before entering the
National Forest, then following the road up the mountain,
past Crystal Reservoir, until the pavement ended and the
gravel ground loud beneath his tires.

Up through the clouds, beyond the trees and granite
fields and alpine tundra, up fourteen thousand feet, to the top
of the world. There, he parked in the lot of the Summit
House, and stepped from the car. It was cold, probably
somewhere in the twenties, with a wind chill that must have

taken it way down below zero. He pulled the collar of his shearling coat tight to his neck as he walked away from the Corsica.

On a clear day, from the peak, it was possible to see as far as Kansas to the east, and New Mexico to the south, and miles of snowcapped mountains to the west. To the north was Denver. But today, as he walked to the low metal guardrail on the edge of the mountain and climbed over, his shoes skidding down the short, steep embankment to a another, rockier ledge, all he could see was the clouds, wrapped so tight around him that they formed a shroud.

He unzipped his coat enough to slide his hand in and get a hold of the Smith & Wesson. Everything about him was trembling as he brought the gun clear of his coat; he wasn't sure if it was the fear, the disease in his body, or the wind that cut him like the frozen blade of a knife. Was he crying, or were his eyes watering from the battering that he was taking? If he leaned forward, he could see down, through a wash of tears, along the jagged rock face to a sheer drop. If he fell forward he would disappear into that deep unknown. His hand was shaking as he lifted the barrel of the thirty-eight and pressed it against the roof of his mouth. The steel tip was still warm from the heat of his body.

Do it fast, squeeze. Don't think. Squeeze.

He thought of his mother, crying big watery tears, the way she had all those years ago. Then he could see other eyes looking into him. John Reed's eyes. The baby was with him now, way out there on the edge of the universe. Trying to tell him something. Trying to get through. *Don't think. Squeeze.*

The holding cell measured six feet by eight feet, with gray walls, a low ceiling with a light bulb in a cage, a heavy, reinforced steel door with a single, sliding observation slot, and a metal cot, covered by a thin mattress. There was no toilet or sink inside the room. It was obviously not a place for long-term internment.

That thought, after three hours, gave Casey Armstrong at least a ray of hope. She'd run the full gamut of emotions in the time she'd been there, from extreme fear to a strange sense of relief that she was being restrained. She didn't have to go any further on her own.

She sat on the cot with her back against the cold, uneven plaster. She was exhausted but too terrified to shut her eyes, believing that if she shut her eyes, it was all going to end, without resolution, in a series of disjointed fragments and associations.

She didn't want it to end like that, so she sat, in the sickly yellow light and tried to remember the face of the child, staring down at her from the window.

The child was the key. John Reed.

Another half hour passed. She checked her watch. They hadn't taken her belongings, not all of them, anyway, just the wallet containing her ID, and the Myotron. There seemed to be a lot of curiosity about that. Legal or illegal in Colorado? Had she committed a felony? They'd never seen one before.

How long before something happened? How long before the footsteps that she occasionally heard from the hallway would stop outside her door? And then what? She wasn't under arrest. The short man, the man in charge, Lochart, had told her that much, several times. He was strange, the way he'd acted, like she was something to be kept at a distance. He'd never even looked her in the eyes.

Then she heard it. Recognized it immediately, even before she could decipher a single word. In reaction, her feelings balled into a fist inside the pit of her belly. That voice was the last thing she wanted to hear.

The footsteps stopped in the corridor, outside the lockup. Then the first door opened, and she could hear his words clearly.

"We're very grateful. It could have been incredibly embarrassing for the army. Taxpayers don't even know the RV Program still exists, let alone that some of its employees are, well," the voice hesitated, "less than stable."

"I understand," Lochart replied. "And I respect the fact that you've been so open with me."

"This is strictly on a need-to-know basis," the hushed voice continued. "I know you'll respect that."

He really was a ham, laying it on, like something out of a Bond movie, and Lochart, with his wide ass and cowboy boots, was buying it big time.

The observation slot slid open and she saw Nick Hughes, looking in at her, as if she was some sort of laboratory animal, a rat or a guinea pig.

"Case, everything's okay now."

The fucking gall of the bastard.

"I came as soon as I got word," he continued. "We've got a private jet to take us back home. Don't worry about a thing. It's all under control."

She stared into his eyes. They looked topaz, like crystals, throwing off colors, yellows and browns. They had betrayed her. Taken everything she'd had. Stolen it all. She hated those eyes. Hated him. More than she had ever hated anything or anyone in her life, she hated Nick Hughes. She wanted to scream, to cry, to break through the door that separated them and to bite him, to sink her teeth into his flesh and tear at his body like a rabid animal. To maim him. The way he had maimed her.

"It's going to be all right now, relax," he continued as Lochart turned the key and pushed the door open, causing the first splinter of light from the corridor to fall across the cement floor.

She sat on the cot, with her back against the wall, and her legs folded up, the front of her thighs pressed against her chest, arms wrapped round her shins, like a scared little girl. A time bomb, ticking.

Finally, both men were inside the cell, and all three of them crammed into the stinking, little stone box.

Nick was dressed in loose corduroy pants and black suede shoes, wearing a cashmere overcoat over a dark sweater. The coat had cost her seventeen hundred bucks. She remembered buying it at Bloomingdale's in New York City, three months ago, because he'd said he'd always wanted a cashmere overcoat.

"Thanks," Nick Hughes said to Lochart. "Now I'd like to talk to her on my own for a few minutes, if you wouldn't mind."

"Sure," the policeman answered, turning toward the door.

"Case?" That smooth voice, those big, sure hands, reaching for her.

What happened next, Casey could never really be sure of. It was all so fast, and so crazy, like an explosion, her whole body and mind letting go at once, everything rushing out of her. She could hear herself scream, but it was more a war cry than an actual scream, and she thought she could feel the collar of his coat give beneath her fingers as she ripped down against the soft wool. She wanted his throat between her teeth, wanted to destroy him. She felt him struggle beneath her weight and lose his balance, toppling over. Nick Hughes. She was beating the shit out of him, holding a clump of his hair in her hand while he shouted for help. She wanted to laugh at the bastard, but she couldn't laugh because she was growling. Her insides had exploded; her animal had broken loose from its cage. She was rampaging.

"We've got restraints!"

Then she realized she was on her back, and the bastard was straddling her, his hands pushing down, hard against her biceps. She bucked but he moved with her, heavy, but loose like a blanket, covering her body. She bucked harder.

"Help keep her steady," Hughes ordered. "Take her arms. Squeeze tight. I need a vein. That's it," leaving him free to uncap the preloaded syringe.

He pushed the needle into the underside of her forearm.

"You fucking bastard," she hissed, twisting in one last attempt to get free.

She saw a cowboy boot, planted on the floor beside her, a few inches from her face. She extended her neck and bit in, toward the shank, and got a mouthful of wool, thick, and musty in texture, then the acrid taste of leather. She bit harder, intent on getting to the man's flesh. The boot tried to pull backward, but she clenched her jaw and clung on, struggling to wrench her arms from his hands.

"Christ, Jesus Christ! I can't hold her forever! Do something, will ya'?!" Lochart shouted.

There was a man bending over her and a fist raised above her face.

"Hold on, Mister! That's not necessary." It was Hughes's voice again.

At first, she felt dizziness, like she'd been hit with a blunt truncheon, soft and rubbery, but packing a wallop. After that everything was out of focus, and there were a lot of people looking down at her, lots of eyes and faces, with a light above, a small, tight beam, shining directly into one eye, then the other.

"Back off." She heard Hughes order. "Let her breathe. The show's over."

More lights, and more faces. She was moving, staring up at the ceiling and moving, turning corners. It was a bumpy ride.

By seven o'clock in the evening the clouds had opened and there was a light snow falling but the temperature in the past week had been unseasonably warm—the thermometer had hit fifty, two days before—and the ground had retained its heat, causing the powder to turn to slush as it landed, giving Thomas Reed a hissing warning as the tires of the car cut through it, rolling slowly down his driveway, stopping in front of his house.

He stood up from the lounge chair that he'd been cocooned in for almost two hours as the sound of the automobile's engine died, then watched through the plate glass of the front door, as the lights of the car were turned off, and the door opened.

Thomas was in the habit lately of leaving the outside lights on and by the time the man had mounted the single step of the front porch he could see that it was the detective, Caruso. But what was he doing? What did he want?

Then it hit. There was only one reason that Caruso would have come to their house. Only one. And for a moment, Thomas Reed considered making a run for it, out the back door and into the woods. It was a desperate thought but he could feel it inside him, trying to break out.

He didn't run.

He stood still, almost mesmerized as Caruso rang the bell.

Molly and the infant appeared at the top of the stairway as the bell rang a second time.

"Who is it?" She asked.

"A policeman," Thomas answered flatly. "I think I'm about to be arrested."

She clutched the baby tightly to her body and started down the steps as Thomas went to the front door.

It all seemed so unreal to him, yet so inevitable. He knew what would come next. He'd seen it enough times on TV. The cop was going to read him his rights, cuff him, and take him away. He hadn't even called a lawyer. He didn't even know a criminal lawyer.

Thomas opened the door and met Caruso's eyes. There was something in them that confused him. They were neither hard nor threatening, instead they were somehow apologetic.

"Mr. Reed?" Caruso's voice was very soft.

"Am I under arrest?" Thomas asked.

Caruso shook his head and answered, "No."

"Then why are you here?"

Thomas suspected something, maybe some kind of trap, maybe he was supposed to panic and do something to incriminate himself.

"Why?" he repeated.

The question seemed to stop Caruso in his tracks and the apology in his eyes amplified.

"I'd like to talk to you, off the record. May I come in?"

Thomas stepped back, still suspicious, as Caruso entered the room, wiping the soles of his shoes on the entrance mat.

"I ... " Caruso hesitated, looking from Thomas to Molly, to the infant in her arms.

The baby looked beautiful, white-blond hair streaming out like a halo around its head, and the extraordinary blue eyes were looking directly at him.

"I came to talk to you about your son," Caruso continued.

"I don't understand," Thomas said.

Caruso stared at the infant, answering, "Earlier today I removed a woman from your property." He walked across the room toward Molly and the child. "I think she'd come here because of the baby."

"What exactly are you saying?" Thomas asked, stepping in between them. Something didn't feel right about any of this, and suddenly he wondered if the cop was off his rocker and dangerous.

"I'm sorry," Caruso said, stopping. "It's just that the baby ... I have reason to think that recent events may in some way be linked to the baby and I ... " He stopped a second time. He was talking crap and he knew it.

"I got some bad news earlier today; it was personal," he said, changing tack.

The baby had turned his head toward him and Caruso was again looking into John Reed's strange, knowing eyes.

"After I got the news, I was about to ... " He stopped and thought. How could he tell these people he'd been a hair's breadth from blowing his brains out?

"I was about to do something very stupid," he said finally. "The only thing that stopped me was the thought of your son. Ever since the day I first saw him, my life has changed. John ... " he spoke the name and paused, giving it weight, "John is very different, isn't he?"

Thomas felt ill at ease. The tough cop was suddenly all too human.

"What's your point, Detective?" he asked. His voice sounded aggressive, which belied the fact that he was scared again, scared that something beyond his control was taking place. Something that seemed to affect everyone who came into contact with the baby.

"I wanted to see him again," Caruso answered simply.

The baby had by now released his grip on Molly's lapels and was reaching out with his hands toward Caruso.

"We shouldn't be frightened of the things that we feel," Molly said, looking at Thomas, not in condemnation, but with compassion before turning back to Caruso. "Here, he wants you to take him," holding the baby out, away from her body.

"Are you sure?" Caruso asked.

"Yes, I am."

Caruso took the child in his arms, drawing him close. He could feel the warmth of his body and the tiny hands as

they gripped the collar of his jacket, surprised by the infant's
strength and coordination.

"I've never seen eyes like his," Caruso said, meeting
the blue. Then he felt the vertigo begin and looked away.

"I've just got this feeling—" Before he could finish
his sentence John Reed reached up with his right hand and
touched Caruso's forehead with the tip of his index finger.

Caruso experienced what felt like a current of
electricity, entering him through the point of contact and
heard a voice, as clearly as if it were directly inside his ears.

"Mikey, don't worry kid, you're fine."

Mikey? Only one person had ever called him Mikey.
His father. He stared into the infant's face, shocked, and was
swallowed again by his eyes. The next thing he knew he was
on one knee, with Molly bending over him, removing the
child from his hands, while Thomas Reed held him beneath
his armpits, supporting him while he regained his feet.

"I'm sorry," Caruso stammered, finding his balance.
He was embarrassed and humiliated. "I don't know what just
happened to me." Then he noticed that he was hot, burning
up inside; it was as if he had a raging fever. "I don't feel good
at all."

"Do you want to sit down?" Molly asked. "I'll get you
a glass of water."

"No," Caruso answered, backing away from the child.
Who was this baby? What kind of power did he have? "No,
thank you. I've got to get going. Just a little air. That's all I
need."

He could sense a tremor in his right hand and was
afraid the shakes were about to begin. *Please no,* he thought.
Not here, not in front of these people.

Thomas watched as the man—he wasn't a cop
anymore, not a tough guy, or an oppressor, just a man, like
himself, scared and bewildered—backed all the way across
the room to the front door of the house.

"I'm sorry about this," Caruso said again. He
wondered if he was sweating, the heat inside him was so
intense that he felt as if he must be flushed red. God, what
did he look like now? Some kind of lunatic? Then, trying to

recover a modicum of dignity, he looked at Thomas and said, "I'll be in touch with you."

Thomas nodded his head, walked toward him, and opened the door as Caruso stole a last, quick glance at the baby.

But John Reed was gone.

"Jesus Christ," Caruso exhaled the word in a single gush, looking at the ball of fiery light being cradled in Molly Reed's arms.

Caruso continued to stare, and in the next instant the outline of the baby created a visible perimeter around the light, giving it form. Then the child materialized, as if he had been born from the fire.

Caruso stood in awe. What was happening to him? Was the illness affecting his mind?

He tried to speak but no words came so he turned abruptly and walked as fast from the house as he could.

By the time he was inside his car, with the windows rolled up and the doors locked, the heat inside his body had escalated. He was a furnace. Then the cramps hit and he screamed as his body convulsed in a million knotting spasms, wringing him till he prayed for release.

Seconds later, when the spasms had ended, Caruso sat completely still, his hands resting on the steering wheel. He felt empty, both physically and emotionally, as if everything inside his body and mind had stopped, both breath and thought, leaving a void.

In front of him, through the sliver of unfogged glass at the top of his windshield he could see the sky. The snow was no longer falling, the clouds had parted and the moon was bright and full, etched with gray shadow and hovering like a white beacon above his head. He felt as if he could reach out and touch it, actually hold it in his hand. The feeling was so compelling that he raised his arm and pressed his fingertips against the windshield and closed his eyes. He had the sensation of warmth, running down from his fingers and into his body.

He could still see the moon, as if its energy had penetrated his closed lids. It was right there, inside the void, its light filling him, infusing him with a glorious peace.

~ 14 ~

"Can you hear me?" the voice asked.

He looked different without the toupee. His head was totally barren of hair, and his skin was a thin, shining hide, covering a misshapen, lumpy skull. He had no eyebrows or lashes and now that there was so much surface flesh above his half-lensed glasses, his black, slanted eyes looked like small beads of obsidian, hard and without depth.

"Dr. Armstrong?" Another blast of spearmint mouthwash from the circular mouth. It reminded her of the mouth of a fish. She tried to move her eyeballs in their sockets, away from him, but the effort sent sharp pains through her skull, and produced no results, as if the controlling muscles had been frozen. Then she attempted to close her eyes and shut him out. That didn't work, either, leaving her staring straight up, beyond his face, at the low ceiling.

"You are going to feel a bit unusual for the next several hours," he continued. "It's nothing to worry about, just the effect of the medication. It arrests the action of the motor neurons. Do you understand me?"

The ceiling appeared low, right above his head, and seemed to be made of some smooth, porous substance, like plastic, or rubber. A rubber ceiling? It was uniform in color, a yellowed white, like his skin. Maybe he was part of the room. Maybe he'd grown out of the ceiling, morphing from the rubber. She was dreaming. She had to be.

"It's good to see you again," he continued, with his perfect elocution. "Very good indeed."

He moved his head, blocking her view of the ceiling, so that she could not avoid his eyes.

"My name is Mishima, Dr. Ken Mishima, and I'm going to run a few tests on you. Standard stuff, just to see if you're in working order." He cuffed her arm as he spoke, pumped a ball, tightening the cuff, released it, and recorded her blood pressure.

Ugly. He was the ugliest man she had ever seen. Please God, let this be a dream.

"You have been asleep for a long time. Nearly seventy-two hours, off and on, three days. You were exhausted, also extremely agitated and it was necessary to sedate you. Mentally, you may require a bit of stimulation."

His head turned and his right shoulder lifted, then his hand appeared. He was showing her something. It was a long, full-barreled syringe.

Her fear mounted. *I need to wake up now)* she told herself. *Wake up.* It was a command that she could not obey.

He bent down, dropping out of her field of vision, leaving her eyes fixed on the ceiling.

His voice continued from somewhere close beside her.

"Memory and recall are my specialties. This is a rather long injection, a full minute actually. Quite painful without the other medication, the curare. Be grateful that you are insensitive to it."

By the time the sixty seconds had elapsed, and the fluid from the syringe had emptied into her vein, Casey's heart rate had risen from forty-eight to one hundred and sixty beats per minute, her blood pressure was soaring, and the only thing she could remember was the face of the baby in the window. She held onto the thought of John Reed's eyes as if it was sanity itself.

In the next room, Professor George and Preston Dix sat, relaxed in their leather office chairs, watching the monitoring screen. The professor leaned forward and switched from the wall mounted to the overhead camera and zoomed in.

Casey Armstrong's pupils were so dilated that her entire eyes appeared black.

George commented, "She looks absolutely transfixed."

Mishima noticed the movement of the zoom lens of the camera above his head and bent over, looking up and talking to the men in the control room.

"I believe her cerebral cortex is fully functional," he said, then he stood, picked up his medical bag, and walked from the room.

"Yes, just like he believed that the memory implant would hold," Preston Dix said quietly, glancing at Professor George.

They both disliked Mishima, but Dix particularly. Everything about the Asian rubbed him the wrong way. He'd been interested to discover that the Japanese man had been born in Nagasaki, on August 9, 1945, the day the United States had dropped the second bomb. He wondered if the fact that Mishima did not possess a single hair on any visible part of his body had anything to do with atomic radiation. He also suspected that, in spite of his Oxford education and time in the United States, Mishima hated Westerners. It didn't matter. He had received permission to terminate the Japanese doctor at the completion of Black-Out. It would be one less person who would know the truth.

Particularly since Molly Reed's blood work had come back yesterday and confirmed the evidence of a chromosomal split, indicating the initial phase in some form of cloning process. The device had a purpose and the technology that had created it was beyond any technology known on Earth.

Dix looked back at the monitor, studying the frozen features of Casey Armstrong's face. He needed her one more time.

In the days that followed, Professor George assessed her. Sometimes his tests were obvious, short-range taskings. Objects—a set of dice, playing cards, a chess board with the pieces positioned in a specific configuration—placed with him in one room, while she sat in the next, drawing or, describing them.

The other tests involved holding objects in her hands, a Mayan wood carving, an ornament from the Ming dynasty, and verbalizing their history and origins as Mishima compared her ramblings with the factual data. It was during the tests that she became aware that something had changed, or was changing, inside her. Her mind felt, somehow, more open and receptive. She was experiencing a deeper contact to the test objects, a clearer perception of some interconnectedness between herself and her targets. It felt as if a veil was lifting, and that the windows of her mind were being cleansed.

John Reed was with her.

If she closed her eyes and thought of him, she could recall the features of his face, staring down at her from the window. It was as if his eyes had become ingrained upon her subconscious. In that way he had become a sort of guide or teacher, leading her to her own self-realization.

Her new room was large by comparison to the padded cell. It had a single bed and table, both bolted to the floor, and a chair that she had positioned to look out of her barred window, at a mountain vista, misty in the mornings, gold, green, and blue in the afternoon sun, and covered in cold, lonely shadows by early evening.

Her door was always locked from the outside, as three cameras quietly recorded her movements within the room. She wondered if they were taping her or if one of them, either the hairless Asian, or the bearded man actually monitored her at all times. There was even surveillance in the bathroom, and, although she could not locate them, she was sure there were also listening devices.

Nick Hughes visited her daily. Maybe he even stayed there, in the hospital, although she wasn't certain of that, just that he was part of whatever was being planned. She understood that it was important that she displayed a trust in him, something she didn't feel. One afternoon she'd made love with him. Instigated it herself. Insisted. Right there, with just the sheet protecting them from the eye of the overhead camera.

It no longer mattered to her what games she had to play, and what indignities she had to suffer. Casey Armstrong was determined to survive.

She sensed a higher calling.

She was permitted access to the recreation room on the seventh day of her incarceration, following her request for a jump rope and enough space to exercise.

Neither of the orderlies seemed concerned with the other five men in the large, stark white, room. Two were glued to a television screen, mounted high on the wall, watching a daytime soap, one was standing in the corner, at strict attention, as another walked a tight circle, head down, his rubber flip-flops making soft, shuffling sounds against the cork flooring.

No one seemed particularly interested as Casey staked out her territory, well away from the frozen man on guard duty and the shuffler, and directly opposite the fifth man, who seemed immersed in a game of cards.

She watched him a few moments, then said, "I hope this won't bother you."

He continued with his cards in silence.

With no timer, she relied on the sweep hand of the wall clock, skipping for three minutes then standing at rest for one, and it was during these recovery periods that she had a chance to observe him.

At first it was just something to do, because he was there, and because his appearance was so unusual.

He had a mane of silver-gray hair which draped his shoulders, its ends reaching all the way to the waist of his green hospital pajamas, and a full, unkempt beard that concealed most of the features of his face. His hands were both repulsive and captivating with fingernails so long that they had folded under, like claws, yet he employed them with a precise and practiced dexterity, like a man who was accustomed to using his hands. His fingers were long and slender, not like a workman's, but like a musician's or a surgeon's.

She watched as he handled each card deftly and surely, gripping it between the nail of his thumb and index finger, while turning and examining it, before laying it purposefully on the surface of the table.

She went through another round of skipping, then stopped. She wondered if he could sense that he was being scrutinized. If he could, it did nothing to break his concentration.

It was the intensity of his cobalt blue eyes that attracted her the most. The way he focused on his task.

Casey was drawn to him. Did he ever blink his eyes? She had never seen him blink. He simply sat, manipulated his cards, and concentrated.

She was into her fifth round when she noticed that his activity had changed. He had laid all the cards out on the table, in two even stacks, and he was staring at them. It reminded her, both in the level of his apparent concentration and the materials he was using, of a psi experiment.

Then he began, the long and clawed fingers of his hands twitching with anticipation as he leaned forward and picked two of the cards up from their opposing stacks, leaning one of them against the other, carefully, until he found a point of balance. Then another two, and another, as the structure developed.

Casey stared, stunned and disbelieving, placing the rope down on the floor as he added another card to the intricate pattern.

She hadn't remembered it like that, not quite. The roof line had seemed less radical, at least in her memory, but as he continued, working faster, one card then another, balancing higher and higher, she realized that he was working from his own plans, his own vision. He had been there, somehow, seen it. He was connected.

They were connected.

She walked toward him, not knowing whether or not he was aware of her presence, hovering above him as he worked, like a student watching a teacher, awed by his ability to concentrate, to recreate the detail. She was frightened that it was all coincidence and terrified that it was not.

It looked like the house in Colorado. The house of John Reed.

She felt as though she had to speak, to communicate with him.

"Hello?"

She could see the orderly in the periphery of her vision. He appeared curious as to what was going on and was walking slowly in their direction.

She felt she had to make contact. It was urgent. She reached out.

"Sir?"

Her touch apparently startled him, and his entire body appeared to jump, his right hand pulling backward, brushing against the house of cards. It teetered. Then, walls caving inward, it collapsed, scattering the pieces across the table top and floor.

She gripped his arm.

"Was that a house?" she asked.

He turned, clutching her hand with his, looking up at her, and in a voice, muffled as if unused to speech, he answered.

"That was the house of God."

Someone shouted in the background.

"Step back. Step away!"

Then, still holding on to her, the long-haired man spoke again.

"Why do they kill what they don't understand?"

The orderly grabbed her from the side, wrapping both arms around her but the man's grip was desperate, and the desperation gave it power.

"Damon! Damon!" the orderly shouted, but it was as if their flesh had merged, forging them into a single entity.

Then Damon Raye spoke again, harsh and rasping.

"I was chosen."

After that there was pandemonium as a burly male nurse arrived and Casey was hauled backward.

He's mad. Crazy, she thought, watching him rear up from his chair, transforming as he found his feet, waving his arms, his eyes wild and his hair a great, flailing swirl around his head. He was shouting at the nurse, "I have been chosen!"

She saw it then, as he lifted his hands to defend himself, and the sight of it changed everything. She stared,

riveted by the mark on his palm, pink and rubbery, a mound
of scarred flesh identical to her own. Marking him. Marking
her. Binding them by some secret crucifixion.

"Damon!" she shouted.

She found his eyes for an instant and held up her left
palm. Pushing it toward his face as if in a gesture of peace.

"Stop!"

Damon stood still and stared at her hand, a bemused,
half smile playing on his lips, just as the nurse drove the
needle into the side of his neck, above his jugular, holding the
syringe like a dagger.

He clutched his throat as he fell, banging the table
and sending the remaining cards to the floor. Then he lay
with his body jerking, until finally, reduced to a soft rubble,
he surrendered to the drug.

"They have no right to destroy the future," he
mumbled. "No right."

Casey felt her emotions gather and swell.

"What have you done to him?" she demanded. "You
didn't need to do that. It was over. He wasn't resisting. It was
all over. Why?"

The nurse who had used the syringe, turned on her,
meeting her emotions head on.

"That's none of your fucking business."

Then, as quickly, he glowered at the orderly.

"She's your responsibility. What's she doing here?!
You know the rules. No contact!"

The orderly took Casey by the arm and guided her
toward the door, hustling her down the corridor, through the
security doors, toward her room.

~ 15 ~

Mr. Caruso?"
"Yes," he answered.
"Dr. Mitchell for you."

It was the call that he had been dreading, especially since he'd been feeling so good in the past ten days. There had been no tremors, no cramps, nothing but a heady sense of well-being. But wasn't that the way it always was when you were in denial? And now he was about to get a double-barreled blast of reality, the medical hex, the final word. At least he was in the private office, away from the other cops. He could hear his death sentence alone. Afterward he intended to live it day by day, always aware of the thirty-eight caliber option.

"Hello, Mr. Caruso?" Adrian Mitchell's voice sounded positively cheerful, but then that's the kind of woman she had seemed when he'd met her at the University Hospital eight days ago. She looked like she was in her late thirties, slightly overweight, with the sturdy features of a farm girl, honest brown eyes and corn yellow hair.

"Hello, Dr. Mitchell," Caruso replied, steeling himself.

Her words seemed to begin quietly and then explode down the phone.

"Mr. Caruso, your tests were negative, all of them."

Caruso took a moment to allow the words to settle.

"There was absolutely no trace of ALS. You're clear," Mitchell stated.

Nothing wrong? No trace. What was she saying? She was telling him the impossible.

Caruso swallowed hard and asked, "Are you sure?"

"Yes."

"But Dr. Rogers ... " Caruso broke off, his emotions welling.

"ALS is a difficult disease to diagnosis," Mitchell explained. "That's why Dr. Rogers sent you to see me. That's also the reason my tests were more inclusive." Had she been in Rogers' position, and without her experience with the disease, she would have come to the same conclusion that he had. There had been something there, but it wasn't there anymore.

"I don't understand," Caruso said.

"When we first spoke you mentioned that you'd noticed the muscle cramping in your hands directly following a practice session at the shooting range."

"That's true," Caruso replied.

"I think what may have happened is that when you were first tested you still had traces of lead in your system. That kind of poisoning can cause cramping and mimic the symptoms of ALS," she continued. "It can also fool some of the diagnostic tests."

It was an educated guess on the neurologist's part, but it was the best she could do. She'd done extensive tests on Caruso, been over them meticulously, and found nothing at all to indicate ALS. It was possible that his body had rid itself of the contaminant but that still didn't explain all the dramatic changes in the workup between Roger's report and her own. She'd even considered the possibility that there had been a contamination in the lab at Colorado Springs.

"How have you been in the past week?" She asked.

"Fine," Caruso replied. "No problems at all." He was thinking of himself on that day in the mountains, with the gun in his mouth. What if he had pulled the trigger? Then he thought of John Reed. John Reed had saved his life.

Mitchell's voice suddenly sounded distant.

"What I'm going to suggest," she said, "is that you call me immediately if you experience anything resembling a cramp or tremor. Then we'll do another twenty-four-hour urine collection and take it from there. Other than that I'd like to see you in three months, just to do a follow-up."

"And that's it. I'm ... " Caruso hesitated until the word came that best described his feeling. "I'm free."

"As far as I'm concerned," Mitchell replied.

In that moment Caruso's heart felt full in his chest.

"I feel like telling you I love you," he said.

"That's always nice to hear," Mitchell answered, then added. "I'm really happy to be able to make this call."

"Thank you, Doctor, thank you very much," Caruso replied.

He was feeling well, wonderful, as he placed the phone down.

Days passed and Caruso was obsessed, attempting to recall every detail of his last interaction with John Reed. Had the infant's touch cured him? Was that the reason his hands no longer trembled and his feet no longer cramped?

He'd read about faith healers and spontaneous cures, but the stories had been in newspapers and magazines, things to think about and ponder, a million miles from his reality. Now it had happened to him, something had made him well. Was it John Reed? What power did the infant have? And was it because of that power that people had been murdered?

He had lots of questions and not a single answer, until the call from the police crime lab.

"Detective Caruso? Regarding the material that we received from your office earlier this month, I believe we have something for you."

"A match?" Caruso asked anxiously.

"Department policy, Detective," the Denver officer reminded him. "We require you to collect the information in person."

It took him less than an hour to make the journey, north, up Interstate 25, driving himself crazy all the way, full of doubts and contradictions.

Caruso had come to view Thomas Reed as a victim, not a perpetrator. Now what if he was proved wrong? What if Reed was guilty? If that was the case, Caruso was in trouble. He'd procrastinated by not making the arrest, wasting time and money while calling attention to the investigation, and to his department.

Caruso broke the seal of the envelope and opened it quickly, slipping out the photocopied picture and details beneath.

He held it in front of him, at first smiling, but it was not a happy smile. It was the smile of someone who had just discovered the fool living inside his own skin. The kind of smile that deflates rather than enlarges, as his stomach tightened, and his mouth turned dry.

He should have known. Should have suspected something, at least put the pieces together. He'd been so close.

The eyes in the photograph, deep and trusting, stared back at him, searching, the way they had then, and the lips, turned up, almost in a smile, were mocking him.

Caruso swallowed what remained of the moisture inside his mouth. He fumbled for words, almost whispering, "Not exactly what I expected."

"Sometimes it isn't," the Denver officer, in charge of records, replied.

The man was young, and his manner seemed arrogant, or maybe it was Caruso's acknowledgement of his own stupidity that was poking the finger into his gut. He felt something slipping away from him as he gripped the edges of the sheet with the fingers of both hands, bringing it closer to his face, as if he could breathe life into it. He knew exactly who it was, but he read the name anyway.

"Catherine Lee Armstrong. Also known as Casey Lee Armstrong. United States Army. High-security clearance. Special Branch."

"I had her," Caruso said to no one in particular.

The officer cocked his head.

Caruso looked up from the photograph into the man's eyes. His voice sounded resigned to defeat.

"I picked her up in Colorado Springs a couple of weeks ago, but the army sent somebody for her .... She's gone."

"What she'd do?" The man asked.

Caruso almost answered "Killed a priest," but something held him back.

He held the young officer's eyes a moment without answering his question.

Finally he said, "I'm going to take a copy of this and be on my way. Thanks."

He found Lochart in his office, seated behind his wraparound desk, reading the *Gazette* and puffing on a Monte Cristo mini. The cigarette-sized cigar looked thin and effeminate in his fat hand, and the sight of it along with the newspaper, as if the captain had the time and composure for such luxuries, added fire to Caruso's anger.

"What the hell's going on, Yale?"

Lochart looked up. He wasn't used to being interrupted unannounced.

Caruso continued. "Are you using me as your fall guy?"

The detective's aggressive manner threw Lochart off-balance. He put the newspaper down and gathered himself quickly.

"Actually, Mike, I'm reading about a murder that nobody's solved. It involves a priest, a local celebrity. Wouldn't know anything about it, would you?"

Caruso walked closer, until he was standing with his thighs just touching the edge of Lochart's desk, glaring down through the expensive smoke.

"That Cuban shit's illegal, isn't it?"

Lochart was getting angry.

"What do you want?" he asked.

Caruso picked the small yellow, gold, and red cigar box up from beside the ashtray on the desk.

"Never seen you smoke anything that costs more than a buck. What are these, a gift from your buddies in Washington?"

Lochart stubbed the Monte Cristo out in the ashtray and sat straight in his chair, letting the silence between them linger till it mixed with the smoke and faded into the air. Finally, he spoke.

"Anybody else would have put a wrap on the Barnes case about an hour after it happened. Anybody else. But you ... you needed to confuse things. Get yourself on TV. What is it? You get some perverse kick out of seeing yourself looking like an asshole? Does it make you feel important?"

Caruso smiled. It was the same kind of smile he'd smiled when he'd first seen the FBI picture of Casey Armstrong. It wasn't a winner's smile. He knew he couldn't win, but he'd gone this far, he was going to see it through. He lifted the folded sheet of paper from his pocket.

"Here's the match on the prints."

He laid it flat on Lochart's desk, facing him.

Lochart looked down at the picture, staring, then up into Caruso's eyes. Something was building. It was a look that Caruso had never seen before, somewhere between dangerous and repentant.

Lochart shook his head. "I don't believe this." He looked down again. "I swear to God I didn't know."

Caruso held on, silent.

Lochart picked up the FBI sheet and studied it.

"I had no idea," he said.

Caruso had never experienced this side of Yale Lochart. He almost trusted him, but not quite.

"Come on. They had to tell you something before they came to get her."

Lochart raised the hand that had held the cigar and stroked the stubble on his chin.

"I'm giving you my word. I would never have dropped you into a situation like this. When the call came back from the army base in Maryland, to verify Armstrong's credentials, whoever was on the other end of the line asked for me by name. I was told that I was dealing with an employee of a top-secret government agency. That under no circumstance was that employee, Dr. Armstrong, that's what they called her, not captain, but doctor ... That under no circumstance was she to be subjected to questioning or interrogation of any sort."

"That's it?" There was still some aggression in Caruso's tone.

Lochart bristled. "I'm being honest with you." He placed the ID sheet down and pushed back in his chair. "Sit down, will ya'. You're making me nervous.

Caruso remained standing.

Lochart eyed him a few seconds and continued.

"She was alone in one of the tanks downstairs for about three hours, until some agent from the National Security Agency came and got her. Then it was out of my hands."

"And that's it? All you know?" There was suspicion in Caruso's tone.

Lochart took a good, long breath. His nostrils flared.

"You're pushing me, Mike. Why?"

"Cause I want to know the whole story. I've got a right to."

Finally, Lochart opened up. "The woman had been the subject of some kind of psychological testing, something to do with mind control. I didn't get details, just that she'd had a breakdown. That's what I was told. Period."

"So what was she, some sort of assassin?"

Lochart's guilt had faded, replaced by the first embers of anger.

"I don't know." Each of the words was pronounced slowly and clearly.

Caruso looked down at the FBI report.

"What was she doing at the Reed house?"

"Stop it, Mike."

"And why the hit on the priest?" Caruso continued. He was thinking of Barnes's radio broadcast. His murder had something to do with the baby. That made sense. Everything kept coming back to John Reed.

Lochart swallowed his ego once more.

"Mike, I'm a cop, same as you. Do you think I wasn't curious about who she was and what she was doing here? I made a few calls to the hotels, the airlines. And do you know what? Nobody had any records of her ever being here. Nothing on paper anyway. No credit-card slips. No signatures. Nothing."

"That's impossible."

"That's the way it is, goddamn it! Don't you hear what I'm saying. I don't want to play against these people."

Caruso leaned forward, rested his hands on Lochart's desk and drummed lightly with the fingers of his right hand.

"So we don't have anybody to arrest, do we?"

Lochart had a terrible sinking feeling in his stomach. He'd seen two friends in Boulder lose their careers over the Jon Benet Ramsay case in '96. He didn't want a similar situation in Colorado Springs. He looked down again at Casey Armstrong's picture, thinking of the crime scene. Could a woman have possibly done that? Then he remembered the way she'd fought in the cell, tearing the shank of his boot with her teeth. He'd actually been frightened of her.

"I don't know what to tell you, Mike. Yeah, it stinks. Everything about it stinks, and I want it to go away."

"Do you think arresting Thomas Reed for something he didn't do will make that happen?"

Lochart swallowed. Is that what he wanted? A sacrifice?

"I'm not saying that," he answered.

Caruso looked at him in silence, squeezing him with his eyes.

"Goddamn it!" Lochart growled. "I don't know who these people are. Maryland? Washington? I don't even know where they come from. Maybe they orchestrated the press leak, maybe they can kick you and me right out of here and on to the street. Maybe they can tie us down to our desks and blow our brains out. It seems they've got that kind of power." His short, fat fingers, were leaving salty prints on Casey Armstrong's picture.

"Thomas Reed is in the clear," Caruso stated.

Lochart inhaled audibly and his expression changed, as if his skin had tightened against his bones.

"Mike, I'll go with you as far as I can on this, but you've got to understand, there's a limit to everything."

It sounded like a subtle warning and Caruso tried to shake the feeling off as he walked from Lochart's office.

~ 16 ~

Thomas Reed listened to the telephone ring and waited for the answering machine to pick it up. He'd changed their number to an unlisted one three days earlier and, somehow, two reporters from the regional newspaper had already accessed it. Sympathetic voices, men with hearts, trying for a story, a new angle, promising to portray his point of view, to give him a chance to air his perspective.

Thomas didn't want to know about their promises. The death of Robert Barnes had already wrecked his life. Helped, of course, by the same people who were now offering him their unbiased ear. Then there were the religious nuts, the few who had put Barnes's radio broadcast and the illegal TV footage of Thomas and Caruso together, and come up with John Reed. Cultists had called or written to offer sanctuary in their churches or or-organizations, promising money and power, and undying devotion, along with the satanic rites of their orders.

Thomas had been outside only half a dozen times since his visit to the police station, all to buy groceries. His job was history. The agency hadn't exactly fired him, but one of the partners, a woman who was also a member of the town council, had suggested he take time off until the case was resolved. Not that they believed he could have done such a thing. Certainly not that, but with the media attention, it was going to make life impossible for everybody at the agency. He'd understood her logic at the time. She'd been a smooth talker. The kind who could boot you out the door and make it feel like a favor. It was only when he'd arrived back at his home, after he had closed and double-locked the front door, that he'd realized that Colorado Springs was over for them. Them? Whatever was left of them. Sometimes he wondered if deep down, Molly believed he was a murderer. It was the way she looked at him, when she didn't think he was noticing, with her eyes full of doubts and questions. Why didn't she just come out and accuse him? But no, she would never do that. She'd bottle it up the same way she had bottled her feelings after the death of their first son, Alex. There was never an open accusation.

He recognized the voice on the answering machine within the first few words, before the caller had given his name. It was the cop, Caruso. The last time he'd seen him, the man had nearly fainted on his floor. Now what?

"Mr. Reed, this is Detective Caruso."

Thomas noticed the difference in Caruso's tone as he left the number for his direct line. His voice sounded more full than during their last encounter, more vibrant.

"I would appreciate it if you would call me. I need your help with something. As soon as you get this message, please phone." He repeated his phone number again and the answering machine beeped and clicked off.

"I need your help." He'd actually said it.

To do what? Thomas wondered.

He placed his cup of cold coffee down on the side table and stood up from the sofa, walking to the big, south-facing window on the far side of the room. He looked out through glass and bare branches of the trees and beyond to the street. He had that feeling again. It was as if someone's eyes were on him, watching and waiting. It was the same feeling he'd had on the day of Robert Barnes' murder, and the worst part of it was that he felt powerless to defend himself and his family against it. It was as if he was playing in a land of shadows, dealing with entities that were not made of flesh and blood, who appeared and disappeared, yet kept closing in. Who was the man that Molly claimed had visited her in the hospital? At first Thomas had discounted the episode, putting it down to his wife's confusion, along with her disjointed memory of her self-proclaimed close encounter in Mexico. Delusions? But what had really happened to Murray Rose? And Robert Barnes?

He drew the curtains, walked back to the sofa, and sat down. Listening.

The baby was sobbing. It had been that way, off and on, for over a week. They'd had the pediatrician to the house, and the woman had found nothing physically wrong, although, like everyone who had been in close proximity, she seemed fascinated with him.

"The way he is developing," she'd said. "I've never seen anything like it. He seems to change every time I examine him. He's exhibiting hand-eye coordination, I'm sure, and he has control of his neck muscles. He's remarkable, absolutely remarkable."

Thomas was relieved that Molly hadn't told the doctor about the infant's alleged ability to speak. At least she'd spared him that much.

Now the sobbing laid a backdrop for the rain outside the windows and the mood inside the house. What had Robert Barnes said? He'd seen God in the eyes of the child. God? Then why this suffering?

Robert had been a friend. Thomas recalled the evening, after the AA meeting, when he'd nearly cracked. Before the child had come. When his fear and apprehension had nearly taken him on a one-way ride to the neon bar on Nevada Street. And Robert had saved him. Why would anyone want to kill Robert Barnes?

The sounds of sobbing grew louder from above. He could hear Molly speaking, her voice hushed and soothing, as he nestled back into the cushions, the phone beside him, the call light on the answering machine blinking, Michael Caruso waiting at the other end of the line.

Thomas closed his eyes as if he could shut it all out. His anger had long ago given way to frustration; he felt powerless to do anything. He thought of the valium that he had stored in the medicine cabinet. It was an old prescription for back spasms. How many pills were still inside the container. Ten? Fifteen? How many would it take? He'd thought of suicide lately, more than once. Everything had turned so bad. Gone so sour. Tears leaked from his closed lids. It was all turning black inside of him. He heard the crying upstairs intensify; the sound seemed to mirror his own feelings, to be in some type of sync with his heart. He thought of John. The tragedy had, at least, given him some perspective on his own feelings. John. His son. It was the first time he'd truly acknowledged him. His only son, a month old, alone and helpless, his daddy in a mess, his mother worn and exhausted. He was a baby boy, trying so hard to survive. Then Thomas looked toward the window, through the crack between the curtains, at the world that waited for them. Police cruisers, and men in uniform, monitoring those who came in and those who went out, but unable to stop the shadows.

What was it going to take to reclaim a normal life, to find some peace? How many new towns, and cities? Running, always running. What if he was arrested? Tried and convicted for a crime he did not commit, the murder of a friend.

The baby's cries pushed deeper into him, until they became an actual presence in his mind, an embodiment of his own fear. The child was frightened. That was it. The baby knew what was happening, sensed it in the simplest of forms. He was tuned to the atmosphere. Of course the baby was crying, fear was everywhere.

Thomas stood up from the sofa, walked up the steps connecting the TV room to the dining room, then up the spiral staircase to the top of the house. The door to the baby's room was locked. He knocked gently.

"Molly, may I come in?"

She was holding John when she opened it, keeping back, away from the door, defensive.

"I'm sorry. He won't stop," she said. There was a silence between them before she broke down. "I don't know what to do. I just don't know anymore."

Thomas wanted to take her in his arms, to hold and comfort her, but before he could do that, he needed to make peace with himself, and with his son.

"Here, let me have him," he said softly. "You go downstairs and rest. He scared, that's all. I'll take over now."

It was the first time he had ever asked. The first time he had displayed any real concern for the child and something inside her began to give way.

"I can't keep going. I'm going to break," she answered, still clutching the sobbing infant.

"Please, it's all right."

As he reached and touched John, she surrendered her grasp.

Thomas continued. "Now, you go downstairs, close the door, get into bed. Just rest. Sleep. That's what you need."

She wanted to believe him. Wanted to believe that he loved the boy, that their nightmares would go away, but she was afraid. The words slipped from her, before she could stop them.

"You won't hurt him, will you?"

He looked away from her. He felt no anger, just shame, deep shame. Then he looked down, into the child's eyes, as if he could escape there, but it was waiting, like the last time, and although instinct told him to turn away, to save himself from the pain, he held on, as the gate opened and he fell into the churning sea. He was feeling it, as he'd felt it then, the water swirling around him, the current dragging him sideways, out of control. He fought it, the feelings and the fear, until something inside him surrendered, and he let go. Sinking down. Deeper. Searching through the sorrow of his life, until he touched its source. It was more than memory. Memory was distorted, tainted by the subtle shadows of time passed. This was clear and alive, raw with feelings and it lay him open, first his mind then his heart.

He could see him.

The child was lying on his back, with the gold chain and cross around his neck. His eyes were open, looking up through the water. He was waiting for his father. He had been waiting a long, long time.

Thomas reached out and lifted him, bringing him close to his body, cradling him tight and warm to his chest.

Then he turned, looking up, and saw the light, shimmering through the watery ceiling above their heads.

He began to kick, struggling toward the surface.

He gulped in the fresh air, hugging the child to him.

I found you. Thank God, I found you, he thought, as he looked down into the eyes of his son.

John Reed stopped crying and it was as if, in that instant, the entire world had gone silent.

"I love him," Thomas answered, looking up at Molly. It was the first time he had ever said it and his words created a reverence between them, as if some integral connection had been rejoined. "I would never hurt our son.

"I'm sorry. I had no right—" she began.

He shook his head, stopping her.

"You had every right," he answered.

She looked first at Thomas, then at the John, who was resting in his arms. Her feelings were of peace. At last.

The phone was ringing as she walked down the stairs. The machine caught it and Caruso's voice came on, again.

"Mr. Reed, this is Detective Caruso calling again. Please return my call. Thank you."

By the time Thomas returned Caruso's call, he had placed the sleeping infant in his crib and was standing outside the door of his room.

"Mr. Reed," Caruso began. "We've had another development in the case, and I'd like to run over a bit of your testimony with you, just to corroborate times and places. There's a few things I'm not clear on. When would it be convenient for you to come to the station?"

Thomas held the portable phone close to his ear, as if to keep the energy of the call from spilling into the tranquility of his home.

He spoke softly so as not to wake John.

"Am I going to be arrested?" he asked, feeling stronger inside, more able to handle whatever lay in store for him.

"No," Caruso answered.

"Then what is it that you want?" he asked.

Caruso's tone changed. It wasn't tough, but it was businesslike.

"Mr. Reed, I need you down here. I don't really have to ask if it's convenient. "

Two-and-a-half hours later, at 8:00 P.M., Thomas was still sitting
in front of Caruso's desk in Homicide.

"Okay," the policeman said, his voice calm. "We've
got two major problems, as I see it. The first is why you
didn't report the gun missing as soon as you got home from
the church, and the second is that no one can testify as to
where you were when Robert Barnes was murdered."

Thomas was tired. It was the fourth time he'd been
over the same story, and his voice was weary from repetition.

"I didn't notice the gun was missing till after I got
home. I'd put it under the passenger side seat, covered in a
towel. Whoever took it, left the towel and I just never really
looked."

"And you didn't lock your car when you went into the
church?" Caruso asked.

"I had a lot on my mind."

"But you didn't?"

Frustration was seeping into Thomas's tone, but still
he tried to think, to recall. Somehow the manner of the cop
seemed changed. He felt a rapport with him, as if the man
had become an ally.

"I guess not," he replied. "I guess somebody could
have been following me and stolen the gun. It's possible." He
stopped and looked at Caruso.

"Come on, you know all this. You've checked my car.
The locks weren't damaged. It must have been open. I told
you about the phone calls. They scared the shit out of me. On
top of that I was angry at Robert Barnes. I was wasn't
thinking straight. Then there was the Jeep—"

Caruso looked up from his notebook. He knew
Thomas Reed was innocent of the crime but he also felt that
he might hold the key to the truth.

"Who would have been following you?"

"I don't know."

"How about your AA group? Would anyone there
have had a grievance with you, or with Robert Barnes?"

Reed answered quickly, "No."

"Please take your time."

"Detective, we've been through all this before. The answer is still no. Nobody from the meeting, and nobody from the church. This isn't about local people."

Caruso looked up from his notebook and their eyes met.

"You know that and I know that, it's nobody local," Thomas said.

Caruso nodded. "Okay, then let's talk about the Jeep again. Tell me about it. Anything. Any detail. Concentrate on the Jeep, and relax, we're on the same side."

Thomas Reed sat quietly, with his arms folded in front of him. He thought of the black Jeep. Remembering the way it had been parked, as if it was waiting and the way, as he'd slowed down, it had followed, turning off only after he'd stopped. He could see it, turning slowly. Then he remembered something else, something he'd not mentioned before.

"It had a broken taillight," he said. "I'm pretty sure of it. A broken taillight on the driver's side."

Caruso answered, "Good, that's good." He wrote it down. He'd been patient, waiting, hoping for another letter, or number off the plate. Sometimes it took repetition and relaxation. A broken taillight was excellent. There might be something in the crime information system on the vehicle. An outstanding violation?

After that, Thomas Reed stopped talking. He was exhausted.

"I'm just going to ask you to do one more thing," Caruso continued, removing Casey's picture from the top drawer of the desk. He'd had it copied, minus the government ID and information. He placed it in front of Reed.

"Take a good look at this and tell me if you recognize her."

Thomas studied the picture in silence.

Caruso needed a result and he felt close. He pushed. "Could she have been driving the car that followed you?"

Reed thought back, again. When he answered, he felt like he was letting Caruso down.

"I can't honestly say. I couldn't get a good look at the driver's face." Then added. "I suppose it could have been .... Who is she?"

"About two weeks ago we removed her from your property," Caruso answered. "She was trespassing."

Thomas remembered the incident with the dark-haired woman in the driveway.

"Why was she there?" he asked.

Caruso thought a moment of John Reed. He had purposefully stayed away from him during their interview. The infant confused him on a very personal level, and Caruso did not want to be confused; he wanted to solve a crime.

"I honestly don't know," he replied, making a mental note to double up on the police surveillance around the Reed house.

~ 17 ~

Lady Blythe-Saxon was dressed in a black Valentino suit and flat, Ferragamo shoes. She didn't like to travel but this trip to Washington had been an absolute necessity. At least that's what Preston Dix had assured her during his brief telephone call.

It was not characteristic of Dix to display much in the form of emotion, but today, standing in the laboratory of the Medical Science Building above the flat metal table, bending over the shallow, circular petri dish, and staring down, he looked positively stunned. His eyes were opened wide and his face was set as if he was concentrating on the final move in a game of life or death.

"At first we thought it was a shard of some kind of glass," Dr. Benjamin Saphier explained to Blythe-Saxon as he escorted her to the table. "But after we discovered the chromosomal split, our entire approach changed. In all my experience I've never seen anything like this." There was unconcealed awe in his tone.

By then they were beside Dix and directly above the blood-filled petri dish.

Blythe-Saxon looked down. Her first reaction was sheer repulsion. The small gray-black thing that seemed to be floating, or swimming in the dish, was pulsing with life, causing the blood that surrounded it to churn. It looked like a very tiny, but powerful, suction pump.

"What the hell is it doing?" she asked.

We're not completely certain, but with the information we've accumulated, we're guessing that this is the beginning of the reproductive process, probably the initial splitting of the chromosomes," Saphier replied.

Dix did not so much as glance up or say a word to welcome Blythe-Saxon to the room.

Very rude, she thought.

So who manufactured it?" she continued, looking down again into the dish as the bug thing continued to throb.

Saphier shook his head. "That's impossible to say, but there's nothing unearthly about its chemical composition."

And the power source?" Blythe-Saxon asked.

Saphier smiled. He was tall, spaghetti-thin, and bald, with the exception of twin patches of wispy, brown hair on the sides of his head. His nose was small and rounded at the tip, and his dark eyes were set close together, in contrast to his wide mouth and yellow teeth. His smile said "I got ya'," which rubbed Blythe-Saxon in precisely the wrong way.

She was under considerable pressure from the people she represented and she hadn't come to play games.

"What's making the damn thing run?" she asked tersely.

Saphier's smile wilted, but not entirely.

Currently," he said, looking down at the bubbling blood, "the direct power source is Mr. Dix."

Blythe-Saxon's entire face hardened in an instant. She didn't like being trifled with, and certainly not by some minion employed by Neo Tech.

"Pardon me?" There was a challenge in her voice.

Saphier kept the remains of his smile intact. He knew he was holding the trump card.

"Please, come with me," he said.

He guided her to the back of the lab, past the darkened area that housed the electron microscope, to a far corner. There was a workbench there with a monitor screen sitting on it.

"Take a look at this."

Blythe-Saxon studied the image on the screen. It was Preston Dix, looking into the dish, while the blood continued its strange undulations.

"Now watch," Saphier continued, pressing a button that had been rigged to the bench. A buzzer sounded somewhere in the room and Preston Dix turned and walked away from his post, leaving the petri dish alone on the table.

"Keep your eye on the dish but think about something else."

"What?"

"Think about ... " Saphier looked down at her shoes, "think about your left foot."

Blythe-Saxon felt mildly confused, looking down once at her left foot then back at the scientist.

"I'm not sure if I understand you," she said.

"Look at the screen," he instructed.

The blood had become stagnant.

Saphier pressed the button, the buzzer sounded, and Dix returned to stare down at the dish. As he did, the device resumed function. Again the buzzer, and again Dix walked away, and again the blood went still.

"The power appears to be psychically generated," Saphier announced with some degree of pride. "In other words the device seems interconnected to the human mind, or to whatever mind created it. It may even function by remote, in other words by indirect mental contact."

"That's impossible," Blythe-Saxon stated.

"Not in terms of quantum physics," Saphier answered. He'd been prepared for this question and had racked his brains for an explanation.

"When an electron is not being observed, it no longer exists in particle form, but as a wave of light. That proves some type of interconnection between mind and matter."

"Yes, but ... " Blythe-Saxon stalled. "Can you reverse the engineering?"

"There doesn't appear to be any engineering," Saphier replied. "Not in a conventional sense ... It's more like a living organ."

Casey Armstrong woke up, but kept her eyes shut, as if the camera, always watching, always peering, always probing, might invade her mind and rob it of its intention. There was only one thing she needed to do. *And after that?* she asked herself. "After that," didn't matter. Maybe there was no "after that."

The lock on the door snapped open with the sound of metal banging against metal. Then a key tumbled the manual lock. She opened her eyes. Something wasn't right. They never came for her this early. She'd always had time to use the bathroom, to dress. Maybe it was later than she'd thought.

"Good morning."

She sat up in the bed as Nick Hughes entered. He was carrying her duffel bag. She hadn't seen it since Colorado and it looked like an old friend, an ally, a traveling companion.

Hughes was smiling, his big, everything's-going-to-be-fine smile.

"You want to go home?"

It was an unintentionally cruel question. Home had become a different place in the past three weeks. Home was not her town house at Meade. There was no security there, and no resolution. Home was the face in the window of the house of cards, and yes, she wanted—needed—to get back there. John Reed had become a yearning.

Tears came to her eyes, and she did nothing to stop or conceal them.

"Yes."

Hughes walked toward her, laying the duffel bag on the floor. She allowed him to take her in his arms and hold her, feeling, even as she did, she was acting the part. The same as he was acting. Their audience was above them, and to their sides, glass eyes capturing their essence, projecting it to a screen inside some hidden room, to be viewed and evaluated.

"As soon as you're dressed, we can get going," he said.

She wanted to ask why? She wanted to ask a lot of questions. The discipline of holding her tongue had been one of the hardest parts of her incarceration.

She replied, "I'll be quick." She slid off the bed, picked up her duffel bag, and took it with her into the bathroom.

Once inside, she closed the door, unzipped the bag, and took out her clothing; it was the same stuff she'd taken to Colorado, but it had been washed and everything, including her blue jeans, had been pressed. The Myotron was gone, so was her wallet, containing her identification and cards. They were letting her out, but they weren't setting her free.

Ten minutes later, she was standing in front of Nick Hughes, trying to look grateful, as if she believed he'd really rescued her.

There was no signing out, no protocol, simply a walk by the guards and out through the same doors that had held her prisoner for nearly two weeks. Out to the parking lot, where Nick's black BMW 528i waited, spotlessly clean, reflecting the early rays of the winter sun.

He waited till they were locked inside the car before he spoke again. "How are you feeling?"

She looked silently across the console at him as he reversed out of the space and drove slowly toward the exit.

Finally, once they were on the main road, driving away from the hospital, he asked again, "You all right?"

This time she answered.

"Oh yeah, I'm wonderful. Absolutely wonderful. It was like a health club in there, the food, the exercise, the medical treatment, five-star all the way."

"Well that's all over now."

She stared. His face was set and his body lacked flow; there was something cold and robotic about him. She felt a surge of anger, bottomed with hatred, as they continued down the narrow mountain road. She didn't feel as if she was leaving or escaping anything. She was merely trading one confinement for another.

"What the hell's going on?" she asked.

He kept his eyes straight ahead, on the road, answering, "We're out of there. That's what's going on."

"Funny, I don't feel out of there. I feel just the opposite."

He didn't answer.

"What's really going on?" she asked again.

He tone was dismissive. "Nothing. Nothing at all."

"Strange," she continued. "How you think you know somebody. Love somebody. Then, something happens, something that takes things down to the life-and-death basics, ripping away the mask, and there you are, facing a total stranger. And you realize that what you treasured, that person who was so good and felt so solid, that person you trusted with your life, was an actor, a fraud. Somebody you never really knew. That's got to be the worst feeling in the world, and I've got it right now."

He listened to her words, digesting them before he spoke.

"Okay. Okay." It sounded like he was giving something up. "They want to use you for another tasking. One more. Then, it's over." He looked at her then, before turning back to the road. "That's all I know."

The energy that had fueled her anger suddenly reinforced her fear.

"Use me. Again?" she asked.

"Yes."

She recalled Montauk with its blood-stained corridor and metal vat.

"I don't think I can do it," she said.

He could sense the first seepings of panic in the car and spoke slowly, as if the slowness of his words could reassure her.

"You have an affinity with whatever it is they're working on. You've got to do it."

"Who's behind this?"

"I don't know," he replied.

"Come on." Her voice turned bitter. "You're a better liar than that."

"I honestly don't know."

"So what does that make you then? My handler, my keeper? You get me there on time. Stand around afterward while they brainwash me, or whatever they do, then tell me lies in the morning—"

"Goddamn it. Listen to me," Hughes snapped. "I want you to stay alive. That's all I care about. That's it."

She looked at his face. It appeared pained. He'd definitely lost weight and the effect had been aging.

She asked, "When?"

He shook his head. He didn't want to answer.

She repeated her question.

Finally, he spoke and his voice had the flat, drained feel of a confession.

"Right now there's a plane waiting for us at Meade."

She thought again of Montauk, with its skeleton buildings and dark shadows. She didn't want to go back.

"To take us where?"

"I don't know," he answered.

Her fear flip-flopped with her anger.

"Bullshit."

He looked at her and said, "I don't want you hurt."

She stayed with his eyes, searching them.

"And I don't believe a word you're saying."

His voice broke, and the emotions, inside, finally sounded real.

"Do you think I want to be involved in this, with these people? Well, I promise you, I didn't have any choice then, and I don't have any now, not if I want you back in one piece. I'm here because you were the best person for the job and I was the closest person to you, and if you hadn't been so damn good, and so damn inquisitive, it would be over by now. But that's not you, is it? No, you had to keep pushing."

"What did you expect me to do?" she asked. "I couldn't sleep. I couldn't work. I couldn't function. What did you expect?"

"I expected the fucking thing to work the way they said it would. A screen memory. That's what they called it. I didn't expect you to be any different. "

"And now, you're going to let it all happen again?"

He took a long time to answer.

"If they get what they need, we walk away, and then maybe we can disappear."

"What?"

"Disappear. I've done it for other people. I can do it for us ... South America."

She stared at him.

He continued. "I can get us new passports, drivers licenses, tickets—"

"Stop it!"

He went silent.

"I like who I am. At least I used to. I don't want to be anybody else," she said.

He looked lost for words as she continued.

"My military ID, my cards. Where are they?"

He turned back to the highway and his voice sounded reluctant, as if he was giving away more than he wanted to.

"You don't need to worry. I've got everything."

"Where?" she asked.

He didn't answer.

"Do you want me to trust you?"

There was a silence, until finally he replied, "in there," motioning to the glove compartment.

She opened it and saw two plastic bags. They looked like police-evidence containers; one held her wallet, the other the Myotron. She tore them out and opened them, first the wallet, then the weapon.

Nick glanced at her and said, "I haven't touched anything since I got them back from the police in Colorado."

She felt better, as if a part of her had been returned. She placed her wallet in the front pocket of her jeans and the stun gun in her lap; she looked across at him.

"Now, I want to know about Colorado."

He looked over and cocked his head, as if he didn't understand her question.

She asked, "Who is John Reed?"

He looked truly confused.

"I don't know any John Reed," he replied.

She continued pushing. "Come on, why are they so interested in a baby?"

Hughes turned and looked at her.

"I don't know what you're talking about. I really don't."

Her tone tightened. "Don't play with my head anymore. I need some real answers."

"Well, I don't have any," he said.

"Who is John Reed?" she asked for the second time.

Hughes exploded. "I don't know anybody named John Reed! I don't know anything about Colorado, or a baby. I don't know. Period."

"That's a load of crap."

"No, that's the truth."

Casey sat back against the seat. She believed him and that made things worse. There was an edgy silence in the car until she spoke again, asking, "What happens if I don't want to cooperate with these people?"

He answered as if he was tired of the question, "I told you."

"Then why don't we keep going? Right now. Just keep on driving. Forget the tasking."

"That's impossible," he said. He sounded agitated.

"Why?"

"Because I've haven't arranged everything. I need time. And I need them off our backs, at least for a while. We've got to cooperate."

"Then take me back to Colorado Springs. Help me get to the bottom of this. We'll go to the police. There's a guy there, his name is Caruso, Michael Caruso, he's a detective in Homicide. I'm pretty sure he'll help us—"

"Michael Caruso? What's he going to do? This is too big for some civilian cop. Way too big."

She reached across the seat and touched the shoulder of his jacket.

"Jesus, Nick. I've never seen you so scared. Too scared to move, aren't you?"

He sat silently as she fingered the collar and lapels of his cashmere coat, expecting to find a transmitter. His mouth tightened but he offered no resistance as she continued inside his shirt with her fingers, running down the length of his chest, finding nothing. Then she looked quickly around the car. Were they being monitored? Was this another experiment, a test? Some kind of setup?

He said finally, "We do the tasking, then we go home. That's the deal."

The BMW slowed, braking for a curve, entering a tunnel of evergreen. As they came out, he accelerated. To her side, and down, she saw a white mist, hanging like a delicate veil across the valley. She was leaving heaven to go to hell, through the blood-spattered corridor and into a room that stunk of rotting flesh, to the metal coffin, to have her brain sucked and reordered. The thought cause her stomach to heave. She could taste it all, the medicine and the fear. Hunching forward, she placed her head in her hands, and retched.

Nick braked and looked over at her.

"What's wrong?"

"I'm going to be sick. Pull over. Please pull over," she said. She retched again.

"There's a town. Five miles—"

She groaned. "I can't make it."

He waited for the road to widen, then pulled onto a patch by the verge of the forest.

"I've got to get some air," she said, trying to open the door.

He pressed the central lock and she was out, breathing the mountains and the sky, walking toward the trees with Nick behind her. Her voice sounded weak.

"Please Nick, just leave me alone. I'll be okay. Just a few minutes.

Nick stayed close, watching, nervous that she would not recover. Scared that they'd be late for the connection that would take them to the tasking. And what if she couldn't perform? What then?

Casey knelt on the dry leaves and pine needles, resting on her hands and knees, spitting the bile from her mouth, then sucked in the cold air. The smell, whole and clean, invigorated her. She remained that way for a few seconds, letting the cold seep up through the palms of her hands.

"Water?" she asked.

Nick ran back to the car and pulled a bottle of spring water from beneath the driver's seat. When he got back to her, she was sitting on the ground, looking at him. The sickness had passed and she appeared calm, as if the crisis was over. He handed her the bottle. She sipped from the lip and handed it back to him.

"Sorry about this," she said, offering him her left hand.

He took it and helped her to her feet, never noticing the Myotron as she brought it around from her right side, cupping it in her palm, bringing it up to his throat, depressing the attack button. There was a dull, humming sound as the battery discharged.

His eyes bulged as he stared at her, disbelieving and unsure of what had just happened to him. Then, as she stepped back, he appeared to be attempting to raise his hand, maybe to touch his throat, but his arm quivered and his hand shook violently as his legs gave way. Not gradually, but with one sudden movement, as if they had turned to liquid and poured into his shoes. His torso followed the line down and he landed on his knees, pitching forward, facedown. Then, in a motion that looked like a pushup, plagued with spasticity, he rose with the strength of his arms, jolted, and flipped onto his back, where he lay trembling.

Another few seconds and he became still, with the exception of his eyelids, which, half-closed, continued to flutter as if they were fighting for the last remnants of light.

It was the first time she had ever seen Nick Hughes helpless. He was a big, muscular man, but more than his physicality, it was the power and grace with which he moved that had given him an aura of invincibility. The sight of him, sprawled at her feet, was completely unnatural to her. It was as if she was standing above a great jungle beast, a lion or tiger, rendered immobile. For a moment, she believed she had killed him and her instincts begged her to go to his aid, to help him. She reached down and pushed in with her fingertips against the skin above his carotid artery, feeling his pulse, good and strong. Bending further to pull the car keys from the pocket of his coat.

"Good-bye, Nick," she said.

After that, she ran for the BMW, got in and drove. She wondered if they could see her, or hear her, if they already knew what had happened, and how long it would be till they came after her.

~ 18 ~

Casey boarded the 10:20 A.M. Delta flight for Cincinnati at precisely the time that Nick Hughes walked into the highway patrol building the outskirts of Roanoke. He gave his name to the officer at the desk, and reported the car theft. The man listened, smiled politely, and asked him to wait while he notified the troopers in charge. He made a call, and a few minutes later, Hughes was escorted to a ground-floor office in the back of the building.

"I believe we have a development on that, sir," the trooper said, picking up his phone and dialing a number that he had written hastily, in pencil on a yellow legal pad.

He kept his eyes on Hughes while he waited for an answer.

"This is Trooper Richard Stanlowsky in Roanoke. I have a Mr. Nicholas Hughes with me here at the station. It's in connection to the theft of a BMW .... Fine, I'll have him wait."

Hughes was screaming inside, wanting to know if they'd found her, but he held his emotions in check, modulating his voice and rubbing down the sharp edges of his nerves.

"Did you guys find my car?" he asked. He thought it suspicious that the trooper, almost casually, brushed the top of his holster with the palm of his right hand, unsnapping it.

Stanlowsky was a big man, big like an out-of-season football player. Not quite in shape, but not more than a training camp away, with a broad face and eyes set way back in his skull and hooded by heavy lids. They looked like they were hiding something.

"Yes, Mr. Hughes, we did," he replied. "Now if you'll just sit tight, I believe we can resolve this."

Hughes couldn't contain it anymore.

"Where was it?" He asked.

Stanlowsky's eyes opened enough for Hughes to see that they were denim blue. Plenty of color, but no emotion.

"Sorry?" he said, as if he didn't understand his question.

"The car. Where did you find it?"

"I believe it was at the airport, in Roanoke," Stanlowsky answered. He sounded guarded.

"How about the person driving it? Any news on—" He almost said her, but kept it to "that."

Stanlowsky eyed Hughes for a few seconds. He'd been asked by the FBI person on the telephone to detain him, and now, Stanlowsky was wondering what Hughes had done, and if he was dangerous.

"Sir, if you'll be patient," he said, "I'm sure we'll all find out what's going on."

The trooper's tone of voice, suspicious, added to Hughes' nerves. He considered getting up and walking out of the building, then wondered what would happen if he tried to leave.

"Please," Stanlowsky said, reading the edginess in Hughes' posture. "This won't take long."

It didn't. At 10:55 A.M. the door to the office opened and a coffee-colored Jamaican in a tan suit entered. The suit was double-breasted, and had the quiet, fashionable shine of a good synthetic, while adding breadth to his slim chest. His patterned tie fell even with his belt. He addressed Stanlowsky first, but there was something dismissive in his tone.

"Sir, thank you for your cooperation. I'll handle this from here." Then, without offering any explanation to the trooper, he turned to Hughes. "Mr. Hughes, are you ready to go?"

Hughes knew him as Larry Fingers, although his real name was Finners, or Finnis. He'd been with the NSA for a little under a year, mostly in the field, and Nick had never been certain as to what his job was. The fingers tag had come as a result of his long, refined hands and manicured fingernails, always neatly trimmed and highly glossed. He was a handsome man, if somewhat delicately featured, one of those black men whose refined nose and thin lips made him look like he'd been born with the wrong skin color. He also had one brown, and one blue eye.

Hughes stood up and followed Larry Fingers out of the office, down the corridor, and through the entrance doors, out into the daylight. His BMW was parked in front of them, in the lot.

He turned to Fingers and asked, "Where is Casey Armstrong?"

Fingers looked nonchalant.

"I don't know anything about that, Mr. Hughes. My brief is to return with you to Meade. That's it."

Fingers removed a set of keys from his pocket. They were hanging on a string, bearing a tag that was stenciled with the BMW's government license plate numbers. He handed them to Hughes, saying, "Sir, would you care to drive?"

They rolled out of the parking area and onto the main road, which intersected with Highway 81. It was a fairly straight run to Meade.

"Would you please take Route 311 north," Fingers said, as they approached the cutoff.

Hughes glanced over, frowning.

"But that's going to lead us back up into the mountains."

"That's the route I've been ordered to take," Fingers replied.

Hughes looked again at his passenger. It was the blue eye that gave it away. It held the fire. The brown was flat and all business.

Hughes exhaled and smiled, as though he'd just caught onto a particularly sick joke. He was going to die. This is how they did it. It was going to happen to him. For some reason he felt relaxed, as if a weight had been lifted, a responsibility removed.

He said, "You know, Larry, there's something that
I've always wondered. What exactly is it that you do for a
living?"

Fingers hesitated, as if the question had taken him
off-guard.

"Security stuff," he replied slowly and softly. "Taking
care of loose ends. Picking up stolen cars."

They both laughed, but it was the kind of joyless
laugh that served only to reestablish a somber equilibrium
between them.

Then Hughes asked, "Is Casey Armstrong still alive?"

"I don't know a Casey Armstrong, sir," Fingers
replied, tightening up again. "I've been assigned to you."

They were about three miles into the mountains,
winding and climbing, when Larry Fingers said, "Would you
mind pulling over? I need to urinate." He was not a great
actor, and his somber tone of voice, and choice of words,
added a finality to his request.

Nick shifted his eyes, glancing quickly from the road
to Fingers's lap. His right hand, long and fine and manicured,
was stretched lengthwise along the thigh of his trousers, while
his left was inside the pocket of his jacket.

That's when the nerves really hit. It was as if they had
been lying in wait, conspiring against him, lulling him into the
false sense that he could handle whatever was ahead, accept
it. When they pounced it was sudden and ferocious, biting a
hole in his belly. He was like everybody else, small and scared.
Very scared.

"Okay, next clear spot," he replied, trying to tell
himself that this wasn't happening. Maybe it was paranoia.

He glanced again, quickly. There was a bulge in the
pocket of Fingers jacket. It was some kind of compact,
Hughes reckoned, maybe a hammerless thirty-eight.
Something he could fire from inside his pocket, with no
trigger to tangle on the cloth, and a hollow point bullet in the
chamber.

Even as the thoughts formed, Fingers shook his head,
and said, "Please, Hughes, I'm really very uncomfortable."

Hughes nodded. He could sense it. Feel it coming. He'd probably get hit a few seconds after they'd stopped. The moment he threw the car into park.

"I'll be very quick," Fingers added. It sounded like a reassurance. There, up ahead. About a hundred yards. I see a spot."

Hughes thought of flooring the accelerator, taking Fingers with him on a one-way flight into the valley below, but even this close to death, he was clinging to something, some vague hope of reprieve.

Finger's firmed up.

"Pull over, Mr. Hughes." His voice left no margin of doubt.

Hughes slowed the car, listening to the gravel grind against the tires. He saw the blue sky and skeleton trees with their branches reaching toward him then stopped about twenty feet from the lip of the drop-off. It was a magnificent view.

A hawk circled above as he put his foot on the brake and his hand on the shift lever, looking at Fingers, straight into his mismatched eyes.

Nicholas Douglas Hughes. He'd never had so much of a sense of himself, of who he was, what he was, both coward and hero. He looked away from the eyes, to the valley and the sky, then back again.

"We're right out there, on the edge, aren't we?"

"Yes," Fingers answered.

Hughes looked down to see the tip of the two-inch barrel, pushing out against the fabric of Finger's suit, stretching the shining fibers like a final punctuation.

Nick Hughes. His book had been written. He thought of Casey. She had been the most important relationship of his life, and he hadn't even known it. Not till now. He should have been kinder, gentler. He should have been stronger. She'd been the love of his life. She had been his chance at being whole. But that chapter was finished, and past, present, and future were crystalizing.

"Has it got to happen this way?" he asked.

"Please, sir, put the car into park."

Hughes turned toward Fingers as his right hand slid the gear stick forward. Then with a shout, he turned the twisting motion of his body into a lunge across the console, his left fist flying toward the Jamaican's throat.

A silent flame burst from the barrel of the thirty-eight, and for Nicholas Hughes, time stopped.

Casey thought she was having a heart attack. The pain was so sharp and intense, causing her to double up, rolling forward in the airplane's seat, clutching both hands to her chest. Nick Hughes? His face flashed in her mind and she wept in a single, purging gush. Then, as quickly as it come, it was over, and the pain inside her was gone with her tears. She sat up. Nick? She turned to look at the vacant seat beside her, as if she was going to see him sitting there.

Maybe she was crazy. She had considered that many times in the past weeks. Whatever had been done to her mind, in Montauk, and at the hospital, had, conceivably, damaged her irreparably. Perhaps she had been operating from some compromised perspective and perhaps that explained her compulsion to get to John Reed. There were a thousand voices in her head telling her to turn around, to save herself, but there was also another voice, a voice that called from another place. Was that the voice of the madwoman? Loud and demented, without restraint or boundaries, demanding that she step beyond what was sane and wise, beyond the fear that could save her and participate in this one final act.

~ 19 ~

It was just after 2:00 P.M. in Colorado Springs. The sky was a lifeless gray, settling down above the mountain peaks like a full belly, and the forecast was snow.

Thomas Reed had carried a stack of logs in from the pile behind the house, lit a fire, and he and Molly were sitting, facing each other, on the twin living room sofas. Their chat had been relatively light, about property prices and California, San Diego in particular. The West Coast had always held a fascination for Thomas. It had only been the ocean that had stopped him, and now, thanks to John, that fissure inside had been healed. Maybe they'd head west. To start fresh. Again.

Things had eased between them in the past days. Molly had relaxed, frequently leaving John alone with Thomas. There was a sense of peace between them, and now that the Barnes investigation had taken a path away from their door, there was also a glimmer of a future. The calls from the press had become rare, and the hate mail now consisted of the occasional, barely literate letter. The short attention span of the world outside had been a surprise to both of them, and, in this case, a welcome one.

John Reed was asleep upstairs, connected to his parents by the small white plastic, Fisher-Price monitor that sat on the low walnut coffee table between them.

At first Molly thought that John had moved, maybe lifting his arm and striking it against the side of his crib, causing the dull thudding sound that came from the monitor,

but when it happened a second time, she put her coffee cup
down and stood up.

"I'll just check on him," she said.

Thomas had heard it, too.

"He's just restless, moving around in the crib. It's
nothing," he commented, wanting to get back to their
discussion about San Diego. The idea of eighty degrees and
sunshine appealed to him, particularly today.

"I'll be right back," Molly insisted.

She walked up the four steps that separated their
living and dining room. From there she could hear without
the monitor. She listened again. There was definite
movement, like a shuffling against the floor, the squeak of
wheels and John's strangled cry.

She took the winding steps two at a time, turning at
the top to see the door of the room closed. She hadn't left it
that way. Twisting the knob, she pushed it open and
screamed at what she saw.

The tall figure stopped in midmotion, staring at her
through the eyes of the knitted hood of a balaclava, the baby
wrapped in a blanket and tucked, slinglike, into the open
chest of a bomber jacket.

The other gloved hand was gripping the frame of the
opened window with its thin, white curtains whipping and
snapping in the wind.

The moment froze, then splintered as the fast, heavy
footsteps came behind her, followed by Thomas's voice.

"What the ... Call 911!"

He rushed past her, brushing hard against her
shoulder as he dove for the leather-clad arms that held his
son, trying to get a grip, to prevent an exit as Molly began
screaming.

"My baby! Oh God. Don't hurt my baby!"

There was another sound, a dull whir, like the hum of
an electric razor, turned on and off quickly and Thomas
straightened, staggering backward, away from the gloved
hand and the rounded tip of the pronged weapon.

"What have you done to him!" Molly shouted, as her
husband fell in front of her, convulsing for a moment before
he lay still.

For an instant, Molly interpreted compassion in the shadowed eyes, because as they met hers there was hesitation, as if a decision was pending. Then, instead of turning and escaping through the window with the wailing infant, the figure turned, and walked quickly toward her, rubber-soled training shoes mute against the pine wood floor.

"My baby. Give me my baby," Molly demanded, extending her arms. She found John's eyes and saw the glaze of fear that covered them. "Please don't hurt him."

The gloved hand came forward quickly and unexpectedly, before she could react. Making contact with her forehead, the metal prongs were cold and hard against her skin.

Once, when Molly had been a child, she'd stuck a hairpin into a light socket. She'd never forgotten the feeling—the surge of electricity, alive and vibrating, magnetic in the way that it seemed to attach itself to her fingers, like the razored jaws of a serpent. Grabbing on to her, entering and slithering through her body to attack every nerve.

Now, as the prongs came alive, the serpent bit again.

It was bitter cold, the wind was howling from the southeast, and the snow was blowing through the opened window. Flakes were landing on the floor and melting, small drops joining to form a puddle, as Thomas Reed dragged the deadweight of his body through the cold water and across, toward Molly. He reached for her, but his arms, hands, and fingers felt detached, as if he was piloting some sort of robotic device, masquerading as his body.

"Molly?" Even his voice sounded far away and disconnected.

"John?" she murmured. "John."

Thomas turned his head toward the opened window and the truth hit him with the icy wind. John? His son was gone.

He dragged himself to the night table and pulled the cord that brought the telephone crashing to the floor. Lifting the handset he fumbled. His eyes would not focus on the digits on the receiver. He couldn't do it. John.

They took my son. He had to get help, had to. Slowly he pressed "9" then "1" and "1" again, mumbling his address to the voice on the other end of the line.

The report of the kidnapping reached Yale Lochart five minutes before the telephone call from Preston Dix.

The message was brief. Casey Lee Armstrong had escaped a special escort transporting her from a high-security unit in Virginia to another unit in Maryland and was believed to be currently in the area of Colorado Springs. She was government property and Dix requested the help of the Colorado Springs police in apprehending and detaining her. It was to be the same procedure as last time, solitary confinement, until an agent arrived to take her into custody.

But this isn't the same as last time, Lochart thought, angered by the dry authority of Dix's tone. The stakes had shot up. There was a baby missing. There was a mess on his plate.

"Mr. Dix," Lochart began. "We've had some developments here that alter things considerably."

"I'm aware of the developments at the Reed house," Dix replied. "That is precisely why I'm asking for your cooperation. We need a low profile in this matter."

"If the kidnapping is corroborated, we're following procedure and bringing in the FBI," Lochart threatened.

Dix hardened. "I'm ordering your cooperation, sir. Our group overrides the FBI in military matters and this is a high-security military operation. Everything is on a need-to-know only basis. You'll do what you're told."

The last remark infuriated Lochart.

"Who the fuck do you think you're talking to?"

Dix's tone changed. It seemed to soften.

"Mr. Lochart. Isn't it true that you have an eighteen-year-old-son? My records show his name to be Samuel. Isn't it also true that in November of 1997 Samuel was arrested by Officer Ronald Delgado while operating a motor vehicle on Highway 24 while under the influence of alcohol and in possession of four grams of cocaine?"

Lochart went silent. He'd buried his son's case personally. Pulled every string and called in every favor. He had made the evidence disappear. Only a few people in the department had ever known about it.

Dix continued. "I show here that the case never went to trial and that his arrest records have been expunged. I can't understand how that would be possible, but I do know that if the matter came to light again, and if there was an inquiry, his future at the academy in Quantico would certainly be in jeopardy. They don't take well to felons in the federal agencies ... I don't believe you would fair too well, careerwise, in this matter either, Captain."

Lochart felt caught. Still he tried not let his feelings seep through to his voice.

"What do you want?" he asked.

Dix continued. "I should be with you, personally, within two hours. Perhaps, I can be more satisfying then. In the meantime, do as you have been told. We're in charge here."

Lochart put the phone down and walked straight from his office to Caruso's desk.

"We've got trouble."

Caruso looked up. The officer responding to the "911" had phoned in. Thomas and Molly Reed were being attended to by paramedics, John Reed was missing, and Michael Caruso was on his way to the crime scene.

"Yes, I know," he replied.

Lochart contradicted him. "You don't know everything. I just had a call from the same supercilious government prick as last time. Demanding our help in bringing in Casey Lee Armstrong. She's here, in the Springs."

Caruso tensed. Now it made sense.

"She's got the Reed baby, right?"

"That's what I figure," Lochart replied. "I need everybody we've got. Get her picture circulated ... But no FBI. This is military. They've got jurisdiction. "

Caruso was about to stand up when his telephone rang. He picked it up, listened a moment, then waved a finger at Lochart, cupping the phone with his hand. His tone was incredulous.

"I've got her on the line right now."

Lochart looked confused.

Caruso met his eyes, and lifted the hand that was blocking the phone.

"Yes, Ms. Armstrong," he said. "I'm here. What can I do for you?"

Casey was on a pay phone, directly in front of a Starbucks. She knew that she was running out of time. She was desperate and Caruso was her last hope.

"What's happening at the Reed house?" she asked.

Caruso's tone remained noncommittal. "The Reed house? I don't follow you."

"There are police cars all over the place. Tell me what's happening?" she demanded.

"Where are you?" Caruso asked.

Lochart remained still, standing above Caruso's desk, willing the detective to keep it together, not to spook her.

Casey was getting a feeling in her stomach. Caruso was different from last time. Something was wrong.

"Why do you need to know where I am?" she asked.

"Because I want to help you."

"Then tell me," Casey demanded. "Did something happen to the child? Something's happened to John Reed. Am I correct?"

Caruso looked once at Lochart, then spoke again.

"Ms. Armstrong, this conversation has got to be face-to-face. I've got people very close to me, here, listening. I can't talk freely. Tell me where you are."

She thought a moment, and couldn't find an option.

"Will you come alone?"

"Trust me," Caruso replied.

She insisted, "Alone. It's got to be alone."

"I promise," he answered.

Casey looked out at the six-lane highway, then up at the street sign. She felt like she was giving herself up, and prayed that she wasn't.

"I'm on North Academy Boulevard. In front of Starbucks coffee. I'm not sure of the exact number—"

"I know where it is. Hold tight. I'll be there in a few minutes."

Caruso put the phone down and looked up.

Lochart said. "The woman's a fucking lunatic and there's a kid involved. We've got to do this by the book."

"No, she's too smart," Caruso answered. "If I arrive in front of a car full of uniforms, she'll run."

Lochart considered. It was the baby that made it tricky. If it wasn't for that, he would have called stakeout.

"Okay," he agreed. "Go on your own but I want Adams and Lake to follow you in a plain car. You take her, but don't let it get sloppy. See if you can get to the kid. That's our primary concern." He stopped and looked hard at Caruso. He was trusting him with a lot. "Don't blow this one, Mike." Then, without waiting for a reply, he glanced across the office and motioned with his hand. "Neil, Dave. Come over here, please."

Casey sat in the parking lot, the doors of the rented Sunfire closed and locked, wondering how long she had this time, and what had happened at Reed's house. When she concentrated on John Reed, her feelings were of pure fear, fear so tangible that she felt she could follow it like a highway to him, but the highway was leading away, to the metal vat, and the slanted eyes.

When she saw the green Corsica pull into the lot she slumped down in her seat, keeping her head back and out of sight from the road. She watched as Caruso parked, turned off his engine, and stepped from the car.

He looked around, toward the pay phone, then at the street sign above the boulevard, as if he may have come to the wrong place.

Casey waited to see if he had been followed. Time passed and he was still alone, his face registering concern as he pulled out a pack of cigarettes, whacked one out against the back of his hand, stared at it, then tossed it to the ground before turning slowly, eyes searching. Until he was staring in the direction of the white Sunfire.

She stepped out of the car and waited for him.

"Ms. Armstrong?" his voice was cautious.

It was as their eyes met that Casey sensed the danger.

"Is the baby safe?" Caruso asked. There was assumption in both his voice and manner.

She remained silent.

"Ms. Armstrong, please place your hands on top of the hood of your vehicle."

She heard other footsteps, flat and loud against the asphalt as Adams and Lake ran toward them from the bottom of the lot.

"Don't do this," she said, reaching into her pocket for the Myotron.

The nickel plate on Caruso's gun flashed in the sunlight as he took a step back.

"Get your hand out of your pocket. Now! Up where I can see it. Both hands!"

Adams arrived first, with Dave Lake a pace behind. Adams patted her down while Lake stood, his 9mm Glock drawn and aimed at her head.

"This is a mistake," Casey pleaded, as Adams removed the Myotron from her leather jacket.

Lake answered. "It's always a mistake."

"Here. Some kind of stun gun," Adams said, holding the weapon with two fingers, up, so that Caruso could see it. "Same thing she'd used on the Reeds ... Now bring your hands down, and turn, facing the automobile."

There was anger in Adams' movement as he cuffed her hands tightly behind her back, so that the steel dug into her wrists. "Now walk."

Inside, she felt lost. It was all going wrong. Completely wrong. Everything was crumbling around her. She was too late.

Adams guided her roughly across the lot to Caruso's car. Once there, he placed his hand on top of her head and forced her down, making sure that she banged hard against the roof as she fell sideways onto the backseat.

Caruso caught Adams' eyes. "Take it easy."

"Easy?" Adams growled. "Give me a break."

Caruso reached in and pulled Casey into a seated position.

"Where's the baby? In the car? The trunk? Come on. Tell me. Where's John Reed?"

She looked up, into his eyes.

"Where is he?" Caruso insisted.

"I don't know," she answered.

Lakes' voice came from across the lot. "The car's clean!"

Caruso ignored him, trying again. "What did you do with the baby?"

Casey shook her head.

"I didn't touch him," she replied.

"What do you want us to do here!?" Adams shouted, standing there with Lake, beside the Sunfire.

Caruso turned away from Casey, toward them. "Lock it and leave it for forensics." A small group of people had emerged from the coffee shop, drawn by the action. A crowd. That was the last thing he needed. He slammed the door of the Corsica, sealing Casey inside, then climbed into the front seat, behind the wheel.

Adams caught up with him as he was about to start the motor.

"I ought to ride with you."

"I'm okay on my own," Caruso replied. He wanted time alone with her.

Adams stalled. "Lochart's going to shit himself if we don't follow procedure."

"That's my problem," Caruso replied. "Go ahead. Get going."

Reluctantly, Adams walked back and joined Lake in the other car.

Caruso watched them pullout, into the traffic, before he moved Casey to the front seat. He didn't want her out of his sight for a second. When they were finally on the road, he looked across at her. Her face seemed vacant. She looked broken.

"If you tell me where John Reed is, we can go there now and get him. Just the two of us. Come on, let's do that," Caruso coaxed as his radio crackled to life and a voice asked for his location. He ignored it, watching as Casey closed her eyes and bowed her head.

Her gesture gave him a sinking feeling.

"Is John Reed alive?" he asked.

She replied quietly, "I think so."

"Take me to him. It's going to make things a lot easier."

She stumbled inside as Caruso continued, "John Reed is not going to last on his own. He'll die. I don't want that to happen."

Casey raised her head and looked at him. "You don't get it, do you?"

Caruso kept cool. "What's that?"

She answered, "I came here to warn you. To warn his parents. I came here to protect him."

"Is that why you took him?"

The radio crackled again. It was loud and insistent, requesting Caruso's location. He went to respond when Casey said, "Let me make it clear to you, Detective. I did not take John Reed anywhere."

Caruso was losing the battle. His orders were to apprehend Casey Lee Armstrong and bring her back to the station. No heroics. No interrogation. He was running out of time. He ignored the radio and tried another tact—risking it—thinking that maybe he could push a button and break the dam.

"Did you kill the baby the same way you did the priest? Did you push a gun in his mouth and blow his brains out?"

She stared at him a moment, stunned. Then she lunged, headfirst across the seat, shouting. "You bastard!"

He shoved her back with his right hand, hard, using the heel of his palm.

"I've seen the FBI match on your prints," he said.

"What prints?"

"I don't know why you're doing it, but I know it's over," he continued.

Pulling the car to the side of the road, he slammed it into park and turned so that he could face her full on.

"Now listen. After we get to the station, I'm not going to be in charge anymore. There's going to be a lot of people. It's going get messy, but now, right now, it's simple. You and me. I want that baby. Take me to him."

Casey searched deep, trying to touch the truth inside him.

She spoke slowly.

"I'd need to be alone. To relax. To see if I could establish a contact—"

Caruso fought the urge to smack her.

"Stop fucking around with me!" he shouted.

His words felt hot against her skin.

"I'm not fucking around," she answered.

He let out a long breath, reaching across to take hold of her collar, gripping it tight.

"Lady, I'm getting impatient."

She held his eyes.

"Detective Caruso ... I broke away from a security guard in Virginia early this morning. I arrived here less than an hour ago. Check my air ticket, it's in my pocket. Whatever happened at the Reed house had already happened by the time I got there. I promise you I didn't touch that child .... We're wasting time."

Caruso swallowed and released his grip on her collar as he reached into her pocket, pulled out the folded air ticket, and studied the times. That part was true. She'd been in the Springs only fifty minutes. Hardly long enough to kidnap the child, hide him, call him at the station, then wait in the parking lot. Unless she'd had an accomplice? He studied her eyes, searching for the con.

"If I could just relax," she continued. "Then I could try to connect with John Reed ... maybe get a bearing on his location."

What if what she's saying is true? Caruso wondered. He considered taking her someplace, maybe the mountains, or the park at the foot of the hills, some place peaceful and solitary, just for a while. At least then he would have tried everything. An hour. An hour and a half. If only he could steal the time. Then his cop voice cut back in, overriding, telling him that an hour could mean the difference between life and death for the boy. Maybe she already knew where he was. Maybe she was tricking him, intending to use the situation to fake a recovery or to create an alibi. He was wrestling with his decision when he saw the car drive up behind them.

It was Adams who jumped out of the passenger side and ran toward them, his weapon drawn.

Caruso rolled his window down and shouted out.

"We're all right here! Everything is under control."

Adams kept his gun exposed, but dropped it to his side.

"What's the delay? he asked. "Why aren't you reporting in? Lochart is going nuts."

Caruso picked up the handset to his radio and called in his location, then ended his communication with, "I'm on my way."

Casey sunk down against the seat. The ax had fallen. It was over.

Caruso looked at her once more and said, "I don't know what else I can do."

~ 20 ~

Yale Lochart was standing there, in front of the main desk, red in the face and seething.

"What the hell are you doing to me, Detective?" he asked, as Caruso, flanked by Adams and Lake, marched Casey into the building.

"Trying to find out the truth," Caruso answered.

Lochart cocked his head back. His nostrils flared, his lips disappeared, and for a second, all that Caruso could see was a crooked row of stained bottom teeth.

"I've just had the governor on my telephone," he hissed through the cracks. "He wants a resolution."

"So do I," Caruso answered. "The right one."

Lochart eyed him, then looked at Casey as he said, "Neil, Dave, lock her up. Mike, you come with me. We need to talk."

Caruso let go of Casey's arm. He couldn't bring himself to meet her eyes. Somehow, he felt like a coward, a terrible coward. The feeling was eating him alive. He was walking away, copping out.

"I'd like to ask Ms. Armstrong some questions," he managed. He sounded, to himself, like a fighter who was waking up from a knockout, and asking if he'd won. Pathetic. He bolstered his voice. "I'm not happy, Captain. Things don't feel right. Not at all. I need to talk to Ms. Armstrong."

Lochart met Caruso's eyes and worked his mouth into a semi-smile, stepping aside, as he did, to allow Adams and Lake access to the door leading to the holding cells. He maintained his position while they led Casey by. Then, Lochart relaxed his shoulders. He seemed to lose height as he did, sinking down, inside his jacket, before reaching out to gently grip Caruso's biceps.

"Mike. You need to talk to me. You really do. Let's take a walk. Get some air."

They walked out, onto South Nevada, and turned left, continuing for five minutes in silence.

Finally, four blocks away from the police building, Lochart stopped, turned to Caruso, and said, "Don't worry. We're going to get the girl back."

Caruso looked at him.

"What do you mean by that?"

"Casey Lee Armstrong," Lochart replied, letting the name hang on the end of his breath. "Once the government people have held her for a while, a day, maybe two. Once they've questioned her." He hesitated. "You know. Interrogated her." Stalling again. "Christ, done whatever the fuck they're going to do with her. After that, we get her back. You follow? We get the collar, and we get closure to the Barnes murder, the kidnapping, we get a result. But for now, we've got to cooperate."

Caruso smelled it, the stench of a lie.

"I don't believe that Casey Armstrong took the Reed baby," he said.

Lochart could feel it building in the back of his throat, like a lump. He wanted to spit it out, to tell the self-righteous prick in front of him that his son's career was on the line, that his own was too, that he'd better shut the fuck up and play ball.

"The baby's dead," Lochart said.

The words went straight to Caruso's stomach. He thought of John Reed. His wonderful blue eyes. The eyes that had looked into his soul. The eyes that had saved him from himself. Then he felt tears well behind his own.

"Oh Jesus ... do his parents know?"

"It's not official, just you and me right now," Lochart answered, looking down at the pavement, then out to the street. "I've spoken to the government people twice since you went after Armstrong. The first time to a psychologist from the bureau and then to an officer with the agency that employed Armstrong as a psychic. This is very serious, very heavy business."

Caruso didn't seem to be listening.

Lochart squared his shoulders and lifted his head, saying, "We need them to close the case, and they need us."

Caruso flared with anger.

"What the hell is this?" he asked. "Some kind of game? In case you haven't noticed, nothing about it works, time sequences, motives, nothing ... "

"Mike, please, let's quit while we're ahead. We're going to make an arrest. Christ, even the governor's freaked. Everybody wants this thing to go away. Far away."

"Yeah, but it's all going to come right back and smack us in the teeth. We can't put Armstrong on trial. You've said it yourself. She's not under civilian jurisdiction."

Lochart took a step closer, looking around again, as if to avoid being overheard by the vacant street corner.

"There won't be a trial. There'll be an official statement. That takes care of us. Armstrong is insane. She gets locked up in some military facility and nobody ever sees or hears from her again. It's over. Finished."

Caruso looked down, at the shadows below Lochart's eyes, and said, "The only problem is, Yale, I don't buy any of it."

"Yes, that is a problem," Lochart shot back. "But it's your fucking problem. I told you before, there's a limit here, and we just hit it. Time's up."

He turned and began to walk back toward the station.

Caruso called after him. "What happens if I keep going?"

Lochart turned again to face him. His eyes were hard and hateful. "You're out. That's what happens. No messing around, I'll get you kicked right off the force. You got that?" Then his eyes softened a shade. "For Christ's sake, Michael, what's done is done. Stop it."

Caruso saw them as he entered the station. The younger man appeared to be in his middle to late twenties; he had very short, sandy hair and his body, even under his winter parka, looked

hard and tough, right down to the thick ligaments and veins that
spread like roots from his wrists, out. onto the tops of his hands.
He was wearing high Timberland boots, with his pressed blue
jeans tucked inside the tops, managing to give his clothing the
appearance of a military combat uniform. He flicked his eyes in
Caruso's direction. They were dangerous eyes. The kind that
Caruso had seen on the streets, wary and ready to strike, with no
gap between thought and action.

The other man was tall, wire-thin, and ashen gray—
skin, eyes, and hair—wearing a wool, single-vented suit and a
maroon ascot tie. He carried a walking cane and spoke with
what sounded, at a distance, to be a mild, Southern drawl. In
spite of his obvious eccentricity, there was a weight to him,
something insinuating in his presence.

They were at the entrance desk, talking to Lochart,
who was standing, arms folded in front of his body. He
looked defensive and obedient, like a whipped dog.

As the conversation ebbed, Lochart turned and
acknowledged Caruso, who had remained on their perimeter.

"Gentlemen. This is Detective Caruso. He brought
Armstrong in. Mike, this is Mr. Dix and Mr. Ames."

Dix nodded, and Roy Ames eyed Caruso suspiciously,
as if he could sense trouble.

Caruso stood silently. He understood immediately
why Lochart was threatened. There was a ruthless quality to
both of the men, mixed with an aura of power and
superiority.

"Detective Caruso," Lochart continued, "would you
go upstairs and send Adams and Lake down."

Caruso hesitated as the three men stared at him, until
their eyes became a unified force.

"Please, Mike we're in a hurry," Lochart added.

Caruso turned and walked away, up the back stairs,
down the corridor, into Homicide.

Lake and Adams were inside the office, standing in
the corner by the filing cabinets, talking. They stopped as
Caruso entered. He looked at them and said, "Lochart wants
you guys downstairs."

Adams caught his eyes.

"Are you okay?" he asked.

Caruso replied, "No," walking toward his desk.

Adam continued to look at him. "I'm sorry, I didn't mean to get on your case out there today," he apologized. "It was just that Lochart was jumping all over us."

"Don't worry about it," Caruso answered. His tone changed, becoming more forgiving. "Look, Neil, he's down at the desk right now, shitting in his pants. You'd better go and help him out."

"Okay," Adams said, turning to Lake.

"By the way," Caruso said, as Adams and Lake got to the door, "has forensics gone over Armstrong's car?"

"They're working on it now," Adams answered.

"I see," Caruso said, watching them leave before he went to his desk and took his notebook from the drawer. He started by writing Casey Lee Armstrong's name at the top of the page, filling in the lines below with what he knew of the kidnapping—approximate time, location—followed by her call to the station, fifteen minutes later. How long had she been at Starbucks, wondering what to do, waiting? How long would it have taken to have rented a car, driven from the airport to the Reed's house, climbed to the roof, stolen the baby, deposited it, driven to North Academy? And then why would she have called him? He studied the page, like it was a particularly frustrating jigsaw puzzle. Then he opened his drawer again and took out the FBI sheet and stared at the print match. It was perfect, no doubt about it, but something still nagged at him. Standing up, he walked to the corner of the office and faxed the sheet through to one of his friends in forensics.

Mter that, he went to the window and looked down. He could see them below, Casey Armstrong, still cuffed, flanked by Adams and Lake, being escorted from the building. The man who had been introduced as Ames was following behind them. A few paces back, Lochart and Dix appeared to have used up their conversation. They were walking together solemnly, the silver-handled cane punctuating their cadence. The whole scene reeked, even from the second floor.

Caruso was about to turn away, when Ames lifted his
hand, aiming his remote at the black Jeep Cherokee.

There it was. The missing piece. Glaring up at him.
The broken rear taillight.

"Hold on!" Caruso shouted.

His voice bounced off the heavy glass of the window,
as the men continued toward the vehicle.

Next, he tried to open it, but the frame had been
painted shut and it wouldn't budge, so he pounded on the
glass till he thought it would break.

Ames put Casey in first, still cuffed, while Dix got in
the backseat, directly behind her. Then Ames walked to the
driver's side, climbed in, closed and locked the doors, and
started the engine.

By then, Caruso was running down the stairway,
stumbling as he sprinted toward the main door.

"Stop those motherfuckers!" he shouted, hurtling
from the building. "Pull 'em over!"

Lochart turned. At first he was scowling but as
Caruso charged forward, his expression turned to panic.

Caruso's voice was breaking with effort. "Goddamn
it! That's the Jeep!"

The Cherokee was twenty yards from him, on its way
out of the lot as he sprinted behind it, drawing his weapon as
he ran.

"Stop!"

"No. You stop!" Lochart shouted. Turning to Adams
and Lake he said, "Get him!"

Lake hit him first, tackling him from behind, above
the knees, and Caruso fell as the thirty-eight flew from his
grip, landing on the asphalt and discharging. The bullet went
wild, missing Lochart's right knee by inches, while Caruso
sprawled forward.

"What are you doing! They're getting away! Goddamn
it, they're getting away!" he repeated, over and over again, as
Lake and Adams hustled him to his feet.

"You're out of control, Detective!" Lochart shouted,
his mouth only inches from Caruso's left ear.

"That's the fucking Jeep that was following Reed!"
Caruso shouted back. "Don't you understand! Those

motherfuckers know. They know!" he said as he was shrugging Adams off and struggling with Lake, watching as the Cherokee pulled away.

Lochart stepped back as the two cops lifted Caruso in the air, one controlling his arms, the other his feet.

"You don't understand," he continued to protest. "This is all wrong. It's a setup!"

Lochart looked out to the road. The Jeep was gone, and he hoped his problems had gone with it.

"Get him inside," he ordered. "Take him to the tank and let him cool off."

Caruso struggled but they held him firm.

"What is it, Lochart? Are you on their team? Are you with them!?"

The captain looked down at him contemptuously and said, "Get him the hell out of here."

~ 21 ~

Caruso sat on the cot, inside the holding tank, with his head in his hands. He'd seen it. The car. The missing piece. The single thing that could have ended his nightmare. A black Cherokee with a broken taillight. A license plate that had begun with GOV. It was not a coincidence. It was exactly the vehicle that Thomas Reed had described. But who was driving it on the day of the Barnes murder. Was it Armstrong? Had she killed the priest, then returned to the Reed house for the baby? There were elements that didn't make sense. Who were the government men, Ames and Dix? What were they doing with the Jeep? Unless they'd been in on it, with Armstrong, from the beginning. Or, maybe Armstrong was telling the complete truth. Where were they taking her? What had Lochart said? A day, two days and they'd have her back with a full confession.

Caruso thought of John Reed for a moment. It was as if the infant was his own flesh and blood. That beautiful baby boy. Those wonderful, healing eyes. Why?

He sat with his elbows supported by his knees, his head in his hands. He felt sick inside, sensing the futility of his circumstances. When he finally looked up, he was facing the same wall that Casey Armstrong had faced only minutes before, the same graffiti, the same names and dates.

It was a terrible place to be, broken inside, helpless and lost. What had he done? To Thomas, Molly, and John Reed? To himself? He'd blown it Fucked their lives. Fucked the case, his job. He stared at the plaster wall, seeing his own turmoil reflected in the gray. Looking at. ... He sat up straighter. Looking at ... he hadn't noticed it before. How could he have? He had been so absorbed in his own thoughts, his own world, his own self-pity. But there it was, scratched into the old paint, staring him in the face.

He stood up and walked closer, kneeling down. Fixated.

The markings were fresh, and the plaster had flaked around them, making the lines appear as if they had been scratched into the wall with a fingernail, or perhaps a pin, but the numerals and letters were clearly discernible, 38N 104W. Caruso had the feeling that they were supposed to mean something to him but he was drawing a blank as to what. Beneath them was a simple sketch of a two-story building and something that resembled the outline of a horse's head. If Casey Armstrong was responsible for what he was looking at, then what was she trying to tell him? He remembered their first conversation, in the car, on the way from the Reed's house to the police station. She'd said that she worked with geographical coordinates. 38N 104W. Where were they?

Seconds later he heard footsteps in the hall, coming in his direction. Then the lock snapped back, the door of the holding cell opened, and Yale Lochart was standing in front of him.

"Mike, you're out of here," he said. Then the gruff voice softened. "Go home and take a few days off. Get some rest."

Caruso caught Lochart's eyes long enough to see the guilt inside them, like a nervous flicker. There was also something else, maybe fear, but he couldn't hold on to them long enough to decide.

"What's going on, Yale?"

Lochart shrugged the question off. "Nothing," he answered. "See you later."

Caruso was walking past him when Lochart said, "Oh yeah, this is yours," handing him his thirty-eight.

Caruso assumed the gesture to be a show of trust but he couldn't see behind Lochart's mask.

"Thanks," he said, taking the gun and holstering it as he continued to walk, out through the entrance of the

building, stopping long enough at the desk to pick up a road
atlas and locate a US map.

The coordinates weren't hard to find. In fact he was
standing on them. It was Colorado Springs, but the low, flat
building could have been anything, and anywhere in the area.
Then there was the other drawing, the one that looked like a
horse's head. That had to be significant. He turned to the
man in charge and asked. "Does a horse's head mean
anything to you? Is it some kind of symbol, or maybe a
landmark?"

The old hospital was situated directly off the single-lane road that
had taken them by a small, red brick guardhouse and through the
main gate of the compound. It was a two-story, wooden
structure, built during the Second World War, and sometime,
during the past ten years, had been issued one coat of white
paint, but now most of that had peeled, revealing the old primer
beneath. The windows were boarded over and it appeared barren
and deserted, like a discarded relic from another time.

It was as Ames turned into the driveway that Casey
first noticed them. They seemed to be part of the shadows,
moving in zigzagging bursts toward the car.

Ames proceeded, leaving the broken concrete of the
main drive and continuing into the dirt and to the side of the
building, then hugging tight to the rear wall. He got midway
along its length, parked, shut off the engine, and sat silently a
moment as the human net closed around them.

There were two to the front of the vehicle and three
more to the sides and rear, dressed in black, their faces
concealed by balaclavas, squatting down, and aiming their
scope-equipped rifles at the Jeep.

Ames turned to Dix. "Sir?" It was the first time
anyone had spoken during the twenty-minute ride.

Dix replied. "Yes, very effective. Very impressive.
Now, go call them off."

Ames looked at Casey, glancing down to ascertain
that her hands were still manacled and secured, then opened
his door, stepped out, and began walking toward the men.

Dix waited till he was several feet from the car before
he spoke again.

"Young lady, you must be very confused."

Confused and terrified, her mind had been a tangled mess since they'd left the police station, but now that they'd entered the military compound, her other senses had begun to overpower her feelings of self. It was Montauk, happening all over again, and Dix's lazy accent was like a drill, digging into her buried stores of memory. She twisted her body against the steel cuffs, until she could see his face across the divide in the seats.

"Who are you?" she asked.

Dix smiled. He wanted her to talk, to cooperate. If there was one thing that George had stressed to him, it was the importance of her frame of mind before a tasking. He could be honest here; he could afford to be.

"I am a member of an organization that has been looking after you for a long time."

"And what organization is that?"

Dix smiled again; he felt very powerful.

"Think of us as a group that supersedes nationality and religion." His voice was as calm as still water, with no trace of Southern accent. "Think of us as the enlightened ones."

"I don't know what that's supposed to mean," Casey responded.

Dix contradicted her gently.

"Of course you do. You know that our world is made up of information. That's been your job. Supplying it. And you know that those who control information have the power over those who do not. Some information belongs to the masses and some is forbidden ... I am one of the keepers of the forbidden."

"I don't understand what that has to do with me," she said.

"We need a conduit to knowledge that, so far, we have been unable to access," Dix answered. "We're counting on you, Doctor." There was a zealous belief behind his eyes.

Casey studied his face, trying to get a fix. What she felt chilled her. There was death all around him.

"How does John Reed fit into this?" she asked.

"That answer would influence your tasking," Dix replied.

"Why here?"

She looked from the window to the derelict building.

Dix followed her gaze, his voice reflecting the irony of their surrounds.

"Yes, you would think that with the resources at our disposal, we could provide a more modern facility." Then his tone firmed. "Anonymity is what we value above all else, Doctor. No red tape, no prying eyes. We go where we are required."

"I don't understand," Casey answered.

"You don't need to," Dix replied curtly. "Just know that the work you will do here, will be the most challenging and important work of your life."

"And then what are you going to do, brainwash me and give me back to Nick Hughes?"

She'd thought about him a lot in the past hour. Nick must have been controlled by these men, locked into a situation without room for compromise. She could almost forgive him.

"Is that the drill?" she asked.

Dix's face never shifted from neutral as he placed his hand on her shoulder and squeezed. His touch brought the darkness back.

"Be assured, Mr. Hughes is out of your life."

"He's dead, isn't he?" It was something that she had sensed but never truly faced.

"Mr. Hughes is no longer with the program," Dix answered.

Then, while she was still reeling, he lifted his cane and tapped on the window opposite him.

Ames turned at the sound and walked to the car. Opening Casey's door, he gripped her roughly by the arm.

"Be careful with Dr. Armstrong," Dix said, as Ames pulled her from the vehicle. "She's just had a shock."

They entered through a back door that had been fitted with security locks, then followed the beam of Ames's Maglight across a dusty wooden floor and through a labyrinth of interconnecting rooms until they arrived at another locked door. Security cameras had been installed above it and they had been standing only a few moments when it was opened and Professor George filled the frame.

"Dr. Armstrong, I am so very happy to see you," he said, a pretentious quality to his voice.

Dix turned to Ames. "Would you please remove the handcuffs from Dr. Armstrong."

Ames took the key from his pocket and freed her wrists. They were numb at first, then the pain came in hot, sharp bursts as her circulation returned.

Dix continued, looking at Ames. "Now, if you will secure the building, we can get on with our business."

Ames nodded, said, "Yes, sir," turned, and walked back through the hallway as Dix ushered Casey into the room.

It was furnished with a metal desk, three collapsible chairs, a small Sanyo tape recorder, twin portable speakers, a microphone, and a monitoring screen.

"We'll keep track of your session from here," George explained.

"What happens if I don't want to perform?" Casey asked, looking for some type of leverage, as the old Montauk fear began in her belly. "Or, if I can't?"

Dix replied, "Somehow, I don't think that's a possibility."

"I need to know more," she demanded, looking at George. "You can't just switch me on, you know that. I've got to feel right. I've got to be able to let my mind go. I can't work if I feel intimidated."

George answered, "I understand, but I'm sure that once you receive your tasking, things will more or less settle into place."

"Like last time?" Casey asked, lifting her hand to display her scarred palm.

Dix's eyes bore into hers and she could feel his will, like a tangible force between them.

"This is a different type of tasking," Dix said, "and you will cooperate." Then he walked across the room and, with the handle of his cane, rapped on an adjoining door. There was no response, so he rapped again.

It opened, and Ken Mishima stood, holding a long strip of paper between the thin fingers of his right hand. He ignored Casey's presence and spoke directly to Dix.

"I've been working with low-frequency flashes of light, and I've never seen anything like this. When stimulated, the alpha reduction in peak power in the right hemisphere is minus sixty percent—"

"Please," Dix interrupted. "Speak in plain terms."

Mishima scowled, but his expression was temporary. He was too excited to hate anyone, even Dix.

"Its brain is a storage cell for latent electricity, with perhaps 60 to 80 percent more potential than any subject I have ever documented, including ... " He finally acknowledged Casey, looking in her direction. "That includes Dr. Armstrong ... and that's in spite of the medication."

Mishima walked closer, so that Dix and George could see the electroencephalogram, allowing Casey a chance to glance down at the sequence of tiny spiked patterns.

"That's from John Reed, isn't it?" she asked.

"Yes," Mishima replied.

She looked toward the adjoining room.

"Is he in there?"

Dix exhaled. He had anticipated problems with Armstrong and, now, he feared they were about to begin.

"Yes, he is," George answered.

"I want to see him," Casey said, starting toward the door.

"You will," George assured, gripping her by the elbow to stop her. "We have you set up in the next room."

She looked at him. "Set up?"

"For the session," George explained. "Please, let me take you in."

She shrugged his hand away, knowing that her only weapon was her refusal to perform.

"What kind of session?" she asked.

"Doctor," George insisted, "let me show you where you will be working."

She turned and met his eyes. Sublimating terror with resolve she said, "I'm not going through another Montauk. I won't do it."

"You don't have to," he assured her. "This is different, very different. Please, let me show you."

He took her by the arm and guided her toward a second door, located to the extreme right of the desk.

Inside, the room was small and visually opaque.

It took her a moment to realize that she was, in fact, standing in a dull metal box, illuminated by two overhead spots, casting a soft, yellow light.

"It's double-walled steel," George continued. "We want you to be acoustically and electrically shielded, no outside influences to prejudice the contact."

Aside from a lushly upholstered armchair, positioned dead center in the beam from the spots, the square space was empty.

"Please, sit down. Be comfortable."

Casey looked up to see the glass eye of a camera following her movements. It was fastened to the track that held the spotlights, and beside it, to either side, were what she assumed to be twin sound sensors.

"What exactly do you want from me?"

"The best way I can put it," George replied, "is to say that we want you to conduct a psychic interrogation. Now please, sit down."

Casey settled into the soft chair as George removed a small object from his pocket. Bending over her, he slid the hand containing the object up toward her ear. At first she thought it was one of the devices from the Montauk session and she pulled away.

"Please, Dr. Armstrong. It's only so you can hear us. It's an audio receiver," he explained, showing her the flesh-colored instrument. "Here.. Place it in your right ear."

She touched it cautiously. Then, lifting it up, she inserted it.

"Good," George said. "I'll go out and get the levels, then we can begin."

Casey looked up at him and said, "I want to see the baby."

"Relax, Doctor," George replied.

"I want to see John Reed."

Her words fell dead in the vacuum of the room as George closed the reinforced steel door behind him.

They set the voice levels and increased the intensity of overhead light, enough to assure a clear view of the session for the audio-visual recording that would be overnighted to the principals at Neo Tech.

Casey sat and waited. Closing her eyes, she settled back into the cushion of the chair. She was frightened, but she was also excited as she heard the door to the room open, the metal edge of the bottom scraping against the metal floor.

Looking up, she saw that George was carrying something in his arms, a small bundle, wrapped in a blue woolen blanket.

Her respiration accelerated and she could feel her heart pounding.

"Dr. Armstrong," he said, leaning over, "I have something for you."

He placed John Reed in her arms.

Finally, she thought, cradling him. *Finally*. She looked down into a face that she felt she had known forever. The features were set against a fine pink skin that looked unusually stretched and thin, perhaps, she thought from dehydration, but in spite of that he was beautiful in a way that defied definition. He seemed somehow ancient and new, both at once, as he molded naturally into her body. His proximity made her feel both protected and protective.

His eyes were open but there was a dullness to them.

"What have you done to him?" she asked.

"Dr. Mishima has been running some tests," George replied. In fact the infant had been sedated shortly after Ames had acquired him. It was in an effort to subdue the aura that the baby seemed to project. It was something that had caused all of them to feel uneasy, indefinable, but it had been there, hovering like a presence around him, threatening their intention, and making their work difficult.

"I'll leave you now," George said, and walked from the room.

Casey cuddled the child close to her while George, Dix, and Mishima studied the monitoring screen, noting the complete relaxation of her facial features. It was almost a surrender, as if she had entered a state of rapture.

"I'd say she's ready to proceed," George commented.

"Get her to talk," Dix ordered.

George picked up the small microphone and depressed the button on its side. "Dr. Armstrong," he whispered. "Dr. Casey Lee Armstrong."

She could hear the voice inside her head. It was already difficult to differentiate between internal and external stimulus. Something was happening to her. Some type of metamorphosis. She knew where she was and she knew that she was being monitored, but that no longer mattered.

"Dr. Armstrong?" George repeated softly.

~ 22 ~

Everything felt like it was dissolving around her.
"Can you tell us what you are experiencing?"
George's voice sounded far away, and the question seemed ludicrous. She was in another land, a land of colors, layer upon layer of red and blue, green and orange, indigo and violet, all the colors of the spectrum, dancing before her like luminous ribbons.

"Where are you?" George asked with increased volume. He could feel Dix bristling beside him.

"Dr. Armstrong, please concentrate."

Concentrate. Casey could hear music, like wind chimes, with notes so full and refined that they seemed to wrap around and envelope her with their vibration. She listened. *Concentrate.* It was George's command that was the catalyst, causing the ribbons of light to stabilize and form images.

Her mother was sitting at a great black Steinway, her hair pulled back and tied in a bun, her long hands moving fast and gracefully along the keyboard. *Concentrate.* She was playing Chopin, a ballad in G minor and Casey was a little girl, seated in the front row of an auditorium. She could feel the soft cushion of the chair beneath her, and smell the perfume, like lilacs, from the redheaded woman who sat directly to her left. Her father was seated to her right; he looked young, his skin smooth and tanned and his hair shiny and black. As the notes from the piano swelled and warmed the air around her, he reached and placed his hand gently on top of hers.

She was experiencing more than memory; it was a shift in reality. Casey was there, inside the scene, experiencing the excitement and joy that she had experienced then, as if every emotional nuance had been stored in a capsule in time, and she had reentered the capsule. She could feel the music inside her, it seemed to vibrate through the pores of her skin, filling her and returning something to her that had been lost and forgotten. She stared at the stage.

Her mother was looking at her, smiling. Then, as if by some gravity, Casey was floating forward, toward her mother as the music changed key, shifting from G minor to A major. It was a prelude, still by Chopin, a shorter piece, less than a minute in length, and one that Casey had mastered as a teenager.

Then Casey was playing, her fingers dancing across the ivory. Playing. Something inside her had been reborn, a part that had been closed down and sealed had been pried open, and Casey Armstrong was whole again.

Dix stared at the monitor's screen then checked the audio speakers.

"Do you hear that?" he asked. "Do you hear music?"

"It's Chopin, I believe," Mishima answered.

"But where's it coming from?" Dix asked.

George turned to him and replied, "It appears to be coming from inside the RV chamber."

Dix looked back at the screen. God almighty, it looked like Armstrong was dancing in the chair, holding the child and swaying back and forth, with some kind of beatific grin on her face. He leaned forward, closer to George, and spoke sharply.

"What the hell is happening in there? Get her to talk."

George depressed the TALK button.

"Dr. Armstrong. Can you hear me?" His voice was barely below the threshold of a shout. "Can you hear me?!"

Casey's eyes snapped open as the words shot through the microphone, disrupting the music.

The chamber became silent again.

"Dr. Armstrong?" George said.

"Yes?" Casey answered reluctantly as the black-and-white keys became wispy waves of light beneath her fingers.

"Please, Dr. Armstrong. Listen to my voice."

Casey snapped to attention, sitting up in the chair, suddenly aware again of where she was and what she was doing.

"Describe what is happening?" George continued.

Casey looked at John Reed and spoke the first words that entered her mind.

"We are being offered a new understanding of our world."

"What do you mean, a new understanding?" George asked.

Casey inhaled. The child was perfectly still against her chest and so light in her arms that she was unaware of his weight, yet he seemed to be controlling her mind easily and completely, making her a conduit to his knowledge.

"There is so much energy here," she said, gazing into the swirls of interconnecting light.

As she observed, the light separated and took form, as if shaped by the power of her mind. She thought of Nick Hughes and sensed his presence in the room.

George's voice was a whisper, "Look at the upper left corner of the screen, just above her shoulder."

Dix and Mishima followed his eyes.

"Do you see a shadow?" George continued.

"I see a dark area," Mishima agreed.

Dix had begun to feel threatened, as if whatever was inside the chamber had the power to burst through its steel walls.

"What's going on in there?" his voice waivered. "Get her back on target."

The image on the screen appeared to be solidifying and gaining in definition.

"What is it?" George asked.

"I don't know," Mishima replied. "It looks to be taking the shape of a human body."

"It's a man. I can almost make out the features of his face," George said.

"Impossible." Dix's voice was sharp. "Make her stop." He was not in control and his anxiety was bordering on fear, an emotion he was not used to dealing with.

"Stop what?" George asked, fascinated by what he was seeing.

"Whatever the hell she's doing," Dix said.

As he spoke Casey seemed to enter a deeper trance state, her body slumping down in the chair, and the sound of her breathing became distant. She could see him now. Nick was standing beside her.

"She's going to drop the baby. Get her attention!" Dix insisted.

John Reed slipped lower inside her arms.

"Dr. Armstrong!"

George's voice was like a cold blast inside her ear.

She sat up, clutching the child.

"Talk to me, Dr. Armstrong. Talk to me." George continued. "What are you experiencing?"

His voice was jarring and it seemed to drag her back into another frame of time. Her body felt stiff and she was aware once more of her confinement, inside the steel box. She sensed energy, like an electric cocoon around her, as the image of Nick Hughes faded, then disappeared.

"Describe your experience," George demanded.

She composed herself, bringing her rational mind back into play, replying, "It seems I am able to manifest my own reality. My thoughts become my world. I believe that is the lesson that John Reed has been sent to teach us."

"Sent?" George repeated.

"Yes,"

"Sent by whom?" he asked.

It was as if the knowledge was all around her, part of the energy that filled the room, like a spinning record. If she tuned in to the frequency, the answers to his questions were there, inside her mind. She had never been more clear, or more positive.

"By a life force that has existed and shaped us from our beginnings," she replied. "A force that supersedes our material reality."

Dix looked over at George, who appeared preoccupied with what was happening on the screen and through the monitors.

"Get everything on tape," Dix said. "Audio and visual. No mistakes. I want this."

George quickly checked his equipment.

"Everything's rolling," he answered, returning his attention to Casey.

"Then what is John Reed?" he asked.

Casey looked down onto the crown of the child's head. The energy seemed to be concentrated there, a visible, swirling pool of light, and as she inhaled, it rose toward her nostrils like a smoky silver thread. Entering with her breath, traveling inside her, down her spine and into her limbs, expanding her and filling the expanse with energy. She had never known such energy—pure and powerful.

She answered, "John Reed is a flesh-and-blood manifestation of a higher, more evolved level of consciousness."

"Where did he come from?"

Casey lowered her head, so that her forehead was in direct contact with the crown of the baby's head. Closing her eyes, she concentrated on Molly Reed, tuning into her thoughts and perceptions.

She was in Mexico City, standing in the street, among closed shops, parked cars, and a throng of people looking skyward as the clouds parted and the moon began its journey across the sun. Then there was darkness. A darkness that sent a shiver of trepidation through her body.

"We're losing the picture," Dix said. "Do something."

George adjusted the tracking knob and attempted to adjust the contrast, but within seconds the screen had faded to black.

"It's not a technical problem," George answered. "I think it's happening inside the chamber."

As he finished speaking the screen burst back to life in a sequential explosion of lights, until the glass appeared to glow with a white incandescence.

At first she thought it was a star, or a ball of fire, but as it descended, coming closer, it began to take on a different shape. What was it? She'd never seen anything like this and she was consumed by a fear unlike any she had ever known.

It was a fear that seemed to touch the core of her being and dissolve it. She was looking at an airship of some sort, a great triangular silver wing with windows and lights, hovering in absolute silence above her. It was not of this Earth. That much she sensed. "Our father who art in heaven." She began to recite the Lord's Prayer. "Our father who art in heaven." She repeated the six words over and over again, too terrified to recall the rest. Praying with her brain on overload, as the lights of the craft began to change, to blink in a sequence of colors. White to ruby-red. Ruby-red to blue-violet. Violet to white, and over again—sending a signal to her brain, causing another alteration in frequency and unlocking another gate to her consciousness.

Then she was going up, into the craft. There was a humanlike figure in front of her, with very thin arms, and no hair on its head. A voice told her not to be afraid.

"But you have no right to do this," she protested.

"We have every right," the voice answered.

"Oh, good Lord, I see it. I see it."

Casey was rearing back in the chair, still clutching the baby, staring straight up into the lens of the camera.

"You're not putting that thing into me!" she screamed.

It was sparkling at the tip and looked sharp. It was coming right at her.

Casey pushed back against the seat. Her legs seemed locked, straight out and open. She felt a burning in her womb as the face looking down at her became more clear within her field of vision, more delineated. She'd seen the face before. It was not developed like hers. The head lacked hair, and the nose seemed disproportionately small for the breadth of the cheekbones. The mouth was more implied than actual, like a thin, dark slit, and the eyes were almond-shaped shadows. She knew the face. She had drawn it once, sitting at the desk in Montauk.

It was the face of the fetus. The face of John Reed.

Then the face faded from her mind and Casey felt as if she was awakening from a dream.

It left her alone inside a wash of light. It was the clearest light that she had ever known, radiant, yet without heat or glare, like a luminous sky above her, free of clouds and mist.

It was a pure and simple place; it was home, the source of her consciousness.

She wanted to stay, but even as this desire dawned she felt herself slipping back, away from the light, being drawn through a tunnel of thought and memory, carrying the baby with her.

Carrying him back from his source.

The picture on the monitor returned as if the channel had been switched, showing Casey, still holding the infant, looking straight up into the camera.

"John Reed is the first to survive," she said. "The first born."

"First born of what?" George asked.

"Of the next phase in the evolution of the human mind," she replied.

"Is he some form of extraterrestrial biological entity?" George continued.

Casey looked down at the baby while Dix leaned across the console and depressed the "talk" button.

"Answer the question," he demanded.

Casey closed her eyes. Her mind had become a direct channel to the child and for a moment she was looking at the fiery wheel, descending to become the silver-winged spaceship of Molly Reed's memory. It hovered in front of her and then splintered into filaments of light. She watched it dissipate and dissolve inside the darkness. Then she understood. It was perception. Imagination flowing into reality, sculpted by the human mind. Time and space; past, present, and future. All of it was no more than a dream. She understood this in one spontaneous burst of revelation. Yet she could not find the words to convey it.

"Is John Reed extraterrestrial?" Dix intoned.

Casey could hear the answer coming in a thousand voices, all speaking at once, as if trying desperately to get through to her.

John Reed is a flesh-and-blood manifestation of a higher consciousness acting upon the human mind. He is an avatar, a messiah, sent to bridge the gap between man and a power that man calls God. He is thought. He is energy. He is body. He is the evolution of human consciousness. John Reed is the future.

As she concentrated, the voices seemed to converge, until there was only one. Her own.

"You continue to ask me if he is extraterrestrial. What does that mean to you?" she asked, suddenly awed by the infant in her arms, by the strength of his mind and the enormity of what he represented.

"Does he come from beyond the limits of this earth?" George asked.

She hesitated, acutely aware of the fear building on the other side of the metal wall.

"Answer the question."

What could she say to them? They could not hear beyond the limits of their understanding. They wouldn't.

Casey sat upright, eyes open, staring at them through the eye of the camera.

"Yes, he does," she said finally, her voice flat.

■ ■ ■

Mishima sat with his back straight, pressed against the chair. His specialty was human consciousness. For years he had worked with the mind, with drugs and hypnosis, studying perception and memory, distorting them to create subjective realities. Yet, on this day, he had witnessed what he believed to be a demonstration of the mind's ability to create an objective reality, followed by an explanation that challenged the limits of his reason. It was as if his entire system of belief had been rocked at its foundation and was now teetering on the verge of collapse.

George was a behavioral psychologist. Humans were like any other animal to him, accurately studied only through the examination and analysis of their observable, objective behavior. He was dry and calculating and, until Black-Out, he had scoffed at the idea of remote viewers, putting their success rate down to chance coincidence. Now he had been confronted with something he could not explain in objective terms, or in fact within the parameters of anything he had studied or learned. He felt suddenly small, threatened, and utterly insignificant.

The silence held until Dix spoke. "Stop the tape and end the session," he said. He was a military man. He'd heard Casey's final answer and his thoughts on John Reed had ended. The baby was a hybrid, half human, half E.T., and Dix was already planning his next move, which was to get John Reed to a secure facility in Virginia.

He also considered Armstrong's fate. She was gifted, but so was the viewer prepping at the hospital. The cover-up would remain. They would hand Armstrong over, Just as he had promised Yale Lochart.

Blythe-Saaxon had informed him that Neo Tech was already arranging a permanent facility for the infant while at the same time continuing their work on the implants, attempting to reverse the process used to engineer them, and decipher their technology.

In the meantime, they needed to observe John Reed, to study him as he developed and matured. That would be the only way they would learn the extent of his capabilities, and his purpose on Earth.

~ 23 ~

Caruso pulled off 115 south, and stopped on the shoulder of the road. Iron Horse Park, with the metal horse's head hanging above its entrance, was about five hundred yards to the east, across the highway, on the perimeter of Fort Carson. There were two buildings near it, an elementary school and a derelict hospital. The hospital was a two-story building with a flat roof, similar to the structure that Casey had etched into the cell wall.

In the early pitch of evening, Caruso could just make out the small gatehouse, separating Route 115 from the single-lane road that led into the compound and, beyond that, through his field glasses he could see the black Jeep, parked beside the hospital. He'd found it. Now he wondered what kind of security they'd have. His question was answered a few seconds later by the appearance of two figures, clad in black, and carrying rifles, walking the perimeter of the building.

M14s, Caruso figured, *probably with night vision, and infrared*. Whatever they were doing, and whoever they were, they were deadly serious. Another thing troubled him. Once beyond the gate, he was off civilian turf. Lochart had been right; it was military business, and suddenly as he weighed his intent against their consequences, he realized just how personal the entire situation had become to him.

During the ride down, he'd been having deep doubts, questioning his own motives. Still he had continued, telling himself that he'd just check it out. Maybe the guy on the desk had been correct about the horse's head, maybe not.

Now as he opened the door of the Corsica and stepped into the cold realization that he was about to cross another boundary, he reminded himself that he could still turn back. He could still phone in the possible whereabouts of the missing child and the suspect, Casey Lee Armstrong, then leave it for the army to act. That would be the correct thing to do.

He reached back inside his car and picked up his phone, punching in the number for Homicide at South Nevada while keeping his eyes trained on the hospital building. He was going to be smart.

Neil Adams answered the phone.

Caruso stalled.

"Adams, Homicide," he repeated for a second time.

For a few seconds Caruso didn't know what to say. Was he about to hand over the reins and hope?

"Neil, this is Mike," he began. " ... Earlier today, before the shit hit the fan, I faxed forensics the FBI printout on Armstrong ... Did anything come back?"

"Yeah, it did," Adams replied, his voice anxious. "There must have been a screwup with the FBI match, cause the prints our guys lifted from the car and the stun gun weren't even close to the ones you brought back from Denver."

"So she didn't kill the priest," Caruso said.

"They weren't her prints on the weapon, that's for sure," Adams answered.

"Thanks, Neil, thanks a lot."

"What the hell's going on?" Adams asked a dead phone.

They'd been quick, entering the room unexpectedly, George gripping Casey's wrists while Mishima slid the needle into her vein.

Now, above her, two cold eyes studied and assessed her condition.

"How do you feel, Dr. Armstrong?"

The smell of spearmint covered her face like a vaporous mask.

"I feel sick."

"That will pass," Mishima assured her, reaching to the side of her head to slip the receiver from her ear.

"Where's the baby?" she asked.

"Waiting for you, in the other room," Mishima replied. "Are you able to walk?"

Casey attempted to stand but her coordination was gone and she pitched headlong toward the floor. George caught her from behind, beneath the armpits, and hauled her upright.

"I need a hand here," he said.

Mishima assisted him, and together they piloted her toward the door.

Mishima injected her with Demerol and Vistaril to sedate her, followed by Versed to induce an amnesia.

Blackness followed. It was more than sleep; it was a sort of death, as if she had been submerged in a thick syrup, a place where time ended.

Mishima looked down at her. The next phase of the electronic dissolution was crucial, it was a static jamming that would wipe out sight and sound, creating an opening for the hypnoprogramming. He held three thin wires in his hand, each ending in a needlelike probe.

The points of the probes sparkled beneath the overhead lights as he inserted two of them into Casey's temples, just under her skin. The third he pressed into the top of her skull.

The portable generator, positioned beside her, had been primed for two hundred volts. He timed the charge for six seconds and threw the switch.

There was an explosion of light and for an instant Casey could feel her fingers, toes, the muscles of her thighs and stomach, all contracting at once. She bit down hard and tasted rubber. There was something in her mouth, like a padded blade. Then blackness swallowed her.

Her next sensation was a pressure against the outside of her eyes, as tweezers squeezed the lids, lifting, first one then the other, then someone peering in. It was if she was adjusting the lens of a camera, the way the face came into focus. Eyes first, yellowish brown and slanted, then the pores of a nose, open and oily, and the surrounding skin, smooth, too smooth, like a sallow wax hardened against bones, as it backed away from her. She saw a syringe, with its thin needle dripping a clear fluid. The fear that it inspired was without an intellectual framework. It was animal fear, pure and instinctual.

He bent over again, too close to her face, like he was going to kiss her.

"I'm going to introduce a thousand micrograms of DMT," Mishira, explained to Dix and George, hoping to improve upon the Montauk procedure. "This is an interesting substance." He talked as he slid the needle into her carotid artery. "It's a tryptamine that occurs naturally in the human brain, also in the spinal column. As strong a hallucinogen as LSD." He projected a false confidence into his tone. Since the RV session he'd felt strangely impotent. "Time ... time is a curious thing," he continued, depressing the plunger. "The human brain perceives time as a straight line, past to present, when in fact, it's no more than a random series of events. We live episode to episode." He removed the needle, tossing the used syringe into a disposal before turning to Dix. "She's ready. We can begin the reconstruction."

After that he was gone, as if he'd dropped through a hole in the floor, and Casey had the feeling of floating, with nothing beneath her or to her sides, until another face appeared above, looking down. She knew him, too. It was just that she couldn't place him. He had ashen skin and gray hair, parted to the side, and he spoke with a slight accent.

"Why did you murder Robert Barnes?" The why sounded like 'wha.' 'Wha' did you murder?

Murder? What was the man talking about? She hadn't killed anyone. She'd never killed anyone in her life. Her mouth opened in protest. She could feel the folds of flesh at the top of her windpipe, forming her vocal cords; they felt like a thick, rubbery obstruction as she strained to speak and nothing came.

"Tied him up," the voice continued. "Rammed a shotgun into his mouth and pulled the trigger. He was a priest. A man of God."

They worked and reworked the scenario, over and over again, until she was inside the picture, walking the steps

between the chapel and the rectory, raging because Robert
Barnes had called attention to John Reed, her target. Carrying
the stolen shotgun in her hands, forcing it down the priest's
throat before she'd pulled the trigger. Watching his blood
splatter against the wall, dripping down the wooden crucifix.

There was a Kevlar vest lying near the spare wheel, and a gun
case next to it. Caruso removed his jacket before putting the vest
on. He was beginning to feel the nerves inside. He'd been in five
fire fights during his two tours in Southeast Asia and he knew
that nothing ever prepared you for bombat. No amount of
training, no simulated action ever even came close.

　　He tightened the upper buckle on the vest, feeling the
adrenaline rising like a second tongue in the back of his
mouth, tasting its bitterness as he told himself that he could
still turn around and drive away, yet knowing somewhere that
he'd made this decision long ago. Maybe it was up in the
mountains, with the gun in his mouth, or maybe in the car
after the boy had touched him, when he'd felt that he could
hold the moon in the palm of his hand. Nothing had been
quite the same since that night. The doctor in Denver had
tried to tell him about lead poisoning, but Caruso had doubts
even then. It had been something else. Something no doctor
could explain. Something miraculous.

　　He looked up at the sky. There was enough moon to
give the scopes plenty of light, so his only chance was on his
belly, moving from the shrubs on the perimeter of the
grounds, then in, following the line of shadow. He'd try to get
to a window well, then climb down, into the basement.

　　He lifted the gun case and unzipped it to remove a
pump-action Remington that he'd borrowed from stakeout
before going after Armstrong. After that he grabbed an old
hunting jacket; it was dirty, and it smelled of mildew, but it
was a dark green plaid, and tonight, dark was what he wanted.
He put the jacket on over the vest and zipped it tight before
walking to the shoulder of the highway, beside the car. There,
he squatted down and dug with his hands, managing to
scrape enough dirt and mud to darken his face.

　　He had a feeling of abandonment as he jogged across
the highway to the outskirts of the base, and by the time he'd

stopped, the hospital had become a dark silhouette in the distance.

He looked one more time at the building, eyes searching for movement, then he began to think of John Reed, and the memory of the infant solidified his resolve.

The ground was frozen and he bruised his knees and scraped the skin from his elbows, right through the coarse fabric of his jacket. Once, as he drew the Remington back with the pumping pulling motion of his arms, he touched the barrel to his mouth and the metal froze against his lower lip. He ripped it free, taking a piece of his lip with the gun.

He was fifteen minutes in, stopping and starting with the movement of the clouds against the moon, more than halfway to the hospital, and too far gone to change his mind and retreat.

He'd counted five men, dressed in black with their faces covered, moving like shadows as they hugged tight to the perimeter of the building. He tried to calculate the intervals between them. They were short, maybe twenty seconds, maybe less, but he figured if he could get close enough without being seen .... If he could get within ten yards, then he would risk a standing sprint, hoping to God that there was a window well at the end of his run. If not, he was going to be stuck behind their line, with the wall to his back. Not much more than a stationary target.

It took what felt like eternity to crawl the next section and by then the guards no longer looked like abstract figures. They were trained men with rifles, M14s, just as he'd thought. He remained still, partially hidden by a mound of earth, steeped in snow from the last fall, and close enough that if one of them had turned and looked through his infrared, Caruso would have been a sitting duck. But the loose formation continued its snakelike rotation, with only the occasional turn of the head, oblivious to his presence, secure in the belief that their whereabouts was a secret, and that no one would be curious or foolhardy enough to crawl three hundred yards on his belly to find out what was going on inside a derelict building.

That thought sustained Caruso through a burst of
moonlight that made him feel twenty feet tall and buck
naked, forcing him to kiss the ground, until the blessed
clouds rolled back in and he could move again. This time he
was quick, not wanting to risk another exposure, crawling fast
for twenty yards. Close enough that he could hear the dull
clumping footsteps of the guard directly in front of him and
the crackle of a walkie-talkie followed by a thin, metallic
voice, declaring, "We're clear on the west side."

Caruso rose from his belly to a crouch. His legs felt
stiff, as if the muscles in his thighs and calves had locked up
and his knees had become suddenly arthritic, but the feeling
lasted only the time it took him to take the first three steps
forward, his eyes searching the darkness for the next man in
line. Unsure if it was his shoes smacking against the ground
or his heart against his rib cage, or maybe it was his lungs
pumping air, but the chugging sound was like an echo in his
head as he sprinted for the shadow of the building, making it
to the wall and looking desperately for a way in. He was on
the verge of panic when he saw the window well a few yards
away. Dropping to his belly he crawled for it, dragging the
gun to his side. He arrived a few seconds before the next
guard rounded the corner then dove headfirst into the well.
Scrambling to his knees, he squatted low with the gun in his
hands, and was staring straight up when the beam from the
Maglight hit him.

The soldier's voice was low and hoarse.

"Drop your weapon. Stand up."

Caruso released his hold on the shotgun and threw
both hands in the air, surrendering.

"Don't shoot me," he stammered. "Please, don't
shoot."

~ 24 ~

A one-month-old baby," Dix vented, outrage spilling through his voice.

"You sick bitch."

Another voice came from behind her. This voice was deeper, and smooth in texture.

"Do you remember the house? It's a crazy, lopsided-looking place, made of cedar wood, with lots of glass. The house looks like a broken pyramid. You've been there. Do you see it?"

From somewhere to her side she heard a low, droning sound as the generator was primed. Followed by a blinding flash of light as her body convulsed and her mind turned to static.

George looked down as Casey Armstrong floated naked in the vat of saline-based solution. It was buoyant, and thermostatically controlled to duplicate the exact temperature of her body, which effectively removed the boundaries between her flesh and the liquid, creating a weightless state of heightened mental sensitivity.

George waited till her eyes had focused then held something above her face.

"Do you see the house?"

It looked like a photograph, but it had dimension. It was hovering in the space above her, all by itself, with its pitched roof and odd angles.

"There is a baby inside that house. His name is John. He belongs to you."

She felt a dull sense of recognition as George continued. "There's a window on the second floor. It's a sliding window and it leads to a small bedroom. Inside the bedroom is a king-size bed and beside it, there is a crib. The baby is asleep. He's beautiful ..."

Her mind created images as his voice held to a steady singsong rhythm, until she was looking through a pane of glass at a baby with blue eyes and golden white hair. She felt a desperation building, a need to possess the child.

"There's a mobile hanging above the crib. It's four bears, blue and soft and cuddly. When you wind the key, a song plays."

The music came in waves, thin and tinny. It was a melody, without words, but she knew the song, and she knew the lyric. "Row, row, row your boat, gently down the stream. Merrily, merrily, merrily, merrily, life is but a dream."

"John belongs to you," George said.

The baby raised his arms toward her as the tinny music echoed in the background.

"Climb through the window and take back your child."

She was hovering above the crib, looking down.

"Take him." The voice was insistent. "He belongs to you."

She bent forward and picked John up. His breath was rapid and shallow and he felt soft, without weight as his tiny body molded to hers. She did know him. They were connected. He did belong to her, but as she turned to leave the room a woman raged toward her, a stranger with intense, frightened eyes. Then, from nowhere, a man lunged.

Another flash of light, another moment without sight or thought, and she was on the ledge, with the baby in her arms and the wind howling in her face, losing balance, falling, as the house began to crumble beneath her.

The ground opened as she hit, swallowing her up, as reality collided with delusion and she lay still, staring up into a white void. Then a face took shape; it seemed to assemble itself from the particles of air above her, as strong hands removed John Reed from her arms, then lifted her from the debris.

His eyes were brown and his skin was bruised and streaked with mud. His voice was soothing.

"Come on, Casey, you're going to make it. Just keep walking. That's right. You're doing fine."

She was lucid only for brief patches as she struggled through the darkness, wrapped in the Kevlar vest and a woolen coat that covered her naked body.

Caruso's distraction at the window well had lasted long enough for the soldier to have a moment of indecision, allowing him time to rise up, clearing the well with his shoulders as he'd looped his right arm around the man's ankles and jerked him forward, feet first. After that he'd moved behind him to intertwine his arms around the thick neck, and squeezed with all his strength.

The man had struggled, hunching his body forward, and Caruso had held on, ripping a muscle in his own back before the guard had lost consciousness. Now, as Caruso cradled John Reed in his left arm and supported Casey with his right, while keeping a grip on the Remington, it was only adrenaline and determination that held him together.

He'd come this far. He was going to make it.

They arrived at the rear door of the hospital. He'd seen the Jeep parked outside.

"Keep going," he ordered Dix. "We're going to walk out of here, climb into your car and drive away. If this turns into a war, I promise that all of you will die. That's a guarantee. Do you understand?"

There was no reply.

"Do you understand me, Mr. Dix?" Caruso asked. The baby was silent and still, like deadweight in his arm.

"Yes," Dix answered.

"Now open the door."

Without hesitation, Dix stepped forward and threw back the locking bolt, pulling the boarded door open to let the cold night rush in.

Caruso continued. "Keep going, very slowly, toward the Jeep." He guided Casey forward.

They had just cleared the building when there was a sharp, snapping sound, followed by a flood of blinding light.

Beyond the light, there was nothing, except a voice, clear and commanding.

"Release your hostages."

Caruso moved tighter behind Dix. His mouth had gone dry, and his words came hard and gruff as he spit them into the gray man's ear.

"Tell them to kill the lights and lower their weapons."

Dix stared into the light and said nothing.

"Mister, you're going die." It sounded like an oath as Caruso jammed the barrel of the Remington into Dix's kidney.

"No lights. No shooting," Dix said. He didn't sound convinced.

"Louder," Caruso urged, his finger tight to the trigger.

"No lights. No shooting!"

The lights died with the thunking sound of air being sucked from a jug, and as Caruso's eyes recovered he could see the hazy outline of the men. Two were standing, and two were positioned in a duck squat, rifles aimed. The Jeep was fifty feet to his right, while Ames stood, arms folded across his chest, directly in front of it.

"Tell them to lower their weapons," Caruso said.

Dix looked at Ames.

"Every fucking one of them," Caruso ordered, knowing that if he showed a grain of weakness it was over.

Dix nodded and Ames unfolded his arms to reveal an Army Colt. He popped the clip, then released the single round from the chamber before dropping the gun to the ground. A moment later his soldiers lowered theirs.

Caruso pushed Dix with the Remington's barrel.

"Walk to the Jeep," he ordered, then as they neared the vehicle he asked, "Where are the keys?"

Ames looked at Dix and wondered what had gone wrong. Until this moment he had believed in the immunity that Black-Out had guaranteed him, from both civilian and military law. If the operation went sour, he wanted out, without complication. He considered an order to fire, to kill them all, but he was wary of Dix, even in death, uncertain as to his affiliations, and the repercussions of his act.

Dix felt the moment of indecision.

"I want the keys. Now, Mr. Ames," he demanded.

Ames reached slowly, and reluctantly, toward his belt and removed the key ring.

"Open the doors of the Jeep," Caruso ordered.

Ames pressed the remote and the door locks disengaged.

"Now open the tailgate, then the car doors nearest the building, front and back."

"Quickly," Dix added. "Let's get to the end of this charade." To him, this was an inconvenience, not much more. Ultimately, the policeman was powerless.

Ames opened the doors, and Caruso guided Casey to the rear of the vehicle, helped her in, then put the baby in her lap. His instructions to her sounded sharp. "Hold him tight."

Then he ordered George to climb onto the roof.

George balked.

"Get the fuck up there," Caruso said, pointing the gun at him. "Then lie down and hold onto the rack."

George grunted his way onto the roof and spread-eagled himself, facedown, holding on.

Caruso shoved Mishima into the front seat of the car, and turned to Dix.

"Walk to the other side. You're going to drive."

"You have nowhere to go," Dix replied.

"Do it," Caruso ordered.

Dix obliged, dragging his cane with him.

Caruso turned to Ames, snapped the keys from his hand, and said, "If you start shooting, you're going to hit one of your own. That's a fact."

~ 25 ~

George lasted till they'd cleared the gatehouse, then he slid from the roof, hitting the ground feet first before falling onto his hands and knees.

"Keep going," Caruso ordered, looking back once to see George stagger to his feet, then fall again.

Dix drove to the intersection of Route 115.

"Turn right and follow the road," Caruso said.

John Reed was silent in Casey's arms. He'd been that way since Caruso had lifted him from her, in the vat.

"What kind of drugs did you give them?" Caruso asked.

There was no answer.

Caruso slid the Remington above the seat and prodded the back of Mishima's head.

"Every drug, everything you did. I want details."

He pushed hard with the gun.

"Talk."

The shock of their capture had worn off, and the fear that was pulsing through Mishima had little to do with Caruso. He was terrified by what he had seen and by what he knew about John Reed. He moved his eyeballs in the direction of Preston Dix, settling them on his profile, feeling him listening.

Caruso pressed harder, grinding the barrel inward.

"Talk, or I swear to God I'll kill you."

Mishima's voice sounded faint at first but as he went on, listing the chemicals and describing the procedure and the sequence of eletroconvulsive shock, it became very clear, resonating through the car.

It took them less than twenty minutes to get back to town, and after 115 had segued naturally into Nevada Avenue, Caruso ordered Dix to turn east on Boulder, directing him into the emergency ramp of Memorial Hospital.

Dix stopped in front of the glass doors and threw the Jeep into park. Turning, he looked at Caruso. There was the glint of self-righteousness in his eyes.

"Mr. Caruso. I don't believe you have the faintest idea of what you have just landed in. It's way above your head. Why don't you spare yourself a great deal of trouble and—"

"Shut up," Caruso said. "Now hit the horn and stay on it. Do it now."

It blared till two orderlies rushed out from the admissions hall.

Caruso opened his window to address them, holding his badge forward.

"This is a police emergency. I've got an adult and an infant in here. The child has been sedated and the woman has been given a hallucinogen. I'll phone the details in, but right now they need medical attention."

The orderlies helped Casey onto the pavement, then one of them removed the baby from her grasp.

Caruso watched through the glass doors of the hospital as two men in lab coats assisted Casey into a wheelchair while a nurse attended to John Reed.

After that Caruso turned his attention to Dix.

"Drive," he ordered.

Caruso, Dix, and Mishima had just entered the police building and into range of the security monitors, when Yale Lochart walked from the door at the side of the public-service desk.

He was holding up his hands, palms open.

"You can't bring them in here," he said.

Caruso continued forward, as if he either hadn't heard or understood.

"Detective Caruso, stop right there."

Caruso stopped as Lochart glared at him. The captain's eyes were tight angry slits.

"Do I need to spell it out for you?" He looked up at the security cameras. "Do you want it recorded for posterity?"

"They're my prisoners," Caruso answered.

Lochart's voice hardened. "Come over here, Detective."

Caruso pushed Dix and Mishima to the far wall, away from the door.

"You move and I'll shoot you," he promised.

Then he walked to Lochart.

Lochart lowered his voice. "I've got reports from Ft. Carson coming in by fax, phone, on the computer ..." He hesitated and lowered his tone even more. "You trespassed on a United States military base. You operated out of jurisdiction. You strapped a government scientist to the roof of a stolen car."

Caruso felt it coming. The inevitable. Still, he tried to reason.

"These people have the answer. They know what happened to Murray Rose, to Robert Barnes—"

"The dead man's name is Griffin George," Lochart continued, cutting right through him. "He was a professor of psychology, a former FBI employee. He was aiding in a classified investigation." His voice spit accusation. "Somebody put a bullet through his head."

Caruso felt the walls closing in.

"I was carrying this," he answered, raising the shotgun. "It's loaded with buckshot, not bullets, and I never fired it."

"It doesn't matter," Lochart countered. He was relieved to be out of it on a technicality, with no loss of face and his son's career, and his own, intact. "Lay the gun down. Don't make more of a screwup here than we've already got."

As Lochart spoke Caruso heard the squeal of tires from behind the door to the front of the building.

Lochart's eyes softened as he sensed the win.

"We can't hold these men," he continued. "That's a fact that you're going to have to accept."

Caruso was so close and he was going to lose it. He could feel his control slipping.

"They don't belong to us," Lochart went on. "This is government business."

"But they've been involved in two murders and a kidnapping, right here, in this town," Caruso answered. "I've got Armstrong and the Reed baby at Memorial Hospital. That kid's not safe. Not with them free."

Lochart had won and he knew it, enough to make a conciliatory gesture.

"Okay," he said. "I'll put a guard on the hospital. How many men do you want? You call it." He glanced in the direction of Dix and Mishima. "But as far as these guys are concerned ... They're out of here."

The door behind Caruso opened and Roy Ames entered the building. Their eyes met and Ames smiled. It was a cocky, fuck-you kind of smile. Enough to snap the last thread that was holding Caruso together. He raised the shotgun, stepped forward, and leveled the barrel at Ames' head.

"Here's your assassin. Here's your kidnapper!"

Lochart glanced to his left, at the man behind the desk, and nodded his head. The man reached down and pressed his panic button.

Ames' smile broadened, mockingly.

Caruso continued, but his voice sounded like a rant.

"You're under arrest for the murder of Murray Rose, for the murder of Robert Barnes, for the kidnapping of John Reed. Put your hands up above your head—"

The door behind Lochart opened and four uniformed officers swarmed into the room, weapons drawn.

"Detective Caruso, lower your weapon!" Lochart shouted.

Caruso ignored him.

"Put the gun down!"

The public-service rep ducked down behind his desk as the four officers took shooting stances, their handguns aimed at Caruso.

"This is insane," Caruso protested. "We've got the answers here, standing in front of us. We've got the truth. Jesus Christ, Yale, what's the matter with you?!" He felt like he was begging.

Lochart motioned with his right arm to the officer closest to him.

"Take the gun away from Detective Caruso."

"No," Caruso said, backing away. "Because it won't end here. It won't end in this building."

Dix's voice sliced the air between them. "Captain Lochart, will you please do what's necessary."

Lochart looked like a fox, caught in the glare of the hunter's torch.

"Mike, don't force me to—"

Caruso turned and bolted, pushing through the doors and sprinting for the black Cherokee. Climbing in, he started the engine, slamming the door shut as he skidded from the lot.

He drove hard, checking the rearview mirror, running lights, and taking to the sidewalk to miss a backup of cars before the turn onto Boulder. He was thinking of John Reed. Desperate to get to him before Dix and Ames.

Caruso made it to Memorial Hospital in ten minutes. Abandoned the car in front of emergency and ran into the building.

He showed his shield to the woman at the admissions desk, and asked, "Have you got security in here?"

She answered, "yes," and Caruso demanded that they be brought to him immediately.

There were three men and no guns. He showed them his badge, then explained as much of the situation as was necessary, including a physical description of Dix, Mishima, and Roy Ames. Telling them that under no circumstance was anyone to be given any information regarding the woman or the child, regarding their condition or whereabouts, and every visitor was to be referred to him.

A minute later Caruso was on the heels of an intern, running down a corridor lined with wheelchairs and trolleys, toward an elevator, then, up to a room on the first floor.

Casey Armstrong was asleep with two LV drips connected to her arms.

"How is she?" Caruso asked the attending nurse.

"Dehydrated," the stout, matronly woman answered. "And very disoriented."

"And the baby?"

"Surprisingly well," the nurse replied, her eyes flickering. In fact, the child had astounded her. He was so aware. She had spoken to him, reassuringly, as they'd whisked him to Pediatrics, and for a moment, she'd thought he'd answered back. Of course she knew that was impossible, but something had happened, some sound.

"Where is he?" Caruso asked.

"Down the hall," she answered. "Is this the mother?"

Caruso thought a moment before he replied, "yes." It seemed simpler that way. No explanation. No complication.

He had the beginning of a plan forming in his mind as he walked out, into the hallway, turned right and continued through the swinging doors into Pediatrics, past one of the security guards, and into the children's ward.

John Reed was awake, lying in the crib on his back, sucking from the teat of a bottle.

Caruso looked down at him.

"Hello, John," he said.

The baby released the teat from his lips and made a gurgling sound.

"Do you know who I am?" Caruso asked softly.

The word came suddenly. It sounded like *D Hien*, something that Caruso had not heard in over twenty-five years, not since Cambodia. It meant soldier.

He stared at the small mouth. Had it moved? Had the child actually spoken? Or had he just imagined it?

"What did you say, John?"

This time the infant made a sound like laughter.

At that point a second security man approached from behind him.

"Officer," he said as Caruso turned. "You've got visitors downstairs."

Caruso was still thinking about the word, spoken in what sounded like perfect Khmer, as he took the back stairs two at a time, entering the main lobby to see Neil Adams, Dave Lake, and three men in uniform waiting at the admissions desk.

"What's going on?" Caruso asked.

"Courtesy of the captain," Adams said.

Caruso looked at the uniformed men. He knew them to be good, tough street cops. People he trusted. Then he looked back at Adams, puzzled.

"Why?"

"He said he promised you security," Adams offered. "Maybe he's trying to do the right thing."

"Maybe," Caruso replied without begging details. Then, turning to the cops said, "I want every entrance and exit to this place covered." He looked from Adams to Lake, "I want you two guys with me. Nobody gets close to Armstrong or the baby. Nobody."

"You got it," Adams replied.

Then Caruso walked to the admissions desk and spoke to the nursing supervisor, explaining that he needed secure, isolated rooms.

She suggested two in the back of the building.

Afterward, at 10:10 P.M., with both John Reed and Casey Armstrong resting in their new quarters, Caruso phoned Thomas and Molly Reed, informing them that their son was safe and in good health.

They wanted to see their child immediately.

It was natural and Caruso had anticipated it. Still, it took him a lot of patience and explaining to dissuade them. Until finally, for the sake of their son's safety, they'd agreed to his plan.

Next, he rang the television station. It was the same station that had run the tape of him escorting Thomas Reed from South Nevada. The tape that had jeopardized his investigation. This time he promised them an exclusive in exchange for their cooperation.

~ 26 ~

They assembled in the hallway at six o'clock the following morning.

Caruso was worried about Armstrong. She seemed confused and alienated, sitting in the wheelchair with her head bowed.

The hospital neurologist, who had examined her upon admission, then again at 3 A.M., had expressed his concern as to the long-term consequences of the mental and emotional trauma that she'd suffered. He was reasonably certain that her faculty for speech would return, but from what he had learned from Caruso regarding the drugs and electroconvulsive shock that she had endured, he was doubtful that she would ever remember much of what had happened to her.

Casey was wearing a black, cotton training suit, sneakers that felt too big, and Caruso's hunting jacket, above the Kevlar vest. A man was pushing her chair while another aimed a camcorder at her face. She raised her hands and hid, sobbing, certain that she was being taken to jail. She knew that she had murdered a man and kidnapped a baby. But why? Her mind was so fragmented that she honestly didn't know.

Neil Adams was pushing the chair while Dave Lake carried the sleeping infant.

"It's all right Ms. Armstrong, we're getting there," Adams reassured.

They continued, into an elevator, then down, thudding to a halt as the doors slid open and she was rolled out, along a corridor, through the bowels of a building, in and out of small rooms with pipes above her head dripping condensation, and permeated with the smell of mold and dampness.

Scenes flashed in her mind. She was scaling the side of a wooden house up, along slippery shingles. She was cutting a circle of glass from the window, reaching in to open a lock, crawling through with the wind at her back, picking a baby up from its crib. But why? Why?

Finally they stopped in front of a metal door.

Adams helped her to her feet and guided her away from the wheelchair while a police woman took her place. Then a second officer, carrying a bundle wrapped in a blue blanket, that could have been mistaken at a distance for an infant, took a position beside the decoy in the chair.

The door opened and a dark-haired man, who Casey recognized but couldn't place, entered the room with a blast of cold morning air, leaving the door open behind him.

She could see a limousine outside, with KCTV stenciled on its door, parked in front of the concrete entrance ramp, engine purring and smoke streaming from its tailpipe. The driver's side opened and a short man in a dark suit got out. He looked at the man she felt she knew and said, "We're ready, Mike."

"Let's go," Caruso answered.

Once the decoys were in the limousine, two police escort vehicles rolled into position, one in front and one behind, and the procession pulled away with the news van following.

Caruso came back inside and closed the door.

Minutes later, there were three loud knocks, a pause, and three more.

This time there was a black Chevrolet Blazer parked in front of the ramp.

Caruso stood a moment, his eyes searching the deserted lower level of the parking lot, then up, scanning the back of the main hospital building. He stood quietly, watching and listening, until, satisfied that they were in the clear, he turned and motioned to the others.

Lake carried John Reed tucked tight to his shoulder, one arm wrapped around him, the other folded across to form a shield with his forearm. He slid quickly into the rear seat of the Blazer and sunk low so that the baby's head was not exposed from the outside of the tinted window.

Next, Adams ushered Casey Armstrong into the vehicle, pushing her tight to Lake and the baby before he slid in.

Caruso ran to the front, got in, and took the wheel.

"Ready?"

"Yep," Adams answered.

Caruso stepped on it. He felt better with the vehicle moving.

Casey buried her head in her hands and watched the pictures flash against the blackness of her closed eyelids. She could see John Reed, staring back at her. Reaching for her from his crib.

Caruso turned and looked back, across the side of the headrest, and caught Adams' eyes.

He spoke softly.

"The parents should be at the studio when we arrive. It's a hell of a way to set up a reunion but I want the public to get a good look at them, all of them. I want to get this story out there. Right now, that's our only insurance policy."

KCTV was located at 3200 North Nevada Avenue. Less than a twenty-minute ride through the vacant streets. Twenty minutes that felt like an eternity in a car taut with nerves, with only Casey's sporadic sobs to punctuate the silence.

The decoy limo and its escort of cars had slowed so that the Blazer could make up time. Although they were traveling by different routes, the plan was to keep a distance that would correlate to about three minutes between the first group of vehicles and the Blazer, so that while the limo and its team were unloading at the main door of the station, the Blazer could slip into a designated bay at the rear of the studio and quickly discharge its passengers.

Caruso slowed as he rounded the corner at Tejon Street, then took a small side street that intersected with Nevada, a block from their destination.

He could see the limo and its escorts. They had pulled to the curb in front of the building and the driver had stepped from the car. From a distance, everything appeared to be running smoothly.

Caruso accelerated, took his next right, and traversed an alleyway, which brought him out at the back of the studio. He could see the chain-link fence in front of him and the opened gate, leading to the loading bay. There were two uniformed police officers at either side, motioning him inward.

Everyone in the car was alert.

"Almost home," Adams said as they drove toward the cops and into the compound.

Caruso looked from his window at the shadowed face beneath the brim of the hat of the officer closest to him.

"I don't recognize this guy," he said. "He's not from South Nevada."

"Yale probably got him from uptown."

"Yale?"

"Lochart set this up," Adams answered. "I couldn't have gotten this kind of manpower without him."

Lochart. Sure. He'd sent the men to the hospital, too. That made sense, Caruso told himself as he drove slowly toward the loading dock, checking his rearview mirror. The uniformed cops had closed the gates and were walking behind, following them in.

Caruso kept driving, straight to the bay, then stopped with the Blazer's front end facing the concrete platform and threw the car into park.

"That's supposed to be open," he said, looking up at the big, steel-fronted door.

Adams glanced across the seat at the clock. The digits read 6:29. They had been scheduled to arrive at 6:30.

"We're a minute early," he replied.

"Yeah," Caruso agreed.

"It's okay man, we're almost home," Adams reassured, hearing the nerves in Caruso's voice.

It was hard to pinpoint the feeling, but something felt wrong to Caruso. Off-center. He turned and looked through the rear window of the Blazer. The two cops were standing about twenty feet behind them, each equidistant from either side of the tailgate. One of them was unsnapping the strap to his holster.

Caruso had a dreadful moment of indecision as the clock hit 6:30 and the big bay door to the studio door swung open. A third police officer stood in the frame, raising his right hand, his thumb and index finger forming the "okay" sign. Right on schedule.

"I think we're good," Caruso said, trying to get a handle on his nerves as he looked up at the smiling cop.

The man's breath was a white mist and his hat was pulled down low across his forehead. It was hard to see his face in the light from the rising sun, but his body, and his bearing, powerful and efficient, even as he stood still, rang familiar to Caruso.

Caruso took his right hand away from the wheel and rested it on the butt of his thirty-eight, knowing yet not knowing, as the man walked from the building.

Ten feet in front of the Blazer, Roy Ames began to draw his weapon, squeezing the wooden grip tight into his palm, wanting to be close to his target, to be sure.

Casey looked up, across the seat and through the windshield.

Ames's dead shark eyes stared back at her.

She knew. The baby screamed as the moment splintered into jagged shards of shouts and screams and Caruso slammed the Blazer into reverse.

The windshield splintered into a cobweb of milky lines.

Adams died instantly, caught by the hollow point between his eyes, his skull breaking apart as his body pitched back against the seat.

Another bullet tore through the rear window, grazing Caruso's neck.

"Take the baby!" Lake shouted, jamming the sobbing infant into Casey's bosom before shoving them both hard to the floor as the Blazer careened backward in a blind semicircle.

Caruso shifted into drive and floored it, crushing one
of the phony cops as he smacked into the side of the
building.

The impact sent Caruso flying through the shattered
window and onto the hood. He slid down the warm metal
and hit the ground, conscious only of the sound of shoes
smacking concrete, coming fast toward him.

He made it to one knee, in time to see a man with his
gun raised, flame spurting from the barrel. Caruso returned
fire. Three rounds and the man fell. Then he turned to see
Dave Lake half-climb, half-fall from the opened door of the
wrecked Chevy, his weapon hanging limp in his hand, looking
toward him, eyes pleading for help, a moment before a 9mm
bullet tore a hole in his throat.

Caruso ducked down, taking cover against the side of
the car, and squeezed off a final shot before his Smith &
Wesson was out. Then he reached for his leg holster and
grabbed his backup, a subcompact Glock 27, discharging
three rounds as Ames made another run at him.

One bullet grazed Ames's shoulder and he changed
course, skirting wide along the Blazer's perimeter. The next
two rounds shredded the fabric of his uniform and thudded
into the trauma plate below, while the last tore off his left ear
in a spurt of blood.

Still he came. Holding on till he was right on top.
Then he fired twice, fast, catching Caruso in the center of his
chest, above his kelvar vest. The impact felt like the kick of a
horse, winding him, stopping his heart for an instant as he
dropped to his knees.

Casey turned, shielding John Reed while looking up into the eyes
of the shark. Recognizing them. Feeling the heat of the bullet in
her mind, as she had at Montauk, an instant before it cut through
her side, behind the vest, hot, as the hollow point opened and the
metal mushroomed, shredding her right lung.

Ames fired again. The second charge broke her spine,
pitching her sideways, her full weight crashing down on the
baby.

Finally Ames leaned into the car, intent on claiming
John Reed. Reaching forward with his free hand to get a grip

on the baby's arm, he had begun to pry him free when
Caruso fired again.

The bullet entered Ames just below the strap of his
vest. He bucked and fell, tucking and rolling, coming up
unsteady to wobble two more steps. Three. Lifting his head
to suck at the air. Finding his balance before cutting to his left
and running once more toward the Blazer.

Face on, into the black hole of Caruso's gun.

~ 27 ~

Paramedic Randy Lourdes had seen enough roadkill in his eight years on the job to know a dead one when he saw one, and this woman was a goner. So was the baby. He reckoned there to be four or five pints of blood fanning out from their bodies, enough to fill the floor, between the front and backseat of the Blazer.

It was one of the saddest sights that he had ever seen. Yet there was a strange, almost surreal beauty to their faces, so close together, staring breathlessly into the void of each other's eyes, as if in death they had somehow merged to form a single expression of peace, like a Madonna and child.

His partner, Vincent Cinque, with six years less job experience, bent over and touched his fingertips to Casey's carotid artery. Checking twice. Then he felt the throat of John Reed.

Looking up at Lourdes, he declared, "No pulse in either of them. Nothing at all."

No shit, Sherlock, Lourdes thought, bending down to repeat the procedure, although his action was primarily a show for the cop who hovered above them.

"Gone," he said, his tone solemn, looking up at Caruso. "Both of 'em.

I'm sorry." Then, gently, he closed the lids of their eyes.

Caruso didn't move. He stood, looking down at Casey and John Reed. It all seemed so crazy, so futile, and so tragic. Then he glanced back toward the loading bay, and at the steel door leading into the studio. It was closed and locked, in order to contain the TV people and camera crews, at least until the crime scene had been secured. Caruso knew that somewhere behind it, held back with the crowd, listening to the panicked speculation as to what had happened outside, Molly and Thomas Reed would be trying to get through, desperate to see their son. Who was going to be the first to tell them?

"Please, sir," Lourdes said, indicating that Caruso should move back so that they could work.

Caruso stepped away, turning toward the steel door, preparing himself for what he had to say to Thomas and Molly Reed, when Cinque shouted, "She's moving!"

Lourdes could feel the surge of emotion, even before Caruso stepped back into frame.

"No," Lourdes said. "That's a spasm. She's not alive, keep pulling."

Cinque felt foolish. "Sorry," he mumbled, tugging with his hands around the baby's back, without result. "The muscles in her arms have seized," he said finally.

Lourdes had seen this type of death-response a few times and the last thing he wanted was to break a bone before the coroner had examined the bodies.

"Leave the baby where he is," he replied. "Let's get a stretcher over here."

Caruso watched as they carried Casey Armstrong and John Reed away, still intertwined, the thick blue blanket covering their bodies and faces. He felt sick inside, as if someone had plunged a dagger into the center of his chest and pried him open, then wrenched and twisted without mercy, ripping out his heart.

He held back his tears as he watched the Flight For Life helicopter lift off and gain altitude, hovering a moment above the tops of the buildings before taking them away, disconnecting him from a promise, and leaving him desolate.

Then he began to feel something else. As intense as the pain in his heart had been, this feeling grew and spread like a fire in his belly. It demanded another kind of release. Wanting one thing and one thing only. He turned and walked to the group of police officers who were measuring the

distances between the chalked perimeters where the bodies
had lain. He cornered Jake Abbot, one of the rooky
Homicide cops.

"Where's Lochart?"

Abbot didn't answer. He was twenty-nine years old
but looked forty-five. His face was too pale, too thin, and too
angular, and he had dark blue-black circles beneath his eyes,
like he'd spent a year of sleepless nights, worrying himself
into premature middle age. The cold fury of Caruso's
demeanor unnerved him.

"He should be here," Caruso insisted, stepping so
close that he could smell the spiced sausage on the rookie's
breath, even through the flap of his half-open mouth.

When he spoke, Abbot sounded scared. "Sir, don't
you know?"

"Know what?" The only thing Caruso knew was that
Lochart had killed a lot of people and that he was going to
return the service.

"The captain's dead," Abbot stammered. "Blew his
brains out when he heard about this ... must have been too
much for him. He did it at the station, right at his desk. I
thought you knew."

Caruso turned and walked away. He felt cheated.

He also felt lost inside, and more lonely than he had
ever been in his life. Stranded in a bad dream from which
there was no awakening.

He felt dead.

~ 28 ~

48 hours later

london, england

Preston Dix walked into the monitoring room, placed his cane against the leather-covered console, noting the silver end cap had come loose and was in need of repair. He wondered if he'd damaged it during his termination of Mishima. It had taken place in the car, while leaving the police station in Colorado, with the late Roy Ames at the wheel. The Japanese doctor had been in the front seat, still sweating from his ordeal with the crazy cop. Babbling and laughing in short hysterical bursts, as if he'd just had a last-minute reprieve from the gallows. He had been asking questions, too many, spilling his guts in front of Ames. Talking about the child, John Reed. "The alien child," that's what he had called him. There was nothing that Dix loathed more than a loose tongue. It was then that he had decided to act, slipping the cap from his cane, lining up Mishima's throat, listening to his fast, high-pitched voice, his pretentious accent, watching his jaw waggle. Letting the hatred fill him like the Paraquat Compound-267 that seeped from the concealed 10-ml barrel into the one-inch hypodermic needle at the tip of the ebony wood. He'd lifted it level with Mishima's throat before he'd said, "Ken. Calm down. Please ... Ken!"

It was the first time that the Japanese doctor had ever heard Dix use his first name and it surprised him. He'd turned, relief oozing from his insipid smile. In time to see the dripping point of the needle thrusting toward him, embedding in his neck with a soft thunk as Dix twisted it with a corkscrewing movement, ensuring the complete discharge of the paraquet, while Mishima struggled, managing to get both hands up, his fingers just touching the wooden shaft. He was already convulsing, his lips twitching and his limbs shuttering as his central nervous system closed down. He'd frozen like that, with his head turned, staring wide-eyed at Preston Dix.

They'd driven to the outskirts of town, opened the door, and dumped him like a bag of garbage, his body still in a seated position, with his arms raised, and his marbled eyes fixed straight ahead.

The execution had been very satisfying to Dix, serving as a temporary release from the setback that Black-Out had experienced because of the cop. His single regret was the spring-loaded mechanism of his cane. He'd had the weapon for nearly thirty years; it had been crafted in London, on Jermyn Street, in the days when he'd been an operative for the CIA. The cane was his lucky piece.

Dix cleared his throat.

"I'm going to monitor the session myself, if that's agreeable to you," he said. "I don't trust this information with anyone outside these walls."

Information? Blythe-Saxon bristled at the word. The lab had drawn more blanks as to the origins of the implants, which had now, without explanation, ceased to function in the petri dish. One of the Washington brain boys was currently speculating that the collagen-encased crystals had actually formed inside the bodies of the woman in which they'd been found. He had compared them to religious stigmata, blood or objects that manifested physically—the wounds of Christ, the nails of the crucifixion—in reaction to certain forms of hysteria. In other words, of natural, if not yet understood, origins. Leaving Neo Tech no closer to a definitive answer as to what they actually were and how they functioned.

The tape of the last RV session, with Casey and the hybrid, had caused a furor in Vatican City, with its religious implications, while security agencies in all four of the governments involved with Neo Tech were reopening their close encounter files.

On top of that, Dix had lost the hybrid.

"Shall we get on with it, then?" she said.

Dix pressed a button on the console. In response to his touch, a panel of walnut directly in front of them, separated, revealing a two-by-three-foot plate of one-way glass.

They looked down, through the glass, into a sunken room, four feet below the level of the one they occupied. The room was small, seven feet long and seven feet wide, and with the exception of the glass partition, was completely lined with sheets of laminated copper making it a self-contained electrical conductor. It had a reddish-brown glow in the subdued overhead light. There was a wraparound desk in the center of the room. The desk, also, was covered in copper, as was the chair that the man sat in.

He was dressed completely in white. It was a silk, one-piece overall, which conformed to the shape of his lean body and zipped to his neck. His hair was silver-gray and cropped short. It appeared to shine, like a polished metal, beneath the overhead light, and his hands were resting on the top of the desk. They were beautiful hands, long, well formed, and recently manicured. He looked up. The features of his face were refined and symmetrical, but it was his eyes that gave him an other worldly quality. They were large and cobalt blue. Perfectly clear. He studied the area of the wall that had moved, looking at the dark side of the observation glass. He studied it for a full minute, and never blinked.

Dix pressed his TALK button.

"Are you ready?"

The man responded with only the slightest nod of his head.

Blythe-Saxon's voice seemed to grow more caustic with use. "I find it difficult to believe that with your so-called contacts inside the intelligence community, you cannot locate the hybrid by a more conventional means."

Dix swallowed hard. *Hybrid.* Even the way she used the term infuriated him. He'd tried everything. There had been an unofficial sighting of the child in Venice, California, and also one in Dallas, Texas, but nothing was confirmed.

"Please, Eleanor, be patient," he replied, with just enough edge to his own voice to intimate that he did not like being held to answer. Even to her.

The atmosphere in the monitoring room had grown silent and hostile by the time the man in the RV chamber lifted the silver tube from the table.

Dix held on, allowing several minutes for him to handle it. Watching as he smelled it, then rolled it between his fingers. Wondering what the hell he was doing.

Finally, the man placed the tube in his mouth, like a cigar, and sucked on it.

Blythe-Saxon was fuming. She did not have much faith in these psychics, these viewers, or whatever they were called. She had the interests of her group to protect. The last thing they needed was John Reed. A miracle. They did not want miracles, at least miracles that they did not control. They wanted a tamed humanity. A world economy that they could command. Wars when they needed them. Pharmaceutical breakthroughs when they deemed them appropriate. Diseases to cull the flock. Cures when required. Religion without bite. Control was the name of the game. They did not want a miracle. And now what were they facing? Something extraterrestrial? Or interdimensional, as another of the scientists had hypothesized, some type of reality shift, a new way of looking at the universe, a fresh paradigm?

She stared across at Preston Dix, despising him for letting the situation get this far out of hand.

"What the hell is going on in there?" she asked.

Dix stared through the one-way glass, understanding that he was at the mercy of the freak in the RV chamber and feeling unusually close to panic.

For once his tone was humble. "Sir, can you hear me?"

Damon Raye removed the tube from his lips and exhaled. He was following his flow of breath with his eyes, as if he was watching a ring of smoke. He looked very satisfied.

"Damon?" Dix said softly, hating the weakness of his own voice. He was asking this maniac for something. Begging for it.

Damon looked up through the glass, as if it did not present an obstacle between them. They were eye-to-eye, all alone.

Dix continued. "May I have your cooperation please?"

Raye looked pensive, as if he was weighing each of his thoughts before translating them into words.

The long silence made Dix nervous and he fidgeted unconsciously with the tip of his cane, causing the spring-loaded device to make a clicking sound.

Blythe-Saxon's tone was sharp. "Please Preston, no distractions. Not now." She snapped the cane away from his hand and lifted it away from the console. "I have put up with your damnable incompetence for long enough. Make him respond."

Dix sat back. On top of everything else the woman had spoken down to him. Humiliated him. In all his professional career, he'd never been made subordinate to a woman. Until now. He stared at the man behind the glass, hating him completely, yet feeling powerless in his presence, unable to rein him in or control him.

Dix felt suddenly small and insignificant, realizing finally that he had fumbled the ball and lost his position on the playing field. His authority was gone. He had a madman in front of him and a bitch to his side, riding him, ridiculing him. He could feel his self-control slipping.

Allowing his anger to color his tone, he hissed, "Mr. Raye. Open the tube."

Damon Raye looked at him and nodded his head slowly.

"Open the fucking thing now!" Dix shouted.

When Raye finally spoke his voice was low, smooth, and vaguely mocking.

"Where do we come from ... ? What are we ... ? Where are we going ...?" He held the tube, containing the Colorado implant, away from him, looking at it lovingly. "Are the answers to our future inside here? Is this the key to man's evolution?"

"Goddamn him," Dix swore under his breath.

Raye smiled.

"When someone tosses you the truth—catch it! Catch it with your gentle hands. Catch it with your skillful mind!" he said, then hurled the tube toward the window.

It hit with a sharp cracking sound, leaving a chip in the thick glass before dropping to the floor and rolling back toward his desk.

Blythe-Saxon stared at the window, snarling. "The man is insane. This is a waste of my time." At that point she made a decision concerning Preston Dix. He was superfluous to their operation, he was incompetent, and he knew too much.

"Damon," Dix pleaded, "goddamn you. Don't do this."

Raye looked from the tube to the monitor's window then up at the ceiling.

"Our father who art in heaven. Hallowed be thy name. Thy kingdom come. Ah, yes, it's coming. It's coming—knock on the sky and listen to the sound." Then he began. Chuckling at first, but after a few seconds he was laughing, the peels distorting with the amplification of the speakers.

Furious, Dix pressed a button and two uniformed guards rushed in and dragged Raye from the room.

Turning to Blythe-Saxon, Dix opened his mouth to offer an excuse and was met with a steely glare. He hardly noticed that she was holding something in her hands as she stood up from her chair, swinging both arms toward him in a fast flailing motion.

Seconds later Preston Dix was slumped over the console, his hands making a trembling effort to clutch his throat. There was a hole that resembled a bee sting above his carotid artery and his cane lay discarded on the floor beside him, the silver cap missing from the point of the needle.

~ 29 ~

C asey awakened to the sight of Preston Dix staring down at her. His eyes were dark and shadowed and his lips were pinched tight with anger. Still, he looked smug, as if he was in control. She felt him first in her stomach, souring it, before the fear crawled up her spine.

She pushed back against the bed, away from him.

The sound had been muted and it was a still picture, a grainy black and white, taken from a frozen frame of the police security video.

She turned her head against the pillow and saw Michael Caruso seated in a chair beside her bed. He was wearing a brown corduroy suit and sitting upright, watching the television, his back not touching the back of the chair, rigid, as if it hurt to sit that way. The features of his face looked lean, closer to the bones than she had remembered, as if they had been recently chiseled, and his eyes seemed alive, reflecting the flickering light from the TV.

He was close, less than five feet from her, but Casey felt distant and it disturbed her. She needed him to acknowledge her, to affirm that she was alive and not watching from the other side of death. She attempted to move toward him but she was constricted by tubes and wires. Then she felt the obstruction in her mouth and throat. Reaching up, she removed the respirator, drawing the slippery tube from her larynx as a bank of warning lights flashed beside her and an alarm bleeped.

Caruso turned.

"Michael?" Her throat felt scratched and raw and her voice was barely audible above the voice on the television.

He stared at the discarded intubation tube.

"Don't move," he said.

The ward nurse was there within seconds, a doctor following behind. They were a perfect contrast. The nurse was broad-shouldered, short, and stocky, with a pale complexion and olive-green eyes; the doctor was a tall black man with a short salt-and-pepper beard, brown eyes framed by gold-rimmed glasses, and a shaved, shining head.

"What's going on here?" he asked, trying to affect a calm he didn't feel while quickly checking her cardiac monitor, then her IV tubes. "How did this happen?" He picked up the respirator, amazed that she was functioning without it.

"I don't need it," Casey answered, suddenly alert to the man on the TV screen. He was wearing a shiny suit and too much face makeup. She recognized him immediately, from the first time she'd been in Colorado Springs. He'd covered the story on the murder of the priest, Robert Barnes.

The man was talking, his lips moving rapidly, without disturbing the plaster mask of skin above. His eyes were set, but focused on the camera. For once Tennyson Albright wasn't using his teleprompter. His face was deadly serious.

Casey reached to the night table and retrieved the remote control, increasing the volume.

The doctor, whose name was Charles Berry, stared at her in disbelief.

"You just moved your arm," he said.

He bent down slowly and began cautiously to examine her wounds, beneath the surgical dressing, as Tennyson Albright's voice filled the room.

"The United States Army and the National Security Agency have disavowed any knowledge of an operation acting under the command of former CIA employee, Preston Willard Dix. Speculation exists that Dix's group may be connected to a privately funded supernationalist organization, but that information is still speculative, as is the question of what Dix and his organization were doing in Colorado Springs. One thing, however, that is fact, is a growing death toll. New information, released by the FBI within the last hour, has linked the January 15th murder of priest Robert Barnes to the death of local doctor Murray Rose, along with the alleged suicide of Springs police captain Yale Lochart. That brings the count to five people, including an infant of six weeks." A picture of John Reed at one-day-old filled the screen; it had been taken by the hospital photographer. His eyes were open and his face was serene. Angelic. "A child's death is always a tragedy. A terrible tragedy. For a child to be murdered is a sin against everything that is civilized in our society. A child. A baby. And the question remains, why?"

"Are you able to move your toes?" Berry asked, oblivious to the television.

Casey moved her toes while staring up into the pale blue eyes on the TV screen. Unable to comprehend what she had just heard.

"I can't explain it," Berry continued, looking at Ruth Halliday, the nurse. There appeared to be a complete regeneration of the ligaments and spinal cord. It was the first time he'd come close to believing what he'd been told by the paramedic who had briefed him upon Casey's arrival. The man had claimed that she had been eighteen minutes without vital signs. That was impossible. What was he dealing with? Lazarus, back from the dead? And now she was breathing on her own and moving her limbs.

"How do you feel, Ms. Lovell?"

Casey continued to stare at the screen. John Reed. Dead? No, that couldn't be.

"Ms. Lovell?"

Casey looked at him, realizing that he was addressing her.

Caruso covered quickly.

"Nancy. How do you feel?" he asked.

For an instant her confusion returned. What was happening to her? What had happened? Nancy. Who was Nancy Lovell?

The plastic news commentator continued to speak but she was no longer aware of his words. She closed her eyes, gathering herself in, struggling for clarity. Then it came, as if the last dark clouds had parted, and she remembered everything as it had happened—the chemicals, the hypnosis, the shock treatment, and the lies.

She remembered Roy Ames, running toward their car, fulfilling her premonition, finding his mark as the bullets had torn into her back.

Opening her eyes she repeated, "How do I feel?" As if asking herself the question.

Berry and Halliday waited, focused on her, Halliday's head nodding, almost imperceptibly, as if to coax a positive response.

Casey's voice was flat. "Like I've been through hell." Then she looked at Michael Caruso and asked the question that she was afraid to ask. "Is he really gone?"

Caruso stared at her a moment without answering.

"John," she said. "Is he—"

Caruso felt a mixture of awe and fear, and something else, something shared and sacred.

"No, he's alive," he answered. Then he walked from the room.

When Caruso returned, Thomas, Molly, and John Reed were with him. Both Molly and Thomas's eyes were red from crying. They knew what had to happen next, but no matter how many times Caruso had explained it to them or rationalized it, or imposed hopeful limits—one year, maybe two—they knew.

Casey met Molly Reed's eyes. Then she was crying too, as the sorrow from the other woman spilled into her and, slowly, Molly Reed walked to her bed. She stopped and smiled a sad, faint smile before handing her the baby.

"Thank you," Casey whispered, cradling him.

She felt John Reed as she had felt him then, after the shooting, clinging warm to her breast. It was as if he was adhering to her flesh, opening her to transmit his energy inward. She remembered awakening inside the helicopter and having no sensation of her body, as if her mind had become detached from her broken flesh and bones. It was a wonderful feeling, pure freedom, and had lasted until the first trickle of pain in her spine. Then, gradually, she'd become aware of the bullets lodged inside her. They'd felt thick and heavy, foreign to her flesh, and with her awareness the pain had intensified, spreading from the bullets to infect the flesh around them, until everywhere was pure heat, searing her from the inside, igniting every nerve, overpowering her will to resist it. She had begun to scream, loud and piercing, and that's when the medics had come.

Now, the proximity of the infant seemed to increase her sensation of being alive, as if her energies were being boosted and her senses heightened. She became suddenly aware of the minds that surrounded her, filled with fear, sadness, and uncertainty.

Caruso looked at Charles Berry and Ruth Halliday.

"Could we have a moment, please. Would it be possible?"

Berry considered. He had witnessed a miracle. Some type of spontaneous healing. There was no emergency here. Maybe the presence of God, or some divine intervention, but no medical emergency.

He replied, "Of course."

Caruso waited till Berry and Halliday had gone and the door was closed before he turned to Casey and spoke.

"I had to protect you, both of you, and there was only one way to do it," he explained. "Casey Lee Armstrong is dead and so is John Reed. Right now, that's the only way I can see .... The people here, in Denver, think that your name is Nancy Lovell and that you and your son, John, got caught in the middle of an armed robbery. I put the story together fast and it won't hold up for long, but it will be good enough to get us out of here and onto the next place."

"The next place?" Casey repeated. It was to be as she had feared, a life of running and hiding.

"I'm working on a safe house," Caruso continued. "Some place that you can convalesce while I set up something more permanent, further away. In the meantime it will give me a chance to work with Interpol. There's already word that Preston Dix's body turned up in London, floating in the Thames."

"He's dead." Casey said softly.

"Yes," Caruso replied.

Casey looked from Caruso to Molly, then at Thomas.
She knew what they'd been through and she sensed the
questions inside them.

"We'll find somewhere secure, until we're sure that
John is safe," Caruso promised, turning to Molly and
Thomas. "Until we do, I need you to be strong. You won't be
away from him any longer than is necessary."

"But—" Molly started and stopped. They had been
over it so many times, through the night and during the
morning. They had argued and rationalized, finally
understanding, but at the bottom of it all was the thought of
separation and the heartache of the loss. Another child was
leaving them.

"I'll arrange visits," Caruso promised. He met Molly's
eyes and his voice softened with compassion. "I don't know
any other way. I really don't. I'm sorry."

Casey felt a great gap opening in the room and she
held the baby tighter to her chest as if to close it while Caruso
tried to find the bridge. He looked at John Reed, then back at
Casey. His mouth was a line of soft shadow.

"The boy is special," he said. "We all know that. Now
we have to do whatever it takes to protect him."

Casey felt, at that moment, that she was returning to
life for a second time, following a trauma that had broken
more than her body. She could not reassemble all the pieces
of her mind, not here, and not now. It would take time for
her to fully understand what had happened. She looked down
at John Reed and felt a new consciousness dawning. She was
alive in a different way. She sensed it through her body,
through the hands and fingers that held the child.

Then she looked at Michael Caruso, and saw him
through the eyes that John Reed had given her. The
policeman looked fierce and protective, brimming with
feeling and emotion, well intentioned, but governed by fear.
He appeared almost primitive. She looked at Thomas and
Molly Reed and saw the same thing, understanding that if she
gave them her knowledge of the child, about his origins and
powers, a knowledge that was still incomplete, not fully

understood even by her, that it would make them more
fearful and threatened.

"John saved my life," she said finally. "I don't know
how, not exactly, but I know that he did, and I believe that
he's been sent to us all for a reason. He has a very special
purpose, but right now, he needs us. He needs our love and
our protection. His safety has to come first and whatever
sacrifices that will require, well, we've just got to make them.
We have to do whatever we can to give him a chance to
grow. It's important. It's the most important thing any of us
will ever do."

EPILOGUE

It had been a year of change, from the mountains of Colorado to the deserts of New Mexico, working through church organizations and trusted friends. Still, within months, no matter where they had taken refuge, news of the child spread.

John Reed was a miracle.

Within ten months he could speak in any language that was spoken to him. At first, those close to the child thought he was merely imitating sounds but soon learned that he could understand and communicate, forming words with his tiny voice and his precise diction. He could heal the sick. He had raised the dead.

To some, John Reed was the devil. To others, John Reed was the new messiah. John Reed was all things to all people. And everywhere there was danger, from the attentions of the well-meaning to those who would try to exploit him for their own purposes.

In the wake of every gathering of people came the media, always clamoring for a story, and as soon as their reports began, it was time to move on.

Molly and Thomas were often with their son, for a day, or a week, and during their time with him they had grown to accept their role, less as parents, and more as guardians, custodians of the miracle.

It was Caruso who thought of the last refuge. His idea had come after three weeks in seclusion on a cattle ranch in Montana, their isolation ended by the arrival of a busload of

spiritualists, calling themselves Truth Seekers. They claimed
to have heard of the child through a Unitarian newsletter, and
stayed patiently in their bus, or camped in tents on the
outskirts of the ranch, while waiting for an audience with
John Reed.

Caruso knew it was time to go, again.

It was actually the child who had planted the idea in
his mind, way back in the hospital in Colorado Springs, on
the night of his rescue. In a way, John Reed had foretold their
fate. He had called Michael Caruso *D Hien*, "soldier." It was
true, Caruso had been a soldier. And now, he felt like a
soldier again.

He knew the place.

It was forty-four miles from the temple city of Angkor in central
Cambodia and the land mines, planted twenty years ago by the
Khmer Rouge, had still not been cleared.

The six robed men walked slowly and carefully, their
bare feet kicking up dust from the red dirt. It was a dangerous
journey, but three times each week, they made it, forty miles
by car and the last four on foot.

The baby had arrived in early February, after the rainy
season had ended. Carried from the old Ford truck by a
Western woman with short, dark hair and aviator-style
sunglasses. She was tall and graceful and there had been a
quality to her, a certain presence, as if she had a sense of
some great purpose. Perhaps she was, as one of the small sect
had suggested, enlightened. It was something in the way she
acknowledged them, with a wonderful feeling of compassion,
mixed with a detachment, as if she knew each of them and
could sense their purpose. As if she had known that they had
been waiting for the maitreya. Searching the eyes and faces of
the newly born children in every town and village.

Recognizing his incarnation in her arms.

There had been a man with them. Taller even than
the woman, broad-shouldered and muscular. Compared to
the monks, with their delicate, almost childlike features,
shaven heads, and slight bodies, he had seemed a giant, with
dark, shoulder-length hair and a full beard. He resembled one
of the mighty soldiers whose effigies had adorned and

guarded the ruins that had once been their temples. He'd
carried four duffel bags, draped over his arms and shoulders,
as he'd led the woman and the child to a rusted military Jeep,
a remnant from the Pol Pot era.

The mahayana monks had watched as they drove
north, into no-man's-land, headed toward the arid forests and
unexploded mines.

Two days later they had followed, bearing food and
gifts for the child and following the tracks of the Jeep. Then,
when they could no longer drive, they had traced their
footprints to a small temple on the outskirts of the sparse
jungle, amazed that the building had been restored and fitted
with a power generator.

The soldier had stopped them, stepping from the
arched doorway to aim his gun at their heads. Then, as if
sensing that their intention was benign, Michael Caruso had
lowered his weapon and led them into the temple, through
passages lit with electric lights and made cool by clean filtered
air, into an inner sanctum of woven carpets and wooden
furniture, scented with flowers and incense. To the woman
and the child.

There they had worshipped at the feet of the future
Buddha, sensing his presence and communicating with his
limitless mind, finding peace in his infinite solitude.

It was understood that no one would learn from them
of his existence, not until the world of man was ready to
accept his gift, for each of the six monks had taken the vow
of silence.

R ichard La Plante began his working life as a special
education teacher in Bucks County, Pennsylvania, where
he spent a great deal of time playing the guitar and
working on songs to the amusement of his students. Following
his dismissal, he formed the rock band Revenge and toured and
recorded till egos clashed and noses were broken.

His first book, *Tegné: Soul Warrior*, a fantasy-fiction
novel, combined his longtime study of Japanese martial arts
with his interest in metaphysics and love of adventure tales.

He wrote a sequel to *Tegné*, entitled *The Killing Blow*,
then switched from fantasy-fiction to hardcore thrillers with a
popular series featuring the characters Josef Tanaka, a
Japanese-American medical examiner and shotokan karate
master, and Bill Fogarty, an Irish-American police Lieutenant.
Mantis was the first novel in the series, followed by *Leopard*,
Steroid Blues, and *Mind Kill*.

A great deal of the money earned from his books
ended up in the chrome and steel accessories that adorned his
custom Harley-Davidson, a 1989 Springer, an obsession
which became the inspiration for his motorcycle memoir, *Hog*

Fever. Detours, written in 2002, continues the motorcycle theme and traces a solo cross-country journey ending in Sturgis, the famous motorcycle rally in the black hills of South Dakota.

Richard and his second wife, Betina, an accomplished photographer and mother of his two sons, built their first home from the ground up on a bluff overlooking Gardiner's Bay in East Hampton, New York.

In 2004, the family moved to Ojai, a small town in the high desert of Southern California, where they built their dream home on a mountaintop, inspiring his latest memoir, *Never Again.*

Richard's other interests include anything paranormal, western boxing, and competitive swimming.

Also by Richard La Plante

FICTION
Last Day
Fogarty-Tanaka Series
    Book 1 - *Mantis*
    Book 2 – *Leopard*
    Book 3 – *Steroid Blues*
    Book 4 – *Mind Kill*
Tegné: Soul Warrior
Tegné: The Killing Blow

MEMOIRS
Hog Fever
Detours: Life, Death and Divorce on the Road to Sturgis
Never Again: Building the Dream House

EAR MOVIE
Hog Fever

www.ingramcontent.com/pod-product-compliance
Lightning Source LLC
Chambersburg PA
CBHW071519260626
47170CB00002B/430